SELECTION

KNOT THEIR OMEGA

E.J. LAWSON

Copyright © 2023 by Thorn House Publishing Inc.

All rights reserved. No part of this book may be reproduced in any form or by any electronic or mechanical means, including information storage and retrieval systems, without written permission from the author, except for the use of brief quotations in a book review.

Cover Design: Pretty in Ink Creations

Edited by: Jennifer Jones @ Bookends Editing

ONE

—

MADDIE

"LESS THAN TWENTY-FOUR hours until we meet the Omegas who will be participating in this year's Mating Trials, ladies and gentlemen," a disembodied voice says from the speaker of someone's phone as I make my way to the library.

"Indeed so, Dave. The selection committee has sifted through thousands of nominations from across the globe. Tomorrow, we'll find out who has been chosen."

The *Royal Watch* talk show is everywhere as I hurry along the crowded corridors of Omega Academy, careful not to bump into anyone or trip over my own feet. Every Omega I pass has their head bent to their phone to watch the show. No one has bothered with their earphones because they're all tuned into the same thing.

Of course, this means none of them pay any attention to me, which suits me just fine. But it also means it's up to me not to bump into any of them. Where some students seem to weave effortlessly through the throng of moving bodies in the Academy hallways between periods, I just barely stumble through, muttering apologies as my wide, bony hips knock into sides and my elbows jab into ribs.

"For those who are only tuning in now, we're discussing the upcoming Mating Trials during which Royal Pack Eaton will select an Omega to finally bond with."

I pull a face, a soft sound of ick pushing up my throat. I'm so sick of hearing about the Trials, but this close to the start of them there's no escaping it.

At the Cambridge Omega Academy, the students live and breathe for it. All of them, it seems, except for me.

Maybe I'd care more if I had any chance of being nominated.

I scoff to myself, shaking away the bitterness my mum says is unbecoming of an Omega, especially one with absolutely no bonding prospects on her horizon after graduation.

You'd think in revered halls such as these, at one of the oldest OAs in the world, slightly more important things would be occupying the minds of the students than three—admittedly good-looking—royal Alphas choosing a non-royal Omega.

It's to the point where the staff are just as enamored as us. Screens have been brought into our instruction rooms to replay grainy footage of previous Trials while professors and students alike sigh and swoon at the fantasy. We even had to sit through an entire unit on the historical significance and importance of the Trials in Omega History this past month.

The crowds thin when I turn into the corridor leading to our majestic library. I exhale a quick sigh of relief. If I've made it this far without incident, I'm confident I'm in the clear.

CHAPTER ONE

At least for now.

Lifting my head properly, I shake my hands out at my sides and smile. The comforting scent of paper and ink fills the air around me, and I breathe it in as I stride into the library. The wide open room with its high, vaulted ceilings and stained-glass windows offer me space to take my first full breath since I started classes this morning.

This is my happy place. My sanctuary.

My footsteps are silent on the padded carpet as I turn left toward Ms. Frampton's office. I tap my knuckles on her door before I walk in.

I won't find bullies like Clara behind this door. There aren't professors waiting for me to mess up. There's no sick mum, no money troubles, and most importantly, no damn Trials.

If only I could take all my classes from the sanctuary of Ms. Frampton's library office.

Ms. Frampton looks up as I walk in. She pushes her black-rimmed glasses to the bridge of her nose before she smiles and shuts the book she was studying. "Just when I was starting to wonder if I might starve waiting for you."

I chuckle and drop down into the chair across from her desk that I've been thinking of as half *mine* for the last two years. "It's chaos out there. Hundreds of zombie Omegas entranced by their phone screens."

"Better call security then."

I snort.

"*Royal Watch*?" she asks sympathetically as she reaches into her lunchbox and picks up a sandwich. "It'll be over soon. Did you finish that book I gave you yesterday?"

I nod, rummaging through the satchel on my lap before locating my slightly squashed sandwich and taking it out of its brown paper bag. "I loved the way the Alphas treated the Omega in this one, but I especially liked the Omega herself. She was such a badass lead character."

Ms. Frampton smiles. "I knew you'd like her. I have a surprise for you today, though. Guess who got her hands on the new Riley North?"

I nearly fall off my chair. "You did? How? I thought it wasn't out until next week."

She shrugs, a coy smile playing on her lips as she picks up the paperback and hands it over. "There are some perks to being the head librarian and a literature instructor here, you know. It's not all about having lunch with you every day."

"It's not?" My hand flies to my chest.

I pretend to pout at her, but I'm too excited to keep up the act for very long. "Have you read it yet?"

"Who do you think I am? Of course, I've read it," she teases, getting that faraway, dreamy look in her eyes she always does when she's read something that she claims has changed her life. "It's amazing. I may be a spinster, but if I could get my hands on a pack like that, I'd dig in my fingernails and never let go."

"You're not a spinster." I scoff. "You're barely in your thirties."

"In my thirties and without so much as a single bond. I'm a spinster, darling, but I'm okay with it. As long as I have my books, I'm never alone. Besides, if I bonded, it would likely mean kissing this job goodbye, and I'd miss it too much."

She sits back, running a finger over a clothbound tome she's repairing in her spare time, watching as I carefully slide the new Riley North book into my satchel. When I look

CHAPTER ONE

up again, she waves a hand at her desk. "Now, about that essay of yours."

"Which one?"

She chuckles. "The one you gave me to read last month about Omega obedience?"

"Oh, that one."

My heart speeds up as I wait for her feedback. I scoot to the edge of my chair, wincing at the lengthy silence. "Was it that bad?"

"Your essays are never terrible. I have to say this one surprised me. At first glance, it's a truly gushing account of a system I happen to know you don't agree with."

"The sarcasm wasn't obvious?"

She laughs. "It was to me, but to any outsider, it definitely wouldn't look like satire. They'd take it as gospel and crown you a queen. Or they'd give you a job here as an instructor in Omega Etiquette Studies."

My nose wrinkles.

"Hard pass. I don't need a crown or a job brainwashing the next generation."

Her pale-blue eyes light up as she laughs and shakes her head. "Is that what you think I'm doing, brainwashing the next generation?"

"No, but you teach Literature. Omega Etiquette Studies, though? One of those things is not like the other."

"Well, at least it would be a job," she says gently. "Have you thought about what comes next, Maddie? You're almost 21, in your final year, yet, every time I ask, you change the subject."

I exhale through my nostrils, closing my eyes for a moment and trying to center myself as the icy fingers of panic wrap around my heart. I tell Ms. Frampton everything. She's one of my favorite people of all time and my only real friend here, but I can't tell her the truth about this.

"I don't know," I hedge, aware of the fact she won't let me change the topic again now that she's put me on the spot. "I used to think I might like to continue my studies in either journalism or literature at a postgraduate level."

"Used to?"

"Well, that was before I realized it's not possible, is it?"

Because I would need to be bonded into a pack to be able to attend on my own, but there's also the problem of money…"Getting a scholarship for an undergraduate degree wasn't so difficult, but—"

"Most would disagree with you on that."

I roll my eyes. "Fine, it was difficult, but I managed. Being awarded a scholarship at postgraduate level is next to impossible. It would also mean I wouldn't be earning an income for a few more years and…"

I can't bring myself to finish the sentence, but Ms. Frampton doesn't need me to. She understands. As my closest confidante these last couple of years, she knows exactly what struggles I'm facing.

She considers me for a moment, then she nods. "What about the Mating Trials?"

I frown. "What about them?"

"You're an eligible Omega, Maddie. For all you know, you could be the Omega who is selected from Cambridge tomorrow."

I've never been particularly ladylike, but the snort that escapes me isn't only unladylike, it's barbaric. "That's never going to happen."

Someone would have to nominate me for me to even be

considered, and I can count the number of friends I have within these walls without the need of a single finger.

"Why not?" she asks like she honestly doesn't understand. "You have as good a chance of being selected as any other Omega here."

"Not really. Even if miraculously, I *am* selected, I won't be the one the Royal Pack chooses in the end. They'd take one look at me and send me home. Besides, I'd be as frustrated as an Alpha in rut with all the primping and bowing and scraping."

"Oh, I doubt that. I think an Omega could get used to living in a castle and being waited on hand and foot, even if there might be some pomp and circumstance to put up with."

"Maybe, but it doesn't matter. You're forgetting that I'd have to be nominated to be considered for Royal Selection. No one would have nominated me. I don't know if you've noticed, but I'm not a part of the social hierarchy around here."

She waves me off. "You never know."

I laugh. "With this, yeah, I think I do."

It's a sour admission. While I have my opinions about antiquated, outdated traditions like the Trials, I wouldn't have minded the security that would've come with being bonded to royals.

But I can't afford to get hung up on unrealistic things like *hopes* and *dreams*. I need to keep my feet on the ground and my head firmly out of the clouds.

And yet, Ms. Frampton's words whisper through my mind for the rest of the day.

You're an eligible Omega, Maddie. For all you know, you could be the Omega who is selected from Cambridge tomorrow.

MADDIE

You never know.

I push through the hedges at the rear of the academy and climb astride my bicycle to head home after class. It's breaking at least one law and three school rules, but I can't afford the Omega-only bus that runs from here to my neighborhood and my dad doesn't have the time or gas money to be picking me up every day. So, I go alone.

On my way down the bumpy trail that leads to the sideroads, I can't shake the seed of hope Ms. Frampton planted. I mean, maybe...

Damn it.

Don't be ridiculous Maddie.

The only thing I should be focused on is reality.

As I let off the brake and let gravity do the work of propelling me down the hill from the Academy, I thank my lucky stars for making it through the day unscathed from the likes of Clara and her minions.

My number-one anti-fan and her demon squad probably spent the day too busy primping for Clara's shoo-in selection tomorrow to torment me. Since the royal family started the first Omega Academy hundreds of years ago and remains the largest benefactor for all of them, they've decided for this year's Mating Trials, the Omegas will be selected from OAs around the world instead of from the usual pool of titled rich kids only a few cousins removed from blood relation.

Our Academy is one of the oldest, founded around the same time as the beta university with whom we share a town. We're affiliated with it, and we're held in the same regard. Generations of Omegas who have attended the institution have gone on to do great things. The self-

CHAPTER ONE

appointed shining star of our year—no, of our entire generation—is Clara Turner.

At least I won't have to deal with her anymore once she's selected.

The fact she'll be gone is the silver lining I cling to at this point. *Well, I also have the new Riley North book to settle in with tonight, so technically, I can focus on two silver linings.*

The state of the buildings deteriorate dramatically as I get closer to home. Litter dots the sidewalks, which are lined by brown, unkempt hedges. Since Fen Road isn't a place where I want to be caught not paying attention, I shove my thoughts away. I'm alert to my surroundings for the rest of the way home.

As I turn onto our block, the first thing that catches my eye is my five-year-old brother, Kevin, playing in our front yard. Alone. At nearly sunset. Again.

My stomach churns, head spinning on a swivel. I don't see anyone who looks too dodgy, but I up my pace anyway, knowing it can only take a second for something terrible to happen.

I nearly fall off the bike in my haste, letting it slide to the ground as I arrive, taking my foot with it, caught beneath the pedal.

Shit. I gasp, regaining my balance just before my head could connect with the rough edge of the sidewalk.

Wobbly but on my feet, I barrel toward my brother and gently circle my fingers around his thin upper arm. "Kev, what are you doing out here alone? It's dangerous, bubba, you know that."

Brown eyes fill with tears as they meet mine. He nods but shrugs his tiny shoulders. "I know, Maddie. I'm sorry. Mummy and Daddy are fighting again. It's too loud."

MADDIE

My heart splinters in my chest. "I know, honey, but let's go inside, okay? You can come play in my room."

He burrows into my side when I wrap my arm around his shoulders and lead him up the steps and to the front door. Thankfully, my parents are arguing, and they don't hear the telltale creak of it opening as Kevin and I tiptoe into the house.

Honestly, maybe we should make some noise so they'll hear us. Maybe they'd stop. But it'd only postpone the fight until later, when they might wake Kevin with their angry voices.

They're both under a lot of pressure, but I really wish they'd be more careful around Kev. At the very least, wait until I'm home so I can keep him busy or take him out while they have their spat.

Once we've made it to my small bedroom and shut the door behind us, I drop my satchel and pass Kevin a puzzle to build. I've always got one in here for occasions like this. He takes it without arguing and sits cross-legged on my narrow bed, drawing the square of cut cardboard from between the mattress and the wall to set atop the lumpy blanket.

Guilt crushes my chest when I realize my parents are arguing about money again, and I do my best to tune out their raised voices.

This is why I couldn't tell Ms. Frampton the truth about what comes next for me.

I have thought about it, but she won't like or support the options I've come up with.

My parents need help.

I need to make some money, and I need to do it fast. I

CHAPTER ONE

can't make my parents wait until I've finished the school year before I earn some sort of income to help pay the bills.

If I want to stay in school, which I do, the only other option I have to make money fast is to sell one of my scent glands. It's drastic, but as I curl up next to my brother with my parents' argument intensifying on the other side of my door, I know I have to do *something*.

While Omegas from all four corners of the globe are spending tonight dreaming about being selected for the Trials and bonding with a pack of royal heartthrobs, I wonder how one goes about selling a scent gland—and where I might find someone willing to purchase one of mine.

TWO

—

KAZ

ON THE FINAL evening of life as I know it, the door to my chambers opens without so much as a knock to precede the entry of my unwelcome guest.

Without bothering to move my gaze away from the twinkling bursts of starlight in the inky sky above, I tighten my grip on my telescope, about to tell the intruder to fuck off until I recognize the crisp voice ringing out behind me.

"Really, Kaspian, have you nothing better to do on the eve of the Trials than to play with that old thing?"

Since not even *I* can tell the queen herself to fuck off, the retort dies on my tongue. I exhale slowly before straightening up. "No, Mother, I don't."

Resisting the urge to shove my hands into my hair, clench my jaw, and demand to know what she's doing here, I turn slowly. I keep my expression stoic and my voice polite but even. "I wasn't aware you were planning a visit tonight, Mother. To what do I owe the pleasure?"

She arches a questioning, manicured-to-within-an-inch-of-its-life eyebrow at me. "The queen needs a reason to visit her own son the night before such a momentous event? Perhaps I've simply come by to check on you."

"Perhaps."

I meet her deep brown eyes directly, aware that heads have rolled for less than the tone of voice I'm about to use on her. "If that's the case, Mother, then if it's all the same to you, I'd prefer to spend my final night of freedom alone."

Her red-painted lips part, chin rising a smidge higher. It's the only indication I get that she even heard me. Instead of responding or leaving, she folds her hands regally over her stomach and moves to the wall of bookshelves to her left.

Every available wall in my chambers has been lined with books and shelving. If it won't block a window, there's a bookshelf there. This is nothing new to her. It didn't happen overnight, yet she studies them now like she's never seen them.

"The announcements will begin at five tomorrow morning because of the time zone differences between academies," she says thoughtfully, like it's only occurring to her right this minute. "I'll expect you and your packmates in the drawing room with me to watch the coverage."

"Yes, Mother." *It's only been on my calendar since shortly after the event of my birth.* "We'll be there. Is that all?"

"No."

She tracks the well-worn spine of an astronomy tome with her fingertip before rubbing the pad of her thumb along her finger like she's ensuring there's no dust on it.

Once she's satisfied not a speck of dust would dare stick to her skin without curtsying, she glances at me over her shoulder. "Five am is going to arrive early, Kaspian. All three of you will have to be in top form for the announcements. The entire world will be watching us. Waiting for your reactions to each of the selected."

I nod. "We're well aware."

"Excellent."

Her high heels clack against the hardwood floors as she strides toward me, her eyes stern on mine as she stops a few feet away. "See to it that Wolfgang and William don't stay up too late. And do not sneak away tonight."

I bite my tongue so hard I feel a sharp pinch of pain before the taste of metal fills my mouth, but I nod like the good little prince she made sure I was raised to be. She can't tell that deep down inside, I'm hurling obscenities at her for treating us like children now when she wasn't bothered to back when we were, in fact, children.

Thankfully, my tolerance for discomfort is fairly high. I'm sure my face won't betray what I feel or that I've bitten a goddamn chunk out of my tongue. Her chest rises in a deep breath as she stares at me, undoubtedly assessing if there's any hint of a lie in my eyes.

If that *is* what she's looking for, she won't find it. Wolf and Tai—not *William*, though it frustrates me to no end that she insists on calling him by his middle name—are right downstairs. I can feel them through our pack bond. They're not planning on going anywhere either.

They're obviously aware of the storm brewing inside me though, their concern flowing freely through our bond. *That's just fucking great. Now I need to appease them before I can go back to my telescope.* I can sense their distress at my discomfort already. If I don't go to them, they'll just come to me.

In all fairness, it isn't their fault. I shouldn't be irritated that they're concerned about me when I'm feeling as strongly as I am right now. If the tables were turned and I felt this kind of intense, negative emotion coming from either of them, I wouldn't have just been concerned. I'd already be by their sides, ready to raze the world to the ground to make the responsible party suffer.

My mother nods curtly as her palms move to her hips, I know what's coming. She's been in lecture mode for weeks now. Whenever she takes this pose, she's about to drone on about things I'm so sick of hearing that I may lose my dinner on her shoes.

"The Omega Trials are a necessary and important part of our history, Kaspian. You would do well to remember that. In the coming weeks I will not have the three of you making fools of us by not taking this seriously."

"Yes, Mother. We are taking it seriously. Very seriously. However, it is worth mentioning"—*again*—"that we're the only nation left doing anything like this."

Her full lips purse as her brow smooths out and annoyance flashes in her eyes. "Look out your window, Kaspian. Does it look like you're in Jordan, Eswatini, or Denmark?"

She waits a long moment, but I do not peer out the window to the manicured gardens and the walls of the castle estate in the distance.

"No."

"Are we clear on this?"

"Crystal."

Arguing with her won't change her stance. I've tried, but she's dug in and will defend her position like it's a fortress under attack.

Although I don't make a habit of giving in, in this instance, I do. Ultimately, she is queen. If I push her too hard, she could retaliate in some way I'd like less than this.

CHAPTER TWO

She's my mother, but she's as cold and ruthless as they come.

Which is saying something, coming from me, but I digress.

After giving me a final, meaningful look, she reminds me that we're to be in the drawing room at a quarter to five. Then she takes her leave. When she's gone, I heave out a breath, sink down on my haunches, and scream into my hands with my palms clamped tight over my mouth to muffle the sound.

It won't make a damn bit of difference, but heaven help me, I wish I could make her see reason. Unfortunately, she already thinks she does. She views this as part of our faithful and honorable duty, and refuses to consider the possibility that the Trials are not necessary anymore.

Secretly, I think the entire outdated tradition is a ploy for her to be able to handpick the next queen. While my pack and I might have some sway in who stays and who goes among the selected at first, ultimately, my mother will 'guide' the final selection.

As I rise again, I smooth out my shirt and start toward the door. Wolf and Tai will be on their way up soon if I don't beat them to it.

After briefly looking in the mirror to make sure there's no outward trace of my feelings, I head out the door and remind myself once again that I need to play the game. It will only be a few more years until my mother will pass the torch and I'll be king. Then, I'll finally have the chance to do some good with my power. I'll be able to make all the changes I want to make to the system.

Maybe I'll abolish the Omega Trials so no future generation will have to subject themselves to the absolute absurdity of it all.

Until that happens, I have to keep up appearances. Even if it feels like it might bloody kill me long before my mother starts thinking about retirement.

Doing my best not to look as pouty and doomed as I feel, I stride into the hall of our pack quarters at the palace. Wolf and Tai are in our rec room, enjoying our last official night of freedom, when I walk in.

Tai stands at the pool table with a tall glass of whiskey in one hand and a Beta's ass in the other. Another Beta is draped across his side, although I'm sure it's difficult for him to take a drink with her positioned the way she is. She's got her tits pushed into his arm, though, so I doubt he minds much. Not paying too much attention to the Betas, he's watching our resident playboy packmate in action, getting turned on by seeing Wolf receive pleasure.

Wolf, in all his golden-haired glory, has his head thrown back and his lips parted on a silent O as he thrusts his swollen cock into a Beta's mouth. She's on her knees between his spread legs, her eyes rolled back, watery, with mascara smudging their rims.

His strong hand fists her hair, ropes of muscle rippling in his forearm where they disappear into his rolled-up shirt sleeves. Strands of the beta's blonde curls stick out between his fingers as they flex and release on her head.

Empty beer bottles are scattered around his feet.

Judging by the level of the ghastly expensive bottle of whiskey standing on the bar, that's not Tai's first drink either.

As the door slams behind me, another wave of frustration tightens in my gut despite the swell of hunger beginning to grow low in my groin.

It isn't often we bring in *outside* affection, but both my

packmates know how riled up it gets me watching them with anyone else. It's one-part jealousy, one-part sweet torture, the two mixing together to create the best and worst sort of drug.

"Jesus, you two do know that we're expected to be up at the ass crack of dawn, right?"

Tai's russet-brown eyes dart away from Wolf to meet mine. They're so warm and cozy that it makes me itch to take the place of both Betas at his side.

"There you are," Tai says. "We were just talking about cutting this short to come check on you."

I shake my head, pinching the bridge of my nose as a pang of frustrated pain kicks through my skull.

"Awe, come on, Kaz...partying tonight won't change our fate tomorrow. We could show up looking like absolute shit and they'll still ship the Omegas here."

I sigh, knowing Tai is probably humoring Wolf because our packmate can be such a knothead, but he's also not wrong. Besides, they've proven time and time again that a cold shower and a bucket of hot coffee can set anything to rights by morning if they're needed in any form of royal function outside the usual duties.

Wolf finally breaks out of the haze of lust he's in and looks at me from beneath heavy lids. Some of the heat melts out of his sea-green eyes even though the Beta's head bounces enthusiastically between his legs. "We're just getting in our last kicks before we're bonded to an Omega, mate."

"Being bonded didn't stop my father from getting in his kicks," I mutter as I stride deeper into the room and head for the bar. I don't know why my mind went straight there, but there it was, and there was no dialing it back.

KAZ

I need a drink.

One won't hurt.

As the whiskey splashes into my tumbler, I see Wolf pushing the Beta off and Tai extricating himself from his two. In no time, they're next to me. Their heat radiates into my sides, making me feel like someone has gently applied a soothing balm to the deepest recesses of my soul.

Before we formed a pack, I had no idea it would be like this. I'd read so many books about it and not one came close to doing it justice. These guys know me better than I know myself. Where some packs are a mix of classes or a mix of sexualities, we're lucky that we found ourselves with one another. That all of us want the same things. Namely, each other. In ways more than what platonic bonds can offer.

We're insanely attracted to each other, and none of us have any qualms about acting on it, but it's not…romantic. Not really. It's a mutual understanding. A meeting of souls. We were friends first. We would always be friends first. A brotherhood before anything else.

It's *pack*.

Unfortunately, I can't act on my attraction to them nearly as often as they do with each other, but it's because *Mother Dearest* keeps me too busy. Someone has to be the killjoy who takes care of the important things. Tonight, though, I'm not too busy, and I'm in desperate need of losing myself in the only two people I trust completely.

Tai pushes a hand into his silver-white hair as he regards me, his gaze cautious as it sweeps across my face. "Are you okay?"

"No. Are you?"

He shrugs, drawing in a deep breath as his free hand finds mine and his long fingers wrap around it. He strokes the inside of my palm with his thumb, those reddish-brown eyes still drinking me in. "We will be, Kaz. We'll all be okay."

Wolf slides his arms around me from behind, pressing his erection into my ass nonchalantly as he rests his chin on my shoulder. "Are we going to stand around gossiping all night or are we going to have a bit of fun before the cameras move in?"

I push back against him, feeling my heartbeat speed up as my cock grows against my fly. "Maybe just a taste of fun."

Wolf smirks and then winks at me before he goes back to his Beta. Tai hangs back with me. "I can tell them to leave if you want."

"No, it's fine. Wolf might strangle you with his bare hands if you make him stop again right now."

I incline my head toward where the Beta has resumed her position. Wolf is fucking her mouth in earnest now, clearly chasing the release he denied himself when he pushed her off to come make sure I was okay.

My dick swells more as I keep watching him, but I'm too reticent to join the fun. To be honest, I'm jealous Tai and Wolf managed to have any fun at all with the pressure of tomorrow looming over us.

A Beta notices the growing bulge in my trousers. When he does, he links his arm with mine and makes bedroom eyes at me. "Want to show me your chambers?"

"No, thank you," I decline politely, my mood already souring. "I think it's for the best I hit the hay by myself tonight."

I try to chase the taste of my own bitterness down with the last of the whiskey from my tumbler before setting it down with a dull thud on the bar counter.

KAZ

Tai cocks his head at me, and I tip mine back at him. "You boys have fun. I'll see you bright and early. I'm not doing anyone favors hanging around here tonight with the mood I'm in."

Tai's sleek jawline hardens as he stares back at me. "She give you any shit?"

Leave it to him to know exactly what had me in knots earlier.

"No more than usual," I say, but as I turn around to head to bed, Tai's hand catches my forearm and he follows me out into the hall.

Once we're out of the rec room, he tugs me back so hard that I'm jerked around and my chest crashes into his. His hand is in my hair and his mouth claims mine with heated desire. Slivers of pain shoot through me as he tightens his grip until my scalp stings. It feels so good that I groan and rock my hips forward until my cock is tightly pressed against his.

"I hate that you feel like this," Tai murmurs between rough kisses as he pushes my back to the wall. His fingers are already skating down my side. "Let me help you blow off some steam, yeah? You know you'll never sleep otherwise."

I bite my lip, looking down the shadowed corridor on either side.

Right here? Now?

"The queen is roaming the halls tonight."

His teeth take over for me, nipping my lower lip hard before sucking away the sting. "If she's roaming these halls this late at night, that's on her. This is our territory, and I want to mark it. You in?"

CHAPTER TWO

I practically growl, tossing away the reins of the infallible self-control I pride myself on. "Fuck yes."

Tai grins against my lips before he runs his hand to the front of my trousers and unbuckles my belt.

A dark chuckle escapes me, but as he lowers himself to his knees, I can't help but wonder how things will change tomorrow. When the halls are filled with strange Omegas and—

I moan when Tai's warm lips brush against my cock, his tongue licking a hot path along the underside of my shaft.

Oh, fuck.

I work to shove the pestering thoughts from my mind.

There'll be plenty of time to worry tomorrow. Tonight, right now, all I want is to feel. As always, Earl Taiyo William Althorpe knows exactly how to make me do just that.

He takes me deeper into his throat, covering my length with the glistening of his saliva as he pulls back, grasping the base of my cock where my knot has already begun to swell. He pumps it while sucking on the tip, his eyes rolling back as he tastes the salt of my precum and drinks it down.

"Fuck, Tai," I groan, fisting my hands in my dark hair as my hips flex, pushing harder into his mouth.

He nods on my cock, urging me to take him. To use him.

A soft moan falls from my mouth as I thrust past his lips and he opens wide for me, letting me fuck his mouth.

Tai's hands come around to roughly grasp my ass, urging me harder, faster, even as he chokes.

His eyes water and the phantom of a triumphant smirk turns the edges of his lips up as he twists his hand around my knot, wringing me into him. I buck, almost pulling out, but he keeps me there, holding on with the grip of his fist and the vacuum of his dirty mouth as he sucks until I'm coming undone.

Tai works my knot in the way only he can, teasing the sensitive ball of nerves until I know any second now I'll be absolutely fucking lost to sensation. His to control. Malleable as clay in his capable hands.

He chokes on my cock again, and I feel the walls of his throat constrict around the head of my cock. The sensation tips me right over the edge. My hands drop like stones, fingers violently twisting into his hair to hold him to me as I come hard down his throat.

I haven't even finished shuddering when he lifts to his feet and presses a salty kiss to my mouth, gripping the back of my neck fiercely. "Remember, Kaz, it's us against the world. *Us*, before anyone else."

He presses his forehead to mine, and I nod against him. "I know."

THREE

—

MADDIE

MY BODY PROTESTS more than it should as I stretch my arms above my head, yawn, and eventually heave myself out of bed. I'm only twenty. My joints shouldn't feel like they need to be oiled before I can move in the mornings.

I peek over at Kevin's sleeping form and tug his thumb gently from his mouth. While it's a habit he's broken while awake, it's one he can't seem to shake while asleep. I snort quietly to myself, noticing how his legs are stretched on a diagonal across the single mattress, leaving me only the tiny sliver I currently occupy. The stiffness in my arms and shoulders makes more sense now. We were pretty crammed in last night.

"Kev?" I murmur quietly, brushing my knuckles gently across his cheek. "It's time to wake up. Come on, sleepyhead. Let's go."

He groans and rolls over, covering his face with his arms before pulling the blanket over his messy brown curls.

"Not yet, Addie," he whines in a sleepy voice, and I

smirk at the accidental nickname born of an inability to make his m and n sounds when he was a couple years younger.

"You're too little for that," I chuckle, bunching my fingers in the blanket before tugging it down. "Sorry, bubba. You'll be late if you don't get moving. I'm going to take a shower and then I need to get dressed. If you're not up before I get back, I'm going to dump a bucket of water on your head."

He pulls the covers down to glare at me over their edge. "You wouldn't."

I raise a mischievous brow at him. "Wouldn't I?"

His eyes widen and I laugh to myself as I push off the bed. My door squeaks softly as I pull it open, but the house is otherwise quiet. Faint sounds drift from the kitchen, telling me that Mum is there waiting for us. Probably having a cup of tea. But there's no clanging of pots or pans. No scent of breakfast wafts through the house.

Just like it does every morning when this realization hits, my heart pangs painfully in my chest. *It never used to be this way.*

Before Mum was diagnosed with Cervus, her energy knew no bounds. She worked all day, was up late at night completing the household chores with me, and then she'd be at my door first thing in the morning to wake me up, breakfast already on the go. She wouldn't have any of my protesting that a piece of half burnt toast was plenty.

My parents used to be laughing together by the time I finally walked into the kitchen. They were happy, in love, and excited for another day—regardless of how dreary that day might turn out to be.

Now, I'm not even certain Dad is home at all, though I

suspect he is. Just still in the bedroom or out in the backyard shed, puttering and muttering to himself. Between that and endless job applications that go unanswered, he'll keep busy enough not to go totally insane from being out of work.

They don't realize I know the extent of our troubles. Fear and guilt trickle into me like ice cubes sliding down my spine. I haven't decided exactly what I'm going to do yet, but my mission for the day between classes is to research—both part-time jobs and selling Omega scent glands.

As I walk into the bathroom and strip down, the irony isn't lost on me that every other eligible Omega has woken up with hope in their hearts while I woke up with resignation.

I step under the dribble of cool water that counts as spray for our shower and race through washing only the most necessary bits before I get out again, not wanting to rack up the water bill on top of everything else.

Once I'm dressed, I pull my damp but unwashed hair into a ponytail and then I'm done.

The bargain shampoo I bought on the last grocery run leaves my long wavy deep copper hair like straw, so I only bother washing once a week, sleeking a drop of conditioner through just the ends to keep them from puffing out like Clara Turner's pom poms.

Since cosmetic products are also a luxury, I've been saving the last dregs of my single mascara tube for graduation because I know Dad will be there snapping about a million photos I don't want to cringe every time I look back at. So, I apply nothing today save for a smear of the moisturizer Mum and I share over my cheeks and jaw where my skin tends to dry out this time of year.

MADDIE

When I look into the minimally fogged-up bathroom mirror and my reflection stares back at me, I sigh. Since my hair got a bit wet, it looks dirty even though I washed it just three days ago. The smattering of freckles across my nose and cheeks makes me look dirty, too. I love freckles on other people, but mine aren't cute. They're like these light brown smudges that won't come off. None of them quite perfectly round, like they could have been drawn on by my kid brother as opposed to the skilled hand of life's artist.

Tiny bits of errant string and fluff sit on the collar of my shirt where it's fraying. My jumper is definitely on the threadbare side, dull patches of the shirt underneath visible through the fabric. I found both uniform items in a thrift store a couple of years ago. They were already well-loved at the time I bought them, but now, they're a bit worse for wear. Too bad they're all I've got until graduation.

Spinning around, I hang up my towel before heading to the kitchen. As I predicted, Dad isn't here. Mum sits at our small, round dining table, nursing a cup of tea.

My heart gives another, more painful pang at the sight of her, but I hide it behind a smile she can't see anyway.

"Good morning," I say cheerfully as I stride across the kitchen to drop a kiss on her mop of dark curls. "Is it just us this morning?"

She turns her head toward the sound of my voice, the green eyes I inherited—ones that used to be so clear and bright—now almost completely clouded over. A few months ago, Cervus rendered her legally blind and began to eat away at the hearing in her right ear. I can't believe how quickly the disease has progressed, but the evidence of its cruelty sits right in front of me. It's bad enough to watch it

CHAPTER THREE

take from my mother, but it's also a reminder of what could be waiting for me in the years to come.

Cervus isn't hereditary as a rule, but it's a lot more likely for those who've had a parent with it.

"Well, Kevin is supposed to be up, but Dad's gone out already."

Although she's trying hard to match my cheerful tone, there's a definite strain to her voice. I know, I *know* she hates it just as much as I do. She manages a soft smile as she points toward the kitchen counter. "The cereal's out. How are you feeling, baby? Today could be the day, you know. For you *and* for Dad. He has a promising interview, and you might be selected for the Trials. You know, I heard there's compensation for your time even if you aren't selected in the end. Not much, but a little something." She sighs wistfully. "It's a big day."

As if on cue, I can hear the radio mutter something about the trial coverage beginning in just *a couple short hours!*

Damn it all.

I should've known she'd bring it up. She's been hinting at it all month, asking if I know whether or not I'd been nominated.

Like always, I don't want to crush her hope, so I pretend like I have a chance, guiltily glad she can't see my face. "Who knows? I might be sleeping in a castle tonight."

She chuckles. "Do you think the toilets are made of gold?"

"Probably."

I get a jumpstart on Kevin's breakfast even though my little brother isn't here yet. When he finally stumbles into the kitchen, he's got his shirt on the wrong way around and the waistband of his trousers is bunched up.

Without saying anything about it, I continue the conversation with my mother while heading over to help him when he shoots me a pleading look. We don't like her knowing when we need help. The last thing she needs is to feel guilty about not being able to see when he's done something like bungled dressing himself.

"Wouldn't it be amazing?" she croons, pressing her hands to her chest as her features soften in that dreamy way. "My daughter—*royalty*. But even those royal boys don't deserve you."

I shove a bite of cereal into my mouth, scoffing quietly to myself, probably looking like a savage. I'd be banned from the castle before I've even set foot in it if any royal saw me eating this way. Thankfully, it doesn't matter because I can't be banned from a place I've never been and will never see. So I can eat like an animal all I damn well please.

Kev raises a brow at me as he drinks the milk from his bowl and that only makes me intensify the speed at which I shove the cereal into my face, earning myself a giggle from him.

"Oh, Kev, slow down." I chuckle as he tries to copy me and spills milk down the front of his shirt. I wouldn't get points for being the best role model, but at least I made him smile before school.

Mum drops her head, going back to drinking her tea with a pained knot between her brows.

"I bet the royal pack are really nice," I offer her, playing more into her fantasy to cheer her back up. It's the image the media would have you believe, but who knew in reality. They could be a bunch of spoiled rotten assholes.

CHAPTER THREE

She hums her agreement, the ghost of a grin on her lips as the radio crackles and dies.

"Not again," she gripes, throwing her hands up. "It's been doing that for days."

I try to get it working again, but it's useless. Something has shorted beyond repair. Mentally, I count the meager few dollars I've managed to keep saved under my mattress. Not enough to help with any bills, but maybe enough for a new radio at the thrift store.

"Sorry, Mum, I can't get it going but maybe I can borrow one from school to bring home for you."

She wouldn't like me buying a new one for her.

I finish breakfast and a quick tidy up of both the kitchen and my little brother before kissing them both goodbye. Mum's soft hands cling to mine for a moment before she lets go of me. "I can't wait to hear how it went when you get home."

"I'll see you later. Love you."

"I love you too, sweetheart." She gives my hands a final squeeze. As I turn to leave, I bump my hip into the counter and jarring pain shoots through me.

My hands fly to my likely bruised hip, but I don't want Mum to worry. Biting back the howl of agony that wants to escape, I hobble out, muttering a string of silent curses until the front door shuts behind me. "Ow. Motherfucker, that hurt."

Being clumsy is downright dangerous, but as I look around our front yard, I realize it's not as dangerous as forgetting to bring my bicycle inside.

Unsurprisingly, it's found a new owner overnight. Now, I'm definitely going to be late. Great.

Oh, for the love of the king's unfaithful bullocks!

MADDIE

Clutching the straps of my backpack on my shoulders, I grit my teeth and gingerly make my way down the steps. If I've already missed the city bus, I'll have to walk the four miles to school with a bruised hip.

Just. Bloody. Great.

WHEN I FINALLY ARRIVE AT the Academy, the rest of the school is already heading into the auditorium. The buzz of excitement among the crowd is palpable, making my heart flutter in my chest.

Everyone else is dressed to impress. They look like they've spent hours at hair and nail salons, with perfectly applied makeup, pressed uniforms, and jewelry that could pay my family's rent for a month. I've never felt more like the scholarship Omega than I do right now, but I keep my head up and my back straight.

"Why did she even come?" Clara says snidely to one of the male Omegas in her demon squad when I pass them.

"Oh wow, is that an actual hole in her blouse?"

I ignore them, hurtling back acidic retorts only from the safety of my mind.

My gaze remains on the back of the head of the Omega in front of me as we wait in the long line of students waiting to take their seats inside. My chest burns when Clara continues. "It's a wonder they're selecting someone from our academy, seeing that we've been letting in the street rats."

What is this, Aladdin? I roll my eyes, but my hands press tighter between my knees.

"They're not selecting *someone*, Clara," an adoring

CHAPTER THREE

minion says to her with a pointed look. "They're selecting *you*. We all know it."

If you're so sure about that, why are all of you, her loyal friends, equally primped and pressed? I let out a long, slow breath before inhaling just as deeply.

"Just because I'm the class president doesn't mean it's definitely going to be me," she protests with such obvious immodesty that I have to work hard at holding back a frustrated scream.

"You're also the student representative to the faculty *and* you're an excellent swimmer."

"And your father owns, like, half of Cambridge."

Clara chuckles with false modesty. "I mean, you're not wrong, but you know the nominations are blind. I was just nominee number five or something to the Selection Committee."

Her minions laugh nervously at that, not wanting to give credence to the thought in their leader's head that one of them could very well be selected over her. But let's be real. With all the money in the world, there's nothing Clara's Daddy Dearest can't buy, including her spot among the selected.

It's about at that point that I can finally get away from them, and I bounce on the balls of my feet eagerly. Instead of following the masses toward the front of the auditorium, I veer to the right, fighting against the flow, and find a nice seat at the back. Just enough light filters in through the window behind me that I'll be able to read my Riley North while the rest of them wait for Clara's name to be called out. I only got halfway through it last night after Kev fell asleep, and I'm dying to see what happens next.

Headmistress Hartigan strides onto the stage as soon as

most of the Omegas are seated. I snort at how smug the strict woman looks today. Her hair is pinned up in a severe bun as always, but she's positively gloating as she reaches the podium and welcomes us all before the reason for her smugness is revealed.

"I have been informed that Cambridge OA had the most nominees submitted of any school across the globe!"

She smiles into the camera set up in front of the stage. "Of course, that speaks not only to the caliber of students we have here, but also to our commitment as a school to the Royal Family as well as to the proud tradition of the Mating Trials."

She motions to a man at her side who stands so straight and so still, it looks like he has a carrot up his arse and he's doing his best to keep it there.

"Without any further ado, allow me to introduce the Cambridge Coordinator from the Royal Trials Department, Mr. Mitchell."

The auditorium bursts into applause when she starts clapping, and the sharp-suited, carrot-clenching man takes her place behind the podium. "Thank you, Headmistress. As you all know, the Mating Trials are an age-old, important tradition that occurs every third generation. As such, it really is an opportunity that only comes around once in a lifetime."

Before he continues with his flashy speech, he pauses for a moment to let the weight of his words sink in. "This year, the Royal Family decreed that one Omega from each of the forty academies around the world shall be selected to participate in the first round of the Trials. These Omegas were selected by an independent, neutral committee based

CHAPTER THREE

on nominations from Academy staff, dignitaries, and instructors at their individual schools."

I frown. There weren't nominations permitted by the student body?

I figured that's where most of them would come from, but...

Well, anyway, I knew the professors could nominate students, but it's only now just occurred to me that there could be one professor—or more accurately *librarian*—who could have nominated me.

My stomach flips painfully, and I clutch my book against it, swallowing hard as a cool, clammy sweat slicks my chest.

"Omegas from academies in different time zones ahead of our own have already been announced. We'd like to congratulate the selected Omegas from Australia, Japan, India, Dubai, and Ukraine."

He inclines his head as more applause breaks out. When it dies down, he gets to the part where he'll announce Clara.

"The Omega who was selected from this academy was chosen based on her studious, subservient nature and having a track record of excellent grades. The nomination committee would also like to note that the essay she wrote on the importance of the Omega system in modern society was *remarkable*. A true credit to everything Omega Academy strives to teach its students."

As I process his words, my heart stutters, and my lungs seize.

No.

My scalp stings, the pins and needles falling until they pinch and stab into every part of me.

This can't be happening.

MADDIE

This is not *happening.*

Clara could've written a similar paper, I tell myself. Anyone at the academy could've. And then I remember Ms. Frampton specifically mentioning that she'd finally read my essay. Could she have submitted it to the nomination committee?

Oh shit, oh shit, oh shit.

I'm going to pass out.

"Omega Academy Cambridge, please welcome to the stage and assist me in congratulating your very own, Maddison Darling!"

He says it like he's expecting a roar from the crowd. Instead, there's a rush of gasps and only scattered applause before the auditorium goes so quiet one would be able to hear a kitten fart.

Mr. Mitchell clears his throat uncomfortably, his brows lowering, confused by my academy's reaction. He'd expected bigger fanfare.

I wish I was invisible.

I wish I could sink into my seat, down into the floor, and disappear into nothing.

The cameras in the cavernous hall pan slowly, obviously expecting an eruption to occur around the selected Omega, but I'm seated between people who don't even know me.

They're craning their necks, looking around like they're trying to find me.

"There she is," I hear someone shout. "Up there."

My teeth clench so hard they might crack.

A spotlight overhead clicks on, the warm white light streaking over the student body until it lands squarely on me.

Holy fuck.

CHAPTER THREE

Fuck. Fuck. Fuck.

I rise, so nervous that I can't hear anything over my heart jackhammering in my chest. My vision is black around the edges, and I clutch seat backs from the row ahead as I robotically turn and try to scoot past the knees of the other students in my row.

"Congratulations," one of them whispers as I pass.

I don't even know what to say.

"Try not to trip," another teases, and a fresh bolt of unadulterated fear rips through me.

They totally just jinxed it. I'm screwed.

Hushed murmurs break out all around me as I pause for a shallow breath, my knuckles turning white from their grip on the seat next to me.

Don't pass out. Do *not* pass out.

Do not trip over your own feet, Maddie.

I repeat. No. Bloody. Tripping.

When I finally make it to the aisle, I focus intently on putting one foot in front of the other, hyper-aware of the cameras following my every move. *Fucking hell, how many people are watching me right now?*

Nope.

Can't think about that.

It occurs to me that it could be in the millions, but that not one of them actually knows me. My family and Ms. Frampton are the only people who do. My mum can't watch, my dad is hunting for a job, and Kevin is at school.

The knowledge that absolutely no one in the world except my literature instructor is supporting me from afar right now settles like a lead weight on my chest. The weight gets even heavier when I look up to find Headmistress Hartigan watching me with her nose scrunched up like

MADDIE

she's smelled something vile. Like she wants to squash me like a bug and announce an understudy to take my place.

I might like that, too.

Tearing my gaze away from her hostile expression, I make eye contact with the faculty onstage behind her.

Ms. Frampton winks at me.

I'm going to murder her. That's how I'll get out of this. Prison. It's perfect.

She mimes taking a deep breath and gives me an encouraging smile that's just warm enough to make me reconsider the murder plan as I manage to reach the base of the stage.

Once I'm beside Mr. Mitchell, he grins like he's about to hand me a check for five million dollars, but he also seems confused when he notices no one else seems to be as excited for me as he is, Ms. Frampton excluded.

"*Er*, right. Congratulations again, Ms. Darling."

He shakes my hand for the cameras, placing a gentle hand on the back of my shoulder to guide me to face the cameras for a clear shot.

I grimace into the lens, squinting through the brightness.

Mr. Mitchell lifts the microphone out of its cradle and dread coils in my gut like a poison slicked snake.

"How do you feel, Maddison, knowing you were selected above hundreds of others to undergo the trials to be bonded to the Royal Pack?"

My heart about gives out when he moves the microphone to my mouth.

Every drop of blood in my head races out.

I'm dizzy, probably about to sway, yet he still waits for an answer.

CHAPTER THREE

"I, uh." A rogue wave of vertigo almost takes me, and I step out, widening my stance in a last ditch attempt to stay standing. "I-I'm honored, and shocked, to be honest."

The coordinator grins again, laughing in a way that's meant to put me at ease.

"That's to be expected. Is there anything you'd like to say to your friends and family at home, to the school, or to your fellow selected Omegas?"

"I, *uh*, yes, *uhm*, thank you, and good luck."

I stop short of quoting fiction about forces being with us or the odds being ever in our favor, but only just.

Mr. Mitchell seems to realize I won't become any less awkward and blessedly removes the microphone. He hands it back to the Headmistress before rushing me offstage.

"Well, what a joyous day," Headmistress Hartigan says and the tension in her voice is anything but ambiguous as Mr. Mitchell whispers something in my ear that I'm beyond hearing. I think it was something congratulatory though, so I mutter a thank you as he hauls me out of the auditorium through the back of the stage and the chaos begins.

All the while, I wonder if this nightmare of a morning has been nothing but a dream.

Maybe I'm still in bed next to Kevin.

Maybe when I wake up, it will all...disappear.

FOUR

—

MADDIE

IT DID NOT DISAPPEAR.

No matter how many times I pinched myself.

I'm in a state of detached disbelief by the time a representative from the Royal Trials Department drops me off at home. Mr. Mitchell had to get back to the RTD offices to do…coordinator-y things after subjecting me to an afternoon of paperwork and questioning. He was horrified when I mentioned I'd better go catch the city bus, so he sent me in one of their cars instead.

I wondered if he was going to try to find some way to undo my selection and trade me in for someone more like Clara Turner…

But then I signed the form and he declared it 'official.'

"No turning back now," he joked, leaving me to wonder if refusal had been an option.

Except, I couldn't refuse. How could I even entertain the idea? Mum was right. There was a clause about compensation for my time. It was minimal, but it would increase the longer I stayed at court. Any money was good money if it meant keeping a roof over my family's heads a little longer.

It's almost impossible to believe that after all the cameras, the smiling, and the signing of a dozen documents, it's very possible my family doesn't know yet.

When we pull up to my house, the RTD driver interrupts my thoughts when he turns to me with a dubious look on his face. "Is this the right address?"

I glance at our ramshackle little house with its peeling paint, sagging gutters, and long-forgotten flower pots on the porch. "This is the place. Thank you for the ride."

"Of course." He hesitates. "Are you absolutely certain this is the correct address?"

I am aware it looks abandoned, but his repeating the question irks me more than it should.

I smile over gritted teeth at him. "This is it."

Students from the Omega Academies do *not* typically live in houses that look like they're a mid-winter sneeze away from collapsing.

"You don't have to walk me to the door. I'll be fine from here."

Once again, he hesitates, but then he nods. "I'll be by at seven am to pick you up. We can't be late."

"I understand. I'll see you in the morning."

As soon as I'm out of the car, he speeds away, probably casting furtive glances in his rearview, fearful of being followed. In a ride like that, he probably should be.

I sigh as I trudge up the walk to the front door. Before I go inside, I organize my thoughts. I haven't had a single moment alone since the announcement was made. My hands are still shaking. Coherent thought left the building when my name was called, and it hasn't returned yet.

CHAPTER FOUR

My mouth is drier than cotton left out in the summer sun and yet I know I've sweat through both my undershirt and blouse from the anxiety of it all.

After dragging in a deep breath of air, I hold it in my lungs, then blow it out slowly. Feeling a touch more clear-headed but by no means anywhere near normal, I reach for the door handle. I push down, smiling when I experience my first moment of normalcy in hours. My parents aren't fighting today. Not yet, anyway.

I hear them chatting to Kevin in the kitchen, debating the issue of him wearing a cape to school in the morning. It makes me smile, and I pause in the doorway, wanting to stay in this moment of normalcy for just another few seconds.

The scent of frying onions and potatoes wafts in the air. I inhale it gratefully, feeling grounded by the smell of the simple fare. If we're lucky, there might be a bit of chicken with it, but it'll likely only be joined on the plate by a sprinkling of discount cheese.

Following the sound of their attempts to dissuade my little brother, I walk into the kitchen. Mum and Kevin are already seated at the dining table while Dad stands behind the stove. He's got on an old, stained apron. Dark smudges show under his brown eyes, and his auburn hair sticks up in all directions.

Days-old, graying stubble on his jaw makes him look at least ten years older than his thirty-eight, but he smiles when he sees me walk in. "A bit late, aren't you? We were starting to worry. Ms. Frampton keep you?"

"Simon," Mum admonishes warmly. "It wasn't Ms. Frampton. Today was Selection Day. I'm sure there was a lot going on at the Academy. How did it go, baby? Are we packing to send you to the palace tonight?"

I can't tell if she's joking or actually hopeful, but I suppose it doesn't really matter. Before I can answer her question, Dad frowns. "That was today?"

He turns to me with sympathy already softening his features. Until he sees whatever expression I've got on my face. "Maddie? Are you okay?"

"I...yes. Yeah, I'm good." I stumble the few steps to the closest chair, sitting down as my knees go weak. "Actually, *uh*, Mum's right." I scoff, baffled at the words about to come out of my mouth. "I should probably start packing."

My family falls deathly silent for a moment. Then they erupt in a mixture of surprise and excitement as soon as Dad drops the spatula he was holding. Oil spatters all over the floor, but he doesn't seem to realize as he races toward me.

"You were chosen?" he murmurs into my hair as he envelops me in a bear hug. "Omega mighty, that's...that's..."

"Unexpected?" I fill in in a mutter against his shoulder.

"Amazing news," he corrects me, pressing a kiss to the top of my head.

Another pair of arms join his, thinner and much gentler as my mother squeezes me as hard as her frail body can. "I knew it was going to be you. I just had a feeling. I mean, it had to be. You're the best Omega they've got at the Academy."

A chair shoves back and Kevin patters over to us, his little face bright, hands out, fingers spread wide like he can't contain his own electric excitement. "Addie's going to be a princess," he shouts in his high-pitched little voice.

CHAPTER FOUR

"You are, aren't you, Maddie? You're going to be a princess, and I'll get to play at a castle." He gasps, racing closer, his eyes going impossibly wider. "Will I be *a prince*?"

My heart squeezes, and I laugh-sob into Dad's shoulder, loving his optimism and hating that I know I likely won't make it past the first trial.

Mum mutters about how much she'd have loved to watch the announcement, and Dad putters on about the stability this could bring. "Even if you're not bonded to the Eaton Pack in the end, you might meet another aristocrat at court. You could be a...a duchess! Or a, *um, oh blast,* what is it called? Oh! A countess!"

Finally extricating myself from his arms, I turn to soothe my mother as warm tears press at the back of my eyes. "I wouldn't get your hopes too high, but Mum was right. There's a small compensation they offer, and it increases the longer I'm in the running. It should help, at least. You know, until you find work."

By the sinking expression on my father's face, I know his interview today didn't go as well as he'd hoped, so I don't ask him. Instead, I say, "I'll send you whatever they send me, okay?"

"Nonsense," Mum says. "You'll keep it. Save it. Leave your father and me to sort out our own finances."

"But—"

"Hush," Dad says, squeezing me one last time before letting me go. "We should be celebrating."

Mum chuckles, burying her face in my hair as she adjusts her grip to hold me tight now that she's the only one hugging me. After a few minutes of not saying a thing, she draws back to cup my face in her cool hands.

MADDIE

Dad carries on about the various aristocrats I might meet. Kevin shrieks about how he'll be a prince. But Mum's voice is quiet and genuine as she looks into my eyes like she can see me.

"I hope you find happiness, Maddie. That's the most important thing in this world. Just happiness."

The tears that have been welling in my eyes finally slide out, tracking hot and heavy down my cheeks before I lean forward to rest my head against hers. Breathing in her lavender scent, I realize there's another scent too. A much less pleasant one. The slightly acrid tang of her Cervus tainting her natural Omega pheromones. "Thanks, Mum."

The doctor promised to send a health visitor to check on her and help with the adjustment since she lost the last of her sight, but I don't think that's happened yet. While Dad's been at work and I've been at school, she's been going through this all alone without help and months-long waits between appointments with her primary physician.

Guilt spears through me all over again. *I should've thought about this.*

If the promise of financial support didn't exist, I would've turned the Trials down. However, last night I was praying to every god out there for an opportunity—any opportunity—to help my parents. And this is the opportunity I got.

Dad's eyes meet mine over the pan of potatoes and onions he's back to frying, and I know, no matter what Mum said, he will take any help he can get. If I stay in the trials, he'll let me help them. He doesn't have another choice.

All through dinner, my mind races with possibilities. Ways I could try to stay in the running longer.

CHAPTER FOUR

Blackmail the prince, perhaps?

No.

My beheading won't put food on the table.

Do they even still behead people?

"Shall I help you pack?" Mum asks quietly, bringing me out of the hurricane of my own thoughts once we're finished eating.

"That would be great." I nod, taking her hand as Dad nods at me to go up, taking my usual chore of clearing the plates and doing the washing.

"You'll be all right while I'm gone, won't you?" I ask once we're alone.

Mum sits down on my bed and gives me a soft smile. "Of course, we'll be all right. Don't you dare squander this opportunity by worrying about us, Maddison. All your life, you've worked so hard. Never had a damn thing handed to you. Just this once, do something for yourself. Do whatever will make you happiest."

"What if it's not being bonded to the Eaton pack?"

She chuckles. "Then you escape the palace grounds in the dead of night," she says, lowering her voice to a conspiratorial whisper. "And we'll all run away together."

I laugh, teary all over again but happy all the stress she's been through since Dad lost his last job a month ago hasn't stolen her sense of humor. Honestly, it's ridiculous that those with family members who have been diagnosed with Cervus don't get more leeway to take care of their loved ones.

With the rapid spread of the disease among Omegas these last couple of decades, there really ought to be more focus on support. Financial. Familial. Emotional. Just...*anything*.

MADDIE

I huff out a breath.

Well, if I don't blackmail the prince, perhaps I can at least bring it to his attention that the Crown and their Government are bloody useless in this regard.

I mean, I'd have to phrase it better, but it's the thought that counts.

Mum and I make idle chitchat about what we think the palace and the royals within will be like. Then she says good night and leaves me to get some sleep before the big day tomorrow. Once again though, I toss and turn for a long time. I've barely drifted off when my alarm clock starts blaring.

Groaning as my arm shoots out to silence it, I roll over and promptly fall right out of bed, landing with a dull thump on the floor. *Ooff!*

Pain shoots through my already injured hip. When I finally open my eyes, I realize I fell because Kevin crawled into bed with me during the night and is currently doing his best impression of a starfish, which once again left me with frightfully little space. Regardless of the pain and the rude awakening, I smile when I look at his little sleeping face.

His unruly dark hair is matted, and his delicate features are relaxed. His chest rises and falls evenly as he snoozes, regardless of the alarm and my fall.

I'm going to miss him so much.

"Maddie," Mum calls up the stairs, surprising me since it hasn't happened in so long. "They're going to be here soon, honey!"

When I glance at the clock, I realize she's right. I must've silenced it a bunch of times because now, I've got all of fifteen minutes before the RTD driver will be here to pick me up. Racing to the bathroom and through a quick shower, I thank the rare foresight I had to lay my outfit out last night and rush through getting dressed. It's nothing special, but it's the nicest long sleeved shirt I own and a hand-me-down skirt from Mum.

I've barely pulled my hair up when Dad calls out from below this time. "There's a fancy car outside, Maddie. Is that for you?"

"Yes!"

I run back to my room to grab my ancient suitcase—the kind we used way before the wheeled ones. Then I kiss Kevin on the forehead before heading downstairs. My little brother is still sleeping, but it's better this way.

Saying goodbye to Mum and Dad is hard enough. I'm quite sure saying goodbye to him would've killed me. As it is, I'm crying again when my parents envelop me in their arms, murmuring their well wishes and goodbyes before I'm rushed into the backseat and the door is closed, forcing me to watch my parents wave through the tinted windows as they floor it out of the rough area of town as quickly as they came.

The driver smiles excitedly in the rearview mirror once we've left Fen Road behind us. "There will be more formal paperwork for you to sign this morning. Mr. Mitchell will be there to help you with it. After that, you'll be headed to London with a palace chauffeur!"

More paperwork? That seems impossible after everything I signed yesterday, but lo and behold...

At the Academy, Mr. Mitchell, Headmistress Hartigan, and even Clara are waiting for me. Mr. Mitchell is the only one who seems faintly happy to see me as he gets up to shake my hand when I walk into Hartigan's office.

"Good morning, Maddison. Sleep well?" He doesn't wait

MADDIE

for me to respond before he sits me down and pushes another pile of paperwork toward me. "Just a few more things and then we'll be off. I'd like to start with the NDA and then..."

I tune him out as I stare at the document at the top of the pile and the words NON-DISCLOSURE AGREEMENT written in bold, capital letters screaming at me from it. *Well, there goes the midnight idea to sell my story or write a book about this to capitalize on the experience to see my family fed for years to come.*

Crap.

I sigh, but once he's taken me through the content, I sign on the dotted line. When I'm done, I look up to find both the headmistress and Clara glaring at me. Mr. Mitchell must notice me frowning at the latter because he suddenly explains the reason for her presence.

"Clara is here as your Class President. The press will want an interview with you before we leave, but they'll also want to interview a friend. Since we couldn't find one..." He gives me an apologetic smile as he trails off. I close my eyes.

I wonder what horrible things she'll say about me. But since there's nothing I can do to stop it, I simply resign myself to being smeared in the press. *I suppose I should probably get used to it.*

With the world watching my awkward, clumsy self interacting with royalty, I'm sure a bunch of unkind things will be said about me before this is over.

When I've signed the last of the papers, Mr. Mitchell gets up. "I'll go tell the cameraman you'll be out in a moment so they can be ready for you."

Oh yes, the televised exit from normal life. No doubt they'll also film my first steps on the palace grounds.

CHAPTER FOUR

My stomach flutters, but I tell myself from here on out I'll pretend they aren't there. It's better that way. If I try to make myself look a certain way, it'll one hundred percent just wind up looking like I'm constipated.

"I'd like a word with her before she leaves," Ms. Hartigan says suddenly before turning to Clara. "Would you mind watching Ms. Darling's belongings while Mr. Mitchell speaks to the press?"

Surprisingly, Clara agrees graciously and exits behind Mr. Mitchell, leaving me alone with the stern-faced headmistress. Once the door closes behind them, she leans back in her chair and raises her chin, literally looking down her nose at me.

"We don't have long, so I'll get straight to the point," she says primly. "Do not embarrass the school, Ms. Darling. It shouldn't be too hard for you to behave for just a couple of days. I don't expect you'll be there much longer than that, so keep your head down and do your best to represent the school in a good light during your stay."

I nod instead of rolling my eyes at her thinly veiled attempt at not stating the obvious. She doesn't think I'll last past the Scenting Ceremony. Just a few minutes ago, I didn't think I would either, but now, I'm determined to last at least a few days longer.

"Thank you, Headmistress."

She waves toward the door. "We'll be watching, Ms. Darling. Remember what I said."

In other words, if I embarrass the school, she's pulling my scholarship. *Good to know.*

Feeling like Atlas with the weight of the world on my shoulders, I leave her office and find Clara guarding my suitcase that I was told to leave outside. She gives me a

MADDIE

simperingly sweet smile when I pick it up. "Good luck, Maddie. You'll need it."

Luckily, I don't have to hold back my eye roll this time, so I don't. "I'll be seeing you, Clara. I'll let you know what the palace is like inside."

She scowls, her hand already lifting to give me the middle finger when Mr. Mitchell appears in the doorway to the headmistress's outer office. She immediately drops her hand back to her side.

"Are you ready, Maddison?"

"It's Maddie," I repeat for the umpteenth time since I met him, but I doubt it'll stick this time, either.

As we emerge from the administrative building, a different private car waits at the bottom of the stairs, but that's not what catches my eye first.

I slam to a stop just outside the wide double doors as I stare at the scene playing out on the other side of the fenced-off perimeter. Hundreds of people are gathered there. They burst into cheers, hollers, and applause when they see me.

My breath leaves me in a rush. Spots dance across my vision again, but then Mr. Mitchell takes my arm in a gentle grip, grinning as he leans in to speak quietly in my ear. "Smile and wave, Maddison. Just smile and wave."

And so I do.

I smile. I wave. And when a man with a massive video camera sticks the lens in my face and a microphone to my mouth, I even manage to say a few words about how wonderful the Academy is before Mr. Mitchell tells the interviewer that we need to leave. I'm stuffed into the backseat of the car, the cheers from the crown outside the

CHAPTER FOUR

academy gates—muffled from the interior of the car—turns to background noise as we pull away and I watch Clara waggle her fingers at me in the rearview mirror, a devious smirk twisting her pink-painted lips.

FIVE

—

WOLF

THE PALACE BUZZES with preparations for the welcoming of the Selected and the Scenting Ceremony to take place later today. The constant drone of conversation and rushed bodies in the hall is reminiscent of a beehive. The noise just as annoying. What it foreshadows is just as violent as a bee's sting.

I sniff, rubbing my itchy nose as I lift a glass of Tai's famous hangover remedy smoothie to my lips. Tastes like absolute shit, but it lives up to the name.

Footsteps outside the door to the pack quarters wander close and my ears prick, but then they fade away again. Tai's mum and my parents have flown in for the occasion, so they're around here somewhere. I should go try to find them, but it's all I can do to sit here and nurse this smoothie right now.

I catch the faintest whiff of Omega coming from the open window I've holed up next to and somehow manage to both cringe and salivate at the same time. I haven't seen them in person yet—the Omegas—but roaming around elsewhere in this very building is the one we'll be bonded to before this spectacle is over.

While we watched the announcements yesterday morning, I spotted a few candidates I wouldn't mind warming my bed, but none I can picture spending the rest of my life with. Since the latter is inevitable, though, I plan on making the most of the opportunity I'll have over the next month to indulge in the former.

Trying the milk before buying the cow and all that.

"Wolf," a warm voice calls from the doorway of the lounge in our pack quarters. I wince slightly when my head throbs as I lift it up to see who's there.

Yeah, drinking again last night was not a good idea.

Regardless of my slight hangover, I grin when Tai's mum sweeps into the room with him hot on her heels. Yua Althorpe is one of the people I love most in this world, along with my own mother and my pack. And maybe my sisters, but heaven forbid they ever find out about that.

Immediately lifting my lazy ass off the couch I've been crouching on, I open my arms to throw them enthusiastically around her narrow shoulders. "Yua! You're a sight for sore eyes. How have you been?"

"I'm good." She chuckles when I take her hand and make her do a little twirl to show off the elegant, emerald-green dress she has on. "Aren't you supposed to be saving your charms for the Omegas?"

God, I love that lilt of the Japanese accent.

Hearing it takes me back to my teenage years when we visited Tokyo with her as often as we could. We escaped the monotonous drone of palace life and hit the vibrant streets.

CHAPTER FIVE

I wished we could jet off there now, avoid this whole ridiculous spectacle.

My mind's eye flashes on seeing the cherry blossoms in bloom and eating sukiyaki from a hole in the wall restaurant in the middle of the night. My taste buds tingle with the memories of satiating our teenage appetites with the best food on the whole bloody planet.

Good times.

I dip into a low bow as I release her hand, pushing my hair off my face when I straighten again. "I've got enough charm to go round. Don't you worry. Do you have any tips you'd like to share with the class before we're thrown to the wolves?"

Through our pack bond, I feel Tai's nerves skyrocket when I ask the question. It's a well-known fact that my filter is on the fritz more often than it works. I want to kick myself for phrasing it that way, but I don't.

We're all nervous. Not that we'd ever admit it, but we're about to be the stars of what is essentially the most widely watched reality dating show on the planet.

Tai and I have grown used to being in the public eye. We weren't necessarily raised for it the way Kaz was, but I knew what my future would hold as soon as I fell into a bromance with him from the moment I met him.

It was the same for Tai. While we certainly don't feel the same sense of duty and responsibility as our packmate, we put up with feeling his through our bond because we love the bastard. Despite the press and the Trials, I wouldn't have it any other way. I know Tai wouldn't either.

Yua regards me through gorgeous almond eyes, her worry shining clear as day from their onyx depths. "Do you really feel like you're being thrown to the wolves?"

She steps forward to help me with the bow tie I've given up on. I knew either Yua or my mother would tie the infernal thing for me. They're motherly, unlike Kaz's Mum, who wouldn't know a show of maternal affection from a declaration of war.

Once she's done, I shake my head and wag my eyebrows at her as I stride over to the kitchen. A lock of hair falls over my forehead again, but I leave it this time. "Nah, we *are* the wolves, and other wolves won't feed on us even if we're thrown to them."

I don't have the energy to figure out if that even made sense. Omega Mighty, I've always been so shit with words.

Pinching the bridge of my nose to stop the aching behind my eyes, I try again. "Let me try again," I say as I grab three beers and uncap mine. "We *are* being thrown to the wolves, but we will return leading the pack. Better?"

Yua and Tai both shake their heads when I offer them their beers, then Yua fusses over both of us some more for a minute. She glances between us with a stern expression suddenly on her face. "Have you told Kaz how you feel? What happens if you don't fall in love with one of the selected Omegas?"

"Has any royal pack ever declined to bond with one of the selected?" Tai asks rhetorically. We all know no pack ever has.

Yua's gaze grows stormy. "I suppose it doesn't matter. Catherine likely wouldn't allow it."

Tai sighs and takes the beer from me after all. Yua and the queen have a turbulent history. It's no secret there's no love lost between them. If I had been William Althorpe, however, I would definitely have chosen Yua over Catherine as well. No contest.

CHAPTER FIVE

My gaze lifts briefly to the ceiling, and I raise my bottle discreetly to the heavens far beyond. *Good choice, mate. Good fucking choice.*

"This is part of Kaz's duty to the Crown, Mother," Tai says quietly. "Which means it's our duty now as well. He's our Alpha."

Yua's chin dips in a curt nod, but when she finally picks up the last beer, I know his response wasn't what she wanted to hear.

As she, Tai, and I bring our bottles to our mouths and take long sips, a knock sounds from the door.

I don't need to look to know it's not the missing member of our tripod coming to take one last drink with us before the games begin. Judging by the intense strain and disdain I feel coming from him, Kaz is still with his parents.

At least the hair of the dog is helping to calm my stomach and soothe the ache in my head so the others don't have to feel the ghost of my raging hangover for the rest of the day through the pack bonds.

"Enter," Tai calls, and the door opens to reveal one of the queen's personal servants.

He casts a disapproving look at the beers in our hands, but since he can't very well admonish us for it, he simply lets out a quiet sigh before he nods. "You're expected in the Grand Hall before the ceremony."

"Of course," Yua replies, instantly draining her beer—a definite sign of frustration, but kudos to her for being able to put it back like that—before offering Tai one arm and extending the other to me. "Escort your old lady to the proceedings, won't you?"

Tai nods, but I see the flash of sadness in those reddish

eyes. I feel it reverberating all the way to my soul as the emotion takes root.

His father should've been here to escort her, and that's who he's thinking about as we make our way down the ancient corridors toward the Grand Hall.

As one, we stop at the doors, take a moment to collect ourselves, and then I nod at the guard to let us in. He and his counterpart reach for the ornate brass door handles, pulling them open in unison to reveal the room within.

Almost immediately, I notice my fathers are already here. They and the king consort are old mates, and they're talking with their heads bent together. Turning to Tai and his mum, I release her arm and incline my head to them as I meet Tai's gaze.

"I should go say hi before all hell breaks loose. See you in a minute?"

Tai's eyes lock on mine, his jaw tight as he nods. "We've only got about fifteen before the ceremony begins. Don't disappear."

I wink at him in an attempt to ease his obvious tension. "Not without you, my dear earl. I'll be right there."

He rolls his eyes but then tightens his grip on his mother's arm and leads her further into the hall while I head to my fathers and the king. I haven't reached them yet when I see the annoyance flickering in their eyes. As soon as I join them, I realize why it's there.

"Wolfgang!" King Edward slurs slightly as he smacks me on the shoulder. His ruddy cheeks rise on a wide grin. "Good of you to stop by, son."

My face wants to frown, but I don't let it. He might be drunk already, but he's still the king.

CHAPTER FIVE

I offer him a shallow bow. "Welcome home, Your Grace. How was Canada?"

He flashes me a salacious smirk before he glances around, obviously not so far gone yet that he's completely forgotten where he is. "My dear wife may think sending me on all these trips abroad is a punishment, but—"

My father cuts him off by clearing his throat. "Wolf, are you ready for this?"

I move my gaze to his, instinctively standing up a little bit straighter when faced with the duke's militaristic posture. "Of course, sir. I was born ready."

My other father, Demetrius, blows out a quiet breath through his nostrils. "No, you weren't," he says on a laugh. "But here we are."

"Here we are," I agree. "Good of you both to come."

I'd half expected only my titled father, the Duke of Bavaria, to attend this thing. My other Alpha father, Demetrius, loathes being at court. But he's putting on a brave face for the sake of everyone else.

"Are Mum and the girls around?"

Demetrius shakes his head. "Regrettably," he says in his 'court' voice, the single word dripping with enough sarcasm to earn him an elbow jab from my other father. "They had to stay in Munich. Ingrid has a dance recital coming up, Hannah couldn't get away from work, and Emilia said she'd rather stab herself in the foot than watch you sniffing a bunch of Omegas."

I snort, but of course, Duke Otto Von Damme doesn't seem quite as amused by my youngest sister as I am and gives me a sharp look that has me schooling my features.

"Perhaps when this is over, we'll all make time for a visit."

The king laughs heartily as well, drawing my fathers' attention back to him while a sudden zing of rage from one of my packmates sets me on edge. My head immediately turns toward Tai. When I see him and his mother greeting the queen, I know the source of his anger.

"Excuse me," I say, but I'm already walking away to support Yua and Taiyo.

Queen Catherine is always snippy with them both, and it's no different this time. She arches a brow at Yua, looking her over from head to toe before her lips purse. "I didn't realize *you* would be here. Although, I should've known William would've invited you."

My eyelids slam shut. *Dear God, would it kill her to stop using Tai's middle fucking name?*

Yua gives her a cool smile. "Oh, I wouldn't have missed it for the world. It's not every day a proud mother gets to see her son when he first lays eyes on the love of his life."

In just one sentence, she's encapsulated the very foundation of the difference between her and the queen. To Yua, this is about love. Finding it, keeping it. Catherine doesn't give a rat's arse about love. All she cares about is keeping up appearances.

"Well, yes. I suppose I understand how a commoner might misunderstand the purpose of the Trials."

I cut a glare at Kaz, wishing he'd step in to set his mother straight, but he doesn't. Since I want to but I can't, I simply grind my teeth and vow to put a bag of marbles under his sheets tonight to teach him a lesson in discomfort.

His obsession with decorum and duty regularly gives me a headache worse than any hangover ever has. Thankfully, the announcement is made for us to move into the ballroom for the ceremony to begin.

"She's a bitch. Ignore her," I mutter to Yua as she departs to take her place among the other dignitaries at court. She covers her mouth to conceal a surprised flush at my vulgarity, swatting my arse as I rush to catch up with my pack mates.

Tai, Kaz, and I take our place on the raised dais. The queen makes a short speech before the Omegas will be brought in, but I can't focus on anything she says. The roil of emotions spinning and jostling through the pack bonds are enough to strike me both deaf and dumb and all I can think about is getting my knot wet as the first hints of Omega scent reach my nose.

Kaz tenses at my other side and hisses, "Not now, Wolf."

I roll my eyes, but I keep my mouth shut since the door is already opening and the first Omega is shown in. As he walks toward us, I rake my gaze over his square face and crew-cut hairstyle. *Nope. Not my type. Next.*

The crier announces him by name and academy, and the Omega wipes sweaty palms on his tailored slacks as he walks the long channel of deep eggplant carpet up to the dais with his head bowed.

"Your highness," he all but croaks to Kaz, blushing.

"My lords," he says in greeting to Tai and myself as he shakily rolls up the sleeve of his right wrist and extends it to each of us in turn to lean in and take a long inhale.

When it's my turn, I get hints of lemon, stronger than I scented before now that he's close up and I think maybe I judged too harshly...but as the lemon fades there's something more like pond scum in its wake, and it's all I can do not to rear away.

Yeah, that's a no from me. Thanks.

At least with all of the Omegas on a rigorous heat suppressant and scent blocker regiment we won't be overwhelmed by any scents too strong—good *or* bad.

I give the Omega, Stephen, a nod as he descends the dais.

Looks aren't supposed to matter much in this thing, but let's get real. Of course they fucking do. To me, at least.

A few of the Omegas who approach for us to scent are attractive, but their scents don't really tempt me. There's one, Casey something or other, a pretty girl who looks like the sweet type, who has a nice scent. Warm and vanilla-like, like she bakes cookies in her spare time and the scent has permeated her very blood.

When I glance at Tai and Kaz, they're both wearing softer expressions than before, so I know they feel the same way. None of us reacted primally or viscerally to her scent, but it's not bad. I could get used to it. And she was cute, too.

Antonio Ramirez doesn't have a horrible scent either. It's strangely aquatic and makes me think of all things summer. With warm eyes and a hard body, I think I could get on board with that.

We're almost to the end of the Omegas now, I think. Thank fuck because their scents are all starting to run together and I'm getting bored as hell.

"Maddison Darling," the announcer calls next, and something sparks in my hazy memory of watching the televised selection yesterday. Wasn't she the one who looked like she wanted the floor to open up and swallow her? What had the queen said?

Poor thing looks skittish. Like a spooked deer, she'd tutted. *That one's not fit for court.*

CHAPTER FIVE

Maybe it's because I know the queen wouldn't approve, but I sit up a little straighter, wanting to give this one my full attention. I sniff hard to clear my nose, already catching something absolutely delicious wafting in from below the dais as Maddison Darling ascends to meet us.

SIX

—

MADDIE

FUCKING HELL, I'm so sweaty, that's all they'll be able to smell. Sweat—and not the musky, clean kind. The horrible anxiety kind. The kind that's sour and bitter.

I can't help it, though.

Today has been an ordeal to say the least. As I stare at myself in an ornate mirror out in the hall, I'm not even sure who I am anymore.

The girl staring back at me now looks completely different to me. Even my freckles are covered, but now that they are, I'm not sure I like them being gone.

Even so, I've felt like an impostor since I was selected, so I might as well continue being someone other than myself. As Headmistress Hartigan pointed out, I won't be here long enough for it to matter.

It's for the best too.

I doubt I'll be going home with my ankles intact if I do stay very long. The heels they put me in are sky high. Well, maybe three inches isn't sky high to other women, but I

MADDIE

might as well be expected to balance on the pointy ends of two blades.

My ankles wobble even while standing still.

Walking through the castle halls from my chambers without snapping a femur was a feat. I feel like an unsung hero for having achieved it. I tried to tell Mary, my lady-in-waiting, not to put me in these, but she insisted and the look on her face told me she would broker absolutely no argument.

I wished I could have tucked myself beneath the fluffy-looking covers on the bed in the bedroom I barely had a chance to properly get a look at before Mary rushed me away to what they called the 'staging area.' Apparently, we'll be able to get ready for the other events in the privacy of our rooms, but only once the scenting ceremony pairs down the candidates, allowing one ladies' maid to each Omega.

Today, I had to share Mary with a girl called Casey. Lucky for her, she didn't need nearly as much time with the tweezers and curlers and beauty treatments and makeup as I did or Mary wouldn't have been able to finish with both of us in time.

"Maddison Darling!"

I freeze when I hear my name being called. *Oh, crap.*

I'm going to fall flat on my face.

No, you're not. You got this.

You fucking got this, Maddie.

"Maddison Darling?"

Okay, apparently I am expected to move.

The Omega in line behind me gives me a little shove. As I wobble from the hall into the ballroom, arms out to steady myself, I see it in its entirety for the first time. My blood

CHAPTER SIX

runs cold. There are far more people gathered to watch the ceremony than I was expecting. The king and queen watch from their lavish thrones off to the left, and cameras stand everywhere, broadcasting this event far and wide.

Moving more carefully than I ever have before, I make my way toward the steps where the Royal Pack are waiting on a dais. When I finally reach its base, I'm so relieved that naturally, I ruin it, tripping over the edge of the first step and landing on my knees on the next.

Gasps ring out and low giggling ripples across the room, but mostly, there's just uncomfortable silence. Blood rushes to my cheeks, the heat of them practically radiating as I get up quickly, square my shoulders, and keep going toward the pricks who didn't move a muscle to come to my aid.

Though I'd be even more mortified if one of them knelt to help me up. It would only draw more attention.

I haven't looked at them since I've been too busy focusing on getting to them without breaking a bone, and now that I've made an absolute fool of myself, I still can't bring myself to lift my eyes.

When I reach the landing, I clench my jaw, breathing fast.

Mary told me that the scenting is usually quick and is sometimes but not always accompanied by a brief touching of hands. If I don't bring my skin close enough to them, they could take my hand to draw me nearer.

I thrust my wrist out at the first of them, my blood rushing in my ears. I don't know what to say, so I say nothing, counting the seconds until this is over.

These are not royal alphas who could have you drawn and quartered, I tell myself.

MADDIE

They are just three guys. Three alpha males who—
Holy shit.

Their scents hit me like a sledgehammer to the chest, the force of them going straight to my head, making me dizzy. I'd caught a lick of their scents from out in the hall, but I'd barely breathed for fear of tripping on the long walk up here, and straight up held my breath after I *did* in fact trip. But now...

My vision turns hazy and something deep and primal in my lower belly tightens, making my thighs press and my throat go dry.

There's smooth bourbon and musk. There's bergamot and cardamom. And woven through the headier scents is one that ties them all together, brightens them, and lightens them. It's a breath of fresh air inhaled straight from an open meadow. It's oakmoss and birch and heather and just...clean air.

My lips part on a muted gasp as surprisingly warm, tender fingers wrap around my wrist. Nervous as hell, still embarrassed, and with my pulse absolutely thundering, I lift my gaze to look at whoever is touching me.

I've done a bit of reading on this lot since I was selected. Of course, I'd seen the tabloids, but I'd never picked one up. Didn't know a damn thing about the royals aside from their existence.

I know now that the eyes I find myself looking into belong to Earl Taiyo William Althorpe. Half British, half Japanese. He turned twenty-one last winter, supposedly practices archery, and once famously said that the best thing about living in the palace is the never-ending supply of some expensive type of imported tea.

Now that I've made the mistake of looking directly into

his eyes—I'm honestly not sure if we're supposed to—I find myself unable to look away. They're warm and the most intriguing shade of brown I've ever seen, with hints of honey and rust shot through them and a ring of bright copper around the pupil.

The pictures I've seen of him didn't do his sleek jawline justice, nor did they accurately portray how bright his silvery white hair is. It's shorter at the sides than the top, carefully styled away from his face.

A face which, as he brings my hand to his arrow of a nose, contorts in what I can only assume is disgust. His fingers tighten on my wrist for a moment before he drops it like my skin has burned him. Then his gaze tears away from mine, his throat working as if he's struggling to swallow the bile that raced into his throat. Like he might choke on it. He grips the arms of his throne-like seat until his knuckles turn white and I rush to the next royal, praying to finish this as quickly as possible.

Hot tears sting my eyes at the first royal's clear rejection, but I swallow hard and extend my wrist again, ready for another kick square to the chest. Mistress Hartigan was right. I'll be out of here before dawn.

If it were up to me, I'd have cut and run, but the entire world is watching so I have to continue with this farce. Knowing my father and little brother are watching, I lift my head up high as I extend my wrist to Lord Wolfgang Von Damme.

His gaze isn't nearly as intense as the earl's. In fact, if I didn't know any better, I'd say he's amused by his friend and packmate's reaction. Light dances in his blue-green eyes, and it looks suspiciously like barely restrained laughter. As he takes my wrist in a sure grip and practically yanks my hand to his mouth, a lock of golden hair falls over his forehead, but he doesn't bother brushing it away.

It's...strangely endearing and some unconscious part of me wants to brush it away from his forehead just to feel how soft it no doubt is.

Unlike Taiyo's, Wolfgang's nose has certainly been broken a time or two if the slight hook in it is anything to go by. But instead of detracting from his shockingly good looks, it strangely makes him even sexier. Rougher. It suits him.

Although, I've read he's the playboy of the bunch. Up close and personal like this, *Wolf*, as he's known to his friends and conquests, looks like he was built for sex. Not just sex, but fucking. Hard, hot, multiple-orgasm-inducing fucking.

I know he enjoys working out and that his favorite hobby is horseback riding, but honestly, I wasn't expecting to feel attracted to him the way I do. Then again, I was attracted to Taiyo as well. Their scents are *definitely* not helping. Even only allowing myself tiny sips of air, I can't deny what they are doing to me. Or more accurately, what they are doing to my body.

If I have to stand here much longer, the slick dampening my panties is going to push right through the fabric and start to drip down my thighs. I suck in my stomach as if I can hold it in, knowing it's useless.

As I hold Wolf's gaze, he winks at me—bloody *winks*—and then he takes a deep inhale against the almost transparent skin of my wrist and instantly drops my hand, his nostrils flaring and something in his jaw clenching.

The veins in his thick neck bulge until I can see the blue tint of them through his skin.

CHAPTER SIX

If it were possible, it's an even worse reaction than Taiyo had. I should never have looked up. I should have kept my head down. *Stupid.*

I suck in a quiet breath of air, more hurt and offended than I've ever been as I move to the last but certainly not the least of the pack. His Royal Highness Prince Kaspian Eaton casts a dark, almost frustrated look at his packmates, his jaw already ticking before he turns his gaze to me.

Don't look, Maddie.

But...I can't help it.

Despite the anger simmering in my gut over how the other two reacted, I'm taken aback by how dark and deep the prince's eyes are in person. I don't think I've ever seen eyes in such a glittering shade of brown. Looking into them is almost like looking up at the sky in the darkest part of the night, except technically, his eyes aren't supposed to be black. I've read they're brown. *But jeez...*

Thick black rows and long, pitch-black lashes frame them, a stark contrast to his smooth, pale skin. His hair, as jet-black as his eyebrows, eyelashes, and probably his soul, sits atop his head like no strand would dare shift out of place without his express permission.

On the other hand, I'd be afraid of a face like that myself. I know he's a prince, but I've never seen a more regal-looking person in my entire life—his pictures don't do him any justice at all.

His cheekbones and jaw are sharper than any real person's should be. He's even got a slight dimple in his chin. He's unfairly handsome, but in a way that's almost brutal.

It hurts to look at him. The kind of hurt that comes from knowing you can never and *will never* know that kind of beauty.

MADDIE

In all my reading, I never came across a single mention of a misstep he's made or a time when he misspoke, and I thought someone had simply buried it all. Looking at him now, though, I don't think it's been erased. I think there's no mention of it because it never happened.

All three of them are Alphas.

Apparently, they presented at around the same time when they were fifteen or sixteen. Rumor has it that they went through their first rut together. I've never spent much time around Alphas, my father aside, which is probably why I have the strangest urge to both whine and purr at the same time.

I can do neither. I've already embarrassed myself enough.

When Kaspian takes a tiny sniff of my inner wrist, he exhales sharply before turning his head away, his eyes darkening.

Well, fuck.

They didn't have this strong of an aversion to *any* of the other Omegas. At least, not from what I could see on the silently playing monitors out in the hall. This is possibly the *worst* thing that could've happened here.

At least it's over.

Walking back the way I came is a study in bottled emotion. The knifepoints I walk on have become even more perilous as I take cautious steps across the tightrope of the ballroom.

It's everything I can do to tune out the whispers of the other royals in attendance and keep myself from crying before I'm out of sight of the cameras, but at least I don't trip again.

Silver linings.

CHAPTER SIX

Tell that to the ocean of slick in your panties.

While I know for a fact that I took my mandatory heat suppressant just before I went into makeup, I have *never* felt like this before.

Maybe it's because of my lack of experience with Alphas, but as the ceremony finishes, the effect doesn't fade. A few more Omegas take their turns to be scented, and the queen rises again, but I can barely pay attention to anything going on around me. The need rising from deep within threatens to engulf me. It's so bad that I don't know how I got down from the dais.

I barely remember the walk back. Their scents are stuck to the inside of my nose. Of my lungs. And I can't seem to shake their images from my mind. The clear discomfort. The revulsion.

The ceremony finishes, but I'm so focused on pressing my legs together to relieve the ache that I don't know if they were as disgusted by anyone else who came after me. Between the heels and the ache, the walk back to my room is a painful blur. It doesn't help my mental state that above everything else, I'm ricocheting between need and embarrassment.

The entire world just saw that.

Omega Mighty, that has to be the worst part.

The Scenting Ceremony is one of the most widely watched parts of the Trials, which means millions of people probably just saw me squirming while the royals didn't even try to hide their revulsion.

By the time I reach my room—chambers, whatever—hot tears sting the backs of my eyes. I don't know if I want to cry, touch myself, kick the Royals, screw their brains out, or do all four of those things, but I do know it's horrible.

MADDIE

It's even worse that Mary immediately picks up my shoes when I kick them off. She's been so kind to me that I feel terrible about snapping at her, but shit...

"Don't worry about those," I say sharply. "I can pick them up myself. Why don't you go help the other Omega, Casey? Go help her get undressed. I can do the rest myself."

The woman blinks at me, her gaze sweeping across my face before she nods, fucking *curtsies*, and then takes off. A frustrated scream builds in my chest, but it lodges in my throat as the tears finally leak from my eyes.

Finally, *and mercifully* alone, I claw at the skintight gown they put me in, nearly ripping the metal zipper open before I finally find the tab. Once I pull it down, I peel the silky fabric off my body with sobs heaving through me.

My soaked panties join the dress on the floor and then I join them, too. Sinking down, I sit my naked butt right there on their thick, royal carpet, pull my knees up to my chest, and wrap my arms around them. Then I really let it rip on the crying.

What I should be doing is mentally cataloging every inch of my chambers so I can describe it to my mother in vibrant detail when I get home in the morning. At this moment, there's also absolutely no doubt in my mind that I *will* be going home in the morning, but I can't bring myself to get up and study everything in sight.

The Royal Pack's reactions play on a loop in my mind. Eventually, the disgust on their faces gives way to the memories of what it felt like to be in their presence. To be touched by them, even if in such a seemingly insignificant way.

Taiyo's warm eyes and Wolf's amused ones flash in my memory, followed by Kaz's cold, but steady gaze. Well,

CHAPTER SIX

steady until he scented me, but I block that part out. I remember the earl's gentle touch, the lord's much more confident grasp, and finally, the almost touch of the prince's long fingers before he pulled back, leaning in to scent me instead.

The thought of it all is enough to drive me crazy, and eventually, I stop fighting it. My clit pulses like a homing beacon, and my nipples are so stiff, they're sore. It's not just them that hurt either. It's my entire body—and my pride—but I'm not too concerned with the humiliation right now.

Denying myself is torture. Since my obvious rejection being witnessed by audiences worldwide was torture enough, I decide to hell with it. They might not want to touch me, but it doesn't mean I can't do it myself.

Pushing to my feet, I head into my en suite bathroom where the shower is the size of my bedroom at home. For once, I turn on the faucet and wait until I see steam rising before I take the longest shower I've taken in, well, ever.

The water pressure is incredible. I'm still so worked up that the warm spray on my skin makes me moan. When the first streams of water run over my nipples, a shiver races through me. *God, I'm already trembling and it's only water. What is wrong with me?*

Also, if this is what being around Alphas does to an Omega, I really should have brought the tiny vibrator I kept hidden under my mattress. *Well, I would've had to if I was staying, which I'm not.*

It's almost a relief to know I'll never see them again, but that doesn't ease the need. Sliding my palm across the slippery length of my stomach, I pause with my fingers right at my mound.

My breathing hitches.

MADDIE

As if in response, my inner muscles clench, and I realize that yes. *I am absolutely doing this.* My hand dips lower. When the tip of my index finger brushes against my clit, the sparks of pleasure are so intense that it's nearly paralyzing.

My legs buckle and my knees go numb. *I'm definitely going to have to sit down if I don't want to fall and crack my head open.*

Thankfully, there's more than enough space in the cubicle—which is more of a room—and I sit down with my back against the cool tiles, facing the showerhead and that amazing water pressure. Unfortunately, the showerhead itself isn't detachable, but I scoot forward a little until there's a constant stream of water covering my pussy.

Oh, fuck. That's good. My muscles tense and my toes curl. When I reach for my clit again, I know I'm only seconds away already.

Allowing my mind to wander to the Alphas responsible for this, I imagine what Kaz's full lips would feel like clamped around that sensitive bundle of nerves. I remember Wolf's confident grip and wonder if that same confidence would be present if it was his fingers on me instead of my own. I think about Tai's warm eyes and imagine them clouded over with heat and lust.

As I get closer to the edge, my mind conjures up images of their facial expressions earlier, but this time, instead of disgust, their features are contorted because of pleasured agony as they breathe me in. In my head, the water running over my pussy is their seed, and that's what sends me barreling into the most powerful orgasm I've ever had.

It's so powerful that I have to shove a fist into my mouth to muffle my cries of ecstasy as I shake and clench against the shower floor.

CHAPTER SIX

When I can move again, I realize I'll need to get out of the glorious shower. I'm suddenly a little sad this will be my last night here. I've certainly started something of a love affair with this shower, but after I climb out, dry off, and get in bed naked, I resign myself to leaving my latest and best lover behind.

If I ever get rich, I'm having a proper shower installed at my place. *God knows, I could certainly do with a few more orgasms like that.*

Relaxed and sated, I lie back on my bed. As the clock strikes ten, a bell suddenly goes off, and I struggle to remember what it means. I'm sure I was told.

Grudgingly, I haul myself out of bed and go to pull the little folder from the desk—the one that Mary assured me should answer any questions I might have.

I flick through the pages, wondering if it's a late night snack bell, since we've already had dinner delivered to our rooms. It was there, sitting on my desk, after I got out of the shower.

But then I find it.

It's in the procedural instructions for the Selection.

"Those who will be going home the morning after a trial's completion will be visited by a representative of the Mating Trials after the tolling of the selection bell," I read aloud, my grip tightening on the page.

Traditionally, the most Omegas to be sent home from the Trials on a single day are dismissed after the Scenting Ceremony. According to my research, it's not uncommon for up to half of the Omegas to fall out after it.

My mood sinks like a stone when I hear the knocks begin down the hallway.

MADDIE

Knock. The creak of a door opening. Then a door closing.

Knock. Door open. Sob.

Knock. Door open. Protesting from a male Omega and a door slam.

The knocks come closer as the representative makes their way closer to my door.

"Shit!"

I remember I'm ass naked and run to grab the fluffy robe I saw in the bathroom just as a knock sounds so close I think it might be my own door until the door to the room next to mine swings open and I listen, ear and palms pressed to the wooden pane as the representative tells the Omega in the neighboring room that she should pack her belongings and a car will take her home tomorrow.

My mouth goes dry as the door closes.

I step back from my door, holding my breath.

Although the footsteps stop right outside my door, there is no knock.

Hang on, there was no knock.

A knock sounds on a door maybe a few rooms down from my own.

It's a mistake.

It has to be.

But I wait and...they don't come back. I wait until there are no more knocks. And then I wait some more.

Somehow, I'm moving on to the second round. *What the fuck?*

An expected bolt of excitement shoots through me, and I grab a pillow to muffle my squeals.

SEVEN

—

TAI

"WELL," my mother prompts with a gentle smile. "What did you think? Did any of the Omegas stand out to you during the ceremony last night?"

I consider her question before I shrug. "A few. One in particular, but it's not my decision to make alone."

She chuckles as she pops a bite of fresh fruit into her mouth, chewing it slowly as she regards me. Once she's swallowed, she takes a sip of her sparkling water and licks her lips. "With breakfasts like this, it's a wonder you're not all as big as houses."

I smile. "Wolf has found a way around it. He makes us work out at least two hours every day, and then he keeps going for God knows how much longer."

"That boy," she says fondly with a soft shake of her head. "I don't suspect you and he will have much trouble deciding which Omega you want. Kaz is the real wild card here."

"Our bond is strong," I assure her. "I suspect they favor

the same Omega I do after the ceremony, but we've agreed not to talk about it until we've spent some time with them."

"How serendipitous then that that's the plan for the day," she muses sarcastically. "Have you decided what you're going to do while you're getting to know them?"

I shrug. "My first *date* will be tea in the gardens. After that, I think it's a stroll to the lake, and later, I'm having a picnic lunch near the stables."

Ripples of exasperation pass through me, and Mum notices, her head tilting slightly to one side as she reaches out to take my hand. "You might find your true love through these Trials, darling. I can't imagine what it must be like doing it on such a public stage, but when you're spending one on one time with them, there won't be any cameras. Forget about the Trials and the queen. Just focus on the Omega you're getting to know."

I blow out a breath, but I know she's right. "I don't like having everything scheduled this way. It's unnatural. There are twenty Omegas left. I already know who I don't want to spend time with, yet everyone will get a date with each of us over the coming days. Why? We should focus on those we want to focus on."

"There is a method to the madness, Taiyo," she says quietly, squeezing my hand before she releases it. "Sometimes, these things take time. Feelings develop that aren't always there at first sight. If an Omega is still here, then it's for a reason."

"Yes, but that reason is political in some instances," I murmur after looking around to make sure none of the staff are close enough to hear me. "Kaz is so aware of Catherine's expectations that I worry he'll deny what his heart is telling him."

CHAPTER SEVEN

"Your bond is strong." She repeats what I said just a minute ago. "The three of you have been leaning on each other and counting on each other for years. Kaz needs you and Wolf now, just like he always has, and you'll guide him just like you always have. It's all part of being pack, isn't it?"

I nod, filling my lungs with a deep inhale before I swipe a strip of bacon off my plate. "You're right. We just need to take it day by day."

"Exactly." She grins. "Tell me about this Omega you favored. Which one was it?"

I shake my head, flashing her a sly smile and making a show of checking my watch. "Well, would you look at that? It's almost time for tea. I don't even know which Omega it's with, but I do love the tea."

"It's the one good thing about living in the palace, right?" she teases.

I roll my eyes, but I get up to give her a hug before I leave her to finish her breakfast in peace.

I swear, I'm never going to live the tea thing down. That quote is everywhere, and it was a damn joke. Wolf and I were giving Kaz shit one day about being forced to live in a palace because we formed a pack with him.

We were *bantering* while on a goddamned yacht, but it turned out that Wolf's socialite friend never made her staff sign the obligatory NDA. One of them overheard us and made a quick buck telling the press all about it.

That wasn't the only thing he told them about, but it's the only thing that stuck with the public. No one seemed to appreciate the irony of a reject being on the fucking yacht to begin with, let alone that *reject* saying something so unimportant about fucking *tea*.

Instead, the most interesting thing about my person-

TAI

ality became my love for herbal tea. Now, I get asked about it during every interview. *How's the tea, Taiyo? What's the brand, Taiyo? How much tea do you drink every day, Taiyo?*

A heavy sigh falls out of me, but as I approach the old oak where the tea has been set up, my footsteps falter and my heart lurches. I wasn't expecting to see her so soon, but sitting at the little metal table in the shade of the giant tree is none other than the beautiful redhead with the scent that almost had me tenting my damned trousers on the dais. Maddison Darling.

Omega Mighty, that female's scent did things to me last night. Fuck, it did *all* the things to me last night. Judging by what I felt through the bond, I wasn't the only one either. Wolf nearly drowned me in his lust, and even Kaz seemed to be toeing the edge of his never-ending self-control.

As I approach, I take the opportunity to *really* look at her. She hasn't noticed me yet, seemingly fascinated by what I assume is her first unimpeded, unhurried view of the palace from the grounds.

Last night was such a blur that I hardly realized the next Omega had been announced until Maddison fell. Then she kept her head down and her eyes on the stairs as she ascended. I only had a few moments to look at her face before I scented her, and then, she was already moving along to Wolf while I was fighting the most ridiculous wave of desire I've ever felt.

Now, though, she's dressed in casual jeans and an oversized cardigan instead of a ballgown. Her rich mahogany locks are down, tumbling in a wave of loose curls nearly to her waist. Her expression is one of unashamed awe as she stares at the spires, the light, blue-gray stone walls, and the large windows of the palace we call home.

CHAPTER SEVEN

My footsteps are muffled by the lawn as I draw closer, but she notices me anyway, sitting up a little straighter as she schools her features and presses her lips into a thin line. When I sit down across from her, I stare into eyes that bring back memories of springtime on the French Riviera.

She stares right back at me, but neither of us says anything. We're silent for so long that it becomes awkward, but in that silence, I won't deny that I'm entranced by her scent.

Having caught a whiff of it last night and replayed it a hundred times since, I'm attuned to it. That zesty, energizing burst of citrus combined with the spicier notes of pink pepper and rounded off with a grounding, almost woodsy hint of patchouli.

I've never smelled anything like it, but it's a perfectly balanced combination of the sexiest female scents around. Sweet and crisp, but with *depth*. It's alluring as fuck that it even has undertones of spice and woodiness usually more reserved for male scents. On a female, it tells me right off the bat that she's different. More nuanced than the sweet freckles on her face would have me believe.

"So, Maddison—" I start at the exact moment she says, "I've never met a earl before."

An easy chuckle slides out of me as I motion for her to continue. Her eyes widen, but when I incline my head at her, her cheeks flush the most gorgeous shade of pink and her scent grows just a little in the air around us.

Then, she smiles.

It's small and embarrassed, but the sight of it knocks the breath clean out of my lungs. "What I mean is that I don't know what to call you. I've never met a earl before, so I'm uncertain about how to address you."

"Tai," I say, extending a hand toward her. "It's nice to meet you, Maddison."

"Maddie," she corrects me lightly as she slides her palm into mine. My skin sings where it's connected to hers.

"Tai, really?"

She crooks a brow.

"My lady-in-waiting said to address you by your proper titles, but she neglected to tell me what yours was."

"Your lady-in-waiting said what the queen probably instructed her to say. The queen likes to pretend. I don't. So, call me Tai."

Her dark eyebrows rise slightly. "Now there's a conversation starter if I've ever heard one. The queen likes to pretend. Is that true?"

I bite the inside of my cheek, knowing I need to tread carefully, a niggle at the back of my mind warning me to be cautious. All of the Omegas have signed NDAs, but it doesn't mean this beautiful, delicious Omega won't share my thoughts on the queen with the woman herself.

"Perhaps it's more accurate to say she likes to control the narrative," I reply before I can stop myself, surprised at how easily the words fall out. Like I've subconsciously decided to trust her before I could consciously make the choice.

I clear my throat at the surprised way her eyes widen at my candor.

"I'm not interested in having the narrative controlled right now," I continue. "We're potentially going to be bonded to you, right? I don't see the point of pretending when the possible outcome is being together for the rest of our lives."

She stares at me for another beat, her eyes unfocused

CHAPTER SEVEN

until she blinks and smiles at me again. "Okay. I like that. If you'll be candid with me, then I'll do my best to be honest with you."

I don't miss the part about *doing her best* rather than just offering unrestricted honesty, but I'll take it. Besides, I'm not the type to pry information out of someone who isn't ready to share it willingly.

"Great," I say, pleased this is going so well, so fast. "Ask me anything you want to know and in return, I'll answer honestly."

"Oh, okay, *um...*" She trails off, thinking, but as she reaches for her tea, she knocks the cup over. It spills quickly across the white tablecloth and even though only a few drops roll over the edge to drip onto my lap before I can move, she groans and reaches for a wad of napkins.

When she moves like she's going to mop up the tea from my lap, I gently catch her wrist and shake my head.

"That's really not necessary. I'm fine. See?"

I scoot back a little so she can see I'm mostly dry, but then I realize what I'm doing is presenting her with my crotch. And that she's staring at it. And that I'm half hard through my dark trousers.

Fucking hell.

Clearing my throat when my cock swells harder against my fly, I move my chair back under the table.

A butler comes to replace Maddie's drenched saucer with another. A fresh cup is brought too, then the table is flipped with a new cloth, the pastry tray reset.

Finally finished, the butler looks at me. "Are you all right, William? Shall I have a maidservant fetch you new trousers?"

"Tai," I say automatically, unable to conceal the flare of

annoyance from my tone. "I'm fine. Thank you. You can leave."

Once we're alone again, Maddie blushes like she was caught naked in the archbishop's favorite chair. "I wish I could say that doesn't happen often, but since we're being honest, you should know that I'm incredibly clumsy. It's a curse."

Clumsy?

My...the queen will *love* that.

I smile even though something in my stomach twists at the realization that this Omega, as perfect as she may seem to me, may not be one of the few the queen will give her blessing to bond with. I ache to reach out and take her hand, but I resist the urge.

This Omega has a rather interesting effect on me. Touching her *isn't* a good idea.

She cocks her head before frowning in the direction of the server who's resumed his post just out of earshot. "Wait, why did he call you William?"

"Oh, it's nothing."

She lifts a brow dubiously.

Right. Honesty.

"It's only that the queen likes to pretend that the scandal of my birth never happened."

"Scandal of your birth?" She leans forward, but not in that way some people do when they're hungry for you to spill a different sort of tea. There's concern in the tightening of her brows. In the slight squint of her eyes.

"I'm assuming this isn't about the queen wanting to control the narrative?" She presses and then blinks, seeming to realize something. "I'm sorry, you don't have to share if you don't want to."

CHAPTER SEVEN

I chuckle. "This conversation is getting deeper, faster than I expected, but no. It's not an instance of her wanting to control the narrative. Not really. She calls me by my middle name so she won't have to remember that my father bonded with a commoner and allowed her to choose my first name. Instead of choosing a nobleman's name, she chose Taiyo, which was her father's name. A fisherman."

"I didn't know your mother is a commoner," she muses. "All I know is that your father was an earl. I read he passed a few years ago. I'm sorry."

Pain slices through me, but I was prepared to talk about him. "Thank you. He was a great Dad, even if he was exiled to France for his choice in my mother. He was a romantic, though. Believed in love. Wanted my mother all to himself. Took them years before they finally formed a pack. It was after I was born."

"Exiled to France?" Her eyes widen once more. "That's why you have that bit of an accent, then. You grew up there?"

I nod. "To be honest, I loved it. My mum still lives there with her pack. I visit as often as I can. It sure beats being the Royal Outcast."

"The Royal Outcast?" She scoffs. "I see your version of outcast and raise you mine. At least yours has *royal* in the title. Mine doesn't. I'm just a loner. A scholarship kid in an Academy filled with Haves who hate that a Have-Not managed to infiltrate their ranks."

"You're a scholarship kid?" I ask, genuinely surprised.

Her lips slam closed, and her shoulders hitch up, and I realize I have the same effect on her as she seems to have on me. She's shared more than she wanted to and she's worried how what she's shared will land.

"I didn't realize anyone who didn't have the *proper pedigree* had been selected to enter the Mating Trials." I say it as lightly as I can, with a teasing lilt so she'll know I'm unbothered.

She raises her hand, gifting me with a smile so sheepish that the last bit of tension inside releases, and I laugh. "Guilty," she admits. "I'm sorry, I don't know why I'm telling you this. You didn't ask."

Losing the urge to resist, I reach out to cover her hand with mine. "I may not have asked, but I'm glad I know."

As soon as I touch her, my Alpha instinct roars at me to claim her already. It's much too fast, and also, *why haven't those rut suppressants we took last night kicked in yet?*

We took them precisely because our reaction to her was much too visceral. Or at least, I know it's why *I* took them. Knowing we needed to avoid any lapses in control during the Trials, even Wolf agreed it was necessary after he scented her.

Maddie looks up at me through her lashes and sighs, her hand beneath mine stiff with nerves. "Well, at least for me, this is just another place I don't fit in. Only with a bigger audience."

"You can say that again," I scoff, giving her hand one last squeeze before I have to force myself to let her go. "And just so you know, I would never blame someone else for the circumstances of their birth. Not after having lived my life being shunned by everyone in the court except for Wolf and Kaz."

She falls silent for a moment, those intelligent green eyes flicking from one of mine to the other. "My parents are devastatingly poor," she admits freely. "I wouldn't even be here if my literature instructor hadn't sent in a tongue-in-cheek essay about the Omega system to the nomination committee." She gives a nervous laugh. "And honestly, I'm just hoping I can stay long enough to earn a little bit of compensation to help them keep a roof over all of our heads."

She bites her lip and looks down into her lap. My heart hurts for her.

"So, that's my story, Tai. I guess you'll probably send me home now?"

I keep looking directly into those eyes, wondering if it's good or bad that after one date, I've already got a feeling I'm looking at the Omega who will eventually become part of our pack. "No, Maddie. I don't think so."

She grins sweetly to herself, thinking I can't see it with her head bent.

Omega Mighty, she's the sweetest fucking thing, and I'm dying to sink my teeth into her.

I ball my fists in my lap beneath the table and clear my throat. "Who have you got next?"

Surprise flashes in her eyes as she lifts her face back to mine. "Wolf. Tomorrow, I think."

"That'll be fun," I tease with just the slightest hint of sarcasm in my voice. "Good luck with him."

She tips her head to the side, but before she can ask, our thirty minutes together is up. The butler returns, and I'm whisked away to my next date, knowing it doesn't matter who I'm seeing next because unless something significant changes, she's the only Omega I'll be thinking about today.

EIGHT

—

WOLF

HAVING ALL these new people around is making my horses fidgety. Usually, this is one of the few places where I feel at ease. The stables are fucking magnificent, with gleaming wooden doors, high ceilings, large stalls, and an earthy scent thanks to a constant supply of fresh hay.

It's by far my favorite place on palace grounds. I'd move in with the horses if I had my way. But since the invasion of the Omegas it's no longer a place of serenity. The majestic beasts who are ordinarily as restrained as Kaz are tossing their heads about. They anxiously pace their stalls, their snorts ringing out in the quiet air as I wait for my next date to arrive.

After I moved to the palace permanently more than seven years ago, much was made in the press about my affinity for horses and horseback riding. For some reason, it's still something the tabloids feel the need to report about. As a result, the powers that be decided my dates should be centered around the activity.

I wouldn't have had a problem with that if I didn't come

here for the peace of hanging out with these animals. They get me and I get them. It annoys me to no end that even *their* sanctuary has been thrown into disarray by the Trials. I'll be requesting a different setting for the last few dates to be held tomorrow, if only to give them some peace.

The black stallion I'm saddling up for my date nuzzles my hip and I chuckle, running my fingers through the coarse hair of his mane. "Hey, big guy. Just stay close to me and do your best to be nice to our guest, okay? Last one of the day and then you don't have to have any other strangers on your back, 'kay?"

As if the mention of a guest summoned her, the next Omega appears from behind the large barn doors at the far end of the row. Recognition quickly turns into an attraction that ripples through me when I see the shock of mahogany hair and the delicate features of the Darling girl.

Her scent damn near undid me the other day. I almost want to rub my palms together at finally having the opportunity to spend some time with her. As she walks toward me, though, it's not me she's looking at. She's staring at my horses with apprehension practically pouring off her.

Interesting. The others have all come in with bright, pretentious smiles, ready to throw themselves at my feet or on my dick. Certainly without any hesitation getting astride a horse to try to impress me.

Maddie doesn't appear to be aware of my presence. Intrigued but amused, I hand the stallion's reins to the groom and stride over to meet her halfway, clearing my throat once I'm in spitting distance. She *still* hasn't looked at me, but as I near her, she jerks, her body freezing. No doubt she's finally caught my scent through all the other scents lingering in the stables.

CHAPTER EIGHT

"First time?"

Her back snaps straight like I've startled her.

She swallows audibly and slowly turns her head toward me.

When those green eyes meet mine, her eyelids flutter on a few more blinks before she finally speaks.

"Excuse me?"

"Is this your first time at the stables?"

A few of the Omegas have taken the liberty of showing themselves around, hence the nervous behavior of my horses. From the muttering of the servants who followed them, it's become apparent they came here looking for me, and upsetting the animals has been merely an unintended consequence.

Maddison Darling certainly doesn't seem to have been one of the more explorative Omegas. She frowns and then looks at me like I've got a dildo growing out of my forehead. "*Um*, was I supposed to have been here before?"

"No," I say, grinning, which seems to confuse her, but she falls into step beside me when I motion toward the stallion. "His name is Sergeant Pepper, and he'll be your mount today. Don't be scared. It's true what they say about horses sensing your fear."

"Oh, well, that's great," she mutters. I swear I detect a hint of sarcasm in her voice. It's scintillating really, since the majority of the Omegas I've met today have been incurable brown-nosers.

Half-facing her as we walk, I slide my fingers into the pockets of my jodhpurs and grin. "Have you ever been on a horse?"

"Nope."

She eyes Sergeant Pepper cautiously as we draw closer to him.

"You don't happen to have something smaller? Maybe, like, a pony? Or an old mare or something?"

I chuckle. "Ponies aren't meant to be ridden by grown-ups, and the old mares are retired. The Sergeant here will take good care of you. He looks far more intimidating than he actually is."

She glances at me from the corner of her eyes. "Is he the only one?"

My eyes widen as she clamps her hand over her mouth almost like she wishes she could stuff the words back in. A loud, albeit muffled groan escapes anyway and I laugh. "I'm so sorry, my Lord. I shouldn't have—I mean, I have no idea why I just—"

"It's fine. Really. It's nice that there's someone here with a sense of humor, and no, he's not the only one who might look more intimidating than he is." I wink at her and she flushes scarlet which only makes me want to keep going.

"And regardless of the things people scream when they're in my bed, I am not, in fact, a deity. There's no lord here, Maddison. Call me Wolf."

Her eyes brighten with a surprised laugh, and she removes her hands from her mouth to smile curiously at me.

"Maddie," she replies so fast that I know the correction is instinctive.

"Maddie," I repeat, tasting her name on my tongue. Savoring it as her scent pushes through the hay and dung odors clogging my nose from a day spent in the stables.

"If ending up with your foot in your mouth is a disease, then I'm terminal, I'm afraid." She groans again then

CHAPTER EIGHT

mutters to herself under her breath, "I really don't get why I'm even still here."

"Ah, I can help you there," I say as I reach for Sergeant Pepper's reins once we're beside him. "We'll talk about it on the ride. Come on, up you get."

I pat the stirrup with my free hand. "Just put your foot in there, grab the pommel. Good. Now just do a bit of a hop on your standing leg and lean your weight into the saddle as you heave yourself up."

We've got a step for the ladies, and the grooms are well-versed in giving leg-ups, but I'm interested to see how she handles this. For a moment, it looks as if she'd rather throw herself under the Sergeant's hooves instead of getting on top of him, but then she breathes out slowly and gives it a go.

I don't miss how her hands shake, but I'll take care of her. Between the Sergeant and me, she's in safe hands.

Drawing in a deep breath, she lifts her leg, but she's too short to get her foot anywhere near the stirrup. The groom swoops in, but I stop him with a curt shake of my head before I turn back to my date. "Allow me."

She frowns but shakes her head in turn. "I can do it myself. Just give me a sec to figure it out."

Oh, so she's stubborn.

Hmm.

I step back, gesturing for her to go ahead. It takes much longer than a moment, but eventually, she manages to get her foot wedged into the stirrup at an angle that looks severely uncomfortable, but I don't offer to help again.

With a swift lift, she gets herself up but when the Sergeant starts as she drops down in the saddle, she lets out a little squeak and hangs onto the horn like she's clinging to life.

I chuckle again before I help thread the reins into her hands while she's still gripping the saddle. "I take it you've never ridden?"

Her wide eyes land on mine as I easily climb astride Lady White and take the reins in my hands.

"Am I really that obvious?"

"Yes," I say without hesitating. "If I'm being honest, you're not very good at hiding your fear."

She glances down at her mount and tentatively releases one hand to pat his mane. "He's beautiful, but he's massive. It's a long way down from here."

"True, but we'll go on a very slow walk, and I'll guide you through the process. Now, the first step is to get a good seat. Your legs have to be firm, but your butt needs to be relaxed. Squeeze your thighs against him if you feel unsteady and let your body move with him when we get going, okay?"

"Firm, but relaxed," she repeats after me before her eyes close. "Sure, I can do that."

Lady White starts moving with the barest prompt from me, and Maddie's eyes grow even wider when Sergeant Pepper falls into step with us. Once we're out of the stables, we're moving at a snail's pace. Slowly, her features smooth out of the pinched concentration they've been taut with since she got on top of him.

"This isn't so bad," she breathes after a moment, perking up before glancing at me. "Thanks for letting me work it out by myself."

"You're welcome," I say, enchanted by the sight of her as she eases into it. All the other Omegas I've taken out on a ride so far have been quite comfortable on the back of a horse. It intrigues me that she genuinely doesn't seem to have ever been near one before.

I'm strangely eager for her responses.

"Tell me, Maddie, how is it that you've never been on horseback before? Are you allergic or something?"

"Or something," she says lightly. Then she sighs and turns to me more fully than she has until now. "I'm not like the others here, but let's leave it at that. I'm sure Taiyo has told you all about my dreary existence, and I'm not one to rehash things."

"Your dreary existence?"

I know I shouldn't, but I laugh anyway. "He hasn't actually told me anything, but I'll spare you the rehashing and ask him about it later. What would you like to talk about, then?"

"Uh, what do you talk to everyone else about?"

"Family and kinks. Pick your poison."

She stares back at me for a long beat before her head drops to one side. It's obvious from her assessing gaze that she's wondering if I'm serious until she finally realizes I am.

"Family it is, then. I have a younger brother who's only five. He came as a huge surprise to us all but was the biggest blessing our family could've had. My mum is an Omega and my father's an Alpha, of course, though he's never felt like one to me."

Odd, but not unheard of. There are Alphas out there who don't display the usual traits, at least, not as obviously.

"They're not part of a pack outside our family and you guys are the only Alphas outside of family I've ever spent time with."

I'm an excellent rider, but I'm so surprised that I nearly fall off my horse. "Is that true?"

"Yes. How about your family? Or would you rather discuss your kinks?"

She's so frank about it that I once again come close to a very ungraceful dismount. Thankfully, I recover before I lose my balance. I can't hold back the laughter that rises from deep within me, though. *She's definitely something, this one.*

"Okay, let's do family first," I say. "My mum is an Omega as well. My two fathers are Alphas. I have three sisters, all of whom still live in Munich with our parents."

"How did you end up here, then?"

"Not a royalist, then?" I tease.

Surprisingly, she rolls her eyes at me. "I don't subscribe to the magazine if that's what you're asking. I did some light reading when I was selected, though."

Another surprise.

"But I don't believe everything I read. I'd rather hear the truth directly from you."

"Refreshing," I say honestly. "Okay, well, the basics are that I came to court for the first time when I was thirteen. My dad and the king are old friends, so we were invited for a visit. Kaz and I became fast friends and we were pretty much inseparable. Eventually, just before my sixteenth birthday, after Tai joined the picture, we begged the parentals to let me move here permanently. Everyone knew how well we got along, so they agreed, and they arranged for me to live here as a mentorship of sorts. We went through our first rut together."

I flush scarlet.

CHAPTER EIGHT

"And then, uh," I clear my throat. "I guess you decided to form a pack?"

I nod, looking directly into those eyes again, and I have the most ridiculous urge to tackle her off that horse and mount her myself.

A slow smile spreads on her lips as she stares back at me. Then the bushes rustle nearby and it must spook Sergeant Pepper because the next thing I know, the horse takes off and Maddie dives down to crush her chest to his neck, holding on with everything she's got as she lets out a strangled cry.

"Fuck," I mutter. *I knew the horses have been under too much strain.*

A little field mouse or squirrel wouldn't ordinarily have affected him quite as much, but...*fuck*. I curse, spurring White Lady as we watch Sergeant take off at a wild sprint.

"C'mon! Let's go, girl. Move!"

Digging my heels into Lady White's sides, I race after them, calling out to the Sergeant as the wind whips through my hair and my mount's hooves pound into the ground. "Whoa, boy. It's okay. Calm down. Whoa!"

Just as we're drawing up beside them, I reach for the reins, but the Sergeant has other ideas, suddenly rearing and throwing Maddie right off his back. Panic nearly incapacitates me, but I manage to yank on Lady White's reins. I'm off her back before she's even fully stopped, running toward Maddie.

My heart feels like it's about to fly right out of my chest. Rivulets of sweat run down my spine.

"Are you okay?" My knees hit the ground beside her, and I reach for her with shaking hands.

She's lying flat on her back on the ground. Frantically

searching the dirt around her, I'm so relieved when I don't see any blood that I feel dizzy.

Her eyes open, and she winces, but then she lets out a low groan and nods. "I-I'm fine. Just bruised, I think."

"Wait! You shouldn't move. I'll call for help."

She waves me off, wincing as she pushes herself up into a seat and rubs her lower back.

"Maddie," I warn. "You really shouldn't—"

"I'm fine," she assures me with a pained smile that twists my stomach, and then she lifts her brow pleadingly at me. "Do you think we can walk back?"

I chuff out a laugh, relieved she's all right.

I *knew* we were pushing the horses too hard. I should have said something earlier. If I had, this never would've happened. She could have been seriously hurt.

"You'll ride with me," I grind out decisively as I glare at the Sergeant.

He's calmer now, suddenly back to nipping at the long grass, but his ears are still too flat against his head to trust him with her.

"It wasn't his fault," she says when she sees the way I'm glaring at him. After sitting for another moment, she rises with help from me and dusts herself off, seemingly running a quick body check for injuries as she stretches out her arms and cranes her neck.

"It's me. It was my fault. You warned me not to be scared, but I was. I must've put him on edge."

Although she's trying to play it off, I shake my head and offer her my hand, gently pulling her in and looking her over for any obvious signs of injury. I pull an errant dried leaf from her hair and the way she looks up at me...

I clear my throat, stepping back. "He's, *uh,* been on

CHAPTER EIGHT

edge these last couple of days and it has nothing to do with you. Here, let me help you onto my mount. Do you see how flat the Sergeant's ears are? That means he's still annoyed."

She sighs, and I know she'd really rather walk, but she's being a good sport and lets me help her. Once she's nicely cradled on the saddle, I lift myself up behind her, tucking her into my chest.

I realize, *belatedly*, this might not have been such a good idea. With her pressed so tight to my front and her hair right in front of my nose, her scent is much too intoxicating. *Much too close. Much too...much.*

Logically, I know I need to restrain myself—especially since she could be injured, but my Alpha nature is at war with my logic. As I spur our mount back into action, Sergeant follows like a meek little puppy.

With Maddie practically in my arms, my frustration with Sergeant and the whole damn debacle of the Trials, soon makes way for a much more familiar sensation.

Again, I'm shocked by the intensity of it.

I'm no stranger to lust, but this is next level.

She's injured. She's injured. She's injured.

Regardless of my internal chant, the farther Lady walks us back in utmost silence, the more I find myself in tune with exactly how my body is rubbing against her. The way Lady's movements roll my hips against her.

My cock grows in the suddenly tight jodhs and my eyes close as I inhale her scent.

I catch myself nuzzling her neck but before I can stop myself or apologize, she arches back into me, and I groan when she lets out a little whine, obviously getting aroused herself.

"This is, *uh*," I clear my throat, rolling my hips into her lush ass and letting out another groan. "Should we—"

Maddie moans, and I see her hands, white knuckled with their grip on the saddle horn. Her back arches and my lips part against her neck, the words *just one taste, just one taste,* a deceptive mantra echoing in my testosterone filled head.

Before I can suggest that we stop and take a little break —either to fuck or to stop myself from wanting her so damned badly, a shrike calls and the moment is broken. Remembering myself and that I need to be proper, I lift my head, holding my breath. Holding out for fresh, un-Maddie-tainted air.

She must sense the shift because she lets out a little sound of surprise, and her body goes rigid in front of mine. I grind my teeth, still struggling not to spur Lady out to the forest and take this Omega for myself.

I agreed, I remind myself. Kaz made dead certain to dash my dreams of Omega orgies in the dormitories just this morning.

Be a fucking gentleman, Wolf, he'd pleaded. *For once.*

"I apologize for that," I force past my clenched teeth.

"For what?" she asks, her voice husky, and I know she's wondering if I'm apologizing for my own behavior now or the horses.

Both, I decide. "This was not how I planned the afternoon to go."

Another groan sticks in my throat, but thankfully, we're at the stables and a groom helps Maddie dismount. I don't follow her, though, giving the groom a stern look instead. "The Sergeant bucked her. Make sure she gets looked over."

"May I take Lady for you, my Lord?"

CHAPTER EIGHT

"No," I decide. "I'm going out by myself for a bit."

Maddie smiles when she looks up at me, dusty and with a few smears of dirt on her skin and a couple of sticks in her hair, but somehow, she's more beautiful to me now than she was before.

"I had a nice time," she says with a little snort that goes straight to my dick. "Despite everything. Do you think maybe we can just have some tea for our next date?"

I laugh, keeping my forearm on my thigh to hide my erection even though I know she just felt it straining into her ass. "Tea is more Tai's style. How about you ride with me from the beginning next time?"

Her gaze dips to my lap, and she catches her lower lip between her teeth as she nods.

Fuuuuuck.

I'm out of here before I can do something stupid. I'm halfway out of the stables before I throw my hand up in a casual wave without looking back. An hour later, when I return, I'm still fucking turned on.

Stalking to our living quarters, fully intent on doing something about this goddamn erection other than hammering nails into a wall—because honestly, I'm hard enough to manage it—I stop short when I find Tai lounging on the couch alone.

"Where's Kaz?" I ask as I slam our door behind me.

Tai's eyes find mine and he shrugs. "Off moping, I suspect." His gaze lowers. "Good date?"

I know he can sense it through the bonds. He doesn't even have to ask.

"No." I huff out a breath, close my eyes, and shove my hands into my hair. "I don't know what's going on with me, but my Alpha came out to play at the worst possible moment. The Omega I was with got thrown, so I put her on my horse with me, right? I mean, it's only proper. But then, BAM!" I point at my crotch. "That happens, and it's been over an hour and it's not fucking going away."

He cocks his head, gracefully rising and keeping his eyes on mine as he walks over. "Which one was it?"

"Maddie."

"Ah."

He takes my hand and leads me to my bedroom. "She did the same to me."

I suck in a breath, and his grip tightens to the point of pain on my fingers. "Why didn't you say anything?"

He shrugs. "We agreed to not talk about them until we've all had a chance to spend some time with each of them, right?"

"Right."

I kick my door shut behind us, then I use my grasp on his hand to tug him into me. He crashes into my chest, but it seems he expected the move because his mouth is on mine the next second, hot and hungry as his tongue delves into my mouth.

I groan, too worked up to waste any time as I reach for the hem of his t-shirt and tug it off. "Think it's going to be the same for Kaz?"

"I fucking hope so," he mumbles between kisses as he grabs the front of my shirt and walks us backward to my bed.

As he falls back on the mattress, I pull off his shirt.

He and I do this often enough that it's like a synchronized dance and neither of us ever misses a beat. I pull my shirt off before planting my knee on the mattress between his and covering his body with my own.

CHAPTER EIGHT

His erection matches mine, a hard, massive pipe that seems to have a mind of its damn own. He growls into my mouth when I rock into him, but I tense my muscles when he tries to roll us over. "Uh-uh. I'm the top today."

Nipping at my lower lip, he tries to gain the upper hand again until I chuckle darkly into his mouth. "It's not going to happen today, Taiyo. Give it up. You had tea with her. I rode all the way back from the lake with her hair an inch away from my mouth."

He groans, though I'm not sure if it's sympathy or lust, but he stops fighting, so I win either way. My jodhpurs are more difficult to get off than his jeans, but the grappling only takes a minute before we're both naked.

Under any other circumstances, we're both fans of foreplay, but it looks like he's not into it today, either. Instead, as soon as we're naked, he gets up on all fours and reaches for my nightstand to grab the bottle of lube sitting on top of it. He hands it to me, practically mewling as I squirt a generous dollop onto his skin and my own iron rod.

We're both feral today, almost animalistic as he pushes back onto me when I position myself against his hole. Reaching around, I lean into him, sliding into his heat as gently as I can while wrapping my lubed fist around the length of his cock.

He hisses, hips already rocking as my hand moves with my thrusts. A howl of protest tears out of him when I let go to grab the lube again. Once my palm is properly lathered up and I bring it back to his cock, he moans and moves again.

Neither of us fuck around. He thrusts into my hand as I thrust into him, feeling him squeeze around me. Within no time, I feel my orgasm building. His knot swells in my hand

and mine makes pounding his ass a little more difficult as it grows.

Unable to get as deep as before, I move faster instead, fucking him with the generous length leftover from the start of my knot to my tip.

Tai moans and heat ignites at the base of my spine, building in that space low in my stomach.

The coming explosion builds with more force than I remember ever feeling before, the detonation imminent, primed for a glorious eruption.

Tai's thighs tense, and his back arches, his head dropping forward as I feel his movements falter.

He comes on a loud roar, but neither of us has any qualms about the staff hearing us. Tai and I are in-the-moment Alphas. We're passionate, and we don't care who knows it. When he clenches around me, his orgasm triggers mine. As I lose it, Maddie's face pops into my head, her name on my lips before I collapse on top of my packmate in the wake of the most mind-blowing climax I've had in a good, long time.

And I know it's because of her, the Omega with the scent that has intoxicated two-thirds of our pack to the point that I could barely walk earlier. All that remains to be seen now is whether she's Kaz's undoing as well. If she is, I think our decision has been made and the Trials may come to an early end this year.

NINE

—

KAZ

"HOW ARE YOU, ERIC?" I ask the mild-mannered head gardener with his arms elbow deep in a rose bush, pruning away the dying leaves and buds.

I've always preferred small talk with all our household staff as opposed to the lifted nose faces of the royals and dignitaries at court.

There's no requirement to be polished and perfect with them, and though it's taken some time, they've all but entirely stopped being terrified to speak to me.

Eric shoots me a sheepish smile, and I'm reminded again that we've yet to find a replacement for the his second. Eric looks like he's been out here since dawn to make up for the now-one-man-short team. I'll have to see to that.

"Very well, thank you, Your Highness. Are you waiting on a date?"

"Yes, I am."

I glance down at the watch on my wrist and heave out a

KAZ

frustrated sigh. "Though it seems this particular Omega is averse to punctuality, which I'm not sure bodes well."

"Perhaps she's lost, sir," he speculates out loud before shooting me another sheepish grin. "Apologies. It's not my business."

Despite my severe irritation about the Omega's tardiness, I manage a polite smile. "No, you're right. I suppose it's possible they may have lost their way. Although, there are enough people around to ask."

"Too right, sir."

It looks like he's about to say more, but then he focuses on something behind my shoulder and inclines his head a bit. "It seems she's found you, sir. A pleasant day to you."

"And you."

I turn to find the Omega who tripped the other night hurrying toward me. Her face is so flushed it looks like she's been stung by nettles.

So why is she still so damn beautiful?

Honestly, I was taken aback the other day by how affected I was at her scent, but it wasn't just that. There was a strange defiance about the tilt of her chin and the set of her jaw as she stared me down that stayed with me long after the ceremony ended.

As she gets closer, I take a deep breath to tame my annoyance about her tardiness, but when I do, I notice the air is tinged by that sweet citrusy scent of hers. Like candied mandarin and patchouli.

I'd never be able to forget a scent like that. I know for a fact it belongs to her, but it's stronger than it should be. More alluring.

If she's taking her suppressants as she's meant to, it has

no right to be that potent. Not unless she's in the shadow of a dawning heat.

Impossible.

All the Omegas participating in the Trials have received clear orders about their suppressants. My pack and I have started taking rut suppressants of our own. *And yet...*

As soon as she stops two feet away from me, my Alpha nature is already urging me closer. *To* take *her.*

Moving a step back instead, I fight against my instincts and don't say a word as I spin around and motion for her to follow. "This way."

She falls into step beside me, almost tripping again in her haste to keep up.

"I'm so sorry, Prince Kaspian. I—"

"It's Your Highness," I snap, struggling to breathe with her scent so incredibly close to me. Turning my head away from her, I focus on the rose bushes surrounding the garden we're in and the bright green lawns stretching in all directions to the forest at the edge of the property. Anything but *her.*

"I apologize, Your Highness. I got turned around and then I asked for directions, but I must've asked someone who wasn't quite sure herself. I ended up on the other side of the palace. By the time I realized I was in the wrong place, I was already late."

"*Hmm.*"

Unfortunately, the disinterested hum doesn't stop her from speaking. Then again, it never does. All these Omegas are exactly the same, only concerned with the sound of their own voices and the pot of gold at the end of the rainbow that is our pack.

"I do apologize," she repeats. "I—"

"I've heard your reason for being late. Let's just walk, shall we?"

"We *are* walking," she says.

Even though I'm making a point of not looking at her, I can hear that she's frowning from the confused tone of her voice. Changing tact from the constant apologizing, she decides to make polite conversation instead, which is just as annoying as the fact that she was late. "The gardens are beautiful."

"Yes."

"It must take a ton of work to tend them."

"I'm sure it does."

A soft sigh slides out of her. "Well, *uh*. What else do you enjoy?"

Silence. I truly enjoy peace and silence.

When I don't answer, she remains undeterred. "I like reading. Do you like to read?"

Yes, which is probably the only reason you're claiming to enjoy it.

It's not the first time one of the Omegas has taken my hobbies as their own. Just this morning, one claimed to be an avid astronomer. So, I bit. I started talking to her about it. It took me less than thirty seconds to establish she didn't know a telescope from a telegraph.

"Look, I know I was late, but I've apologized. Have I somehow done something else that has offended you? You've barely said a word to me, and we're almost to the turning point in the pathway. I...I can just head back if you want."

I sigh, but she's so interested in the sound of her own voice that she just keeps speaking before I can answer the

CHAPTER NINE

question she posed. "Is there something I can do to make it up to you? I feel like we've gotten off on the wrong foot and—"

"Good God, do you ever stop talking?" I snap.

It hardly ever happens, but I can't help it, my control slipping just an inch.

An inch too much.

Her scent is fucking everywhere.

Between that and the incessant sound of her voice, I can't think. "Look, it's not you, okay? I'm just...it's been a long few days."

I finally turn to face her and her scent smacks me in the face and makes the whole thing worse.

I groan to myself, keeping my breaths short but it's no use. That scent has gotten under my skin, burrowed there, making a home in the marrow of my bones, and I can't rip it out. I shiver, demanding self-control, but unable to catch it as it slips away.

It *has* been a long few days. And a long afternoon of hours spent entertaining Omegas who mostly would rather prattle on about fake hobbies and boast about their grades and pedigree than say a single thing to me that has any meaning.

"This whole tradition is fucking ridiculous," I say, detached, my vision wavering, unable to stop myself as I continue. "You're all a bunch of spoiled, rich Omegas who will lie and cheat to try to win the crown and the affection of me and my packmates. And then we'll be trapped, bonded together with an Omega none of us really know because once the bond is complete, there's no way in hell my family will allow it to be broken."

Fuck! It's like I'm watching myself from the outside and

there's no way to rein it back in. I feel the muscles in my back flex and I clench my fists, but it brings me no relief, no sense of control.

Until the look on her face strikes me still.

I'm not sure which one of us is more surprised by my outburst, but her widened eyes narrow to slits and her own jaw flexes. For a frightening, fantastic second, I think she might hit me.

"Oh, boo hoo," she bites out, huffing. "The poor prince and his poor packmates have a bunch of the most eligible Omegas in the world vying for their attention. You're right. This whole thing *is* ridiculous, but at least you have your pack. You have a fucking palace and all these amazing staff members to support you. I never expected to be nominated or selected. I didn't ask for this. To be torn away from my family, fucking primped and poked and painted and pushed out for all the world to watch me fall on my face. But you don't see me being a prick about it, do you?"

I rock back on my heels.

She seems to realize the gravity of everything she's just said as a flash of fear crosses her face, but the stubborn Omega shoves it down, lifts her chin, and waits for me to render my judgment.

Huh.

"You forgot to tack on a *Your Highness* somewhere in there."

She snorts, giving her head a slight shake. She does *not* apologize, which is perhaps an alluring thing about her. She's...*real.*

"I didn't forget," she says with a coy inclination of her head and a whisper of a smirk on her full lips. "I simply

CHAPTER NINE

thought that if we are already well enough acquainted to be shouting at one another, formalities aren't necessary anymore."

My gaze catches on her vibrant, determined green eyes. I pause for a moment, considering my response now that I'm suddenly a bit calmer. "It's been a long time since anyone's spoken to me that way."

Anyone who isn't Pack...

"What was your name again?"

"Maddie," she says, then rolls her eyes. "Though everyone here seems intent on calling me Maddison or Miss Darling."

"Where are you from, Maddie?"

"Cambridge," she says, staring at me for a beat. "Why are you so eager for this thing to be over? Shouldn't you be enjoying the attention?"

A bench nearby catches my eye, and I motion her to it, sitting down heavily and putting my head in my hands.

"This isn't what I wanted," I admit, unsure when I'd become the type of man who *shares* his thoughts. "I've always known that I would be bonded as a result of the Trials because of the generation I was born in, but if it was up to me, I'd have chosen to bond with someone based on..."

"Love?" she offers when I can't seem to bring myself to say the word, unsure if it's even the right one.

I nod anyway. "Something quiet and meaningful. Not forced."

It's more than I've ever shared with anyone other than Wolf and Tai.

I cock my head at her, trying to read her thoughts

through the bottomless depths of her eyes. They convey so much and yet I can't pick out any one emotion. Not a single clear thought.

What are you thinking?

A soft breeze sweeps through the garden, kicking up her scent, mixing it with the bouquet of florals surrounding us in a way that makes my stomach clench.

It's fucking with my head. It must be, because I don't do this. I don't *talk*. Not like this.

Maddie hesitates for a moment. I feel when she finally comes to sit next to me.

I've still got my head in my hands, but her tone is gentle and surprisingly soothing when she speaks again. "You're clearly frustrated by all of this. If it helps, I didn't want to be here either, but now that I am, it's not so bad. Maybe if you give it a chance, you will find someone to love here."

I scoff.

"Do you honestly expect me to believe you didn't want to be here? Every Omega in every Academy around the world has been salivating for this opportunity since it was announced that one Omega will be selected from each of them."

"Yes, but when that announcement was made, I wasn't *in* one of the Academies and there wasn't much of a chance I ever would be. Your family made the announcement when I was sixteen, working hard for a scholarship I didn't think I would ever be awarded."

My eyebrows draw together as I process what she said. Slowly lifting my head, I turn toward her and look back into those green eyes that have been in my dreams since I got my first whiff of her scent, though I don't recall it having been quite this strong before.

CHAPTER NINE

"Hang on, am I correct in my understanding that your family is not well off, then?"

She frowns, her fingers fidgeting in her lap as she nods with skepticism flickering in her eyes. "Do you guys not talk to each other, like, at all?"

"Excuse me?"

"You, Tai, and Wolf. They told me to call them that, by the way, so don't get pissy because I didn't use their titles. I told Tai all about my family on my second morning here, yet Wolf didn't know my story either."

"It's not that we don't talk. We have an agreement not to discuss the Omegas until we've each had a chance to spend some time with every Omega individually. It seemed fairer to do it that way, once we've had the chance to come to our own conclusions before we start influencing each other."

She rocks her head from side to side before she shrugs. "I suppose that does seem fair. How's it going so far? It doesn't seem to be going very well if the mood you were in when I arrived is anything to go by."

I sigh, surprising myself once again when I laugh a little. "It's not going very well, but that wasn't the reason for my mood. Have you ever heard the expression *timeliness is next to godliness*?"

"I thought that was cleanliness," she says without skipping a beat. "I've heard it both ways, though. So, you really were in such a terrible mood because I was ten minutes late?"

When she says it like that...

"In any event, tell me about yourself. That's the point of this, isn't it. I'm curious to know...how does a scholarship Omega with no apparent connections to high society get selected for the most highly anticipated Mating Trial of the century?"

TEN

—

MADDIE

THE ROYAL PACK has surprised me, but none more so than the prince. It was pretty clear when we started our date that he was frustrated, angry, and just wanted to go through the motions rather than getting to know me at all.

Now it's blatantly obvious he meant everything he said. He wants to bond for love instead of being forced into it. For some reason, his sharp features have also softened since our brief stand-off and now, he's looking at me like I might have a shot of winning this thing.

Coming in here, I didn't expect it for a single moment, but as those infinitely dark eyes hold mine, I see a certain tenderness in them. Combined with how pleasant my dates were with the others, it makes me wonder if I stand a chance. My heart skips more beats than what could possibly be healthy at the thought of it.

Contrary to how I thought I would feel, I actually like these Alphas. They're easier to get along with than I could've imagined in my wildest dreams. Even though their proximity does strange things to me, I enjoy every minute I spend with them.

"How did I get selected?" I repeat his question as I try to think of where to start. "Well...because I'm a scholarship kid, I'm not particularly popular, but I've always been a bit of a loner anyway. Reading and writing are basically how I spend every day, and I don't need anyone else for them, so I haven't made many friends, and I've never really wanted to."

I drag in a shaky breath before I continue. "The librarian at our Academy is also my literature instructor. She...*Ms. Frampton* became more like a friend than anyone else there. We're very similar, and we get along really well. A couple of months ago, I wrote an essay on the merits and advantages of the Omega system and gave her a draft to read over. That's what she used when she recommended me to the selection committee."

I laugh a little uncomfortably before I decide to make the admission. "It—*um*—was meant to be satire."

Surprise flickers deep within those dark depths.

"That bit obviously went right over their heads, so here I am."

"You're really not from a family who is *at all* part of the high society?"

"Nope."

I smile, but when I see the sympathy creeping onto his features, my stomach plummets.

"What is it?"

"I'm sorry, Maddie. I really don't know how to tell you this, but I would feel like a complete bastard if I don't."

My chest constricts, and my palms get all clammy. "What is it?"

CHAPTER TEN

"You can't be chosen. My mother would never approve of such a match and it's...well, it's not expressly her decision, but I do need to stay in her favor."

"What?" I breathe, my voice stolen by the shock and disappointment currently snaking like shards of ice from the very center of my chest to my extremities.

I shouldn't be surprised. I really shouldn't. But after the last couple days with Tai and then Wolf, I thought maybe...

Kaz dips his chin in a nod, seeming honestly disappointed, himself. Maybe a little bit sad, judging by the sudden downturn of the corners of his mouth.

"I would risk my own happiness if it meant I had the chance to improve the lives of my citizens. I hope you understand. Truly. I can do a lot of good if I'm to become king. I can do a lot of good even now if the queen sees fit to involve me in making decisions that could affect the country as a whole. She's insisting on regular meetings with me throughout this process so I can update her on our feelings with regard to the Omegas. If I so much as hint to her that we've taken a fancy to...well, to someone like you, I'm certain she'll do something to sway us. Or worse, to ensure you are no longer eligible. Ultimately, it remains our decision who we choose, but if I don't become king, if she doesn't share her power, I can't do the great things I want to do."

Stunned, I stare back at him with my heart stammering and flip-flopping, strangely feeling like it's crumbling even if it has no right to. I'm so attracted to them all, and I get along with them so naturally that I thought...

Never mind. It doesn't matter.

"I understand," I murmur with my pulse thundering in

MADDIE

my ears when I realize what this means. I'm wasting my time here. Time I should be spending helping my family.

"Why am I still here, then?"

"Well, my mother doesn't know there's interest in you yet, but my real guess?" he says, his voice as quiet and contemplative as my own, but there's an apology in his eyes, too. "Entertainment purposes and appeal to the masses. A true Cinderella story. Nothing captivates viewers quite as much as a rags-to-potential-riches situation."

"Wouldn't I need to win the heart of Prince Charming for it to be a true Cinderella story?"

"No," he says, eyes gentle as they refocus on mine. "It's all about the façade. The illusion. Get people rooting for you, keep you here until the end so it looks like you've almost made it before someone swoops in and takes the win from you at the last moment."

"Are you sure?" It's a long shot, but I won't forgive myself if I don't at least ask.

A sad smile curves on his lips as he nods again. "As awful a reality as it is, I am sure. Has Tai told you much about his family?"

"A bit. Why?"

He exhales deeply through his nostrils. "Taiyo's family has held their title for generations. It was bestowed on his great, great-grandfather more than a century ago."

"Wow."

"Yes, but that's not really the point of this story. The reason I'm telling you this is so that you'll understand why you will never get the queen's blessing. She'd known Tai's dad since they were children. As a result of his family's connections to my own, they spent a lot of time together."

CHAPTER TEN

"Okay?"

He leans back on the bench, and his jaw tightens as he stares absently into the hedges, his throat bopping as he swallows heavily. It's plain to see that he doesn't like talking about this very much, which must mean he feels it's imperative to tell me this story so I'll understand the truth of what he's saying.

"When he took over some of his family's duties, Tai's father was sent to Tokyo on business for the Crown. He met a young Japanese woman there, a waitress he claimed to have fallen into love with at first sight."

"Should you be telling me any of this?"

He sighs. "Probably not, but I need you to understand the extent of my mother's disdain for commoners."

The use of the word stings, but it's not incorrect. At the thought, the pieces fall together in my head, and I finish the story for him. "That woman is Tai's mother. Your mother sent a childhood friend into exile because he fell in love with a commoner. That's why they moved back to Tai's father's home country."

"And why this is only the second time the Duchess has returned to court since Tai's birth." Kaz's chin lowers before he finally looks at me again. "Do you understand now?"

I hate it, but... "I do."

The weight of reality bears down on me when I realize I can't stay here. That I may have to sell one of my scent glands after all. If I can even sell it. I haven't wanted to ask any of them why they reacted to my scent the way they did at the ceremony, but I'm beginning to suspect it may not have been because they were repulsed by it after all. A strong reaction doesn't mean a bad one.

MADDIE

As I think it over, the hopelessness of my situation sinking in, an idea suddenly sparks in my head. "You said I could possibly stay until close to the end, right? Give viewers the opportunity to root for Cinderella?"

Curiosity flashes in those eyes as he tilts his head ever so slightly. "Yes. Who stays and who goes is our decision. We shouldn't get any pushback if we decide to keep you in the running, particularly not if that's the very reason why there hasn't been any pressure to get rid of you thus far."

The gears are turning. The longer I stay, the more compensation I could get to help my family. But maybe there could be something more. Something that'll last longer than a couple thousand quid.

"Maybe I can help you."

"Excuse me?"

"Before you tell me I'm crazy, just hear me out."

He frowns but nods. "Okay?"

"I share living quarters with the other Omegas, right? We eat most meals together. We share recreational areas. What if I get some insider info for you? I could watch out for any disingenuous behavior and report back. They'll speak more freely and act differently in front of the rest of the Omegas than they do when they're with you. I could let you know what they're like when you're not there. I could be your eyes on the inside. There's no getting out of this tradition, but maybe I could help you find someone who wants you for you and not for the crown."

Those dark eyes flare wide open, but then he swipes his tongue across his lips. Surprisingly, he doesn't turn me down right away. When his gaze focuses on mine again, he arches a dark, knowing eyebrow at me.

"Say I agree to this. What do you want in exchange?"

CHAPTER TEN

Excitement bubbles deep down in my gut. This isn't exactly winning, but at least it's a chance to help my family. "My dad is unemployed, but he has experience in culinary work as well as gardening. You give him a job. Anything steady that pays a decent wage. Oh! And living quarters where my little brother and my mother could stay with him. You promise me that and you give me your word that he won't be fired as soon as the Trials are over, and I'll get you the information you need not to wind up with a gold-digging asshole for the rest of your life."

He regards me for a long time as he mulls it over. Then, slowly, he reaches that elegant, long-fingered hand out toward mine. "Gardening, hmm?" He rolls it around in his mouth, eyes flicking to the bushes. "Okay, Maddie. You've got yourself a deal. If we can't find love, then at least you can help us find a good person."

We shake on it. Once again, I'm disturbed by how much his touch stirs up in me, but I shove it all down. This is for my family. For their future. For mine, too.

Kaz's grip tightens before he withdraws, quickly swiping his hand over his thigh like he's trying to rub my scent off his skin, making me rethink whether or not my scent is repulsive to them.

It will confuse me until the day I die that they didn't get rid of me after the Scenting Ceremony, but maybe I'll have a chance to ask one of them at some point.

A day when Tai doesn't immediately launch into the queen's vendetta against him, and Wolf doesn't get me chucked off a horse. A day when Kaz isn't breaking my heart by shattering dreams I was only now starting to dream.

Not today, but one day, I'll ask my new ally about it.

MADDIE

"Give me your phone," he says suddenly. "You'll need my private number so you can text me."

After we exchange numbers, he gets up. I realize we've been together for much longer than our appointed thirty minutes. He doesn't seem to be as concerned about his tardiness for his next date as he was about mine for ours, but I don't say as much.

In fact, we don't say another word to each other as he dips his head in a goodbye and then strides away to find the next Omega who's waiting to spend time with him. I sit back down on the bench for a while, thinking about everything he said and how bittersweet it is that I will never be their Omega.

There's definite comfort in the fact that I managed to achieve what I came here to achieve in the end, though. I wanted to find a way to monetize this experience to provide income and stability for my family, and I've done that.

When I see Kaz walking in the distance with another Omega, though, I decide it's too soon to watch him on a date. A date with someone who *does* actually stand a chance. Instead of subjecting myself to a sight that hurts more than I thought it would, I head back inside the palace.

The Omega living quarters are an entire wing of the south side of the building. It consists of multiple sitting rooms, TV rooms, and even a small library—which, of course, I adore. Then there's a dining room, our bedrooms, and a parlor, and that's where I find the bulk of Omegas when I walk back into the palace.

Rachel, a horrible snob of a female with a nose that's literally slanted so that it's permanently up in the air, is bullying Antonio, a gorgeous albeit reserved male I've spoken to once or twice in the library. Rachel stands with

CHAPTER TEN

her hands on her hips, a smug smirk on her lips as she rakes her gaze over him like she's already the queen.

"You should stop wasting everybody's time, Antonio," she sneers. "You're the runt of the litter around here. Everyone knows about your family's solvency issues. Your business almost went belly up last year, didn't it? Do you honestly think they're going to choose an Omega who's on the verge of being penniless?"

My teeth grind together as I watch him stare her down, itching to say something in his defense, but I really have no idea who Antonio is. If I'm going to be a valuable spy, I can't make enemies.

Antonio can stand up for himself, if he thinks it's even worth his time to waste his breath on someone like Rachel.

"You're a joke, Ramirez."

Antonio's jaw tightens, his face turning a light shade of pink.

"All of Barcelona knows it," Rachel drones on. "We know it all the way over in California, and London knows it too. Do us all a favor and—"

Yeah, that's it. Maybe I *shouldn't* make enemies, but that doesn't mean I *can't*.

Antonio stares at the floor now, shuffling on his feet and biting his lip like he's about to start crying. I don't know if what she's saying is true, but it doesn't matter.

"Actually," I cut her off as I step farther into the room and march to his side. "Why don't you do us all a favor and stop trying to intimidate your way to the top? It's not going to work, you know. They're smarter than that and none of them will choose a vapid bitch to bond with."

Her eyes flash with the challenge as she turns to me. "Aren't you the Darling girl?" She smiles. "My pen pal,

MADDIE

Clara, sent me a message about you. I wonder if the Royals know there's a commoner in our midst."

My eyes roll so hard, I catch sight of the memories of my first birthday buried deep inside my brain. "Of course, they know. I'm not the one who seems to think they're stupid. The real question here is whether they know they have a bully as a selected candidate. They don't care so much about me being a commoner, but from what I've seen of them so far, they won't take so kindly to the quintessential mean girl trying to scare off her competition."

Rachel huffs out a breath, but one of her friends drags her away before she can say another word. Once they're gone, Antonio finally looks up, surprise written in his wide, teary eyes as he shakes his head at me. "Thanks, but you've really done it now. She won't forget that."

"Nor should she," I say honestly. "I meant what I said, and I stand by it. If the pack finds out about this, I'm sure they'll send her home."

He arches an eyebrow at me. "You have no idea who she is, do you?"

"Nope, and I don't care." I incline my head toward the corridor where the bedrooms are. "Want me to walk you to your door?"

"No, thank you. You've effectively transferred the target from my back to yours. I'll walk you instead."

I smile, deciding I may as well get some intel for Kaz now that I seem to have made an unexpected friend. "How have you found the Trials so far?"

"Good, I guess." He shrugs as he follows me out into the hall. "My dates have been fine. The Royals seem okay."

"Okay?" I echo disbelievingly. "Jeez. You're lucky. Have you not, you know..."

CHAPTER TEN

I trail off but he isn't picking up what I'm putting down.

"I mean, their scents are just—I don't know—maybe it's just me, but every time I'm around them I feel like my suppressants aren't working. I guess I thought it would be that way for everyone."

He frowns, obvious confusion etched into the furrow of his brow. "Well, their scents are really nice—"

I give him a look and he chuckles, amending his statement. "Okay, they are more than *a little nice*. But the suppressants are doing their job. I don't feel any indicators of an oncoming heat."

Well, shit.

"This has got to be extra stressful for you. I saw your selection on TV. And your—*um*—little trip during the scenting ceremony. I take it this sort of thing isn't your strong suit. It's probably the anxiety. Either that or if you aren't used to being around Alphas in your life outside of OA then your body could just be having a strong reaction."

My head drops back, and I groan when I realize he's got a point I haven't considered yet. "Yeah, you're probably right. Stress might be the most obvious answer."

"Not that you asked for it, but my advice would be to increase the dosage of your suppressants to one and a half. It should sort you right out. My brother went through something similar when he first left the Academy. He upped his suppressants, and everything went back to normal."

"I'll do that. Thanks."

When we stop at my door, he gives me a strange look. "If you ever need any, I brought a huge stash of suppressants. Because it happened to my brother, I couldn't rule out that it might happen to me. Just let me know, okay?"

"Okay."

MADDIE

He scratches his jaw, his eyes taking on a faraway quality. "The expiry date on yours might also be off or something. Either way, if it doesn't work, talk to me. I owe you one."

"You don't owe me anything, but I'll let you know."

He smiles as I reach for my door. "See you at dinner, Antonio."

"Sure thing. See you, Maddie. Watch out for any meerkats."

"Meerkats?"

He winks as he starts walking backward away from my room. "It's a nasty little mongoose-type creature that has a pointy snout and a pretty nasty bite. They're especially aggressive to people they don't know, and they work in groups."

I think of Rachel's pointy nose, her sneer, and the group of minions she's already gathered here. "Oh, right. I'll be careful. Thanks for the warning."

He blows out a breath, shaking his head at me again. "Seriously, watch your back. Court isn't like you've seen in the picture books. Not really. Not if you look hard enough."

Before I can answer him, he's gone, and I'm left with a hollow pit in my stomach that tells me he's right. And very perceptive to have already deduced as much on his own in barely a few days.

I've gotten to know the predators at my school, but I'm not in Cambridge anymore. I'm starting to understand why Kaz was willing to give me everything I asked for in exchange for this information. As it turns out, this seems to be a bit of a feeding frenzy, and Kaz and his pack are the chum. I'm only just starting to realize what they've gotten themselves into, but he's known all along.

CHAPTER TEN

At least he has me now, though. As long as I'm earning my family's keep, I won't allow myself to feel guilty about it. If the tables were turned, I'd have given a lot more than that to avoid having to spend my life bound to someone like Rachel.

ELEVEN

—

KAZ

WHEN I WALK BACK into our quarters after yet another horribly exhausting afternoon, Tai and Wolf are waiting for me at the bar in our rec room. As soon as I enter, I know they're up to something.

"What is it?" I ask curiously, shrugging out of my jacket and hanging it on the coat rack near the door before locking the damn thing behind me. *Screw anyone who wants into these quarters tonight. It's just not happening.*

My packmates exchange a look, and I feel conflicting emotions coming through the bond. There's excitement, nerves, anticipation, and an incredibly healthy dose of lust mixed with a whole bunch of other stuff I'm too tired to unpack.

"You've spoken about the Omegas without me, haven't you?"

They exchange another look, then Wolf smirks at me. "It kind of happened by accident after I spent time with Maddie yesterday. Tai had her the day before, and you had her today, right? I checked your appointment schedule."

KAZ

At the mention of her name, I know what they've been up to and exactly what all those emotions they're feeling are about. My head is shaking before any of us have said another word.

"Absolutely not. She can't be chosen. You both know her history. Her lack of pedigree. The queen would never allow it. I have no appetite for the chaos that would come of even *mentioning* her as a potential candidate."

"How about tomorrow?" Wolf asks. "Will you have an appetite for it then?"

"No," I say firmly, striding behind the bar and fixing myself a stiff drink. Two cubes of ice rattle in the crystal tumbler as I drop them in, but they're soon drowned in the best brandy France has on offer. "When I say chaos, I mean *chaos*. The kind that could see me disowned."

"Maybe the monarchy needs a little chaos to come out better in the end," Tai suggests hopefully. "A little chaos to usher out the old and bring in the new."

"No, Tai," I snap. "Think about your parents and how they ended up. Is that what you want for us as well? A life of exile and offspring who feel like they don't belong? I can affect real change here. *We* can affect change, but only if we're *here*. If we're in Her good graces."

Even as the words come flying out of my mouth, I regret them. I sound...political. Cold.

My words hit a mark they weren't intended for, though, and Taiyo flushes with anger, his eyes narrowing as he rises off the stool he was sitting on. "Oh, I get it. She's a commoner, right? That means she'll never be good enough for you even if we all know you're as taken by her as we are."

"Taken?" I scoff. "You fucking scented her once and

then had one date with her. Barely an hour spent in her presence and you're ready to propose?"

"I felt what you felt earlier, man. How do you think we knew you saw her?"

"Wolf checked my schedule," I say coolly, really trying to remember who I'm talking to here. "He just said it."

"Fuck off, Kaz," he snaps. "Wolf checked your schedule, but only *after* we both felt it. To make sure our suspicion of who you were with at the time we felt it was right."

"So, this was a fucking ambush?" I bring the glass to my lips and take a long swallow as my gaze clashes with his. "You were waiting for me so you could, what? Try to convince me to choose someone that you both fucking *know* we can't?"

Heat rises up the back of my neck to my cheeks. I exhale sharply, shaking my head again as he keeps glaring at me. "Have you forgotten all the plans we have? The good we want to do for our people?"

"We can do all that without the fucking monarchy," he hisses. "Ordinary Betas, Omegas, and Alphas who aren't royal do good every single day. Don't hang that on me, Kaz. You know how I feel about helping people, but we don't need the Crown at our backs to do it."

"Why are we having this argument again?" I set my glass down with a heavy thud on the counter as I glare right back at him. "It's been a long fucking day and we've already talked this topic to death. Ordinary people do a lot of good, but we can do more with the monarchy behind us than any of them ever could."

"Well, all we need to do is wait for your dear mother to drop dead then, don't we? As long as she's alive, the monarchy will *never* be behind us, Kaspian. Meanwhile, we could be letting go of someone who could be perfect for us, who shouldn't even have been selected, by the way, just because you're crawled too far up your mother's royal ass to see Maddie for what she is. Don't you realize it's a miracle she made it in? That has to mean something."

"My mother's ass may be royal, but it's also what's keeping the goddamn roof over our heads. You can't tell me you want back into exile. We *will* change the system, Taiyo. This just isn't the way to do it. How do you not understand that? After everything you've been through."

"We're having this conversation *because* of everything I've been through," he shouts, meeting me halfway round the bar and getting up in my face. "This whole attitude of yours of being better than anyone else is ridiculous. Yes, you're royalty. Who fucking cares? It's an antiquated regime doing more harm than good under your mother's rule, and I know you feel the same way, so why are we dancing to her tune?"

"We're not dancing to her fucking tune," I hiss, my eyes narrowed to slits as I stare into his. "We're playing the game, Tai. You *know* this. You're right about her, but the only way we can change that is to play. The. Fucking. Game. So play it. Forget about Maddison Darling and focus on our goddamn future."

"That's exactly what I'm doing." He's trembling with exasperation now and frankly, I wouldn't be surprised if this comes to blows. Which is odd. It never goes this far with us.

As if Wolf had the same thought I just did, he steps in. "Now, now, boys, let's take this down a notch, shall we?"

He places one palm on my chest and one on Taiyo's, pushes us apart, and then gives each of us a meaningful

CHAPTER ELEVEN

look. "The enemy isn't in this room. You've got different views on the role of the monarchy. We all know that, but this isn't about the monarchy. It's about who we're going to end up bonded to, which isn't a decision we can make when we're about to start throwing punches."

He moves that sea-green gaze to Tai's and pats his chest. "Take a walk, brother. I've got this."

Tai glares at him for another beat, then his chest deflates, and he nods. "Fine, I was done anyway. Like talking to a brick fucking wall."

Wolf heaves out a dramatic sigh, but then he winks at me as soon as Tai stalks out of the room. "Damn, man. It's been a long time since you've gone *full Alpha*. It's nice to know you've still got it in you. C'mon. Let's go."

"Where?"

"I'm going to help you out," he says as he starts toward his chambers. "Let's go, Your Highness. We're burning moonlight here."

If he were anyone else, I'd have told him to shove it so hard I'd be able to take whatever it was out of his mouth after, but he's not anyone else. He's Wolfgang Von Damme, and he's been my best friend since we were thirteen.

Honestly, he was—and sometimes continues to be—a terrible influence, but he was also the one person who made me feel alive. Until Tai came along, then there were two people who made me feel alive. It's still like that, the three of us against the world.

And suddenly, I feel like an asshole. I'll have to find Tai and apologize.

Wolf pulls his shirt off and all rational thought flees as he drags me toward his bedroom.

KAZ

He's already unbuttoning his trousers before we cross the threshold, kicking them off as he walks.

Fuck, he's perfect.

Always has been. Probably always will be.

All the way from those golden locks, to the broad shoulders and chest that tapers down into narrow hips, further to his glorious, long cock that's as veiny and nearly as thick as his neck when his knot's swollen, to his muscular legs and even his goddamn perfect toes. He's just...exquisite.

I know he works hard for every ripple of definition in his arms and torso, and those legs and that ass are the product of hours spent upon a horse, but shit. My throat bobs as I swallow. He's so fucking sexy, it hurts.

"You're really wound that tight?" he asks as he strides over to me and takes the back of my neck in his strong hand. "Do you want me to call that Beta friend of mine? You know, the one who does that thing with her tongue?"

"No." I stare into those breathtaking eyes. Touching anyone who isn't my pack or Maddie right now feels wrong.

Whoa. Back the fuck up? Since when am I thinking about her that way?

I groan out loud, and Wolf offers me a knowing smirk. "You're thinking about her still, aren't you?"

My throat constricts. I give him nothing to indicate that he's right or wrong, but I don't have to. Somehow, Wolf always knows.

Those eyes soften and I swear—I fucking swear—I would go to war for this man. The way he reads my mind...

"Are you?"

"Yeah, Kaz. I can't seem to stop." The words are hardly out before his mouth claims mine in a bruising kiss, one that makes my dick threaten to tear my zipper apart, but it still doesn't feel right. Not until I feel another pair of arms wrapping around me from behind and Taiyo's voice whispering in my ear.

"I forgive you," he murmurs against the back of my neck. "You're a fucking idiot, but I forgive you. This is just—"

"Hard?" I offer on a breath.

"You're goddamn right, it's hard." Wolf grunts into my mouth as his cock rocks into mine. "It's so fucking hard. Get those clothes off him, Tai. I've got plans."

With that, he gives me another searing kiss and then releases me. Tai is right there, turning me around and working to get me out of my pants as his lips touch mine in a much gentler caress.

"I didn't mean what I said about—"

"I know you didn't," he interrupts, shutting me up with another kiss.

Wolf's kiss was all about sex and dominance, about breaking me out of my head and bringing me into the moment, but Tai's is an apology of his own as well as physical proof of his acceptance of mine.

I said some pretty fucked-up things, and I had no right to tell her his story—which he doesn't even know about yet. When I tense up again, he pulls away, but his lips are on mine as he murmurs, "Don't you dare, Kaz. Stay the fuck out of your head right now."

"Make me," I taunt.

He shoves my pants and underwear down in one go and wraps his long fingers around my shaft, gliding his thumb over my wet tip.

"I knew that's what this was about." He groans as his

hand starts moving up and down. "You've got to let us in, Kaz. We're in this with you. You're not alone, yeah?"

"Yeah," I say breathily as pleasure rushes through me, my feet stiffening as I flex my thighs to fight the fast-building climax. "I know. I'm sorry."

Thing is, Tai's not exactly ecstatic to be here at the palace. Never has been. He's here for me, and for Wolf, but he hasn't a clue what his actual role is around here. I've felt the listlessness of how lost he feels. Half the fucking reason I want the damn crown is for him, so he knows how valued he is and never doubts the king is in his back pocket.

He moves his mouth to the column of my throat, kissing and nipping until Wolf comes back. He's fully naked now, his erection pressing into my ass as he comes up behind me, his hand joining Tai's on my dick.

A feral growl escapes my lips as I surrender completely, dropping my head onto Wolf's broad shoulder, giving them permission to unleash their wicked desires upon me.

The seconds blur into minutes. Time spent in the haze of each other as we touch and grab and squeeze and lick and suck and it's not long before Wolf makes his play.

He's a top, but every once in a while...

He gets down on all fours atop his bed, his muscles rippling with anticipation as I sense his desire. Not to fuck. Not tonight. But to *be* fucked.

With a savage hunger, I spit into my palm, slicking my cock before I nudge at his entrance, easing patiently into him at first, letting him adjust before I plunge into him. He lets out a faltering groan. The scorching heat of Wolf's inner sanctum engulfs me, gripping and squeezing with an exquisite tightness that defies reason.

Simultaneously, Tai positions himself upside-down on

CHAPTER ELEVEN

the bed, shimmying through Wolf's strong arms until his lips seal around Wolf's throbbing cock and I feel his core tighten around me in response.

He moves, pushing me deeper before easing forward, asking me without words to fuck him.

So, I do.

Every thrust sends shockwaves of pleasure coursing through my veins, propelling all three of us into a drunken haze of carnal pleasure. Wolf bends his head to Tai's erection, suckling on the tip just as Tai deepthroats his cock beneath him.

Moans blend with desperate cries of ecstasy as our bodies move in perfect synchronization, each motion pushing us closer to the edge of sanity.

"Fuck!" Wolf cries and I reach forward, fisting his blonde locks in my hand, pulling his head back for just a second so he'll look at me. I need to see it. I need to see him loving this as much as I do.

"You like that?"

I fuck him harder.

"Fuck yeah," he says, breathless, his eyes heavy lidded and a smirk on his lips as he realizes he's gotten exactly what he wanted out of this, for me to let go. To lose myself in them. "Faster, Kaz. I don't want to be able to sit right tomorrow."

Something low in my belly tightens and I growl, pushing his head back onto Tai's cock until he's choking on it, redoubling his efforts.

I abandon all control, fucking Wolf wildly. Savagely. The primal beast within me takes hold as I surrender to my nature and my knot swells to the point of agony, begging for release.

KAZ

Begging for the tight warmth only an Omega can provide me.

Tai cries out, his voice merging with the symphony of moans as his hips flex and Wolf drinks him down. Wolf, unable to resist any longer, succumbs, his seed spilling into Tai's eager mouth. A pearl of pure white escaping to roll down the side of Tai's cheek.

I roar as my body wrings out its own release, pumping once, twice more before I see fucking stars. And not the kind I watch in the sky. Not the steady kind. No. I pour into Wolf's ass as a supernova explodes before my eyes with a force that takes the edges of my vision with it and leaves me shaking and weak on uneven ground.

In the aftermath, our bodies lay intertwined, a tapestry of sweat-slicked skin and heaving chests. We bask in it. In each other. Our breaths mingling as we gradually come down from the high. And I finally manage to find the words.

"She's spying for us," I murmur. "Maddie, I mean. I told her she wasn't going to be chosen, and she accepted it, but then she offered to be our eyes and ears on the inside."

"In exchange?" Wolf asks, thoughtful but not surprised.

I sigh. "Compensation in the way of a stable job for her father and someplace for her family to live."

"She could've just asked for money," Tai points out cautiously. "Cold, hard cash to make their troubles go away. It says something about her character that she only asked for a job and a stable roof over their heads."

"I know," I admit. "I was expecting it to be money. And look, I know you're both hesitant, but this is exactly what she asked for. She's being compensated, and with her help, it'll all work out in the end."

Even as I say it though, I know they're not convinced.

CHAPTER ELEVEN

Frankly? Neither am I. I don't believe this bullshit I'm peddling right now, but I need to peddle it.

For our sake as much as for hers, I need to start believing it'll all be all right. It's only the rest of our lives on the line.

No fucking pressure or anything.

TWELVE

—

MADDIE

AFTER A FEW HOURS OF DELIBERATION, I decide Kaz needs to know what happened between Rachel and Antonio earlier. I promised him information. The sooner I solidify my role as his mole, the easier it will be to remember it's nothing more than that.

Plus, my parents really need this to happen. Like, yesterday.

Although I haven't told him how dire their situation is, I need him to hold up his end of the bargain as fast as possible. Whether he even has the power to make something like this happen overnight, I don't know.

I'm hoping it doesn't take months to get it through the *proper channels*. Either way, I made a promise and I intend to follow through. I've been pacing up and down for at least an hour because of all this. Enough is enough. Mind made up, I march to my bed and pick up my phone.

As far as I know, our communications aren't being monitored, but considering how many legal documents I signed, it's not impossible that we're being watched.

Although I'm tempted to type it all up and send it to him, I keep it simple in the end.

Me: HRH, I have a report.

Within seconds, the dancing dots tell me he's typing a response and then, it appears.

PK: Excellent. Meet?

Me: Yes

PK: Hang tight. Sending reinforcements.

A few long, torturous minutes later, there's a very quiet knock at my door. I crack it open to find a surly-faced man on the other side. He doesn't speak, simply looking into my eyes and canting his head to the left.

I nod, tiptoeing out of my room and shutting the door as quietly as I can behind me. The man walks down the corridor and doesn't stop to check if I'm following. If I didn't know any better, I'd say he was on patrol and I was simply up to get a glass of water or something.

But I suppose that's exactly what it's supposed to look like. I follow him to a staircase at the bottom end of the hall, then we take it three flights up before he turns right. A few short paces down another corridor, and we take another staircase, only to climb one flight down before we turn left into—surprisingly—yet another stairwell.

Pretty soon, I'm so lost I'm sure I'll end up in the queen's private chambers if I try to make it back myself, but I pray that won't happen. Eventually, at least a dozen corridors, halls, and stairwells later, we enter through what appears to be the back door of the pack quarters.

I know it's got to be that because I'm suddenly overwhelmed by their scents. In the past few days, I've gotten to know those quite well. I'm immediately struck by Taiyo's bright, warm smell. It's all spicy nettle and bergamot, like

CHAPTER TWELVE

Earl Grey Tea, with cardamom, and sage. The intensity increases as we pass an ornate door I'm sure leads to his chambers.

Uniquely mingled with that scent is Wolf's more outdoorsy smell. To me, he smells like a peaceful meadow—birch, heather, and oakmoss with an undercurrent of crisp mountain air.

Their scents are heavy on this side of the corridor, telling me they spend a lot of time going to and from each other's chambers. Wolf's warm wood and Tai's warm *everything* follow me into what I suspect is Kaz's territory.

The others' scents are fainter here. They're still around, but they're not nearly as infused into the very walls as they are on the other side of the corridor. When the scent of smooth bourbon, musk, and caramel grows stronger, I know we're getting close to Kaz's chambers.

A few seconds later, the guard who was leading me raps on a door without stopping. Then he keeps walking as the door opens and my wrist is caught in a powerful grip. I'm tugged inside, close to losing my balance and tripping from the force of it, which is no surprise. What does surprise me is the soft smile on Kaz's face when he shuts the door behind me and folds his arms.

"Well?" he asks, his hair damp from a recent shower that did nothing to dull his scent. If anything, it's stronger than ever this close to him. The wetness only serving to infuse it with a hint of something like petrichor.

Once again, my clit lights up like a homing beacon. I have to press my legs together as I run my gaze over our crown prince who's in nothing but black sweats and a gray t-shirt. I know I'm not meant to feel this way. I took one and a half times my heat suppressant a few hours ago, but

MADDIE

at the sight of him, I want to whine with need. I want to cuddle up with him and feel that hard body pressed against mine. I want to feel him purr and purr into him in return.

Stop it, Maddie.

His feet are bare, his expression strangely smoothed out and relaxed as he regards me. I've never seen the prince like this before, but he seems a touch...too relaxed.

"What's up with you?" I ask before I can stop myself.

To my utmost surprise, he simply smirks and cocks his head at me. "Nothing. What's up with you?"

"Nothing," I say, but then I squeeze my eyes shut and shake my head. "I mean, it's not nothing, obviously." I look at him again, trying to ignore how much I want to know what he was doing before I came here. "We haven't established what kind of information you want or how often you want it. If I'm wasting your time right now, then I'd like to apologize in advance."

He shakes his head. "You're not wasting my time. What happened?"

Curiosity gnaws at my insides, so intense that it certainly can't be healthy. It's none of my business what he was doing. Plus, just thinking about how he might've ended up so relaxed isn't helping the situation in my panties. *Snap out of it and report, Darling!*

"When I walked back into our quarters earlier, Rachel was being awful to Antonio. She was talking about how his family business was in trouble and how he shouldn't even be here."

Kaz exhales heavily, a light and easy smile blooming on his wicked lips makes my heart skip a beat. "Thank you. Rachel has always been perfectly cordial to me, but she's the daughter of a diplomat. With them, you can never be too sure. She's been in media training since she was about four, so she knows how to put a nice spin on things."

"Will you choose her?" I ask, thinking maybe he didn't hear me. "She's a bully, Kaz."

Kaz's smile morphs, quirking up at one side in a way that seems...almost curious.

"I don't know," he replies after a moment. "Probably not. Neither of the others are too fond of her, and we're making this decision together. Thank you for coming to me with this. It's good to know that what we suspected about what she's really like is true."

"What about Antonio?" I ask even though I know I shouldn't. "Is it true what she said? I don't mean about his family's financial difficulties, of course. I'm talking about how he will never be chosen because of it."

He stares at me through those immensely dark eyes before he rakes a hand through his jet-black hair. "Antonio is a prime example of who we should choose. His family has made a name for themselves over the last few decades. They're affiliated with Spanish royalty. Bonding with him will be akin to marrying into the modern version of royalty, I suppose. Financial troubles or not. Likely, the crown would put an end to those rumors and even right whatever financial mess they've gotten themselves in."

Gaze clouding over as he contemplates it, he shrugs. "Antonio's sister is an influencer. His brother is an entrepreneur who's revolutionizing medical testing equipment. His mother is the picture of a wholesome maternal figure, but she kicks some serious ass from behind the scenes."

"But they're okay?" I ask cautiously. "The way Rachel

MADDIE

was digging into him, it looked like she was going to make him cry. I thought..."

Kaz reaches for my hands and takes one, squeezing it quickly and gently before he lets it go and wipes his palm on his sweatpants. Again. He's nice enough to me when we're talking, but he clearly doesn't want my scent on him.

"They're okay," he assures me as he shows me back to his door. "Last I heard, they fell on some tough times in the past year, but it was a difficult one for everyone. Rachel's family included. But that stays between us. Is that all?"

"That's all," I affirm, but before he opens the door, I take a quick look around his chambers. *I mean, who wouldn't?*

This is my first time in a real live prince's living quarters, and I'd be stupid not to at least look. What I've read in the press about his love for reading is obviously true. There isn't a spare inch of wall not covered by bookshelves. The spines of his books are all worn, telling me that they're not just there for show.

Actually, it doesn't look like anything in here is just there for show. His space is much cozier and more appealing than I thought it would be. We're in some kind of sitting room where comfortable couches hold rumpled throws on the back. A fire roars in the fireplace even though it's spring—but to be fair, it is pretty cold in their stone fortress—and in front of one large window is a telescope.

Excitement coils in my belly when I spot it. "It's true, then. You're an amateur astronomer? Funny, I thought the tabloids wrote that to make you seem smarter. More scientific."

A smile curves on those beautiful, full lips as he shakes his head. "Trust me, the tabloids would never do me any

CHAPTER TWELVE

favors. They wouldn't report something to make me seem smarter. Dumber, definitely, but smarter? Never."

"That must be terrible," I say, glancing back at his telescope. "If I tell you how sorry I am that they won't do you any favors, will you do me one?"

"A favor?"

I nod, swiping my tongue across my lips and wondering if I'm about to go too far. When his smile widens and his brows lift to let me know I can go ahead, I decide to ask him regardless of whether he might think I'm pushing the boundaries of our newfound quasi-friendship.

"I've always wanted to look through a telescope, but I've never had the opportunity. May I?"

His gaze captures mine and holds it hostage for a long moment. "Have you really always wanted to or are you just saying that?"

"I've really always wanted to. My mother used to read me this bedtime story about a girl and the stars, and ever since, I don't know, maybe it's stupid, but I always wanted a telescope like the one she had in the story."

He stares at me for another long moment before he dips his chin in a nod. "Who am I to deny you a lifelong dream becoming reality? Go ahead."

"Really?" I squeak, and to my surprise, he chuckles. When he does, his eyes light up and the corners crinkle a little bit, his features transforming in a way that makes him look so innocent, like he's still just a boy underneath the weight of the man he's expected to be. I never thought I'd see him this way, but it's a moment I know I'll remember.

For some inexplicable reason, tears well in my eyes. He frowns, but then he turns and walks toward one of the

MADDIE

shelves, swiping up a handkerchief and handing it over to me. "Are you all right?"

"I am. I think it's all just getting to me, you know? This whole experience is so surreal, and my emotions have been all over the place. I swear I'm not usually like this."

It's nothing at all to do with the fact that my mother will never read that same book to Kevin now. That she'll never read anything at all.

He flashes me an unexpectedly understanding smile. "We've all been a bit on edge. Come on, let's take a look at the stars. It'll help. It usually does for me."

Nodding as I dab my eyes with his handkerchief, I ball it up in my hand and slide it into my back pocket when he motions for me to follow him. Once we're at the telescope, he bends over to look at something through it, then he makes a few adjustments before lifting his head and smiling at me.

"Ursa Major," he explains as I move forward to gaze at whatever he's focused the telescope on. "It's also known as the Big Bear. It's a great place to start for stargazing. See?"

I feel it when he moves in behind me, leaning closer presumably to do something with the telescope, but I've completely forgotten what I'm supposed to be looking at. Suddenly enveloped by his scent and with his heat radiating into me, I lose focus on everything else. I can't think. Can't breathe.

When I pull back to get some space before I do something stupid like press my ass into him, I wind up with my face only inches away from his. Almost as if on instinct, my gaze drops to his lips.

Kaz's eyes drop to my lips, too, and he leans in as if he can't help himself. I want it so bad that a soft moan escapes

CHAPTER TWELVE

me, but Kaz straightens up like a shot when he hears the sound. He stumbles back like he's been slapped, then he rakes a hand through his dark hair and averts his gaze for a moment.

"Let me walk you back to your room," he says. "We'll have to be careful, though. If anyone sees us together, there will be whispers that I'm spending more time with you than with anyone else. That will only cause drama for the both of us."

I nod, blinking rapidly as I try to gain control of my thoughts. *What was I thinking? I can't go around almost kissing the crown fucking prince.*

Kaz looks at me again. Something about the set of his jaw makes me think he's contemplating saying more, but then he decides against it and puts some distance between us. As promised, he walks me back to my room, but neither of us says a word along the way.

When we reach a familiar corridor that opens into the hallway with all the Omegas quarters, he stops in the shadows.

"This is as far as I go."

He dips into a shallow bow before he spins around and strides back the way we came. I sigh, but I go into my chambers and try to put the whole encounter behind me.

Trouble is, twenty-two hours later at dinner, I still haven't quite managed to stop thinking about his Royal Hotness or our almost kiss. Antonio frowns at me from across the table we're sharing. "They're still getting to you, huh?"

"Yep."

He flashes me an apologetic smile. "That sucks. I'm sorry this is so hard for you. We've got enough going on

MADDIE

without you having to worry about a heat pushing through the suppressants. Have you seen someone on the medical staff here yet?"

I shake my head. I don't want to make a fuss. "No, but I will if it gets worse."

"On the bright side, I may not have to worry about it much longer."

Actually, that's not true. Not for me, at least.

Since I already know I'll be making it through to the next round, I also know I'll need to deal with these issues for at least another couple of weeks, but Antonio doesn't know that. He sighs, lifting his goblet of wine and taking a long sip as he nods.

"Are you worried there's going to be a knock on your door later?" he asks. "I am. I was so nervous during my date with Wolf today that I called him *my Lard*. He was cool about it, but still. They're looking for someone who can handle the pressure of being part of the Royal Pack, and I'm not sure that's me."

"My *Lard*?" I laugh. "Don't worry. I accidentally asked him if he looks more high-strung than he really is."

Antonio's brown eyes flare wide open before a bark of surprised laughter comes out of him. "How does one accidentally ask him something like that?"

"I don't know. How does one accidentally call him my Pig Fat?" I tease. "He was cool about my thing, too, though. I don't think he's going to encourage the others to send you home because of it."

Antonio takes another gulp of his wine. "Well, I'll let you know whether they do or don't. I guess we'll have to wait and see."

"I don't think you have anything to worry about," I say,

CHAPTER TWELVE

thinking back to what Kaz told me in his chambers before the *incident*. "You're a catch, and they should know it. If they don't, that's on them."

"Yeah, well, everyone here is a catch." He takes an exaggerated look around before he reaches for the bottle and tops off his glass before adding another splash of wine to mine. "Do you know what I think?"

"What?"

"We should get at least a little bit tipsy on the Royal Family's dime. While we still can, you know? We might be sent home in the morning. If it's our last day, we should have a little bit of fun. Besides, I don't think I'll be able to sleep otherwise."

I chuckle. "You just want to be able to say you got drunk in a palace, don't you?"

"Tipsy," he reiterates as he winks at me. "And yes. Why not? Let's have some fun, calm our nerves, and badmouth our competitors."

I raise my glass and clink it against his. "That sounds like the perfect potential last night to me."

"Wonderful. I knew there was a reason I liked you."

"Aww, thanks. I like you too." Out of all the Omegas here, in fact, if it can't be me, I hope the Eaton Pack ends up choosing him. At least that way, I'll know for sure the three Alphas who have taken up residence under my skin will be in gentle, caring hands.

I just really wish those hands could've been my own.

THIRTEEN

—

TAI

I SHOULD *NOT* BE HERE. If anyone sees me in the Omega wing, rumors will fly. The last thing we need is for it to get back to the queen that I've been sneaking around with *the commoner*.

The whole situation with Maddie has caused enough tension in our pack as is. If the queen starts throwing her weight around, we're going to end up back at each other's throats.

As I glance from left to right once I'm at her door, relief ripples through me that no one seems to have seen me so far. There are no windows in this corridor. I haven't seen another soul since I walked into this part of the palace.

It's late, though. I waited until I would have the best shot at getting in and out unseen before I came. Of course, it means Maddie may be sleeping, but I need to talk to her someplace private, so here I am. Hopefully my scent is masked enough from the chingara root tea I drank earlier and the heavy cologne I applied before leaving my room. If the knocks have already happened, then hopefully all the

TAI

Omegas are either asleep or too busy packing to be out in the halls.

I didn't want to wait for our next date to speak to her. This deal she made with Kaz bugs me, especially because I don't think he should've told her she's out of the running completely. I respect his decisions, and if we really can't be with her in the end, then I'll find a way to be okay with that.

But I also think it warrants more thought and a few more conversations at least. She's a commoner, yes, but she's participating in the Trials like everyone else. I've checked her ratings online. She's doing well. People like her.

The cameras aren't around all the time—thank *fuck*—but the Omegas have been having these "confessional" sessions at least once a day, where they're recorded giving updates and talking about their experience. It's not broadcast live and not nearly all the footage is used, but the world seems to be liking whatever they've seen of Maddie so far.

I like what *we've* seen of Maddie so far, too. While I'll play the game and do what Kaz said to keep looking at our options, I haven't written her off quite as completely as he has. Which is why I'm here. I need to either talk her out of this deal with him or find a way to change the terms.

For example, she can keep spying for us, but she needs to know she's still in it, too. That I'll do my best to make sure she has a fair shot.

As I raise my fist to knock, it occurs to me that she might think this is *the* knock. The one that means she's going home.

The thought gives me pause, but then I rap my knuckles softly across the wood anyway. I'll just keep knocking until—

"Come in," she calls from inside, and I frown.

CHAPTER THIRTEEN

Is she...drunk?

"Yes, enter the future royal's chamber," another voice calls out drunkenly, and I grin.

I like the sound of that...Maddie as the future royal. Maybe it's a sign.

When I open the door, I find Maddie and Antonio curled up on her bed with a bottle of wine. Surprise flickers behind her eyes. When she sees me, she sits up, pushing a lock of hair behind her ear and nearly tumbling off the mattress with the movements. Antonio sees her teetering, and he lunges for her, pulling her back with a loud giggle before he says in a stage whisper, "Maddie, why is the earl in your bedroom?"

She shrugs as she leans into him. "I have no idea."

Shutting the door behind me, I'm still smiling as I regard the two of them together. They look so happy and comfortable I don't even mind that I won't be able to speak to Maddie while he's still here. Obviously, they're having fun, and I don't want to ruin that.

"What's going on here?" I ask, amused as I walk deeper into her chambers and perch myself right at the edge of her bed.

Antonio immediately plucks a glass of wine off the nightstand and offers it to me with a slight bow of his head. "Want some? We swiped a couple bottles from dinner. *Shhh.*"

I laugh. "Do you two do this often?"

Maddie makes her eyes huge at me as she shakes her head back and forth, her rich locks swaying in the ponytail behind her head. "No, this is our first time. We thought we might be going home tomorrow, you know? Decided we might as well get drunk on royal wine at least once. Our version of high tea."

"A smart decision," I say, even if I am a touch confused about why she'd have thought this might be her last day. My understanding of her arrangement with Kaz was that she'd stay in the game for a lot longer. Did something happen between them? Or maybe she's just holding up the ruse in front of the other competitor. Since I can't ask her, I let it go for the moment. "May I join you?"

"Please," Antonio says, scooting up even though I've already got a space on the bed. "Where are the others? Also, why are you here?"

After sliding my jacket off, I lay it down next to me. "Well, I, *uh*, I remembered the answer to a question Maddie asked on our date, but it doesn't matter. How are you guys?"

"Well, there were no knocks on our doors earlier, so we're good." Maddie smiles, and it's so carefree and gorgeous. It feels like there's a hook behind my heart that's snagged the organ and someone is now tugging on the line.

Her scent is so strong in here that it's almost overpowering. While I know Kaz would shit a brick if I make a move on her, I'm dangerously tempted. Deciding that I need backup, I pull my phone out of my pocket and text Wolf while Antonio launches into a whole host of reasons why he's doing so well. He's rambling, but I don't mind. It's good to see this relaxed side of him just as much as it is to see the same of Maddie.

"No knocks! Can you believe it? I went back to my chambers just before nine to wait, then we heard the knocks and after, I came right back here to celebrate. This wine is incredible. I heard it's such good quality that it doesn't even give hangovers. That's marvelous, isn't it? Wolf and I had a great time on the horses today. Unlike Maddison here, I didn't even fall off. She has a bruise the shape of Africa on her butt, did you know that?"

My gaze snaps up as irrational jealousy rips through me. "You've seen her butt?"

He presses his hand to his heart like he'd have clutched his pearls if he had any. "Of course not. She told me about it. A bruise the shape of Africa. Isn't that amazing?"

"Amazing," I muse, breathing in deeply to tamp down on the jealousy I shouldn't be feeling so intensely. Although, with her, everything is heightened. More intense. I've decided to just...roll with it. "The hangover thing isn't true, by the way. It's good wine, but you'll have a monster of a headache tomorrow."

"Boo," he shouts, then he blows a raspberry. Maddie giggles some more before turning back to me.

"How about you? How are you?" She hiccups, then flushes, then hiccups again. "Fuck. I mean, sorry. I shouldn't be cussing in front of you, should I? No, I probably shouldn't be. I apologize."

"For what *fucking* reason?" I ask, emphasizing the word. Apparently, it's the funniest thing either of them has ever heard because they dissolve into fits of giggles that make me wish I was drunk too.

Maddie leans into Antonio's side as she laughs, and the jealousy flares right back up again until he sees whatever look is on my face and pushes her off. The jealousy is instantly replaced with concern and even anger that he might've hurt her when he pushed her away. He cocks his head at me. "You're making the Alpha uncomfortable, Maddie-poo."

I know he's talking to Maddie, but he's looking right at me. She frowns at him. "What? Why?"

"Not sure," he replies, but thankfully, he's had too much wine to delve into it right now. Eyes still on mine, he gets up, sways, and then sits down again. "Whew, I think I'm going to need help getting to my room."

Wolf walks in without knocking at that exact moment, hears what the other Omega said, and then turns to me. "Is this what the 911 message was about?"

"Yes," I say. "I needed backup, and now you know why."

He lets out a dramatic sigh, obviously wondering what I'm doing here, but then he steps toward Antonio and chivalrously offers him his arm. "Come on, Ramirez. Let's get you to your bed. Are you always such a lightweight?"

He's joking, but Antonio's jaw drops, and he feigns being terribly affronted. "I am *not* a lightweight. I've had at least two bottles of that by myself, thank you very much."

He clutches Wolf's arm and then winks at Maddie. "Look at this, we've got Royals in our beds tonight."

"Absolutely not," I say with a warning look at Wolf, but he simply rolls his eyes at me like I'm being ridiculous.

None of us have touched anyone but each other since the Trials started. While I know it's been harder on him, I also know he doesn't *want* anyone other than us and Maddie right now. Like Kaz and me, he feels off when he even thinks about it. Until he hinted at it, I thought he was trying to behave himself because of the cameras and that was why there haven't been any Betas around our quarters recently, but now, I know better.

Because I know *exactly* how he feels. How Kaz feels. We're all so hot for her that no one else holds even the slightest bit of appeal.

CHAPTER THIRTEEN

Wolf smirks at me when he pauses inside the door. "Don't have too much fun in here without me."

I roll my eyes at him this time, but then Maddie keens like she's been injured. Wolf and I are both suddenly on ultra-high alert. "Is everyone really leaving?"

Fuck. She's not hurt. Thank God. My heart is still racing as I shake my head at her, though. "No, honey. I'm staying right here. I'll tuck you in, okay?"

She smiles brightly. "Okay."

Wolf's muscles finally relax, and he glances at me with uncertainty shadowing his eyes. "You going to be okay?"

"I'm fine." I'm so *not* fine with the strength of her scent in here, but I'll live. "Try not to get seen down here. In and out. Have the staff open the windows at the end of the hall to dull your scent."

It smells like he just came from a workout, his scent, normally already strong as hell, is even stronger now. He gives himself a sniff and winces, nodding that he understands.

"See you in your room?"

He nods, then he gives Maddie a softer smile than I've seen him give anyone other than those closest to him. "Good night, Mads. Sleep tight. Don't let the bedbugs bite."

She arches a teasing brow at him, matching his energy effortlessly. "It's a palace. There are no bedbugs here."

Laughter ripples out of him as he dips his head in concession. Then he and Antonio leave, and Maddie and I are finally alone. As soon as we are, the humor fades from her eyes. "I didn't ask you any questions on our date you haven't answered yet. What are you really doing here?"

"Nothing," I fib. "I just wanted to check on you. Kaz told us about your deal. I came to make sure you're okay. I would've been here last night but, *uh*, I got somewhat sidetracked."

"By what?"

I shrug, flashing her a coy smile I know will tickle her curiosity. "Wolf and Kaz."

Her cheeks flush a deeper shade of pink. The urge to claim her rises again, stronger than ever before. "What were you doing with them that got you sidetracked?"

She's slightly breathless now, her eyes growing steadily more unfocused. Drunk or aroused, I'm not sure, but the fact that it could be both means I need to get out of here before I try to find out. "We got into it a bit, then we made up. Nothing huge. You didn't answer me, though. Are you okay?"

"No," she says, evidently a lot more honest with a few glasses of wine in her. *In vino veritas, I suppose.* "It really hurts that you can't choose me. I wish you could, but I understand."

As if realizing she's saying more than she ordinarily would, she sighs and pulls back her covers. "Are you really tucking me in?"

I nod, rising off her bed and kneeling beside her as she lies down. My head is less than a foot away from hers. Her gaze flickers to my lips before she simply closes her eyes. "You should go now."

"Yeah, I know," I murmur, brushing her dark locks back and staring at her lips in turn. "Sleep it off, Maddie."

"Can I have a good night kiss?" she asks as she opens her eyes again and gives me such a pleading look that I almost give in.

"No, I'm afraid not." Sitting up higher on my knees, I brush a soft kiss on her forehead, hoping it'll suffice.

CHAPTER THIRTEEN

"Why not?" she asks.

I smile, looking directly into her eyes as I rise to my feet. "When we do kiss, you'll want to be able to remember it."

Her green eyes widen.

"Sleep well, Maddison. I'll have some painkillers sent to your room for tomorrow morning."

Before I do something that makes Kaz birth a whale, I rise to my feet and flick off her lights on my way out the door. I'm halfway back to our quarters by the time I realize two things. First, I forgot my jacket at the foot of her bed, and second, I need to be alone right now.

I need to think and for once, I need to do that without Wolf and Kaz. While I won't go as far as trying to block them out of my head, I just...I need some time. Although I've forgiven Kaz for everything he said last night, I'm uneasy about how he effectively took Maddie out of the running without discussing it with us first.

The fact of it is that I don't want to go back into exile. Growing up, it wasn't bad. If we could get away from here, then fine, but it would tear Kaz apart, and I couldn't do that to him. There has to be a way, though. I just need to find it.

FOURTEEN

—

TAI

WHEN I REACH THE STAIRCASE, I go down instead of up. Now that I've realized I'm not ready to head back to our quarters yet, I've decided to head into town. It frustrates Kaz immensely when I do this, but since I'm as frustrated with him right now, I'm going to do it anyway.

I reach the bottom of the stairs, opening the door just a crack before heading into a corridor that runs along the back of the palace. It's used mostly by the serving staff. Although a few might be up and busy, most will have retired for the night by now.

My luck holds as I hurry down the hall, through one of the many kitchens, and slip out the back door. As soon as the crisp night air washes over my face, I inhale slowly.

To be fair, I could've walked out using the front door, but if I did, a contingent of bodyguards would've followed. Which is not what I want tonight. I realize it's for my own safety, but the pub I'm going to isn't far from here.

It's seedy as hell, but I like it, and no one there poses any danger to me. They know who I am, but they really don't care. I don't get treated any differently from any of the other patrons, and I definitely don't need an army of bodyguards to join a friendly poker game.

Keeping my head down, I stride to a pedestrian gate in the perimeter fence and enter the passcode to get out. The hinges creak quietly when I push it open. I glance left and right, checking that no one heard before I slide out, and then, I'm finally on my way.

The sidewalks are empty, but I keep my head down regardless. I'm no stranger to walking these streets at night, but exercising caution has become a constant necessity since I formed a pack with everyone's favorite royals.

A small wooden sign tacked into the stone building is the only indication that a pub is coming up. The sign is so faded from decades in the sun that the words *The Randy Toad* don't have any color anymore, but I'm grateful for it.

It means that few people who aren't regulars ever stumble in here. As I push open the nondescript door and step inside, the scent of stale beer and desperation envelops me like a warm hug.

A few old-school, green lamps hang overhead, but aside from tacky lights behind the bar, that's the only light in here. No one takes much notice of me as I stride up to the packed bar counter, though those who do see me acknowledge me with curt nods.

That's it, though. There's not a single autograph-seeking, selfie-taking fan in sight, and I fucking love it. The barkeep is a codger named Bob—his real name—and he flashes me a yellow-toothed grin as he bends over to swipe a beer from the fridge below the counter.

"Tai," he says as he sets it down before jerking his head

CHAPTER FOURTEEN

to the side. "They're in there. Just got started if you want to join 'em."

"Thank you." I drop a bill on the counter to pay much more for my beer than it actually costs, but I value Bob's discretion. If he wanted to, he could've told the press ages ago that we frequent this place, but he hasn't.

He'd have been able to afford a new sign and a whole lot more if he had, but he's never made me feel like he's considered it. That's definitely worth large tips as far as I'm concerned.

Leaving me now that he's handed me the beer, he heads over to continue the conversation he was having with another codger before he saw me. With my drink in hand, I walk to the door he motioned to and tap out a rhythmic knock as I push it open.

Walking into the smoky room beyond, I smile as I nod at the three men gathered around the table. Dave stubs out his cigar and waves me closer. "I was wondering when you would turn up. Come on, then. I'll deal you in."

The chair doesn't make a sound on the aged carpet beneath it as I pull it out and sit down. Dave picks up the deck of cards he was shuffling when I walked in. Turner glances at me, a cigar clenched between his teeth.

"You lot have brought madness to the world with this dating ordeal, mate. 'Spected to see you day one. It's got to be crazy at the palace right now. Thought you might want to escape."

I chuckle. "I've wanted to, but I haven't been able to get away. You're right. It's chaos."

Same as with Bob, I'm very aware these men could've sold me out years ago. Obviously, they haven't done so, either. In all the years I've joined them on occasion for their nightly poker games, they've learned enough about me that they'd get paid handsomely for their stories. Though I know they need the money, they haven't leaked a single word of what's been said in here.

It's not exactly a private room. Anyone is allowed in and the door is only closed for the smoke, but I still feel safe when I'm here.

Turner sighs as he looks at the cards he's been dealt, then he tosses a quid into the middle of the table. "I bet you've been busy. Bet Wolf's been busy too, what with all those Omegas begging for his knot."

My jaw grinds, but I shake my head. "It's not like that."

Dave arches a disbelieving brow at me, the pronounced grooves on his forehead deepening as he lowers his chin. "It's not? Why not? If it were me, I'd have been taking advantage of the situation."

"Are we playing cards or gossiping like old hens?" Alfred snaps before glancing at me. "No offense, mate, but I don't give a shit what's happening over at the palace."

"None taken. Let's play some cards." As I pick up my cards, I will myself to relax. I got out of the palace, and now I'm here. I should be able to shut it all out for a couple of hours. I usually can, but tonight, it's not so easy.

Maddie's scent must be clinging to me or something, because I can't stop thinking about her. Every time I blink, I see that carefree smile that was on her face earlier. I hear those giggles echoing in my ears. I wasn't aware she'd struck a friendship with Antonio, but it makes sense that she would.

We haven't met him before, but regardless of what his family has been through recently, he's an easygoing, sassy, and witty Omega once he starts opening up. From what I've

CHAPTER FOURTEEN

seen, he's also smart as a whip and surprisingly genuine, just like her. I should've known they'd get along.

Stuck in my head, I lose the first two hands, but then it starts going better. After I've beaten the trio a few times, I smirk at them. "Should I go see who else wants to play? I like a challenge, and it's like you guys haven't even shown up tonight."

"Sod off." Dave laughs. "You're welcome to check who else wants to take a go at you, but—"

He cuts himself off when the door opens. I twist in my seat to see who made him fall silent. Wolf and Kaz stride in like they were invited, which I know they didn't need to be, but still. Kaz moves like he owns the place, and Wolf isn't much better.

"Here you are," he says, pulling up a seat and dropping into it. "What happened to meeting in my room?"

"I needed a break," I mutter, annoyance clear in my strained voice. "What are you doing here?"

Kaz inclines his head at the others before he pulls up another chair and slides it in beside mine. "We came to check on you. Wolf tells me he found you someplace you shouldn't have been earlier."

"He didn't *find* me," I snap. "I told him where I was and asked him to come there. There's a marked difference between the two."

"You boys playing or what?" Turner asks, treating them the same as he does me, which is the same as everyone else.

My pack have been here with me at times. Although these men don't know them as well as they know me, they've grown used to them. Kaz bristles a bit at his lack of formality, but Wolf grins at Dave.

"Deal us in, mate. I hope you're prepared to lose."

TAI

I sigh but nod at Dave when he looks at me to check. "Deal them in."

While he's shuffling the deck, Kaz turns on his chair to face me and his head lowers to one side, dark eyes intent on mine. "Want to tell me what you were doing there? After hours?"

"After hours?" I scoff. "Please. I caught a whiff of a very familiar scent when I left my chambers this morning. I know it wasn't Wolf. Let's not get into anyone being in chambers they shouldn't be when they're not supposed to be there."

It's a pathetic attempt at discretion. Even though I trust my poker group, Kaz doesn't. I also know that if they'll get the general idea of what we're saying, they won't have any specifics that could get us in trouble if the conversation does somehow leak.

Kaz's eyes narrow, but then he gives his head a small shake. "It was for business, not pleasure."

So, she was in his chambers last night because of their deal. *Figures.* "Regardless. You could've given us a heads-up. Might've been nice if we were all present."

He's got his guards up, but I feel his faint guilt along with something a lot more interesting. Intense lust. Okay, so maybe that's not so interesting since I know how much he wants her. What's interesting is that he feels it now while at the same time, he's telling me that she was there for business.

Now, obviously, he can want her even while she's reporting back to him. It's not that. It's the sudden suspicion I have that something happened between them. Or almost happened, at least.

Wolf groans softly at my side, so I know he felt it too.

CHAPTER FOURTEEN

Searching Kaz's gaze for clues, I inhale deeply and wonder when we started hiding things like this from each other.

"Business, of course," I say as I nod at him. "It couldn't *possibly* be anything else. Not like you'd dip the royal wick in muddied water."

The veiled barb lands with a tightening of Kaz's sharp features. "I've never been afraid of a little mud."

Wolf winces on my other side. "Could we stop talking about mud? I understand the analogy—I know, shocking—but do either of you realize how fucking insensitive and offensive that is?"

I know he's right and something grimy coats my stomach. Why did I even say that?

"Just…go home and we'll talk about this later."

"We've been dealt in," Kaz says as if that decides it. Then he picks up his cards and gives Dave a stoic look once he's checked them. "What's the buy-in?"

"A quid."

His brow furrows. "One?"

"Yes, Kaspian. One. We're not here to bankrupt anyone." I cut an exasperated look at him before turning my attention back to the game.

In the end, though, Kaz cleans almost everyone out, and to me, it's symbolic of the way the royal family controls everything. He gets up after the last hand and leaves the money on the table as he nods at the men, turns, and walks out.

Wolf flashes them an apologetic smile. "Sorry, mates. Looks like we're off."

All round, eyes roll and they huff, clearly offended, and I understand why.

I wasn't going to take their money either, but I usually

give them an opportunity to win it back before I leave instead of making them feel like lesser for not wanting to take any of what little they have.

A heavy sigh falls out of me as I stand in unison with Wolf. "I'll see you another night, gentlemen. Thanks for the game. And sorry for my packmate."

Wolf's hand moves to my shoulder, and he squeezes it as we walk out the door. "We were worried about you. Don't be mad at him. He's doing the best he can."

"I know."

The best *he* can do isn't the best *we* can do if he'd simply stop for a minute and listen to reason, though. I know I can get him there, but I haven't figured out how. "We need to slow him down. Get him to think this through."

Wolf inclines his head in a slight nod. "We will. We'll talk, but it doesn't have to be tonight. Let's just get some sleep, yeah? Tomorrow is another day. It doesn't all have to happen right this very minute."

Disappointment fizzes through me, but he's right. Rome wasn't built in a day and all. We've got time. Not much, but what we have will have to be enough. And it will be. I'll make sure of it.

FIFTEEN

—

MADDIE

IT'S STILL DARK when I wake up, thankfully not too hungover but definitely a little drowsy. Since it's obviously not dawn yet, I'm not quite sure what woke me until I become aware of the pounding in my head and between my legs.

A soft moan slips out of me when I squeeze my thighs together. Then I grab the pillow from under my head and crush it over my face, but it smells like Tai.

"Ughh," I groan, tossing the pillow away.

Why is it still this bad?

My suppressants really don't seem to be doing their job. For some reason, the increased dosage isn't helping much. After taking a deep breath, I realize I'm too restless to lie here. There's no way I'll be able to fall asleep again, so I kick the covers off and get up, which is when I spot Tai's jacket lying on my bed.

No doubt it's the culprit of the strong scent still lingering in my room.

MADDIE

Glum weight presses down on my chest as I think about the pack I wasn't expecting to like at all.

After last night, the Omega numbers have been whittled down to ten, but I won't win. Instead of being relieved and elated, I'm a little depressed. The only silver lining is that Antonio made it through as well. As much as I like my new friend, knowing he has a chance isn't the same as having one myself. Over and above that, I haven't heard if Kaz has made any headway on his part of the deal. Uncertainty churns like a living being in my gut.

My parents… They haven't said as much, but I think they're struggling without me at home to help out. Mum is hanging on to hope that I'll win this thing. She's so excited whenever I tell her I've moved on to the next round. I can't find it in me to tell her I don't stand a chance.

The knowledge of how hopeless my situation is only becomes harder to swallow with each passing day. I mean, I saw the way Tai was looking at me last night. I saw that he wanted to kiss me. Instead of simply saying he couldn't, he said he wanted me to *remember* it when he did.

Why?

Urg!

With the way my body is reacting to them—complicating an already over-complicated situation—I'm bordering on insanity. In the last few days, I've rubbed up against Wolf, nearly kissed Kaspian in his chambers, and then point blank asked Tai why he didn't kiss me. If that's not insanity, I'm not sure what is.

Fucking hell, I need to get out of here.

I know my way around our wing of the palace pretty well at this point. I'm sure I'll be able to get outside without

CHAPTER FIFTEEN

anyone the wiser. *Maybe I should go for a walk in the gardens to cool off and clear my mind.*

After rolling out of bed, I dress quickly in jeans and a comfortable sweater with the OA's logo emblazoned across it and head out. The hallway is dark and quiet when I emerge from my room. No one else is about as I shut my door with a soft click behind me.

The palace is peaceful at this hour, though it won't be long until the staff prepares for breakfast. Since only ten of us are left, there will be a lot less food to make. I have a feeling the only people who will be more relaxed are the chefs and servers. I'm certain the atmosphere will be so thick between the rest of us that you'd be able to slice right through it with a blunt butter knife.

If I stood a chance, I might've used this time preparing myself to up my game, but my competitive spirit has died. All I want is to *not* want the RP so bad, but even as I head down the corridor and out into the gardens, I feel the slick between my legs with every step I take.

It's ridiculous. Honestly.

I'm either going to have to double my dose or talk to the palace medical team. I'm almost certain going into heat will mean my immediate disqualification from the mating trials.

Once I'm out of the palace, fresh air washes over my face. I inhale deeply, hoping the crisp predawn chill and the fragrant scent will distract me from the desire that builds within my core. My feet barely make a sound as I rush down the flagstone path leading away from the doors. When I'm far enough away that I don't think I'll be seen by anyone who happens to be up early and bothers to look out the window, I slow down, finding myself near the rose garden where I sat with Kaz.

Pain zings through me as the sight of it brings back memories of the conversation we had on that innocent metal bench. This will forever be the place where my silly dreams came to die. As a symbolic *fuck you*, I turn my back on it and head deeper into the grounds.

Surrounded by tall, old trees and beds of flowers, I draw in another breath, smiling at the woodsy, floral scent that pervades my nostrils. I'm well out of sight of the palace now. The tension from being cooped up eases out of my muscles as I walk, admiring the early spring blooms and how incredibly well-tended the gardens are, even in the shadows of pre-dawn.

Dad would love it h—

"Maddie?" a soft, familiar voice speaks from the shadows of a massive oak tree. The faint moonlight isn't enough to reveal his exact spot, but I'd know that voice anywhere.

"Tai?" I frown. "Where are you?"

As he steps out from around the tree trunk, his silver hair practically glowing as the light of the moon kisses it, he looks like an ethereal figure. His face is partially hidden in shadows, but I see it when one side of his lips curves into a beautiful, surprised smile.

"What are you doing out here?" he asks.

I shrug, hoping he can't see my face flushing while I do my best to sound nonchalant, like I'm *not* on fire for him and his friends. "I woke up early and decided to come for a walk. You? Thanks for taking care of me earlier, by the way."

"You're welcome. How are you feeling?"

"Not too bad, thanks to you." I walk over to him, captivated by the ridges of his chiseled face when they're thrown into contrast by the moonlight like they are right now. "I'm sorry if I was...I don't drink much."

He laughs quietly. "I had a feeling. Besides, I can't judge. After I tucked you in, I sneaked out to a pub to get away for a while. Walk with me?"

"Sure." I shouldn't though. I should put some distance between myself and the Alphas, but I fall into step beside him anyway, his pull too magnetic to ignore. "A pub, huh? I didn't realize you could go to one of those without causing a ruckus."

Tai chuckles and offers me his elbow. Even though I shouldn't do that either, I take it, linking my arm with his as we stroll farther down the path leading toward the forest at the edge of the gardens. "Generally speaking, we can't go anywhere without causing a ruckus, but this particular pub is my personal unicorn. It's the one place I can go where no one cares who I am."

"What about Kaz and Wolf?" I ask curiously. "Does anyone there care who they are?"

"Not really. The regulars there are regular, hardworking people who go to blow off some steam. They don't bother us, and we don't bother them. I'm not sure I'd have survived here if not for that place."

"Everyone needs that one place, huh? Funny, I kind of thought that if you live in a palace, you'd never want to leave it."

"A golden cage is still a cage," he muses before he glances at me. "What's that one place for you, then?"

"The library," I reply without hesitation. "At the moment, it's the one at the Cambridge Academy, which is absolutely breathtaking, but before I went there, it was the small library in town."

"Kaz is the same," he teases, or at least, I think he's teasing. "Show the man a library, and we lose him for the rest of the day no matter how big or small the place is."

Fuck's sake. I already suspected we had that in common. I really didn't need it confirmed. And I didn't want to talk about Kaz right now.

"What about you? Do you enjoy reading?"

"I've been known to crack open a book on occasion," he says easily. "I'm not quite as obsessed as Kaz, or you, but give me the right story and a pot of tea, and I'm happy on the couch until my book is done."

"That sounds like my dream vacation," I joke, once again surprised by how at ease I am around him. "I wouldn't need to go anywhere. Just give me my nest, a pile of books, and some snacks, and I'll see you next month."

He smiles, but something in his eyes flickers with heat at what I've said. His throat bobs.

Tai hugs my arm to his side as he points at a patch of lush lawn in a copse of trees off to our left. I see some archery targets in the distance. "Throw some archery into the mix on that vacation, and I'm there. I've traveled a lot, but it's true what they say. There really is no place like home."

"I wouldn't know, but a good book takes you places no airplane can. I think I prefer my wildest imagination over anywhere real."

"Want to sit?" he asks as we reach the patch of grass. "Kaz uses this clearing for stargazing sometimes. Apparently, it's one of the best places for it on the property."

"Oh?"

CHAPTER FIFTEEN

We sit down side-by-side, then I take it one step further by lying down flat on my back. "He showed me a constellation the other night when I looked through his telescope, but part of me wondered if he's really into it or if it's to make himself seem like the intellectual type."

Tai chuckles and surprises me when he lies down right next to me, seemingly unconcerned to be a royal with bits of grass and earth sticking to him. "He doesn't have to make himself seem like anything. He *is* the intellectual type. The thing about Kaz is that he may be restrained and reserved, but what you see is what you get. He doesn't pretend with stuff like that. Astronomy, for example, is a love he inherited from his grandfather. That telescope in his room used to belong to him as well."

I turn my head to face him, which is when I realize that once again, I've ended up in a situation where my mouth is so damn close to his. I don't know how this keeps happening, but it's freaking torture. With his eyes on mine and his lips so close that I can see the faint lines in the plushness, I suck in a sharp breath, and my heart races.

"Tai," I breathe when his gaze drops away from mine to my lips. The moment grows heated. His fingers twine with mine on the ground between us, and he props himself up on his elbow, his head now hovering only inches above my own. "We shouldn't."

"Do you want to?" he asks, his voice breathier now than I've ever heard it before. He brushes a lock of hair away from my forehead and tucks it gently behind my ear, tracing the line of my jaw with his fingertip in a way that makes me shiver.

Despite myself, I nod, catching my lower lip between

MADDIE

my teeth as I stare up into those warm brown eyes. "We can't always get what we want, though."

"Not always," he agrees as his mouth descends. "Perhaps just this once, though."

He presses his lips to mine.

My world implodes, the reverberations of his kiss tearing through me like grabbing hands and warm water and pressure like I've never felt before.

A moan that's half a cry grows in my throat, and Tai swallows it, easing my mouth open to delve in gently with his tongue, tasting me as I feel his body quake against mine. Tai kisses like he's making love, and I feel every brush of his lips, every flick of his tongue, all the way to my toes.

He kisses me like he'll never stop, like he knows he'll never get enough. Then, just when I think it can't possibly get any better, his hands are on me. He hooks his thigh between my legs and a whimper of vicious need slides out of me as I push my hands into his hair, pulling him closer.

My hips roll against his muscular thigh, and he adjusts it so I'm grinding, practically dry-humping a earl's leg. I should be embarrassed, but I'm not. I need him—need this—too much to care that I'm probably making a fool of myself.

Tai shifts so he's on top of me, his hard cock against my core as I keep grinding, fucking him with our clothes on. Our kisses deepen as sparks of pleasure race from my core to my extremities. He groans loudly into my mouth, his hips moving with mine as he kisses me harder, thrusting his hard-on against just the right spot until I'm whimpering into his mouth.

He trembles above, his hips moving faster. Then he hooks his fingers into my waistband and he works his hand

CHAPTER FIFTEEN

in between us. As he moves his lower half off me to give himself some space, I cry out at the loss of him, but he deftly undoes the button on my jeans and pulls down the zipper.

We can't do this.

Shut the fuck up, Maddie.

His fingers slide into my panties, and I arch into his touch as his hips keep rolling against my thigh, no doubt trying to douse the fire in his trousers.

All the while, he hasn't stopped kissing me, but when his hand reaches my folds, he hisses at the pool of slick he finds there. To his credit, he doesn't ruin the moment by commenting on how wet I am. He doesn't need to. It's pretty fucking obvious.

His fingers are a bit rougher than mine, and they feel like heaven as he drags them through my slit, his thumb gathering my juices before he circles my clit. I moan, removing one hand from his hair to run it down the length of his abdomen while holding him to me with the other.

As soon as I reach the hard bulge between his legs, I squeeze his cock. Even though it's over his jeans, he growls into my mouth, and his hand finds the perfect rhythm on my pussy. Tai plays me like a fiddle. Like he knows exactly what I need and when I need it.

He's hardly slid his fingers into me when my toes curl. I'm right on the precipice of release within minutes. "Tai!"

"*Fuck*," he breathes against my throat. "Maddie, you're so wet for me."

"Tai, fuck, I'm going to—"

"That's it, *ma trésor*, I want to feel this pretty pussy clench around my fingers."

My core tightens at his dirty words, and I grip him

through his trousers, rubbing his hard length as I let the wave inside of me crest.

"Come for me, Maddie," he commands, and I do. He swallows my moans as I surrender, my entire body shaking as pleasure overwhelms me. I'm vaguely aware of him quivering at my side, but I'm too wrapped up in my own euphoria to pay too much attention right now.

White lights flash behind my eyelids when I squeeze them shut, coming like I've never had an orgasm before. To be fair, I've never had one like *this*, but it's like a drug, keeping me coming back for more, aftershocks racing through me until I'm boneless and panting, my mouth dry and my head a little sore.

When I finally come back down to earth and blink my eyes open, Tai is panting too. His forehead is pressed to mine as he tries to catch his breath. "I'm not sorry," he whispers so low I'm not sure I've heard him right. "I've wanted to do that since the first moment I saw you."

My hands tremble as I lift them up to cup his face, planting a soft kiss on his lips and shaking my head as I fight the urge to cry, speaking through the burn in my throat. "Just this once. It can't happen again, Tai. It'll only hurt more when..."

I can't even bring myself to say it.

He groans and runs his nose along the length of mine. "There's no other Omega I want, but I also don't want to get your hopes up. Unlike us, the queen always gets what she wants. But I want you to know, I haven't given up yet."

I shove the emotions threatening to rise inside me down deep, blinking back tears. "We should get back to our rooms."

SIXTEEN

—

KAZ

"THANK YOU BOTH FOR COMING," I say as I rise from the chair behind my desk and motion Eric, the head gardener and the head chef into seats on the other side. Eric and Kay exchange a half-curious, half-frightened look, but then Eric closes my office door behind them and they move toward the desk. "Have a seat."

"We'll stand, sir," Kay says quietly, her hands folded behind her back and her gaze never quite meeting mine.

"Nonsense." I smile when Eric finally looks at me. "Please, sit. Neither of you are in any trouble. In fact, I have a favor to ask of you. I'd rather you be comfortable during the conversation, because that's all it is, a conversation."

Eric blinks back his surprise, but he nods and moves around the chair to sit down. Kay glances at him from the corner of her eye. Her curiosity must get the best of her because a few seconds later, she takes the chair beside his.

"Wonderful." I lower myself back into my leather, ergonomic monstrosity and fold my hands on my desk, intent on not coming across as demanding or condescending. "Thank you for agreeing to meet with me."

"Of course, sir," Eric says easily, but I've spent more time talking to him while I've been out in the gardens than I've spent speaking to Kay in the kitchens. "How can we help?"

"Well, I was wondering if either of you have any openings on your staff at the moment. Anything at all."

"I'm sorry, sir," Kay says, risking a glance at me. "I hired a new sous chef just last month so we'd be ready for the Trials. The queen approved him herself. I—"

"It's all right," I interrupt gently. "You've had your hands full with the influx of guests in the palace. I'm not surprised the queen ensured the kitchens were fully staffed. We needed all hands on deck. It's not a problem. Really. I just had to take a chance."

"Of course, sir," she replies, but she still appears to be on the verge of tears.

"You've been doing a wonderful job keeping everyone fed, Kay. I have it on good authority that all the Omegas are worried about gaining weight as they just can't get enough of your food."

She glances up at me again, a beaming grin appearing on her lips when she sees the sincerity in my eyes. "Thank you, sir. If I may, you've a much softer look about you these days. I hope one of the Omegas is responsible for putting it there."

Fuck. I scowl before catching myself and smoothing my expression over again. She's not wrong. One of the Omegas *did* put it there, but it's the one I can't have. And the one I'm doing this for, which is why I pretend everything is just fine as I turn to Eric.

CHAPTER SIXTEEN

"How about you? I know you recently lost your assistant. Have you managed to find a replacement? Any other openings?"

The man regards me for a moment before he nods slowly. "As it happens, I do still need a new assistant. The few I've interviewed wouldn't suit the position."

"Excellent." *What a fucking relief.* "I'll take care of the paperwork myself. No need to run this up the official chain of command. Your new assistant's name is Simon, and he'll be here within the next few days. He's got experience as a gardener, and I'm sure he's up to the task."

I'm not really, but I'm hoping he is. I desperately want him to be. Either way, Eric seems satisfied, if not curious, about where this is coming from, but he doesn't ask. I don't usually get involved in staffing decisions. I've never been directly responsible for appointing someone without so much as an interview, but I made a promise and I'm keeping it.

As he nods and stands up, he takes another look at me and inclines his head toward Kay. "She's right, you know. Something seems different about you. Whatever is responsible for it, I hope you can keep it close. It's nice to see you happy."

The chef about squeaks when Eric addresses me so casually that I stifle a smirk.

Frankly, I've never had anyone but Wolf or Tai comment on my facial expressions or express an interest in my happiness. I've no clue what to make of it, so I smile and nod. That's what I've been trained to do when confronted with uncomfortable remarks. It works, with both of them suddenly much more relaxed as they say their goodbyes and leave my office.

Once they're gone, I collapse back in my chair and groan out loud. I must really be looking *soft* if it's so obvious that members of our staff are not only noticing it, but commenting on it already. I thought I was putting on a better front than that, but Maddie and I have been texting whenever she has an update for me, and we've spent a bit more time together.

It would be a blatant lie to say she hasn't taken up residence in my head or that I don't enjoy the time I spend with her more than my time with any of the other Omegas. There are a few pleasant ones left, but none affect me the way she does.

She has a true love of reading, and we spent the entire hour of our last date discussing our favorite books, arguing about each other's choices and the pros and cons of the current trends in the literary market. It was the most exhilarating conversation I've ever had about my favorite hobby. Even though absolutely nothing of importance was said, it was the most fun I've had with anyone outside my pack in a long time.

And I can't have her, which is infuriating.

Meanwhile, Wolf and Tai haven't given up. They're respecting my wishes and the deal I made with her, but I see the way they look at her. They both want her just as much as I do.

Yet, what I'm doing right now is the best I can do for her. Now that the job has been taken care of, it's a matter of arranging for living quarters. Picking up my phone, I put in a call to facilities management.

Before I reach out to Simon Darling, I want to have all my ducks in a row. It might take a couple of days for everything to fall into place, but at least I've started. I know the

CHAPTER SIXTEEN

head gardener used to live on the property, in a little cottage just outside the main palace grounds, and to my knowledge, Eric declined the use of it when he took the job. I pray it's still empty.

The call with facilities lasts less than five minutes, but when I get off the phone with a promise from the chief of staff to check if the cottage is in suitable shape, it's time for my next date. Since Maddie is on my mind, I'm not sure which Omega I'm with. I couldn't be bothered to learn anything about them. They might as well not show up for the interest I have in them.

It isn't fair, but it's the truth. And it turns out to be an unfortunate trend that continues for the next few days while I spend all my free time fulfilling the promise I made her.

When the weekend finally rolls around, I haven't seen her again. Although I could easily text her about this, I decide to go to her instead. *I fucking swear, I can't help myself with her.*

I checked her appointment schedule, so I know she's not with Wolf or Tai right now. I text her as I wait in the corridor just outside the Omegas' shared wing.

Kaz: Meet me in the hall?

I hope against all hope that she's not with one of the other Omegas. I'm glad she's made friends with Antonio Ramirez, but I need her all to myself this morning.

I'm so fucked.

It's still early, and I half expect her not to see the message. The sounds of laughter filtering down the corridor from the dining hall tell me that most of the remaining Omegas are at breakfast. My stomach clenches at the thought she may be in there with them, enjoying breakfast with friends when all I want is to see her.

I peer around the corridor, almost getting my head knocked off by the catering staff, but I see her door open, and I'm nearly bowled over with relief.

She looks left and right, spying me in the shadows.

"Kaz?" Maddie whispers, clearly surprised to see me as she opens her door wider to let me in, ushering me forward when she sees there are no other Omegas in the hall.

Bad idea.

Fuck.

I rush over and she quickly shuts the door behind me and locks it just in case. "What are you doing here?"

She glances down at herself. I realize she's not only surprised to see me. She's embarrassed too. Still in a flannel pajama shirt with jeans on, bare feet, a bare face, and her hair still a mess, I must've caught her before her ladies maid could get hands on her.

As I look at her, I see a smattering of freckles across the bridge of her nose and her cheeks I hadn't properly noticed before. They're on full display now, and I'm instantly entranced by them. They're so beautiful, so real, that I completely forget she asked me a question. All I can do is stare at her unashamedly, searching for constellations in the soft stars on her cheeks.

"Kaz?" she prompts eventually. "Are you okay? Why are you looking at me like that?"

"I, *uh*." I clear my throat and manage to bring my gaze to hers. "Why are you blushing?"

"Um, it could have something to do with the Crown Prince being in my bedroom while I'm half-dressed, have

CHAPTER SIXTEEN

no makeup on, and haven't even brushed my hair, but hey. Who knows?"

I chuckle, lowering my eyes, taking notice of the other things. The little things her ladies maid must tame and cover-up. The things that make her even more beautiful. Even more *real*.

"Don't be embarrassed, Maddie. You're gorgeous. Sorry if I was staring."

Her lips part, but not a sound escapes her before she closes her mouth again and shakes her head, folding her arms across her chest. The movement draws my attention down to said chest. When I see her nipples are pebbled under her pajama top, I yank my gaze right back up.

No. Nope. Eyes up top, Kaspian. You're a fucking gentleman. Act like one.

Unfortunately, now that I'm looking back into the stunning green depths of her eyes, I'm going to do something I'll regret anyway. I can't stand the disbelief I see shining back at me. *Why doesn't she believe that she's beautiful?*

Closing the distance between us in two short strides, I capture her face in my hands. Before I can think about stopping myself, I brush my thumbs gently over her freckles. "Freckles suit you, my little spy."

Her eyes close when my breath fans across her skin. Then she leans into my touch, the moment stretching silently between us. When her lips part again and she tips her head back ever so slightly, vulnerability flashing in those eyes when they open again and look right into mine, I'm lost. I'm just...*fuck*.

Fully realizing I'm about to do something I really shouldn't, I snake my arms around her waist and pull her into me, groaning softly as her body fits against mine like she was made for me. My mouth lowers, and she pushes up on her toes to meet me halfway. When our lips touch, I know beyond any shadow of a doubt that I'm good and proper fucked now.

But I don't pull away, I deepen the kiss, a tight squeeze in the pit of my stomach almost wringing a groan from my lungs. Maddie whines into my mouth, and I realize it wasn't a groan at all. My chest vibrates in a steady purr that prods my cock into a soft erection.

Fuck.

Maddie clings to me, and I indulge in this forbidden moment of recklessness to the fullest extent possible, I allow myself this one taste of her, reveling in the softness of her lips and the sweetness of her tongue. Her full curves pressed against me are so different from Wolf and Tai's hard bodies. While neither is necessarily better than the other, this feels really fucking good.

Really fucking right, too.

As she melts into me, I hold her tighter. She winds her arms around my neck, not stopping until we're flush against one another. All rational thought leaves me, and the next thing I know, I'm walking her back toward her bed, my cock straining to get inside her and my hands itching to feel every inch of her soft skin under them.

My instincts roar at me, urging me to claim her as ours right here and now. In the end, it's those urges that force me to pull away from her.

Fuck!

Get it together, Kaz.

Breathing heavily, I break the kiss and take a big step back, my hands clenched into fists at my sides as I fight

CHAPTER SIXTEEN

with the beast within. The beast urging me to fuck. To knot. To bond her to me forever.

Those instincts claw at the flimsy cages deep within me when she opens her eyes. I see the hurt flickering in them as she looks at me.

"Are you okay?" she asks, her voice husky before she drags in a deep breath and clears her throat. "Kaz?"

"I'm fine," I grind out the lie, following her example and filling my lungs with air. *Abort mission. I should never have come down here. I should never have come into her bedroom where her scent is so strong it permeates directly into my skin. I repeat, abort. The. Fucking. Mission.*

Her scent is so overpowering in here that I come *this close* to giving up the fight, but eventually, I remember why I'm here. "I have something to show you. Get dressed. I'll meet you outside in a minute?"

"At the Rose Garden?"

I nod. "See you there."

Before I make yet another mistake, I turn on my heels and flee from her room, not breathing again fully until I'm outside where the air is clear of that incredible, sweet but spicy scent. I fucking love that there's a bit of spiciness to her scent. It's so like her, all soft and sweet until you really get to know her and you discover how strong she is at her core.

My head is spinning, and I'm reeling from that one fucking kiss. *If that's what kissing her is like...*

But no.

I can't let myself go there. Down boy.

When she finally joins me about ten minutes later, she's wearing a sweater and her hair has been brushed, but she hasn't bothered with makeup and those freckles are out to play. For the rest of my life, I know I'll be thinking about her whenever I see freckles.

Any will be a painful reminder of that one time I threw caution to the wind and nearly claimed an Omega who would've sent my world into a state of disarray. *Still, I wonder if the chaos would be worth it.*

Tai seems to think it will be, but then Maddie sends me a puzzled frown and folds her arms again. "Well?" she asks quietly, cautiously almost. I really hate that she feels this way around me now. "What did you want to show me?"

"A cottage," I say vaguely before motioning for her to walk with me. I'd have offered her my arm, but that's probably not a good idea.

"A cottage?" she repeats as she rolls her eyes, but follows when I start toward the path. "Pray tell, Your Highness, why are you showing me a cottage?"

"It's Kaz," I correct her on instinct. "You and I have a deal, remember? This is me holding up my end of the bargain."

Maddie slams to a stop and spins toward me, her eyes wide and twinkling with excitement and relief and some other emotion I cannot name. "You're showing me this cottage because it's where my family will live?"

I nod. "I'll do you one better than that but come on. Showing is better than telling."

With a cautious quality to her steps, she takes my arm and allows me to pull her along. When we press to the edge of the gardens, we round the corner of hedges, and she spots her family waiting across a short lawn on the front steps of the old staff cottage. She's overcome with emotion.

She stops moving again, but then she releases me.

The next second, she's running at a full sprint toward

CHAPTER SIXTEEN

the three figures in front of the old gardener's cottage. We have a bunch of these staff quarters on this side of the property, but most of them are uninhabited these days. The wages now sufficient enough for the staff to live outside of palace grounds.

This particular cottage is a quaint, three-bedroom stone-built home with a fireplace, two bathrooms, heating, and a fully functioning kitchen. I had the staff clean it out and make sure everything was up to par before sending for Maddie's family.

For the first time, I realize the implications of what I've done here. What I may have subjected myself to. When Maddie leaves the trials, will she live here, on my palace grounds, with her family? She will, at least until she's claimed by a pack.

My jaw clenches.

I'll have to watch her take that step.

I'll have to be *this* close to her without being able to touch her.

Fuck. My. Life.

As I watch, Maddison throws herself into the arms of a burly, older man who must be Simon, her father. He's got the same mahogany hair as hers, but his has streaks of gray at the temples and shot through it. She hugs him for a long time before she envelops a little boy who, even from a distance, appears to be a bundle of pure energy.

His shouts of laughter ring out when she tickles him. Then she sets him down on his feet before turning to the final member of her family. Her mother.

She's gentler with her than she was with the other two, and I blink rapidly when I realize why. Shock reverberates through me, but there's no mistaking the telltale signs. The ginger, careful way she moves, the twitch, how she touches Maddie's face like she's making sure it's her, but she can't quite see her, the slight hunch of her back...

Maddison's mother has Cervus.

The realization slams into me like a ton of bricks. Like a punch to the gut.

This is why she needed her father to have good, steady work. The medical bills alone would be enough to put them in debt and that's not taking into consideration the inflated rental costs and taking care of a young child.

I swallow hard, a hand going almost unconsciously to my chest to attempt to quell the ache starting there.

Feeling like an unwelcome intruder, I take my leave and head back to the palace, my heart full but also aching. *I can't believe she didn't tell me. Didn't tell any of us. Didn't make private care for her mother part of the deal.*

Utterly overwhelmed for the second time this morning when I haven't even had breakfast yet, I stride straight back to our pack quarters. I don't know what to do with myself right now, but I know that I need to not be here.

SEVENTEEN

—

MADDIE

"HOW DID YOU DO THIS, DARLING?" my father raves as he leads me into the cottage. "You must've made a heck of a good impression on them. A job and a home? That's incredible."

"I live at a palace now," Kevin croons, clinging to my leg as he follows me in. "That makes me a prince, right? That's what princes do?"

"Not quite." I laugh as I stroke my fingers through his soft, short hair. "Almost, but they do other stuff, too. Royal duties and whatnot that you won't have to worry about."

My dad has his arm around my mum's waist, guiding her in as he makes a sweeping gesture with his free hand once we're in the small entrance hall. "Just look at this place. So much space. I've no idea what we're going to do with it all."

As I get my first good look around, I realize he's right. The cottage is a lot more spacious than it appeared from the outside. While it's nothing in comparison to the cavernous spaces in the palace itself, it's a hell of a lot better than where we came from.

A dining area, lounge, and kitchen make up a semi-open concept living area, with a beautiful stone fireplace and comfortable furniture. The kitchen has a small breakfast nook. Whoever lived here before seems to have had an affinity for ducks since the drapes in the kitchen window as well as some of the décor in the kitchen has the animal on them, but it's cute. Homey.

"Get a load of this," Kevin yells as he grabs my hand and pulls me through the living areas down a short hallway at the back of the cottage. "This will be my room!"

The bedroom and bathrooms are clustered together here, with the master at the end of the hall and two other bedrooms sharing a bath. Kevin has chosen the room on the right, which already has a bunk-bed in it and offers a view of the forest beyond.

I'm sure he'll love it, but that leaves me with the bedroom on the left—with a fantastic view of the palace that houses the Alphas I'll never get to be with. I can see the wing with the pack quarters from here.

Since my family is so excited, I play along, but I won't be able to live here for long. As soon as I can, I'll have to move out for the sake of my sanity. I already know that when the Trials are over, I'll be lying in my bed at night, longingly staring at the pack quarters and wondering what they're doing in there with the Omega who ends up being chosen.

My heart won't be able to take it. Plus, with my heat symptoms acting up so much while I'm on these grounds, there's no way I can stay without losing my ever-loving mind. That only leaves me two options since an unbonded Omega can't live alone. Either I find another pack to claim

CHAPTER SEVENTEEN

me—unlikely—or I work as an assistant at OA and live on academy grounds.

The latter wouldn't be so bad. I wonder if Ms. Frampton would take me on as an assistant. My grades are good enough. I can't see why she wouldn't.

When we're done with the tour, I make a cup of tea for my mother while Dad takes Kevin to explore the grounds around the cottage.

"You're lying," my mum says as soon as we're alone. "I don't like having to call you out on it, but you're not nearly as excited as you would've been if you thought things were really going as well in the Trials as Daddy thinks they are."

"I'm doing the best I can," I say, which is true, but I don't want to give anything else away. When I inevitably get dismissed from the Trials, I don't want my family knowing it has anything to do with who I am or where I come from. "The Royal Pack is nicer than I thought they would be. I think we'll be happy here."

Mum shakes her head at me. "You should probably get back, but promise me one thing before you leave?"

"Anything."

"It's wonderful that you've somehow managed to arrange all this for us, but I can't help but wonder what you've given in return. Promise me you'll think of *yourself* in these trials and what you want. Not just what might help us. We're your parents, Maddie. We're supposed to be taking care of you, not the other way around."

"You do take care of me."

She chuckles. "I'm just worried you sacrificed something to make this happen."

"I didn't." They weren't going to choose me either way. "It's all fine, Mum. I promise. How are you feeling?"

MADDIE

She shrugs. "If you can insist on being fine, then I can do the same. I'll be right here if you need me, okay? You should get back now. I'm sure you don't have time to spend the rest of the day with us."

"As much as I would love to stay, I do need to get back."

My heart protests at the thought of leaving them again so soon, but Mary told me she'd be waiting after breakfast. "My lady-in-waiting wants to give me some lessons before she gets me ready for dinner tonight."

"Lessons?" Mum laughs. "What lessons?"

"Etiquette." I groan and roll my eyes. "I'm having dinner with all three members of the Royal Pack later, and she believes I'll make a fool of myself if we don't have a dry-run first. Apparently, I'm having a charm-school crash-course today. Then, she's going to pluck and polish me until I look like a queen."

Mum reaches for my hand and squeezes it, smiling beautifully as she waves me off with her free hand. "Go on, then. In my opinion, you've always looked like a queen, but I suppose I'm biased. Give your lady-in-waiting all my love and tell her to come say hello to me sometime. I'd love to hear all about your adventures in the palace from an honest outsider. You've been sugarcoating things, I'm sure."

I chuckle. "The only thing she'll tell you that I haven't is that we regularly argue about the height of my heels and that I have to wear them at all."

"You've been wearing heels?" Mum's brows sweep up. "How's that been going for you?"

"Not well," I admit. "During the Scenting Ceremony, I fell. I'm surprised Dad didn't tell you. I've tripped into so many of the Omegas at meal times that they're walking circles around me now."

CHAPTER SEVENTEEN

She chuckles. "That sounds about right. Dinner with the Royal Pack, huh? That seems like a really big deal."

"It is, but we're just friends."

Her brows lower curiously at that comment, and I realize my mistake. "I mean," I correct. "For now, we're just friends."

"Even so, being friends with those boys is quite something." Her cloudy eyes turn sad as she releases my hand. "Now, about that promise."

"I will do whatever I can to make myself happy," I promise before giving her a kiss on top of her head. "I'll visit again soon, okay?"

Regardless of her protests that follow me out the door, I *will* visit them again soon. I don't want them to feel like a burden or that having them here is lessening this experience for me in some way. I've genuinely missed them, and now that I can see them whenever I've got time to myself, I'm definitely coming back as often as I can.

On my way back to the palace, my mind wanders to replay the promise I made to my mum. When I made it, I had no intention of upholding it, but now I'm wondering *why the hell not?*

Seeing the place where I'll be staying as soon as this is over has been grounding. The fact of the matter is that I've only got so much time left in the palace. I'd be a fool not to make the most of it. That kiss with Kaspian earlier was so hot that it nearly ignited my bones, and Tai rocked my world the other night.

Regardless of their reactions when they get a whiff of my scent, they're clearly not as repulsed by me as I thought. I've never been as attracted to anyone as I am to them. Maybe the happiness I feel when I'm with them will be fleeting, but it's better than not feeling any happiness at all.

Mind made up, I sit through all of Mary's lessons without objection. Then, while she's helping me get ready, excitement flutters in my stomach at the thought of what tonight might hold. There's no guarantee anything will happen. If it doesn't, then it doesn't. It'll still be fun hanging out with the three of them, but if something does happen, I'll go for it with everything I've got.

As if thinking about him made him feel the need to reach out to me, my phone beeps with an incoming text from Kaz.

PK: Do not hide the freckles tonight.

I smile, passing the message along to a surprised Mary when I swat her powder puff away.

"If that's what the prince wishes," she says with a kind grin. "I knew you'd come around to them eventually."

"I haven't, but maybe they're not quite as bad as I thought."

She chuckles, then forgives me for knocking the powder to the ground when I lean over to put my phone back down on my dressing table. Mary is getting used to my mishaps, though. She simply laughs and gives her head a little shake.

"I've already agreed not to use it. You didn't have to break it."

I stare at the little container on the floor. "I didn't break it! It was closed."

"Lucky, that," she says. "Chin up, darling. We've only got a few more minutes, and I can't curl your hair properly if your neck is bent at that angle."

True to her word, a few minutes later, my hair is done, and my dress is on. After I've slid a pair of two-inch block-

CHAPTER SEVENTEEN

heeled shoes onto my feet (Mary is catching on!), a knock sounds from the door. Mary wishes me luck before letting Wolf in as she leaves.

The charming blond Lord grins when he sees me, looking like a superhero with his long hair loose and a well-tailored suit hugging every muscled inch of his body. He lets out a low wolf whistle as he looks me over.

"Mads, thank fuck we've got you tonight. I've been looking forward to this dinner all my life. You're breathtaking. Ravishing. Let's go give my brothers blue balls, shall we?"

"Should you be down here?" I ask, trying to hide my blush, peering down the hall to see the other Omegas whispering. "They'll see."

"I wish I could say this escort is a courtesy only afforded to you, darling, but every group dinner date gets a royal escort."

He leans in conspiratorially. "But yours is the only one we had to draw straws for to avoid a full-out brawl."

My mouth drops open, and I flush ever fucking harder.

We haven't gone horse riding again, but we've been on a few walks and we played croquet the other day. I shouldn't feel this *electric* around Wolf still, but I do. I do every time he's close to me. I hope it never goes away. Not for as long as I'm here.

Wolf is...fun. I imagine his boundless energy could get exhausting, but I'm lying to myself if I think I could ever tire of him.

For now, I plant my hand firmly in his outstretched one and do the little twirl he prompts me into. "That mouth is going to get you in trouble, Von Damme."

"Nah, but it could get you off."

MADDIE

I laugh. "Don't make promises you can't keep."

Wolf spins me right into his chest, and heat flickers in those blue eyes as he winks at me. "Oh, I can keep it. Want me to prove it to you?"

Yes! "No, you said something about brothers and blue balls?"

I'm acutely aware of the other Omegas in the hall watching us. I clear my throat. "Shall we?"

"Of course." He purses his lips in mock disappointment but then takes my arm and escorts me to their quarters for dinner.

When we arrive, I'm surprised to find Tai and Kaz sitting at the bar with four empty shot glasses lined up, a bottle of tequila at the ready, and their ties already off.

"I see we're doing away with the formal dinner tonight," he says appreciatively and then gives a whoop before loosening his own tie and waving it in a circle above his head before letting it go. "Thank fuck. These things feel like damned nooses."

It lands at Kaz's feet, but the prince doesn't bend over to retrieve it. Instead, he looks at me like he's never seen me before, his dark gaze roving over my face until it sticks to my exposed freckles. "Perfect," he murmurs. "I hope you don't mind, but we're going with a more informal dinner this evening. We're doing Mexican food."

"Are we having enchiladas? Please tell me we're having enchiladas." I kick off my shoes like I'm actually comfortable here, but since they've all lost their ties, I figure being barefoot is okay. "I could settle for tacos, too. Maybe some nachos with pico and guac?"

"Told you she'd like it," Kaz says, giving Tai a shove.

"All of the above," Tai informs me as I sit down next to

him. He doesn't reach for me, doesn't lean in to kiss me or anything quite as obvious as that, but the way he glances at my lips lets me know he's thinking about our kiss right now too. "How was your day?"

"It was great." I motion at the big, supposedly bad boy prince. "Our Kaz came through. My parents are here. Isn't that amazing?"

"Our Kaz," Tai muses. "I like the sound of that."

Wolf's eyes are like the hottest of flames as he goes to join Kaz at the other side of the bar and looks back at me. "Why do I suddenly feel like you've spent a lot more time with these idiots than you have with me? I'm usually the only one who's this comfortable when the Omegas are around."

I waggle my eyebrows at him, but Kaz surprises the crap out of me when he winks at his packmate, a slight smirk lifting the edges of his lips. "Feeling a bit left out, are we?"

Wolf pouts, then gives me a playful, suggestive look. "How about we leave *them* out for a change? I've got a promise to keep, anyhow."

Wetness pools between my legs, and my nerve endings spring to life at the same time. I promised my mother I'd do whatever makes me happy. I vowed to myself that if the opportunity presents itself tonight, I'd roll with it.

But they promised me nachos, and I've never spent time with all three of them together. I'm making memories here, and this is one I definitely want. I simply flash him a coy smile instead of turning him down like I know he's expecting me to.

"Later," I promise, my stomach choosing that moment to give a loud burble of hungry protest.

MADDIE

"Charlie!" Kaz calls toward the east wing corridor. "Bring in the feast."

He pours four shots of tequila as a line of serving staff starts to bring in plate after plate of Mexican food. Some I recognize and some I'm desperate to try.

"Cheers," Wolf says, lifting his shot glass. "To enchiladas and orgasms."

I flush again, giggling as all of us as one chant the toast before downing our shots. "To enchiladas and orgasms!"

EIGHTEEN

WOLF

HOLY SHIT. I've never met anyone who can keep up with me the way Maddie does. Every fucking time, she surprises the living daylights out of me, and I'm so here for it.

She's outeaten me. No one clears their plate faster than I do. *No one.*

No one except Maddison Darling.

Putting my hands together in applause, I bow down to the Omega who has rendered me speechless. Kaz gapes at me before turning back to her. "I can't believe I'm saying this, but it seems you've out-Wolfed Wolf. Give him a minute to think of an appropriate response. I'll go tell the server we're ready for more nachos."

When he's gone, Tai glances at me. Even if we didn't have a bond that allowed me to feel what he's feeling, I'd have known exactly what he's experiencing right now.

Maddie belongs with us. She gets us all so damn well. While it sucks that we can't make her ours, we still want her. Bad.

Oblivious to what's passing between us, she laughs at something Tai's said about a good 'ravishing' being *almost* as good as a plate of taquitos with salsa verde.

"A good ravishing, huh?" She chuckles. "So, tell me, what do you guys do around here when you're not sweeping innocent Omegas off our feet?"

She bats her lashes at him, and he grins so easily that I'm a little taken aback by it. Tai doesn't naturally get along with just anybody. It's rare to see such a relaxed grin on his face even with us, but aimed at an outsider, it's almost unheard of.

"Don't pretend you're so innocent, darling. You want to be swept off your feet, but to answer your question, I guess we just do this."

"Between bouts of good ravishings," I joke—sort of, anyway. "We hang out. We shoot a little pool. Binge Netflix, and Kaz saves the world every once in a while."

Maddie's gaze drifts in the direction he disappeared to. When he comes back around the corner, I see the moment he sees her looking for him. I thought the guy was made of steel to be able to ignore his impulses with her, but I suddenly realize he's no better than us.

His razor-sharp features soften instantly, his gaze becoming almost gentle before it fills with a familiar heat and his fingers roll into his palms like he's physically restraining himself from reaching for her. He tightens his fists, then his nostrils flare as he collects himself and pretends nothing happened.

"I don't save the world," he says modestly, though he legitimately has had a hand in doing just that once or twice. "Eventually, I hope I'll be able to do some good, but I'll leave the world-saving to the professionals."

CHAPTER EIGHTEEN

Maddie frowns. "Wouldn't being the king automatically make you a professional?"

My brows rise. It's not often that someone is so blatantly honest with him. As I turn to him, expecting him to snap at her or something, I realize he's considering a real answer. He doesn't seem surprised by the question at all, and when he finally replies, I fucking *know* he's been blocking us out at times when he's been with her.

There's no way they've had conversations this intense and this raw without us feeling it from him otherwise.

"I wouldn't say I'd automatically be a professional. I'd be more involved and a lot of people would look to me for advice and guidance, but I'd have people advising and guiding me in turn. Unfortunately, being the monarch means not always being able to get your hands dirty."

"Who are the actual professionals, then?"

"The people on the ground level," Tai chimes in as if he's not shaken about how these two interact with each other. "The people doing the actual work."

Kaz and Tai square off, but before they can get into their favorite argument in front of her, I step in. "You said your parents are here? How are they settling in?"

Maddie's face lights up, and my packmates graciously dismount their high horses while she talks about her family. "They're so excited. My little brother thinks he's a prince now, and my dad can't wait to get lost in the gardens. If a dark-haired preschooler finds you out on the grounds at some point and starts following you around, that'll be Kevin. Just send him home, but be nice about it or I'll tell him where you sleep."

"What'll he do if you tell him where we sleep?"

She smiles. "Crawl into bed with you regardless of

who's already in there. He's fond of pretending to be a starfish in his sleep, and we've been working on his pranking skills."

"Warning received." I touch my hand to my heart and sit down as the server brings in our food. "What about your mum? Does she like her new house?"

Some of the light fades from Maddie's eyes, and her smile loses a megawatt or five. "She loves it, but she's more concerned about my happiness."

Tai's hand twitches like he's about to take hers, but then he sees Kaz watching him and rolls his eyes instead. "It's good that she cares about your happiness, isn't it? Sure beats parents who want to control everything regardless of how we feel."

Kaz's jaw tics. "Some people don't have the luxury of believing the world runs on sunshine and love."

When red streaks creep up Tai's neck, I pick up the tequila and fill the glasses. "Shots!" I announce, immediately dispelling the negative energy in that way only I can. Well, with Señor Tequila's help.

Kaz jerks his head in a nod, but then his phone chimes and he curses when he checks it. "My mother is requesting an audience."

"Right now?" Tai scowls, and I know he suspects her Royal Bitchiness is pulling Kaz away from dinner because she knows exactly who she's pulling him away from.

"Yes. Right now." Kaz gives Maddie an apologetic smile. Once again, he surprises me when he goes over to her and drops a chaste kiss on top of her head. "I'm sorry. I have to go, but we'll talk soon? Thanks for the freckles."

The smile she gives him in turn is equally fond and genuine. "You're welcome."

CHAPTER EIGHTEEN

He chuckles, then reaches out and brushes his knuckles across one of her cheeks. "I'll text you later."

"Okay."

When he turns around and strides out, I stare after him for a beat before snapping my gaze to hers. "The fuck was that?"

Confusion darkens her eyes as she frowns at me. "What was what?"

"That." I incline my head toward the door. "With you and Kaz. Did that really just happen?"

Tai chuckles. "It happened all right. Now that Captain Spoilsport is gone, what is that promise you said you had to keep?"

"Oh, that." I glance at her. "Maddie said my mouth was going to get me in trouble, and I told her I'd rather use it to get her off."

He groans, but then he turns to her as well. "You didn't tell him to go fuck himself?"

As her eyes dart between us, she seems to realize what we want. When her gaze settles on Tai's, she smiles a little. "Why would I do that?"

His jaw slackens as he scrubs a hand over his face. "Here we go again."

She laughs. "You could sound more enthusiastic about it."

Peeking at her between his fingers, he hesitates for a beat before he places one hand in mine and the other in hers. "Trust me, I'm really fucking enthusiastic about it, and I'll prove it to you in a minute, but we promised it would only be that one time."

"We did," she murmurs her agreement, lifting their joined hands to her mouth and brushing a kiss to his knuckles. "Neither of us wanted it to stay that way, though."

"We didn't," he says, getting up and releasing my hand to wrap her up in his arms. She rests her head against his chest, and her eyes close as she listens to what I know from experience is the very steady beat of his heart. While she does, he cradles her against him, stroking her hair and murmuring to her. "I don't know what it is about you, Maddie, but I can't stay away."

"We don't do this with any of the other Omegas," I say as I move in behind her, cautiously sliding my arms around her waist and stepping in so close that her back is pressed tightly to my front.

I've never had my hands on her properly before, and I'm mindful that she hasn't exactly given me her express consent to do so, but she leans into me and drops her head on my shoulder as she looks up at me.

"You don't?"

Tai shakes his head. "I've already told you I don't want any other Omega. Wolf and Kaz don't either."

Those gorgeous green eyes grow contemplative on mine. "We can't get attached. You know I'm not going to be the one."

I snort. "I hate to break it to you, but I'm already attached, Mads. My vote is that we let things happen and have fun while we still can."

"Funny, I was thinking the same thing."

Tai takes her chin gently between his fingers and waits until she looks back at him. "It's not ideal, but he's right. I'm already attached too, and I'd very much like to see where this goes. We can't offer you the world on a platter, but we can offer you this."

CHAPTER EIGHTEEN

"Enchiladas and orgasms?" she asks softly before inhaling through her nostrils and then shaking her head. "I'll probably regret the hell out of this, but I'd rather regret the things I did than the things I didn't."

I grin. "Are you part of the *you only live once* clan, then?"

"No, but that doesn't mean they don't have a point."

She chuckles. Even though I see that she's forcing it, she does her best to relax. "Are we going to make some memories or what?"

"We're making memories," I say immediately.

Tai lifts her against him and carries her to his chambers, looking at her like she's personally responsible for hanging the moon. As he lays her down on his bed, he glances at me and I nod, kneeling behind him to remove her tights.

I slide them off slowly while he sits her up to tug on the metallic zipper of her dress. Once it's open, he crawls onto her and claims her mouth with his own, and I drop her tights before I stand to watch them.

Her fiery hair is spread out around her head, dark streaks against his white bedding. She's got her hands in his hair, her trimmed fingernails dragging over his scalp as she holds him to her, kissing him back as deeply as he's kissing her.

My packmates and I have gotten ourselves into some pretty hot situations over the years, but the sight of her hands in that white hair and her hips rising off the mattress to search for his is easily the most erotic thing I've ever seen. It turns me on and makes me painfully jealous at the same time.

As he maneuvers the dress off her, I move in behind him, undoing his fly and helping him out of his pants while he works on her underwear. Once his pants and shoes are off, he grips his shirt behind his neck and pulls it off, then turns to me when he's naked.

Heat burns from those eyes as he grabs the nape of my neck and pulls me to him, his cock as hard as steel against mine. Leaning in, I kiss him, and Mads gasps somewhere behind us. Our hands meet on the waistband of my pants, working together to get me out of them.

When I open my eyes without breaking the kiss, I find Maddie flushed and sitting on the bed, watching us with her lips parted and her chest rising and falling fast. As much as I want Tai right now, I also want her. Plus, it's her first time with the two of us. We can't leave her out of it.

Smiling against his lips, I slow the kiss before tugging off my shirt and going to her, crawling onto the mattress and covering her body with mine. "Ready to see what this mouth can do?"

She nods enthusiastically, but she's clearly not one for talking much during. *We'll get her there.*

Lowering my head, I claim her lips for an urgent, hot kiss that sends an electrical current straight to my cock before I drag my mouth down, breathing in her scent until my dick throbs so much that I think it'll fucking explode if something doesn't happen soon.

Not only her scent, but everything about her. Her skin is so soft and sweet, and I've just decided her little gasps and soft moans are my new favorite song. Catching her nipple between my teeth, I groan when I feel Tai behind me, his hands running up and down the muscles in my back before he reaches around and wraps his fist around my aching cock.

My heart is pounding, and I feel droplets of sweat forming on my forehead. Maddie moans again when I bite

CHAPTER EIGHTEEN

her nipple gently, and I make a mental note that she likes it before I drag my mouth farther down.

She scoots up a little as Tai's hand strokes me, moving slowly up and down. Tingles of pleasure skate through me, but I don't thrust into his palm. Holding back might kill me, but I don't want this to be over too soon.

As I lower my head and Maddie scoots up, I'm presented with her perfect, pink pussy. I growl when the sight and scent of her arousal hit me with full force. *I really don't want this to be over too soon, but fucking hell...*

Resting my weight on one elbow, I use my free hand to spread her apart. Then I tuck in, tasting her sweet glistening slick. Licking and sucking her while Tai's hand speeds up on my cock. My muscles tense, and I move my knees so I'm in a position where he'll be able to take me from behind.

Thankfully, he doesn't make me stop what I'm doing with her to ask him for what I want. A dribble of cool liquid splashes onto my ass, and I groan when I feel the pressure of his tip against my entrance. Pushing back against him, I graze my teeth across her clit, and she shudders, squirming under me as her hands fly to my hair and she pulls it hard.

Tai thrusts into me. My resounding moan vibrates against her, making her cry out my name as her hips buck, and I buckle down on my efforts. My cock swells, the sea of sensation close to overwhelming me as Tai's fist speeds up, his thrusts grow more frenzied, and Maddie makes little motions against my face, trying to chase her release, but I can tell she's holding back.

I grip her thighs, pulling back just for a second. "Don't be shy, Mads, I want this pussy all over me. Ride my face like you want to break it."

I furiously go back to licking her pussy, adding my fingers to the mix and like a good, good girl, she rides my face like I asked her to.

She screams as her orgasm rips through her, the sound pushing me to my own edge. She shakes, her thighs tightening, trying to squeeze me out, but I keep her spread open, flexing my muscle as I wring every delicious second out of her orgasm that it's willing to give her.

She shudders and whines and her juices flood my mouth.

I let go, shooting ropes of cum onto her stomach while Tai fills me up from behind. He bends over to press his torso to my back, and I collapse beside Maddie as Tai lets go of me to lie down on her other side.

She lifts her head to rest it on his chest, her fingertips drawing patterns on his skin as I curl around her side and try to catch my breath.

We stay like that for a moment. The three of us tangled together, sharing breath, sharing in the silence.

I tense when I realize Kaz will have felt what we've just done. Will he be angry? Fuck.

Sensing the shift, Maddie pushes herself up.

"I should probably go." She tries to shuffle to the edge of the bed, but I hook my arm around her waist and pull her back down, nuzzling her neck as I hug her closer to me.

"I'll walk you back soon. Just stay with us for a few more minutes, okay?"

She fits herself against me, cuddling into my side as she goes back to drawing those patterns on Tai's chest. "Okay, but just a few more minutes."

As silence falls between us, I feel the intensity of the emotions coming from both Tai and Kaz. I know what Tai's

CHAPTER EIGHTEEN

are about. He doesn't want Maddie to leave us tonight. He wants her to stay here, to sleep in his bed, and to wake up with us in the morning.

Kaz's, however, are more difficult to interpret. The usual undercurrent of frustration when he's with his mother is there, but something else is there, too. Something that feels a hell of a lot like despair.

NINETEEN

—

KAZ

WHENEVER I'M SUMMONED to my mother's office, it's for a lecture about one thing or another. At this hour, the lecture she needs to give must not be able to wait until morning, which makes me equal parts curious and angry.

I was looking forward to spending the evening with Maddie and my packmates. The dynamic starting to emerge between them and her when I was called away was interesting—to say the least. Sure, it also brought up an age-old argument between me and Tai, but that's not her fault.

I know how he feels about the monarchy and how he feels about her, but seeing them together suddenly made me wonder for the first time if perhaps he has a point about us not needing the monarchy to do the things we want to do. I'm not an idiot. I'm not about to abdicate in the name of love, but I'm fascinated by the way she matches with each of us.

It's almost surreal that one person can be so uniquely capable of providing all three of us with exactly what we need. She calls me out and forces me to be honest, to be introspective, and to answer the questions I'm not usually called upon to answer. All those questions I usually only answer in my head because most are too afraid to ask them out loud.

It's like she holds up a mirror and shamelessly, fearlessly makes me look into it. But she does it with a certain measure of vulnerability and understanding. She's fierce, but she's not hard. That juxtaposition isn't easy to find in a person.

Then there's the way she keeps up with Wolf. Gives what she gets and doesn't seem to tire of it. To be fair, I only saw them together firsthand for a short time tonight, but it only confirmed what I already knew to be true from what I've felt from him when they've been together.

The rush. The exhilaration of finding an Omega who not only enjoys his boundless energy and great sarcastic wit, but equals it.

And Tai…I've never seen anyone but us draw him out of his shell that way. She gives him the courage to speak his truth to someone outside of our pack. In a way, it's like she's giving him back the voice he thought he lost when he moved into the palace and chose to become part of my pack.

That's fucking magical because it's the one thing I've never been able to give him and the only thing I've wanted to for so long. As I knock on my mother's office door, I know I'm going to have to take it away from him again.

Regardless of how fascinating, how magical, or how perfect she is, the one thing Maddie isn't, is fit to be a royal. Her lack of breeding and connections eliminated her from

CHAPTER NINETEEN

being a true contender in this competition long before she was selected.

"Enter!" my mother calls from inside. I dip my head in a shallow bow as I open the door and stride into the inner sanctum.

This office is just that. It's the epitome of an inner sanctum. The secrets that have been shared between these four walls, the decisions that have been made here...this is where the true power lies. This is where I'll change the world for the better.

If it ever becomes mine—and that's why I can't let Maddie be the one to give Tai his voice back. Because when the sanctum passes to me, I'll be able to do it not only for him, but for millions of others as well.

Even if a sense of deep despair grows within me when I think about not choosing her now. I've often found this office to be a place of clarity. A reminder of why I must diligently carry out my duties without fear or favor, but tonight, even as it has reminded me of that, I can't help but feel like it's not so great in here.

A fire is roaring in the fireplace, but I've got the same thing in my chambers. The regal, ancient walnut desk is cool, but it's dated. With its overstuffed armchairs and flowery drapes, the office lacks a certain...*oomph* tonight.

My mother stands by the fire with a brandy in her hands, staring at the dancing flames before she turns slowly to face me. "Kaspian."

"Mother." I stride over to the drinks trolley and help myself to some of her brandy.

It's the good stuff. She has it distilled by some special guy in France who bottles it only for her. Usually, I wouldn't dare touch this decanter without her say-so, but I'm in a fuck-it kind of mood, it seems.

The queen raises her chin as she watches me pour myself a drink, but she doesn't say anything about it. Instead, once I've got my glass in my hand, she motions toward her desk. "I've laid out some paperwork for you to take a look at. I'd like to know the meaning of it all."

I frown. *So, this isn't a lecture? It's about paperwork? Odd.*

As soon as I see the paperwork in question, however, it's not so odd anymore. In fact, it makes perfect sense.

The documents are laid out side-by-side, a printout of the lease for the cottage, the employment contract for Simon, and finally, a request for medical aid that I put in this morning. *The old bag really doesn't miss a fucking trick, does she?*

"I'm waiting, Kaspian. What is the meaning of this, please?"

I sigh before I straighten and face her again, taking a small sip of her brandy to steel my resolve. "You summoned me here to confront me about her? Why? Maddison Darling is an eligible Omega who was selected to participate in the Trials. I learned of her family's hardship, and as we were in a position to assist them, I thought it prudent to do so."

"Maddison Darling should never have been selected, and you're smart enough to have figured that out by now. Her presence is nothing more than the result of a mix-up within the selection committee. The members responsible for it have been dealt with, and the Omega who should have been selected is named Clara something or other. Don't fool yourself, Kaspian. She's not who you're going to bond with."

"She isn't?" I lower my head slowly to one side as I

regard the woman who was too busy to help me as a child and who now seems to think she can influence my decisions as an adult. "Regardless of how she was selected, the fact remains that she was. I speak for my packmates and myself when I say that in our view, she's a strong contender."

My mother's dark eyes narrow as she studies mine. "Oh, for God's sake, don't tell me you've gone and fallen in love with her."

"Don't dismiss the notion so easily, Mother. She's got a wonderful heart and the people quite like her. Have you seen her ratings?"

"Of course, I have. That's the only reason I haven't taken care of her mistaken participation myself."

"Except that it's not your decision who stays and who goes," I say with absolutely no clue why I'm digging in on this and standing up for her when I've already told her we'll never choose her. "We've grown to care about Maddison, Mother. Perhaps it was fate that dropped her in our laps instead of the Omega who was supposed to have been selected."

"Fate?" She arches a brow at me as she releases a sharp breath through her nostrils. "My dear boy, you cannot possibly be that naïve. It's not my decision who stays and who goes, but I do have considerable influence over the media and as such, over the people you say love her. That might be true right now, Kaspian, but you and I both know public perception is fickle. A *darling* one minute, a pariah the next."

So that's why Antonio and Rachel are being punted as the top two. Good to know. "Careful, Mother. My next interview with the *Daily*—"

KAZ

The door bursts open, and my father stumbles in. His eyes are red and shiny, glazed over as he tries to focus on my mother and me. Reeking of alcohol and sex with his tie askew and his buttons not properly aligned, he grins and sways as he throws his arms out to his sides.

"My family!" he exclaims like he's had the best surprise of his life. "Here you are. Do you think we could have a drink? I—"

"You don't need another," my mother says coolly before she strides to the door and peeks out into the hallway. "Stuart! A little assistance."

While we wait for her pet of a secretary to come take the drunken mess off our hands, the stone that was the mask of my mother's features cracks. Wordlessly, she goes to his side and takes his arm, guiding him to the nearest chair and taking care of him in her own way despite his treachery.

It makes me sick, but when she gets him a glass of water, I see the depth of the pain in her eyes. She's not so stoic now. Not so impenetrable.

She dropped everything to help a man who was balls deep in some other woman earlier tonight, and Mum knows it. Yet, she brings him the water and coaxes him to drink, murmuring softly as she sits on the armrest of the chair he's in and holds the glass so he won't drop it.

Moments later, Stuart comes in and takes the King Consort away. Once we're alone again, she brings her gaze to mine, but her mask isn't back on yet. "This is where love gets you, Kaspian."

She stands and strides back to the fireplace to pick up her brandy. "Keep your little pet project," she says as she stares at the flames. "But you *will* end up with one of the other Omegas."

CHAPTER NINETEEN

Her voice is strangely forlorn now. "Antonio Ramirez is a good match for you, as is the American girl. Rachel. There are a few others too, if those two don't tickle your fancy. Have your fun with Maddison Darling. Get her out of your system, and when the time comes, make the right decision. The sensible one."

"Right," I mutter, too depressed and chastened to argue with her right now. After what I witnessed between her and my father, tonight won't be the night to attempt to win her over anyway. "Good night, Mother."

She lifts her hand in a wave, but as I leave her office, she still hasn't looked away from the flames. My earlier despair rolls back into me ten times as strong. Instead of going back to our pack quarters, I head up to the roof.

Judging by what I'm feeling from them right now, this isn't the time to discuss what I learned with my packmates. Body, heart, and soul, I yearn to join them, but I don't, because my brain is stronger and smarter than that. Our bodies, hearts, and souls are what got us into this mess.

Right now, I need my brain to get us out of it.

TWENTY

—

MADDIE

HAVING my parents so close is amazing. It's the one thing that's been detracting from this experience all along. Now that they're here, it's as close to perfect as it's going to get. As I watch the leaves rustling in a light breeze on my way to the cottage, memories of the other night with Wolf and Tai stream back into my head like an unstoppable current as powerful as the ocean itself.

I've tried to stop thinking about it. Really. No matter what I do, though, as soon as I have a moment to myself, that's where my head goes. My footsteps are silent on the thick lawn beneath me, leaving me with not even the sound of that to distract me.

Despite what they said the other night, I can't quite believe they're not doing the same things with the other Omegas. It's impossible that all three of the Royal Alphas only want *me*. There's no way it can be true. Yet, there were no other scents than theirs in the pack quarters that night.

I don't know where they've been having dinner with the remaining Omegas when the others have had their dates

MADDIE

with the pack, but it definitely wasn't there. Their scents—and theirs alone—washed over me that night, making me feel safer and more protected than ever before.

And hotter. Literally. I've been feeling a bit flushed ever since. The usual first indication of an oncoming heat. I'm starting to wonder if I might be sick. If maybe I'm beginning to get Cervus. The mere thought is so terrifying that it makes my knees numb, but something is wrong with me.

I don't know what it is. Something *has* to be. It's like my suppressants aren't doing anything at all. What's more is that I took Wolf's tie from their quarters the other night. I wasn't aware of doing it at the time, but as he walked me out, I snagged the tie he'd dropped and added it to the little collection I've been growing.

Along with Wolf's tie, I also have Kaz's handkerchief and Tai's jacket. I'm keeping it in my chambers like some kind of shrine to the Royals—or even more worryingly—some kind of *nest*. And not the kind an Omega makes for herself at home to feel most comfortable. No, a nest meant to be used with a pack.

That's how I know something is absolutely, irrefutably wrong with me.

A heavy sigh falls out of me, but I can't afford to dwell on this right now.

My parents *cannot* know that I'm worried about this, so I paste a smile on my lips when the cottage comes into view. Then I frown when I see a woman I don't recognize sitting on the porch with my mother. They're talking and they're both knitting, laughing together as if they're old friends.

As I draw closer, I get a better look at the woman. I'm so surprised that I feel lightheaded when I notice the resemblance between her and Tai. Not only in their delicate features, but also in their scents. She's got the same warm, spicy nettle and cardamom I've grown to love so much, and while the bergamot isn't as strong on her, it's definitely there.

The scent envelops me like a favorite blanket, and I'm strangely comfortable with her before she looks up and sees me. "You must be Maddie." She smiles and sets her knitting aside to stand up. "I've heard so much about you."

I walk up the few steps to the porch, and once I'm there, she comes over to give me a warm hug. "I'm Yua. Tai's mother."

"Oh, uh. Hi." I hug her back, but then I remember all the things I've done with her son and the awkwardness sets in.

As she releases me, she puts her hands on my shoulders and looks me over. "Gorgeous. Simply gorgeous. So much more so in person and up close. I love the freckles, darling. Lord knows why they were covered initially."

My blush deepens as I stammer out a lame response. "I, um, I. Makeup."

She chuckles. "Of course."

When she steps back, I move around to give my mum a hug, and I can't *not* notice how happy she looks. Serene. Peaceful. Smiling as she motions toward her new friend.

"Yua was walking in the gardens and we got to talking," she explains, and there's more color in her cheeks now than there has been for months.

I know she's been lonely, but friendship doesn't cure Cervus. Since she's so excited though, I don't interrupt her but I'm curious. "At first, she was standing down there chatting to me, but then I offered her a cup of tea and she came up to sit with me. We lost track of time after that."

MADDIE

"I was so impressed by your mother's knitting," Yua chimes in. "It's an incredible feat, especially considering her vision concerns. She's marvelous, though. She offered to teach me."

Mum's face flushes. "Yua's a wonderful student."

"I'm not doing well," Yua says modestly and Mum laughs.

Meanwhile, I feel like I've stepped into the Twilight Zone. I haven't seen my mum this carefree in…I don't know how long. I've only been here for a couple of minutes, but I haven't seen the Cervus twitch at all—not even the small ones that have become so much a part of her that I've stopped consciously noticing them.

The lack of them, however, is a whole different ball game. "You're looking good, Mum. Did Yua bring you a miracle tea?"

"Heavens no." Yua laughs before she turns to my mum with an intensely excited smile. "Tell her, Emily. Or would you like some privacy before you do?"

Privacy? What for? Tell me what?

Mum shakes her head and reaches for her new friend's arm like she's silently seeking support. I have no idea what's going on, but the two Omegas in front of me have clearly become fast friends.

"I haven't had a twitch since yesterday afternoon," Mum says proudly, gripping Yua's arm now. "Can you believe that, honey? That new medicine is working. It's no cure, but it's definitely effective."

"New medicine?" I ask, glancing at Yua before looking back at my mum. "Where did you get new medicine? I didn't realize you'd gone to see the doctor again."

"I didn't," Mum says softly, and the gratitude in her

CHAPTER TWENTY

voice is so genuine it sounds almost like awe. "The prince sent his personal doctor to come see me, and they got me on a new regiment of pills. I even spoke to Thane Woods. They've signed me up to go to a Cervus clinic for an experimental treatment that could possibly cure me."

My jaw drops open. "Thane Woods? *The* Thane Woods? Like, from Riley North's pack?"

The man is a superstar. He's one of my favorite author's Alphas, sure, but for once, my excitement isn't about Riley, it's about him. Thane and his family are doctors who have found a cure for Cervus. Well, that's the best-case scenario. There's no guarantee their treatment will cure an Omega, but the worst case is that it significantly slows the progression of the disease.

From what I've read, they're working tirelessly to get their medicine approved and into mass production, but it's not that easy. It's not as simple as taking an aspirin to make a mild headache go away, so while they've been working hard to make it widely available, it's just...not.

Meanwhile, every Omega in the world who has been diagnosed with Cervus is trying to get in touch with the Woodses. I have written them dozens of letters and emails begging for an appointment, but all to no avail.

As soon as my mother was diagnosed, I made it my personal mission to get her in with them one way or another, but I soon learned it was a fool's errand. First, they're based in the States, and without being able to afford to get her there, the plan was basically dead in the water. They're in the process of setting up clinics all over, but it's early days yet for this particular course of treatment.

I've heard it can take years for clinics with treatments like theirs to pop up and be accessible to anyone, and my mum doesn't have that kind of time. Second, Cervus isn't only a disease for the poor. Rich and powerful Alphas and Omegas the world over have used their considerable influence to get their loved ones in with the Woodses. I didn't stand a chance.

I should've known Kaspian would have the means to make something like this happen, but I'm stunned that he reached out on our behalf. It's above and beyond what we agreed to, and there's absolutely no way I'll be able to repay him.

Yua laughs when I keep gaping, unable to process the magnitude of what the prince has done for us. "Kaspian has a big heart. I know that better than most. Don't look so surprised, sweetheart. He knows Thane. They all do. They're not besties or anything quite so colloquial, but they've met at fundraisers and on official business. It's no more than a phone call for an Alpha like Kaz."

"I…" *Have no idea what to say.*

Tears prick at my eyes.

Mum yawns, and she tries to suppress it, but the excitement has obviously become too much for her. Yua's gaze darts to her at the same time mine does, and then she rises gracefully and smiles at my mum. "Thank you for a wonderful morning, Emily. I will most certainly come visit again but for now, I should get back to the palace. Will you walk with me, Maddie?"

Shit. I came here to spend some time with my parents, but my mum nods encouragingly as she gets up. "Have fun. I think I'm going to go have a little lie down. The pills may be working, but new medication is always a bit of a shock to the system."

"Of course," I agree, ignoring the ache in my heart about

having to leave her again so soon. "I'll come by again tomorrow?"

"If you've got time," she says lightly before turning to her new friend and opening her arms. "It was so wonderful to meet you, Yua. Anytime you want another lesson or a cup of tea, you know where to find me."

"I certainly do," she says warmly as she embraces my mum. "You're going to tire of me soon. Now that I know where to find the best company on the palace grounds, you can bet your favorite hat that I'll be here to overstay my welcome again as soon as I can get away."

They hold each other close for another moment before they let go, then Yua takes my arm and holds me tight as we walk down the stairs and start across the lawn. Silence stretches between us for a couple of minutes, but it's a comfortable one.

"Has Tai told you much about me?" she asks out of the blue, laughing when she glances at me and sees that my eyes have popped wide open. "I'm going to assume he has, then. Don't worry, darling. Nothing you can say will offend me."

"I doubt that very much," I mutter. "I have a special talent for ending up with my foot in my mouth. It's no wonder they won't choose me."

"I wouldn't be so sure about that. When it comes to love, it doesn't matter where you are class wise. Love doesn't care about status, or power, or money. Take me, for example. If they've told you about me, then you know I was a waitress at a street-side café when I met Tai's father. I wasn't born into all this."

She waves her free hand around to indicate the palace and the seemingly never-ending grounds.

MADDIE

"God knows, at least you grew up near here. You've heard of the Royal Pack and you had an inkling of who they are before you came. It was different for me. I met an earl on the other side of the world and when I first came here with him, it was like someone had dropped me in an alternate reality."

"Sure, I grew up near here, hearing about them, but Japan has the Imperial Family. You know as well as I do that simply being in a country that has a monarchy doesn't mean much."

She chuckles and dips her chin in a nod. "That's true, I suppose, but that's also my point. Love doesn't care about your past proximity to royalty. Love only cares about love."

"Maybe, but that doesn't mean they're going to choose me. It just...it is what it is. I am what I am, and they're the Royal freaking Pack."

Yua frowns. "The queen is stubborn, but maybe she's grown less so over the years. Are you okay? You're terribly flushed all of a sudden."

I know. There's a terrible ache in my stomach, too, but it's only because of who we were talking about. "I'm fine. It's nothing, really. I've been having heat symptoms recently, but I'm handling it."

Her frown deepens when I fan myself in a futile attempt to make my cheeks return to a color that's slightly less... overripe tomato.

"Have you been taking your suppressant?"

"Yes," I say honestly. "I've increased my dosage, but I think the ones I have are duds or something. I checked the expiry date, and they're supposed to be fine."

Concern tightens her features as she looks at me. "Promise me you'll go see a doctor if it gets any worse?"

CHAPTER TWENTY

"I promise," I say, even though I know I likely won't. The doctor could make a recommendation for my disqualification and I can't...I don't want to leave. Not just yet.

Yua sighs, but then she suddenly stands up straighter and an excited curiosity sparks in those reddish eyes. "There is another possibility for what's causing it."

"What's that?"

"Sometimes, your body just *knows*," she says vaguely. "Heads can be such silly things at times, but bodies? They don't lie, especially not when they find their match. Meds be damned. When your body knows, it knows."

"I, uh, I don't think it's that."

"Well, again, I wouldn't be so sure. If my son wasn't one of the Alphas in question, I'd have asked how they were taking it, but since he is, I'll tell you that we don't want any accidents to happen. It's safe enough to double your dose in the short term. Until the trials are over. Try that, and if it still doesn't work, go to a doctor."

"Yeah, maybe I will." As we approach the palace, I wonder if Antonio is in his chambers. He offered me some of his suppressants. If I'm going to double my dose, then I will definitely need to supplement my stash at some point.

TWENTY-ONE

—

TAI

"CAN you believe this is our last one-on-one date?" I ask as Maddie and I stroll toward the archery field.

Her scent is stronger today, but the notes of pink pepper and patchouli that I've come to adore are there, settling me and making me want to do things to her all at the same time. I've grown used to controlling my urges around her, but it's not fucking easy.

At times, it's almost overwhelming how much I want to make her mine. When she smiles before lowering her head to rest it on my shoulder as we walk, it's one of those times. "It's crazy how fast time has flown by. In some ways, I feel like I've been here with you for years, and in others, it feels like this journey started only yesterday."

"I know what you mean," I muse.

She glances at me without lifting her head off my shoulder, her hands warmly gripping my arm. "Hey, speaking of the start of this journey, can I ask you something?"

"Anything. I thought we'd established that."

A faint flush rises from her neck to her jaw. "I, um. Yes,

we have, but this is kind of embarrassing for me. I wanted to ask you that first day, but then we got sidetracked and eventually, I was just too humiliated to ask."

"Go ahead," I say as curiosity rages through me. "What do you possibly have to be embarrassed about?"

"My scent," she blurts out after pausing for a moment. Then her entire face turns bright red, and she stops walking.

Since we're far enough away from the palace and a decent portion of the forest separates us from it, I move in front of her. My arms automatically encircle her waist as my eyebrows rise. "You're embarrassed about your scent?"

"Well, not my scent, necessarily, but you guys were so obviously repulsed by it during the Scenting Ceremony that I've been wondering ever since why you didn't send me home."

For a moment, all I can do is stare at her. When I see the seriousness and confusion shining back at me from those eyes, I laugh. I can't help it. Maddie groans and punches my arm before covering her face with her hands.

"Never mind. Forget I asked."

"No, it's not that," I manage as the laughter subsides. I reach for her hands, gently tugging them away from her face and shaking my head when she finally looks at me again. "It's just that I can't believe you've spent all this time thinking we're repulsed by your scent."

"Aren't you?" she asks, a crease forming above the bridge of her nose as she pinches her eyebrows together. "I call bullshit. I've seen the way you all turn away from me. The looks on your faces. The swallowing like you're gonna pu—"

I tap my index finger against her forehead as I cut her

off. "Think, Maddie. Use what's in there and think. What else would cause us to react that way?"

"Well—" Her eyes flare wide open as she stares at me. I practically see the realization when it dawns. "I mean, I thought maybe...but it's such a strong reaction that I figured it had to be negative."

I smile and bend my head to run my nose along the length of hers, making no secret of it that I'm breathing her in. It makes me fucking ache for her so bad, but I'm getting used to that, too. Although, at this rate, my dick will have a permanent imprint of the inside of my zipper. "At the Scenting Ceremony, we were the complete opposite of repulsed, Maddie. We were trying to stop ourselves from mounting you in front of a worldwide audience."

"Oh."

"*Oh*," I agree, closing my eyes as I rest my forehead against hers and tug her into me. "There hasn't been one moment since we first laid eyes on you that we haven't wanted you, Maddison Darling. If wanting you was the only consideration, we'd have sent every other Omega home right there, halfway through the Ceremony."

She trembles in my arms, and I hold her tighter, feeling her chest expand on a deep breath before she pulls away from me. "It's the same for me."

"I know," I confess quietly.

"You know?"

I nod. "Omega arousal has a very distinct scent, and yours is the sweetest I've ever smelled, but let's just leave it at *we're definitely not repulsed by you*. If we keep talking about this..."

"Okay. How about we talk about this instead, then. I met your mother yesterday."

TAI

I blink a few times in rapid succession, and thankfully, my cock deflates at the mention of my mum. "You did?"

"Yep. She's befriended my mother, believe it or not. Mum's even teaching her how to knit."

Now it's my turn to look at her with my eyes as wide as saucers. "My mum is learning how to knit? Wow. She must really like your mum."

"I think she does." Maddie gives me that radiant, relaxed smile again. "Why do you say that, though?"

I shrug, releasing her to start toward the archery field again. "My mum doesn't really like sitting still. She's a bit like Wolf in that way. Their energy never wanes."

"Ah." She looks out at the field when it comes into view. "So, you're teaching me how to shoot today. Is that safe? Considering that I nearly scalded your testicles when we were having tea, I'm not sure I should be handling sharp objects around you."

"My testicles are fine," I assure her, raising an arm to point at the targets that have been placed along the length of the field. "You see that roof over there? We'll be under it, and you'll be aiming the arrows that away. I'll stay behind you just in case, but I was planning on showing you how to aim anyway, which means I'll always have been behind you."

She laughs, and the sound makes something inside me feel soothed and safe. When I hand her a bow and arrow and watch as she examines them like they're precious to her, looking a little like a surprised but excited kid on Christmas morning, it occurs to me that I'm absolutely, head-over-heels in love with this Omega.

I could watch her do that for days. I could listen to her

CHAPTER TWENTY-ONE

laughter for the rest of my life and still not hear enough of it. *Fuck*.

The realization is sobering. In just one more week, she'll be gone. A distant memory. *And there's nothing I can do about it.*

The thought sends searing pain ricocheting through me, and I reach for her, gently taking the bow and arrow out of her hands and setting them down on the ground beside her. Surprise flickers in her eyes when I pull her close again, but when I bring my mouth to hers, she doesn't stop me. She also doesn't ask what I'm doing.

She simply wraps her arms around my neck and pulls me down, kissing me passionately and murmuring against my lips, "I'm going to miss you, too."

When her mouth fuses to mine again, things get more heated between us, and fast. Maddie moans and mewls, hooking her leg around my thighs like she's literally trying to climb me, and I'm not much better.

My instincts are in overdrive. If I don't watch myself, I *am* going to claim her this time—regardless of the consequences. The thought breaks my heart a little, but at least it allows me to win back a modicum of self-control.

I won't claim her, but I will make love to her. Mentally going over my options, I realize the grass is probably softer than the concrete under the little roof, so I walk backward and bring her with me, rolling up the hem of her knit cardigan and only breaking the kiss to pull it over her head.

Her hands are on the waistband of my jeans next. We both nearly fall over when she stumbles, but I catch her. Then I lower myself down on my knees and lift my arms to undo her slacks. Once I've got the button through the hole, I hook my thumbs into the waistband and pull them off, leaving her in only a pair of innocent white panties and a matching bra.

A low growl tears out of me when I look up at her like this, her hair a fiery halo around her head with all that smooth, pale skin and the plain underwear as the cherry on top. With every beat of my heart, a single word thunders through my head.

Mine. Mine. Mine.

On my knees like this with my nose just about level with her pussy, her scent pervades my very blood, driving me to the brink before I've touched her. I put my hands on her hips, then tug her closer, watching that she doesn't step in the hole that made her stumble before.

Her pupils are dilated as hell as she stares down at me, wordlessly capturing my cheek in her hand and stroking my skin with her thumb while she watches me pull her panties down. As soon as they drop to the ground, she steps out of them and reaches behind her back to unhook her bra. Then she lets that fall to the ground as well.

We're out in the open here, but I'm not worried about being discovered. Hardly anyone other than me ever comes out here, so we should be okay. Even if we aren't, even if the queen her-fucking-self walks out from behind one of those trees right now, I wouldn't stop.

Not with Maddison bare in front of me, her nipples pebbled and her chest heaving, her scent so strong that my head whirls with the headiness of it. Her pussy is only inches away from my face, her lips swollen and glistening.

Leaning forward, I band one arm around her hips to anchor her while I drag my other hand down, spreading her apart before running my tongue through her folds. She

CHAPTER TWENTY-ONE

keens, grabbing my hair as she bucks into my face, and her legs shake.

Suddenly realizing that she might fall if I don't let her down first, I offer her my hand and wait for her to lie down on the grass. Then I position myself between her legs and pick up where I left off. Maddie's taste, like her scent, is addictive. She's so sweet and warm that I can't get enough.

"Tai," she cries as her body tenses and she pulls at my hair again, hard. "Tai. Tai. Tai."

Chanting my name like a prayer, she comes as soon as I touch my thumb to her clit. Then she comes again when I push my fingers into her channel. My instincts are going crazy right now, filling me with an almost unstoppable urge to claim. Protect. Keep. I have no idea what's going on here, but she's clearly fucking sensitive today, and it's messing with my head.

As she rides out the orgasm, I lift my head to look at her face, her eyes screwed shut and her lips parted as she shakes underneath me. My balls draw up, and I know I'm in trouble. Undoing my pants with the hand not on her, I shove them and my underwear down. I'm so hard, my knot is already swollen.

Fuck, fuck, fuck. I'm so goddamn close. So close.

Her eyes are still closed, but it's like she knows. "Knot me, Tai. Please. Give me your knot."

The begging sends me barreling closer to the edge. My heart is pounding as I crawl over her, pressing the broad head of my cock against her entrance. "I can't, *ma trésor*. I want to, but I can't. If I do, I'll never be able to let you go."

Mainly because I've never knotted anyone before, always imagining I would wait for *the one* before I do. And I think she is *the one*, but I may not be able to keep her, and if I do this... *Fuck!*

I've never been so frustrated in my life. When I take her hands, holding them tight as I look into her eyes when I sink into her, I see the hurt in them as she looks back at me. *Hurt and maybe even a little bit of pain? But that makes no sense.*

She can't be in pain right now. Instead of breaking the moment to ask, I thrust into her as far as I can. She doesn't ask again, but she reaches between us to caress the knot I'm not giving her. It's fucking killing me, but as she rubs it ever so gently, pleasure unlike anything I've ever felt shoots through me.

My orgasm slams into me with the strength of a Boeing falling right on my head. I explode, coming like a goddamn geyser. When I'm spent, she's still spasming around me, her channel milking me for all I'm worth.

"Fuck, Maddison," I groan, closing my eyes and resting my ear against her racing heart. *How am I ever going to let her go?*

I mean, I didn't knot her, but it doesn't seem to have made a damn bit of difference. With her fingers in my hair and her eyes already closing, I doze off, only to be woken up what feels like a minute later by pouring fucking rain—and the sound of horse hooves thundering closer.

Wolf gallops around the corner atop Lady White, smirking at our state of undress as he rides up and Maddie stirs underneath me. I was planning on talking to her now, after, but he quickly dismounts his horse and helps her sit up.

"Would you like a ride back to the palace? I don't know

if you guys have been too busy to realize this, but it's really coming down out here."

She smiles at him. As I roll off her, he helps her up and smirks at me. "Wish I could take both of you, but I can't."

I nod, helping her find her clothes and watching as she puts them back on before she climbs on Lady White with him. Then they ride off, leaving me alone and frustrated in the pouring rain.

Fuck my life. I still don't know what happened there, but I almost completely lost control. She was so warm. And all that slick...and that pained look in her eyes.

It was almost like...almost like she was in heat. Or something close to it.

This is not good.

TWENTY-TWO

—

WOLF

WITH LADY WHITE'S hooves pounding the ground beneath us and Maddie once again tucked tight against me, her scent is so intense I'd have to be dead not to notice it. It seems to have grown even stronger, and it's been pretty damn strong since we met her.

As I adjust my grip to keep her from sliding off the saddle in the rain, a headache comes on. The possessiveness rising from deep within me is like a force of fucking nature. I'm more restless than usual, too. My heart slams against my ribs and I've got that dizziness that makes it feel like I'm coming down with a fever. Strangely, it feels like I'm going into a rut, so close to her that my thoughts are choppy.

It's probably just the flu. As much as it feels like a rut, it can't be. We're still dutifully taking the suppressants. The only thing that would render them useless is an Omega's heat. *If it's not the flu, it could also be the fact I haven't gotten laid as much as I usually do since the Trials started.*

Apart from the few times Tai, Kaz, and I have fooled

around and that one time with Maddie, I've been a good boy. Keeping it in my pants does *not* come naturally to me, but I have, which could also explain why I'm so fucking horny all the damn time.

As we come to a stop once we're under cover at the stables, Maddie turns to me. "Thank you. Are you going back for Tai now?"

I smirk. "Nah, he looked like he needed to cool down. Nothing like bucketing rain to clear the mind."

After I dismount, I help her off and Lady White nudges her side with her nose. Maddie starts, but I smile, running my hand through the horse's wiry mane. "She likes you."

"Does she?" Maddie asks, seemingly surprised before she suddenly rolls her eyes. "Not everything that rubs up against you likes you, you know."

"Well, in this case, that's not true. I was just rubbing up against you, and I like you."

Those green eyes dart back to mine as she runs a hand along Lady White's neck. "Do you?"

"I do."

"Is that why you came to find me?"

I shrug, but I don't give her a definitive answer. The truth is that as soon as I saw the storm approaching and I realized she and Tai weren't back yet, I nearly lost my shit. My protective instinct hasn't reared up like that in years. Perhaps not since I saw my little sister getting bullied by some asshole once.

Even then, it wasn't this strong.

But I don't say any of that.

None of us needs this to be any harder than it already is.

Maddie drops her arm away from Lady White and as

she turns, she spots Sergeant Pepper in the stall behind her and smiles. "Hello, you. Miss me?"

The Sergeant lowers his head over his stable door and I laugh. "He wants a scratch."

"From me?"

I nod. "Definitely."

Who wouldn't want your hands all over them?

She approaches him cautiously, but he's on his best behavior today. Storms have a tendency of unsettling these animals, but I'm right here. Since the Omegas have stopped randomly popping in, they've been a lot more comfortable.

"Wow." Maddie laughs when the Sergeant closes his eyes as she rubs between them. "I thought for sure that this guy hated me."

"Nah, he was just a little unsure way back at the beginning," I explain. "He's a lot like Kaz that way. He only threw you off because he was scared."

"You're comparing your packmate to a horse?"

"If the shoe fits," I joke. "On a more serious note, though, fear makes every creature on God's earth react differently than they ordinarily do. It's instinctive. Fight or flight."

She eyes the Sergeant's relaxed demeanor and eventually nods. "Yeah, I think I know what you mean. I also think I understand this guy a little better now. I was scared. He was scared. I knew even then that he didn't mean to hurt me, but it makes a lot more sense now."

Slowly walking up behind her, I reach around her side to offer him a sugar cube from my pocket. She giggles when she sees him gobble it up, then she turns to me. "Do you have another one?"

"Always." I dig one out and hand it to her, but before

she turns away again to feed it to him, her green eyes latch on mine. "How did you find us?"

From the corner of my eye, I see the Sergeant straining for the sugar in her hand. I trust the big guy, but to get to his sugar... Well, he's pretty determined. I know how he feels. *I wouldn't stop at much to get to the sugar I'm after right now, either. But first things first.*

"You better give him his treat while I explain," I say, and when she offers it to him on the flat of her palm like I did before, she giggles again when his whiskers tickle her.

The sound of her easy giggles brings *another* smile to my lips. I slide my hands into my pockets before I use them for something else. "To answer your question, I knew where you were because of our pack bond."

"Oh, right. I've heard of that. It's a similar concept to, like, twin-tuition, isn't it?"

"Sort of, but not really," I say, realizing that I'm about to get passionate, but our bond is one of my favorite things about being in a pack. It always has been. I've been told that I sound almost reverent when I talk about it, but that's because I genuinely do revere it. "Alphas can feel each other's emotions through our pack bond. It's like this invisible tether linking us to each other regardless of the distance between us. I love it."

"Isn't it...distracting?"

I shake my head. "It's only strong if our pack mate is feeling strongly, but it's dull otherwise. More of an awareness than an intrusive stab of emotion."

"Okay," she says slowly. "How did you know to look at the archery field, though? It's not like you can read each other's minds or see what the other is seeing, is it?"

"Nah, but that's the only place on the grounds that

CHAPTER TWENTY-TWO

bring true serenity to Tai," I reply. "Whenever I feel that sense of peace from him blanketing me, that's where he is."

"That sounds amazing," she says wistfully. "Can you always feel them, no matter what?"

When her cheeks pink, I laugh. "Yeah, pretty much, but don't worry. Even if we can feel it when the others are... doing something, we don't kiss and tell."

She sighs through her nostrils. "I wish someone had told me about that part of the bond earlier. Is that true, though? *Always*?"

"Not *always*, always. We can block our feelings from each other to stop them from being shared through the bond, but it doesn't always work. Sometimes, it only helps to dull it a bit." Like what Kaz has been doing to us recently.

"I mean, it must be weird at first though, right? To feel another Alpha's emotions like that?"

"It was, in a way. In other ways, it wasn't really. It was a little bit like coming home. You know, I've never been asked so many questions about this."

She shrugs as she flashes me a small smile. "I'm curious, and I haven't exactly known many Alphas to discuss it with."

"Do you really not have any Alphas in your pack?"

"No, we don't. We, um, don't even have a pack beyond family. I suppose my parents are sort of a pack unto themselves, and if they hadn't gotten pregnant with me so early, they might've grown their pack and I would've had more family, but as things stand, it's just us."

"Sort of like the queen and the king consort, huh?"

She frowns, but then nods. "I've never thought about it like that, but yes. I suppose it's exactly like them, except that my parents had Kevin as a little surprise years down the line, and Kaz remained an only child."

"Well, he has us, but I guess that's different. On the other hand, they *are* different. It's always been weird to me that they never took on additional packmates." I sigh. "Personally, I think it's because the queen was so upset about Tai's dad and Yua. She was so in love with him that when he chose a different pack, she shut herself off."

Fuck, did I really just say that? I mean, everyone knows I tend to say exactly what's on my mind, but I've never said *that*. Not even I randomly go around sharing theories about the royals.

"Do you really think so?" she asks. "I haven't met Her Majesty, but none of you talk about her like anyone would actually want to be part of her pack."

Right. I guess we're talking about this, then. "Well, you'd have to be willing to put up with a lot, but most people would for the kind of power she offers."

"Yeah, maybe."

Our gazes lock again. She's still so close to me that her scent draws me to her like a moth to an open flame. I lean in, but before I can kiss her, she shakes her head and takes a small step back. "We can't do anything here. It's the stables."

"You didn't have a problem with the archery field," I joke.

Her lips curve into a beautiful, shy smile. "That's different. There are always people coming or going from here, but I didn't see anyone when we were still on our way to the field. As soon as we left the palace behind, it was just us."

"There *have* been a lot of people coming and going," I say, but then an idea pops into my head, and I give her my

CHAPTER TWENTY-TWO

most mischievous grin. "Would you like to go somewhere, then? Somewhere not sanctioned for the Trials?"

She gives me a long look before she tugs her lower lip into her mouth and nods. "Yeah, why not? My time at the palace is coming to an end. I might as well see as much of it as I can."

We'll see about that. "Come on, this will make you feel better."

It's also going to make Kaz's head explode, but hey...he hasn't exactly been a team player these last couple of weeks anyway. Besides, I've been burning to spend some more time alone with Maddie for ages, and this is the one place that, guaranteed, we will have as much time alone as we want. No one will find us, and no one will think to look for us there.

In other words, it's fucking perfect—even if Kaz will kill me for taking her there.

TWENTY-THREE

—

MADDIE

"WHAT IS THIS PLACE?" I ask as Wolf and I stop on the covered porch of a house near the back of the grounds.

The garden around it is overgrown in places, and it's got a distinctly abandoned air to it, telling me that we're not dropping by to visit somebody. No lights are on inside, the drapes are closed, and even though it's raining, the porch we're on is covered in a thick layer of dust.

"The dowager house," Wolf says as he shakes the water out of his long hair. When he looks at me again, he must notice that I'm shivering because he suddenly starts for the door.

It may be spring, but I've been drenched for a while now, and it's not summer yet. There's a definite bite in the air today, but I've been too wrapped up in our conversation to think much about it until now. "Come on, let's get you inside before your teeth start chattering. Then I'll explain more." He grabs my hands and twists the door handle before pushing it open.

MADDIE

A soft creak sounds as it swings in. For a moment, I wonder if we're supposed to be here, but when he walks in like he owns the place and tugs me with him, I follow. He said this place wasn't sanctioned for the Trials, but he doesn't seem concerned about bringing me.

Mustiness clings to the air inside and most of the furniture has been covered by white cloth, but it's still a nice place. Dim light filters in from outside. Even though he doesn't switch on any of the lights, it's not so dark in here that it's as scary as it might be at nighttime.

The living areas are spacious, with high ceilings and intricate details carved into the wooden cornices. As in the palace, large fireplaces are in almost every room with elaborate mantelpieces and what appears to be expensive art on the walls. Abandoned or not, the place has certainly retained an elegant character.

"This is the dowager house?" I ask as Wolf leads me further in, heading for the living room and more specifically, the fireplace and the basket of kindling beside it.

He releases my hand and drops to his haunches, grabbing a few pieces of wood and packing them neatly before he turns to look up at me. "Yep. It's where the widowed parents of the king or queen would stay. Kaz's grandfather lived here until he passed almost a decade ago now. At the moment, it's kept nice for visitors, but it's rarely used, which is why everything is covered."

He pushes to his feet and strides to a small box on the mantel. After reaching in, he comes back with firelighters and a book of matches. While he gets the fire going, I cross my arms to keep warm as I look around.

Wolf was right when he said it was being kept nice. There was dust on the porch, but it's clean enough in here.

CHAPTER TWENTY-THREE

Maybe a little dusty, but not dirty. Thick rugs cover the floor in front of the fireplaces, and the carpets leading away from the living spaces aren't grimy.

Once he's got a few flames licking the stacked logs, he turns and takes my hand again. "I'll give you a tour while this gets going. It'll take a while before it's nice and toasty in here. Come to think of it, we should probably also get you out of those clothes."

"Wow. You're not even going to try to charm me out of them?" I tease lightly. "Are we really at that point in our relationship where you come right out and say I need to get naked?"

He smirks, humor flashing in those eyes as he rakes them over me from top to bottom. "I'd love for us to be at that point, but I don't mind putting in a little bit more work if we're not. That, however, was more of a practical suggestion than a real attempt at getting you naked."

"Since I can't feel my toes anymore, you won't get any arguments from me." I'm freaking freezing, so cold that I wince every time my soaked clothes touch a new part of me as I move, but I don't want to come across as being too needy. I'm the one who fell asleep in the rain. This is what I get for it. It's not Wolf's problem or his fault.

He seems to know how cold I am anyway, though. Leading me down a long corridor, he walks straight to a bathroom with a shower larger than the one in my chambers. After releasing my hand again, he steps into it and turns the faucet, then he glances at me over his shoulder. "Right. Get naked, then. That should warm up in a minute."

"Are you going to leave?"

He grins and cocks a hip against the counter, making a show of getting comfortable before he shakes his head. "I don't think I will. I just need to track down some towels, but I might join you once I have."

"You're joining me?"

"Perhaps. Some Omega fell asleep in the rain, and I heroically swept in to save her from pneumonia. Now I'm soaked to the bone and freezing my balls off. I know how good Tai is in bed, so I'm not saying I blame you, but there was a roof like, two meters away. Couldn't you just have fucked there?"

"You'd still have been soaked," I point out. "On account of the heroic rescue and all."

"Good point." He winks at me before he pushes away from the counter to bend over and rummage through the cabinets. "Or, if we weren't out in the elements, I might have joined you. Although, it looked like I might've been a little late to the party."

"How does that work?" I blurt out before I can stop myself. All the blood in my veins that hasn't frozen over shoots to my face and I groan. "Why does this keep happening to me?"

"What?" he asks, amusement heavy in his tone as he pulls out two towels and sets them down on the vanity.

"I've always had a talent for putting my foot in my mouth. It's like the clumsiness, so much a part of me that I can't get away from it, but it's so much worse around you lot."

"Oh, so we're the problem?" he teases before he shrugs out of his light jacket and grips the collar of his shirt.

The fabric sticks to him for a minute. As he tugs at it at the nape of his neck, it breaks free and rises to expose all those golden ridges and valleys I haven't had the pleasure of properly ogling before.

CHAPTER TWENTY-THREE

That night with him and Tai, I was too caught up by the time he got naked to pay enough attention, but now...my mouth dries up completely. Need blossoms through me, heating me right back up before I've even come close to the shower.

As I gaze at him, drinking in those washboard abs and the narrow V of his hips with the smattering of blond hair leading down from his belly button, slick gathers between my legs again. I almost moan out loud, but I manage to bite it back at the last moment.

I'd have expected him to have some ink on him, but he doesn't. Tai does, tattoos covering every inch of him that will be covered when he's in formal attire, but Wolf's skin is clear of any markings. It's curious that the easy-going playboy of the bunch doesn't have any ink, but I'm too busy enjoying everything on display to ask.

Wolf's eyelids grow heavy as he watches me looking at him, a flush rising on his cheeks as his lips part. The next thing I know, he's striding up to me, crowding me as he grips my sweater and smoothly pulls it off.

I barely have time to raise my arms before it hits the ground with a wet *thwack*. Piercing blue eyes locked on mine, he reaches around me to unhook my bra, his breathing speeding up as he pulls it free before dropping it, too.

"Is this okay?" he asks, his voice raspy.

I nod, finally breaking out of my trance to reach for the button of his jeans. None too gracefully, I manage to get them open and off without breaking his penis—and for me, that's a win considering how wet his clothes are.

As I remove his underwear, he kicks off his shoes and steps out of the puddle of garments around his feet before he gets me out of my pants in turn. My panties go next, and then his mouth is on mine, hungry and intentional as his tongue sweeps past my lips, devouring me like he's never tasted anything as delicious.

At the same time, he snakes an arm around my hips and hauls me closer so my stomach is pressed flat against his engorged cock. This time, I can't bite back my moan. It escapes into his mouth, and he swallows it with noises of pleasure coming from the back of his throat.

Without breaking the kiss, he walks us into the shower cubicle and positions me under the hot spray, waiting for me to warm up before he finally eases his grip. His kisses become more playful until they slow to a natural end.

As we break apart, he cups my face in a large palm and pulls away to look at me. "Your mouth is the best thing that's ever happened to me, even when it's got your foot in it."

"It can't be the best thing that has ever happened to you. What about your pack?"

"Okay, second-best thing," he agrees. "My life has been fucking grand, just so you know. It's just..."

Those eyes blaze into mine before he swallows and drops his forehead to mine, his hand on my cheek and his thumb stroking the soft skin right underneath my eye. "Wolf?"

"Yeah?"

"What are we doing? You, me, and Tai, I mean. I know we said we were having fun, but..."

He sighs, his forehead still on mine. "Yeah, I know what you mean, but I don't know the answer. All I know is that we want you."

"And I want you. So bad that it physically hurts."

CHAPTER TWENTY-THREE

"Now that, I can help you with." He smiles again, but it's a less carefree one this time. It even seems somewhat sad. "Warmed up?"

"All the way through."

"Okay. Let's get you to the fire. It should've taken by now." He wraps his fingers around mine and shuts off the water. Then he climbs out of the cubicle and wraps me up in a huge, only slightly musty towel.

While I dry off my body and my hair, he wraps his towel around his hips after drying off too. Then he takes my hand again and leads me back to the living room. Once we're there, I kind of expect things to become awkward, but they don't.

We're walking around naked, seemingly without a care in the world, but Wolf is so comfortable in his own skin that he makes me feel the same way. He guides me to the thick rug right in front of the fire. Then he kneels down and brings me with him, arranging me to straddle his lap. His hands travel into my wet hair, and he grips it hard as he brings my mouth to his, the kiss so searing and meaningful that it brings tears to my eyes.

Against my core, he's as hard as a brick and yet somehow, he keeps growing. My hips rock against his as instinct takes over. The need to be filled claws at my insides. He growls into my mouth, sounding so remarkably like the creature he's nicknamed for that it would've been comical if it wasn't so damn hot.

"Fuck, Maddie," he breathes as he lifts me in his strong arms and positions me right over the thick length of him. "You're going to have to tell me to stop if you want me to."

"Never," I murmur, rising up on my knees until I feel him nudging at my entrance.

MADDIE

As I slowly slide down, taking him inch, by glorious inch, we both moan, and our mouths crash back together. And that's when all the tenderness ends.

Wolf flips us over so I'm on my back and he's on top of me, pistoning into me like he'd die if anyone tries to stop him. His kisses are so hard they're almost bruising, but I love every minute of this.

It's so primal, so raw, that it makes me feel more wanted than I knew was possible. Slick leaks out of me onto the rug and down my thighs. Wolf's eyes go wide when he feels it against a different part of his skin. His lips pop open and he swipes his tongue across them before he grins down at me. "Look at you," he says, huskily. "So slick for me."

"Wolf," I mewl when he moves again, pumping in and out of me faster and harder.

His hands come back to my face, cupping it as he watches me hurtling toward the edge. "Fuck, I can't wait to feel you come on my cock, Mads. That's it," he croons as I tip my head back, feeling the build of my orgasm tight in my core. "I want to feel this pretty pussy clench. And then...I want to do it again," he thrusts hard. "And again." Thrust. "*And again.*" Thrust.

Given my lack of sexual experience, I've never come across someone with a mouth as dirty as his, but I love that, too. My muscles constrict around him as I come, and he groans, his lids shuttering for a moment before his eyes are blazing into mine again and I'm crying out, praying there's no one around for miles of this place to hear me.

"Do you have any idea how fucking incredible you feel? I'm serious, Maddie. I've never felt anything like this."

Nor have I, but I seem to have lost my ability to speak. Instead of responding verbally, I pull his mouth back down

CHAPTER TWENTY-THREE

to mine and crush my lips against his. Rapidly approaching another intense orgasm, I lift my hips to meet every one of his punishing thrusts, crying out when the new angle makes his swelling knot hit my clit in just the right way.

He's close now, too, I can sense it. See it in the heavy-liddedness of his eyes. Feel it in the swelling of his knot.

But it's still not enough. The climax is so close, I can taste it, but I can't quite seem to— "Give me your knot," I beg for the second time today, but I can't seem to help myself with them. Not anymore. "Knot me, Wolf. Please. I need it. *Please.*"

And like with my climax, his knot is so close that I can feel it, but what Tai denied me, Wolf gives willingly. Eagerly.

His lips part in surprise before he clenches his jaw tight, and I see in his eyes that he's made up his mind. Or that he's given in to his own vicious desire.

I scream as he thrusts all the way in, forcing his knot inside me with a feral curse on his lips.

There's pain at first, but it gives way to something else entirely as he settles inside. I cling to him as a new kind of euphoria overtakes me, an earth-shattering orgasm that makes my core tighten so hard I feel every pulse of his knot as he pours into me. The ecstasy drags me into its blissful depths, keeping me there for so long, I think I might've died and gone to heaven as broken breaths shudder in and out of my lungs and my whole body spasms.

It's my first knot ever, and there's definitely nothing like it. Nothing has *ever* felt this good. Until, like he promised, when I think it can't get any better, he reaches between us and strums my clit, rolling one orgasm into two, making me come again before I've even started recovering.

MADDIE

Pleasure breaks me to pieces. A sob tears through me as I hold him, wishing I never have to leave. As we come back down to earth, he and I seem to be in the same frame of mind. Wolf brushes my hair back and kisses the tip of my nose, but for once, those gorgeous blues are completely devoid of humor. "I shouldn't have done that. How am I ever going to let you go now, Mads?"

"I don't know," I whisper honestly, because I really don't. "Do you feel like we made a mistake? Tai held back. He said he wouldn't knot me."

"Tai's an idiot," Wolf says fiercely, looking at me like he's discovered the rarest gem on the planet. "Maybe it was a mistake for it to happen now, today, but I don't regret it."

"You'd rather regret the things you did than those you didn't?" I ask, and he smiles softly when he recognizes it as the same line I used that first time he and I got together.

He chuckles, and since he's still locked inside me, neither of us try to move as we keep talking. "Something like that, yes. Kaz likes you too, you know."

"I'm not so sure," I admit quietly. "He might like me all right, but he doesn't feel the same way about me you guys seem to."

Those blues are unguarded as they move from one of mine to the other. "Don't take this the wrong way, Maddie, but you have no idea what you're talking about. For Kaspian to have let you see as much of him as he has, it means he may feel even stronger for you than we do."

I frown. "That's not possible. He—"

"Doesn't show his emotions the way he does with you," Wolf insists before he lets out a shallow sigh. "I shouldn't tell you this, but we're going to be here for a while yet before this thing goes down, so we might as well get real."

CHAPTER TWENTY-THREE

I smile, but then I lower my chin in a nod. "Fine, then. Get real."

"Kaz was taught not to show emotion. It was hammered into him by the god-awful witch of a governess who used to do things to him that I think is tantamount to abuse. So trust me when I say that what he's shown you is huge for him."

My jaw slackens, and my heart breaks in my chest for the man who seems so strong and unwavering, or more accurately, for the boy he used to be. "What?"

Wolf nods, his gaze clouded over now as he looks into my eyes. "Yeah, it was awful. The queen knew the methods the woman was using, but she never intervened. Anyway, I've said too much already. Just know that Kaz cares about you. A lot. Don't ever think otherwise."

Tears sting the backs of my eyes. I know Wolf is only trying to reassure me, but his words have had the opposite effect. It's devastating to know that they care about me the same way I do about them. That they want me as much as I want them. And yet, it isn't meant to be.

We'll never be together, and the reality of that has never been anywhere near as painful as it is right now.

TWENTY-FOUR

—

TAI

WOLF and I stare at each other from across the bar in the rec room, bracing for the fit of rage coming our way. We can both feel the storm brewing deep inside Kaspian's being. Since we just had a little tête-à-tête, we're well aware of why he's as angry as he is.

When he storms in, he slams the door behind him. His fists are clenched at his side as he comes to stand in front of us, slack-jawed fury on his face as he stares us down. "What the fuck were you two thinking?"

"About?" Wolf asks, trying—and failing—to play it cool.

Kaz arches a sharp brow at him, lightning flashing in those onyx pools as he turns his gaze to our packmate. "You do not want to fuck with me right now, Von Damme. I just had my one-on-one with Maddie and we had a very interesting conversation."

"Yeah?" Wolf shrugs. "What about?"

"You know exactly what about!" he roars. "You told her about Madame Carpenter?"

Wolf has the decency to flinch. "Yeah, I'm sorry about

TAI

that. I was, uh, I was a little stuck inside her at the time, and it was kind of an honest moment."

Kaz stops breathing, his eyes growing to what appears to be the point of pain as he stares at Wolf. "You *knotted* her?"

At least he's not yelling anymore. On the other hand, the hushed tone is somehow worse. So much more dangerous.

Wolf looks him right in the eyes as he nods, not so much of a shred of remorse on his handsome features. "So what if I did? You're not the only member of this pack, Kaspian. I also took her to the dowager house to do it. I'm not sure if she told you that part."

"You fucked her, knotted her, in my grandfather's fucking house? Jesus, Wolf." He spins to me, breathing heavily as red streaks creep up from his neck to the bottom of his jaw. "What about you?"

I lift my hands to show him my palms. "I didn't knot her, but I wanted to."

"You fucking idiots," he mutters as he paces up and down before he grabs a bottle of whiskey and drinks down a good, long swallow. "We've been over this so many times. I warned you not to get attached to her."

"Well, it's too late," I say. "Just fight back against your mother, Kaz. It's not so hard. You love Maddie. We all do, so tell Mother Dearest that and threaten her with exposing how the whole thing is rigged if you have to."

Kaz refuses to answer one way or another, pacing up and down with his fists clenched and his chest still rising and falling fast. My temper flares and I jump off my stool, ready to make a fucking stand if I have to.

"We're not players in this game of yours, Kaspian. We have hearts. Minds. And we know what we want. We also know what *you* want. For once in your life, stop being a goddamn puppet and do something!"

"A goddamn puppet?" He seethes quietly, eyes flashing as he turns on me. "If that's what you think of me, then why are you still here?"

"Because I love you, but I won't stand by and watch you do this. I won't let the queen be the one pulling the strings in deciding the Omega we have to spend the rest of our lives with."

"This is what you signed up for," Kaz snaps. "You've known this was coming literally from the day you met me. You knew the Trials would be held in our generation and you knew what a political shitshow it would be."

"Yeah, but I didn't know the political shitshow would drop the best goddamn Omega in the world right in our laps."

"An Omega who shouldn't even have been here!" he explodes. "If you two weren't so busy getting your rocks off with her the other night after dinner, I'd have told you, but no. You've been so caught up in her that I haven't had the chance to tell you that she got in by *mistake*. She's not the Omega from Cambridge Academy who was supposed to have been selected, so while she's eligible in theory, she's not eligible in practice."

"I wouldn't have given a fuck even if she *cheated* her way in," I retort. "The point is that she *is* eligible and that she *was* selected, even if it was a mistake."

"You're really not going to back down from this?" Kaz breathes hard as his features tighten and his eyes narrow to slits. "We *cannot* have her, Taiyo. What part of that do you not understand?"

"No, Kaspian. *You* cannot have her," I say, then I turn on my heels and walk out with Wolf chasing close behind.

The door slams behind us. As we leave the pack quarters, I haven't heard it opening again so I know Kaz isn't rushing after us. Wolf catches up to me, passing a flask he must've grabbed while Kaz and I were arguing.

"Drink?" he offers.

I swipe it out of his hand and drain half of whatever the hell is in there, my heart still racing as we leave the palace and head out to the archery field by unspoken agreement. "Thank you."

"Looked like you needed it," he comments lightly before he pauses. "I can't even say that I didn't mean to knot her. I was caught up in the moment for sure, but I knew what I was doing when I did it."

"Yeah, I figured as much."

He sighs. "So, what do we do now? We're all in love with her. We all want her, and yet we'll have to choose another Omega."

My eyes slam shut as I force out words I never thought I would come close to saying. "*We* don't have to choose another Omega, Wolf. *He* does."

"What?"

I don't blame him for not getting what I'm saying. It's such a horrible prospect that I wouldn't have caught the insinuation either, so I spell it out for him. "We could break our pack bonds."

Wolf blinks hard, and his footsteps falter, but he doesn't stop walking. "I'm surprised you've thought about it, but I won't deny that the thought crossed my mind a time or two when I was with her the other day. I didn't think I would ever hear it from you."

CHAPTER TWENTY-FOUR

"Yeah, I know. I love Kaz. You know I do, but pack loyalty should come above all, you know?"

"I know. I also know Kaz hasn't been doing that recently. He hasn't been putting us above all."

"Still, breaking our bonds? Are we really talking about this?"

"Can you see yourself choosing another Omega?" he asks quietly. "Because I can't. I've already chosen and even considering someone else feels like...a fucking crime against my nature. I can't do it. I love Kaz too, but he needs to think this through."

I blow out a deep breath, agony slicing at my insides like I'm being flayed alive, but there's nothing for it. He's right. I've already chosen too, and if Kaz doesn't shape up and choose her, then Wolf and I may not have a choice.

"No, I can't see myself bonding with another Omega." I nearly choke on the words as I try to get them out. "If Kaz doesn't choose her, we might have to consider an alternative."

Wolf grunts, but I feel his pain mingling with my own, just as intense and just as fucking heartbreaking. "Guess you're more like your father than you thought, huh? You realize the whole world will detest her for this when word gets out, right? The Omega who broke up the Royal Pack. Can you imagine what they'll do to her?"

"No, but we wouldn't stick around to find out. It would kill her, and this isn't even her fault. She's not forcing us to do anything. In fact, she's the one who made the deal with Kaz to spy for him instead of asking him to keep her in the running."

"Yeah, but people will want someone to blame and it ain't going to be the future king."

TAI

"True that." I sigh. "Okay, so if it comes to this, we'll get her out before the news breaks. We'll go someplace else. Leave the country and go somewhere far away. Somewhere no one knows who we are and where they don't care enough about monarchies and royalty to find out."

"I mean, sure, we could try, but we're going to have to go pretty fucking far."

I nod. "Have you got your phone on you?"

He frowns. "Of course."

"Good. So do I." We've been walking so fast that we're breaking through the trees surrounding the field already. "Reception's not bad out here. Let's do some research, finish that flask, and then we can go find her?"

"Yeah, okay." Although he's agreeing with me, his voice is ragged. He's just as conflicted about this as I am.

But the thing is that we can't *not* choose her. To the two of us, Maddie already is our Omega and we'll do whatever it takes to keep her. To protect her. To love her.

Even if we have to break our own hearts to do it.

TWENTY-FIVE

—

MADDIE

TEARS BLUR my vision as I stand in front of the door leading to the pack quarters. My date with Kaz is over, but I feel like we just had an hour-long breakup. Even though all we did was talk about the other Omegas and Wolf and Tai, when he left, I could tell he was torn up.

Which tore me up even worse than I was before.

And that's why I'm here.

Kaz and I talked about everything *but* us. If today is the last time I'll get to speak to him, then I need to be honest. I was planning on telling him how I felt during our date, but things went a little sideways when he asked me point blank why he's been feeling like Wolf, Tai, and I are keeping secrets from him.

I told him everything that's happened between the three of us because we haven't been keeping secrets. I don't think Kaz realizes how deep our feelings toward each other have grown. He knew a lot of what I'd said, but I don't know if he's pieced it together because of their bond or if they straight-up told him.

MADDIE

Either way, the one thing I haven't done is the thing I've returned back here to do.

Just as I'm about to knock, the door jerks open. An incredibly pissed-off Kaz appears, apparently on his way out. He slams to a stop when he sees me standing there with my fist already raised.

His gorgeous face is all sharp edges right now, set in a scowl that makes it look like it's been permanently etched onto his features. His cheeks are flushed with obvious anger, and the veins in his neck bulge so much that he looks more like Wolf than he does himself.

"Maddie? What are you doing here?" His voice is harsh, like I'm the last person he wants to see right now.

Part of me wants to tuck tail and run. Especially because it's pretty damn obvious he's already in a real mood, but I can't back down. Not now.

After our date, I went back to my chambers and tried to put it all behind me, but I can't. This is too important. This is *everything*, and he needs to know it.

"I'm here to talk to you," I say eventually, bringing my gaze directly to his, although I'd rather be staring at hellfire than looking at the rage and hatred burning into me from those depths right now. "Could I have a few minutes? Please?"

A heavy breath falls out of him, but he nods and steps aside, waving me into their quarters. As I walk in, it's immediately clear the other two aren't here. There's an emptiness, a silence, that says only Kaz is home right now.

Since he mentioned on our date that they were hanging out here after, I frown. I kind of expected them to be here to back me up on this if they chose to do so, but it looks like I'm on my own.

CHAPTER TWENTY-FIVE

"We just talked for a whole fucking hour," he says, his voice not as smooth as I've become accustomed to hearing from him. There's a rough edge to it that could be either agony or rage. Or both, judging by that look on his face. "What else could you possibly have to say?"

"A lot." It takes some doing, but I manage to keep my tone even. I need to get my point across, not to piss him off more. "You like me."

His jaw grinds, the back of it ticking as he glares at me. "Okay. Is that a question? Because it didn't sound like one."

"No, it wasn't, but it's true. You like me and I like you."

Some of the fury evaporates from his eyes, and his shoulders slump incrementally as he shakes his head. "Is there a point to any of this?"

"Yes, there is." Swallowing every ounce of pride I've ever had, I walk up to him and take his hands in mine. "Choose me, Kaspian. I know it will be hard, and I know you've got better options, but choose me anyway. I'm strong enough to handle whatever gets slung my way, and I'll be more committed to you than anyone else ever will. Tai and Wolf want me, and I know you do too. Just choose me. Please? We can figure the rest out later."

For a moment, I seem to have rendered the Crown Prince speechless. His throat works, and he's blinking hard, but he doesn't say a word until he wrenches his hands out of mine and twists away from me. "I can't do that, Maddison. Life isn't about what we want. Or at least, my life isn't. Going after what I want is a childish notion I've long since learned not to bother with. My life is about duty and honor, and there is neither of those things in choosing you."

"Oh? Because I beg to differ." I don't reach for him again since he's made it crystal clear he doesn't want me touching

MADDIE

him, but he *will* hear me out. "What about your duty to your pack or your honor as Alpha? I realize you were talking about your Royal duty and honor, but we're not talking about asking the kingdom to choose me, Kaz. We're talking about *you*."

"That's why I can't choose you," he hisses as he glares at me over his shoulder, already walking away. "You don't even realize there is no difference. If I choose you, so does the kingdom. I can't separate myself from the royalty, Maddison. I *am* royal. I *am* the next king of the goddamn empire, and I need to act accordingly."

The tears that were stinging my eyes are back at full strength, but they're not only prickling the backs of my eyes now, they're streaming in hot rivulets down my cheeks. "So that's it, then? There's absolutely no way you're choosing me?"

"I've been clear about that since our very first date. I was honest with you. I warned you. And now it's all falling apart. My packmates..." He chokes, unable to continue, and I feel something inside me shrivel.

Oh no.

It wasn't my intention at all, but is it possible I've come between them? In fact, it suddenly occurs to me this is why he was so angry when I arrived, and this is why they're not here. They got into a fight.

Because of me.

The Royal freaking Pack with their super-strong bond is on the outs, *because of me*. A sob rises from the center of my being, but instead of sticking around when he's right that he has, in fact, been crystal fucking clear right from the very beginning, I spin around and run.

And I don't stop until I'm at the door that leads into the

CHAPTER TWENTY-FIVE

Omega wing. Pausing for a beat to collect myself, I swipe the tears from my face and vow that I can hold them in for just a few seconds. Just until I'm back in my room.

I cannot, under any circumstances, let them see me this way. The others can't know that I'm heartbroken. If they see me sobbing my insides out, they'll be stupid not to suspect that's exactly what I am. And if that happens, they'll expect me to go home.

But I won't be because I'm stuck in this hell of my own, personal making because I have to keep spying until the very end. Regardless of everything else, Kaz and I struck a bargain, and he's held up his end of it. Hell, he's gone above and beyond, and I need to put my personal feelings about him aside and do the same.

As I crack open the stairwell door, everything is quiet in the hall. Which isn't surprising, really. It's almost dinner time, and most of the remaining Omegas will be gathered in the dining hall already. They've taken to having drinks there together before our meals—though Antonio and I are never invited. *Gee, wonder why?*

Just as I'm tiptoeing past his chambers, I notice his door is already slightly ajar and I hear movement inside. I paste a fake smile on to greet him, but then my face falls when I see through the opening that he's not paying any attention to me. He's too busy sucking face with one of the few Alpha security staff members to have noticed me.

I stop in my tracks, knowing I should keep walking but I can't. *What is he doing?*

When they break apart, he glances out into the hall, clearly to check if the coast is clear. When he sees me gaping at them, his face turns ashen and he breathes my name. "Maddie."

MADDIE

"Yes, Maddie," I whisper back, then I point in the direction of the stairwell I just came from and glance at the Alpha. "That one's clear. Go quickly."

The Alpha nods, his expression stricken as he steals down the hall and turns from the door to take one last look at my friend. Antonio's jaw tightens, but he nods at his lover and takes my wrist in a gentle grip before stepping out of his chambers and shutting the door behind him.

I feel icky.

This is...wrong. Antonio is supposed to be trying to win over the Royal Pack. Not fucking the palace staff.

But how the hell can I judge?

I swallow, biting the inside of my cheek, trying to figure out how I feel.

Relieved Antonio isn't gunning after my pack?

Or pissed off that he would fuck someone else when he's their first choice to become their bonded Omega?

Both. It's definitely both. But it's enough of the former that I'm willing to calmly hear him out.

"We need to talk," he whispers harshly.

"Clearly," I agree, keeping my own voice low as we rush to my room. "What was wrong with doing it in your chambers, though?"

Heat creeps to his cheeks and he blows out a breath, but he only answers the questions once we're safely sealed in my chambers. "You don't want to go in there right now. It's a mess."

"A—" I cut myself off. "Oh. Right. Because you spent the afternoon having sex in there?"

He snorts, but there's a knowing look in his eyes as he turns the tables on me. "Yes, I have, but I'm not the only one

CHAPTER TWENTY-FIVE

keeping secrets around here, am I, Ms. *I-Regularly-Sneak-Off-With-Members-of-the-RP*?"

I blanch, every drop of blood draining from my face. "You know about that?"

"Of course, I fucking know about that. Who do you think has been covering for you at all the meals you've missed because you've been out with one of them on unsanctioned time?"

"I didn't think anyone would notice I wasn't there," I murmur as shock makes my legs feel shaky. Stumbling back, I sit down on my bed and bury my face in my hands. "Who noticed?"

"Uh, everyone?" he says, sounding considerably gentler now as the mattress dips when he sits down beside me. "There are only eight of us left, Mads. It's kind of obvious when someone isn't there, especially since everyone is on such high alert about who may be spending more time with the pack than others. Where were you yesterday? Wolf didn't show up for his date with Rachel and when you weren't at lunch..."

"Shit. I didn't know he was supposed to be on a date. We went to the dowager house. Do they know I was with him?"

I can't bring myself to look at him, so I don't know if he's shaking his head, but eventually, he says, "No, they don't know for sure. I told them you haven't been feeling very well, and at least that part's true."

I sigh. "What are we going to do?"

Finally, I lift my head as Antonio gives me a pleading look. "Please don't tell anyone about Francis, Maddie. I think...I mean, I know it's crazy, but I think I'm in love with

MADDIE

him. We're still figuring things out, but we want to be together."

"*I* won't tell anyone," I say, but then I shake my head when relief washes over his features. "*You* need to, though. At the very least, you need to tell the Royal Pack you have feelings for somebody else. If you don't, they might choose you and you can't let them do that if you don't want them."

"I can't, Maddie," he breathes like I've shocked the wind out of him and he can't speak. "They'll dismiss me, and—"

"Talk to them, Antonio," I urge gently. "They're good guys. They'll understand. If you don't tell them, I'm not sure I feel right about keeping this secret. Haven't your dates with them been good?"

"They've been fine," he sighs. "But they're all clearly distracted. Clearly not interested in anyone but, well, *you*."

My jaw clenches, and I fight the urge to drop my jaw, cry, smack him, and grin at the same time. I don't know how that's supposed to make me feel, but despite how I should feel, there's no mistaking the preen I feel inside.

Outside the door, we hear some of the other Omegas heading back to their chambers after dinner to get ready for knocks. Antonio looks down at his feet before looking back up at me with discomfort pinching the lines of his face.

"We all have our secrets, Maddie," he says before turning on his heel to leave. "I'll do the right thing. Just... just give me some time."

What I have with the RP is absolutely incredible, but it will be over soon. I hate that fact to the very center of my being, but it doesn't make it any less true. Especially not after the fight I had with Kaz earlier. Wolf and Tai might be rooting for my Selection, but ultimately they'll side with their packmate, and I don't blame them. How could I? I

CHAPTER TWENTY-FIVE

could never be the thing that broke them apart. I would never be able to live with myself.

They're pack, and a damn strong one at that. Me? I'm just a poor Omega with one hell of a story she'll never be able to tell.

TWENTY-SIX

—

TAI

SURPRISE FLASHES in Maddie's eyes when she opens her door and finds me waiting outside. She frowns, but darts a glance up and down the corridor before pulling me inside.

"We have *got* to stop meeting like this," she jokes, but then the humor drains from her eyes as she frowns at me. "But seriously, we need to stop this. Antonio already knows we've been sneaking around, and he may not be the only one. I overheard the other Omegas whispering about catching your scent down here the other day."

I take a step closer to her. "Danger is my middle name. What do you say, feel like being risky tonight?"

She chuckles. "Your middle name is William. But what did you have in mind?"

"I want to take you to my place."

Her chin lowers and her eyebrows rise, understanding taking root. "You want to take me to a pub to play poker?"

"Yep."

She hesitates for a moment, and she still seems wary,

but then she drags in a deep breath and nods. "At this point, why not? You only live once, right? Lead the way, Danger."

Laughing as I slide my arm around her shoulders, I lead her to the door, but I stop before I open it. "You should probably change."

Her eyes widen as they dart down and she realizes she's wearing her pajamas. Cheeks flushing that pretty shade of pink I've come to know and love, she nods again. "Yeah, that might be a good idea."

Slipping out from under my arm, she spins to wag a finger at me. "Wait right there. I'll be back."

She saunters away from me, and I swear she adds a little extra sway to her hips to taunt me, but I don't bite. I'm on a mission, and part of it is getting her to that pub.

After stopping at her wardrobe, she disappears into the bathroom. A minute later, she comes back out wearing a pale-pink sundress that would make even Kaz lose his shit. She hasn't bothered with makeup, and her hair is still pulled into a messy knot on top of her head, but she's so fucking gorgeous that I pull my phone out of my pocket and snap a quick picture.

"What was that?" she asks.

I shrug as I stash the device in my back pocket. "Nothing. Just checking something. And taking a picture."

Her eyes widen, but then she laughs and shakes her head. "Well, I suppose at least it'll last longer."

I don't respond to the statement as I open her door and check that there's no one out there before we sneak out. Hurrying along the corridor and down the stairs, I lead her to the pedestrian gate. Exhilaration rushes through me once we're out on the sidewalk.

CHAPTER TWENTY-SIX

"Our first escape together," I say as I capture her hand and hold it firmly in mine. "How does it feel?"

"To be off palace grounds with you? Amazing." She squeezes my hand, but then she looks around like she's searching for someone. "What if the paparazzi are hiding in the bushes?"

"They're not," I assure her. "There are guards stationed at the beginning and end of this block because it borders on the palace. Besides, if they've never caught me coming or going from here before, there's no reason they will be here tonight."

"Except that it's the Trials and everyone is super interested now that it's getting to the pointy end of the competition."

"Yeah, well, let them be interested. I'm not worried about anyone else tonight." As we walk into the pub, I signal the barkeep for two beers, but I don't stop at the counter to collect them.

When we walk into the back room, my buddies are already there. They do a double-take when she walks in with me, but no one comments on it. They simply deal us in, and since Kaz isn't here, I clean up again.

Only tonight, I don't give everyone the opportunity to earn back their winnings. If I lose the ultimate bet, I'll let them win it back next time, but not right now. Maddie turns out to be an average player, but it's only once the others have given up for the night that I reveal the true purpose for bringing her here.

"Poker is a lot like life, you know? You get what you get and you don't get upset. The stakes are always high, and if you don't call the bluff, you're going to get fucked."

"How profound," she teases lightly until she realizes there's something I'm not saying. "What is it?"

I rake all the cards in from around the table, shuffling the deck in my hands without looking, my eyes never leaving hers. "Draw a card."

She frowns, but plays along, carefully studying them as I fan them out face down. "Okay, this one."

Fingertips dragging the card away from the rest, she moves to flip it over but before she does, I put my hand over hers to stop her. "You made a deal with Kaz. Will you make one with me?"

Uncertainty creeps into those beautiful eyes, but she doesn't say no. "That depends on the deal."

Holding her gaze, I move my hand off hers and tap the card she still hasn't turned over. I know what I'm doing right now is the biggest gamble I've ever taken, but I need to do it. "If that's a low card, you get to keep my winnings from tonight. All of them. They're yours, free and clear. It's not that much, but it's something."

She turns it over in her head before her chin comes up a fraction of an inch. "What if it's a high card?"

Shit, please let this work out in my favor. I'm about to lay it all on the line here. I'm betting the house, and if I lose, I'm not quite sure what will happen, but it won't be good. I might lose Kaz and Maddie in one fell swoop. As it is, I may already have lost Kaz. I don't know for sure yet, but right now, I'm not playing his game. I'm playing my own, and I'm playing for keeps.

I'm playing for *her*.

In the only way I can stomach it: by leaving it to fate.

"If it's a high card, you agree to be my Omega. No matter what."

CHAPTER TWENTY-SIX

"Excuse me?" For a long minute, she doesn't move. She just sits there, staring at me like she can't quite comprehend what I'm saying.

Then her features knit together, her eyebrows mashing into one as she blows out a sharp, disbelieving breath through her nostrils and shoves her chair back. She shakes her head. Her eyes are narrowed to a squint as she glares at me once she's standing, a hand going to clutch her heart like I've physically wounded her. "Wow. I'm done. I can't believe you would...never mind, it doesn't matter. I'm out of here."

With that, she scoffs again and then turns on her heels, storming out while I'm still sitting there, confused as fuck about what just happened. Clearly, she's angry, but that's not exactly the reaction I was going for.

At worst, I expected her to turn me down, but now she's pissed at me. *Why?*

I feel like my head has been detached from my body as I try to figure it out, but when I realize she's not coming back, I shoot up off my chair, swipe the card off the table, and bolt after her. Regardless of why she reacted that way, she needs to know that I was serious.

She needs to know that I want her and that I brought her out tonight to ask her, away from the palace, if she'll be mine. Everything's gone to shit now, but I can't let her get away without making sure she understands I'm already hers.

We may not have bonded yet, but I feel like we have. Sort of. I don't really know what it's supposed to feel like with an Omega, but this, what we've got, is what I want. *Forever.*

When I catch up to her, she's rushing down the alley

behind the pub. She's almost made it back to the road. "Maddie! Wait!"

She stops moving, spinning around to face me with her index finger raised and trembling as she points it at me. "That was a cruel, cruel joke, Taiyo William Althorpe."

"Why the hell would you think it was a joke?"

"Isn't it?" she asks as I stride across the distance between us, her expression tight as she watches my approach. "Why would you tempt me with something like that if it's not a joke? When you know I won't be chosen?"

Slowly, the pieces start clicking into place in my head. "I'm turning the tables, Maddie. Maybe you won't be chosen, but right here, right now, I'm asking *you* to choose *me*. Me and Wolf, that is. I should probably be clear about that."

"What?" She stares at me with incredulity painted across her features, her lips parted and her eyebrows high. "Are you serious?"

"As a rut," I say, though I don't know why I didn't just go with heart attack. All I know is that I'm not thinking clearly right now. As I reach for her hands and take them in mine, I know this is what it's all come down to. This moment right here is make or break. I may not be thinking clearly, but I need to express myself more clearly than I ever have before. "If it turns out that way, will you choose me and Wolf? Regardless of titles, or royalty, or being bonded to the Royal Pack, or the Trials... Will you choose us?"

"How?" she breathes. "That's not possible."

"Well, it's possible, but it won't be pretty," I admit, my voice strangled as I close my eyes. "It would mean that we would break—"

"No," she says immediately. "You wouldn't do that to

CHAPTER TWENTY-SIX

Kaz. This is a joke, right? I was right earlier. It's a fucking joke."

I firm my grasp on her hands when she tries to yank them out of mine. "It's not a joke, Maddie. Neither of us want to do that to him, but we would do it for you. I need you more. Wolf needs you more. Kaz needs you more than he needs the monarchy too, but if he won't admit it, then that's his mistake to make."

"Tai..." she trails off, moisture shimmering in her eyes as she steps into me. "I can't let you do that. I can't let you break your bond to be with me."

"You won't have to let us do it. We just will. It's our bond to break, not yours. And again, I'm not saying it will come to that. All I'm asking is that *if* it does, will you choose us?"

"Yes," she whispers without hesitation. "Of course, I'll choose you. I'll always choose you. In this lifetime and in a hundred lifetimes to come, I will never *not* choose you, but what about Kaz? I can't take you away from him."

"Let's hope it doesn't come to that." I pull the card out of my pocket and hold it out to her. "Well, what is it?"

"It's a high card," she says, her eyes tearing. "It's...a queen."

The emotions that surge through me are the strangest I've ever felt, because on the one hand, it feels like my heart is shattering. On the other, it's never felt more whole. The sensations are so conflicting that I feel dizzy, but when my mouth descends to hers and she takes it, wrapping her arms around my neck and holding me close, I know I've done the right thing.

I bet the house and I won, but there's no telling if the outcome will be the same when I bet the palace. Because that's up next, but for now, I'm going to take my solace in the fact that no matter what happens, I'll have my Omega at my side and so will Wolf.

Maddie is *our* Omega now. Our queen, even if Her Royal Bitchiness might never see her the same way.

She kisses me like she's giving herself to me, deep and with so much love behind it that it's almost like she's suddenly become part of our pack and I can feel her emotions as acutely as I can feel theirs. I know it hasn't actually happened and she's not part of our pack, but there really is such true, pure love in her kiss that it feels like she's as much a part of me as they are.

I've been in this alley so many times that I walk us to a wall without having to open my eyes. Then I brace my arm around her to take most of the impact as we smack into it. She moans into my mouth, effortlessly lifting herself against me as I lower my hands to her thighs and pick her up.

Her soft curves mold to me, and I've never been more grateful for a dress than I am for hers right now. Either way, I would've made this happen, but the dress makes it significantly easier. It means I can get inside her that much faster.

Maddie reads my mind again, reaching between us to undo my pants and shoving them down far enough that my cock springs free. I'm already rock hard for her, but I always seem to be. It might've been a problem if she hadn't agreed to be mine.

Adjusting her so I'm at the right height, I wait until she's lined me up. I feel her move her panties to the side before I thrust into her, moaning as her hot, slick channel takes all of me like it's been waiting for me all night.

CHAPTER TWENTY-SIX

Maddie cries out, and I cover her mouth with my palm, pulling back to give her a warning look.

"I love hearing you, baby, but this is risky enough as it is."

She nods, then her lids slide closed as she arches her neck and drops her head against the rough wall of the building. The column of her elegant throat is right there, begging me to mark her, but I won't. *Not yet, anyway.*

Much faster than I'm proud of, my knot swells.

She bites into her lower lip, trying to rein in her moans as my thrusts pound her hips into the stone wall.

"Fuck it," I say, groaning loudly, no longer caring who hears us. Let the whole damn city hear. I want everyone to know that this Omega is *mine*. I want them to hear how good I can make her feel. How much she loves my cock inside her. "I want to hear you, *ma trésor*."

On command, she releases her lower lip and whines loudly, mewling as I roll my hips into her, working to hit the spots she likes. The ones that will have her melting like putty in my arms.

She whimpers against me as my knot swells big enough to rub against her slick clit. I feel her juices coating my balls, painting her thighs. She's so ready for it.

Her eyes beg me without words and I can sense she's too afraid to be refused again. She won't ask me to knot her, but tonight, she doesn't have to.

This is *my* Omega, and I'm done holding back.

Maddie seems to sense the exact moment I've made up my mind. Her eyes flick wide and her mouth opens in a little 'o.' I feel her thighs brace hard around my waist and her core tighten just as I widen my stance, pressing into the cobblestone ground to get the leverage I need to force my knot into her pussy.

She screams. A scream of pain and bliss and crumbling empires and the purest form of passion.

I swallow that scream with a kiss as her heat clenches around me, milking my seed into her. The pleasure is so fucking intense that my knees go weak and it takes everything inside of me to stay conscious and keep her held up against the wall. My breathing goes ragged. My eyes roll. My vision goes black around the edges.

"Tai," Maddie says on a breath, her fingers clenching into my shoulders. "Tai, are you okay?"

I let my head fall against her collar, breathing onto her chest as I ride out the waves of raw pleasure racking tremors from my muscles. "I'm more than okay," I manage after a minute, lifting my head just enough to plant a warm kiss on her collar, in the exact place I plan to mark her as mine forever. "I'm perfect. *You're* perfect."

It takes a while before I can safely set her down. When I do, I hand over the card and hold her to me as my knot slowly deflates. She holds it between us, considering every ink line in the white card.

When my knot is soft enough to slip out, I kiss her nose before tugging the handkerchief from my jacket pocket. She reaches for it, but I shake my head. "I clean up my own messes."

I kneel before her in the street, running my hands softly up the curves of her legs until I reach her pussy. I use the handkerchief to clean her as best as I can, her sweet scent driving me to another erection before I've even stood back up. I tuck the slick coated hankie back into my pocket.

CHAPTER TWENTY-SIX

She blushes, and hands me back the card, but I gently push it back. "Keep it."

"As a memento?"

"A reminder," I correct her, tucking a stray auburn hair behind her ear. "That you're mine."

She smiles, bringing the card to her heart and holding it there. She nods, but I can still see sadness in her eyes, and I know she may not agree to be mine and Wolf's forever. Not if it means us leaving Kaz behind.

TWENTY-SEVEN

—

MADDIE

SINCE THIS MAY BE my last opportunity to explore the grounds as someone with an actual semi-right to explore them, I walk around parts of the gardens I never have before, secretly hoping I run into Kaz out here. I need to apologize for the other night. I need him to know that I'll respect whatever he chooses.

I run the soft petals of a white rose between my fingers. They really are beautiful, and I almost can't believe that a few days from now, I'll never be able to roam in here freely again.

I'll be living at the cottage with my parents, but the commute to school and back will take up most of my free time. Even then, it's not like the gardener's kids can gallivant around the grounds like I have been so far. Kevin and I will have to stay out of sight of the palace, and it kills me that while the RP will be so close, they'll also be so far.

Unless I take Tai's offer.

The proposal he made last night has been on my mind ever since. I can't freaking stop thinking about it. It's so

MADDIE

tempting, but I just really don't know if I can take him up on it. If it was simply a matter of choosing them, then duh. It's already done.

But it's not that simple.

I can't allow them to break their pack bond for me, but Tai made it seem like they were going to do it regardless of whether I want them to or not. He made it sound like it *was* that simple. Like all I had to do was say yes, and then that would be done as well.

I know how much they love Kaz. Frankly, my feelings for him are just as strong as they are for the others, but he's not part of the package deal I'm being offered. If I take Tai up on it, it'll be me, him, and Wolf.

No Kaz.

Kaz would be alone. Kaz that gave my family a stable income. A *home*.

Kaz who got my mum medical attention even though it wasn't part of our deal.

Kaz who told me the first time I spoke to him that he wanted to bond for love. That he wanted to be with a good person, and not just the Omega who might give the best political advantage.

Kaz, who is willing to sacrifice all of his own desires for a position that will never truly fulfill him. Never truly give him what he really wants: a sense of home. Of love and respect.

And the thought of that makes me feel sick. Sick*er* than I have been feeling, anyway. *We can't do that to him, can we?*

A sudden shove at my back makes my knees hit the ground hard, and I start. I wasn't paying attention, but I didn't trip. Someone—

"Well, well, what do we have here?" a cold voice taunts

CHAPTER TWENTY-SEVEN

before Rachel, the American Omega who was bullying Antonio, walks into my field of vision. It's a fucking wonder she's even still here. I know the RP doesn't want her, which can only mean it's the queen who's pulling the strings there.

My knees are smarting, but I'm so used to this particular sensation that it doesn't bother me much.

As I start lifting myself off the ground, another pair of hands shoves me and I stay down this time, wondering how many of them are behind me. Before I can check, Rachel tuts her tongue and shakes her head at me, her expression cool as she folds her arms and looks me over like I'm a gnat she's about to crush with the heel of her expensive shoe.

"The question is *why* are you here, Maddison Darling?" she says, keeping her voice low, but there's no mistaking the malice in it. "You know, after you stuck up for that Spanish piece of shit, I asked Clara about you. She told me some pretty interesting things."

"I'm sure she has."

Shit. With everything that has happened since, I completely forgot this hyena had it out for me. "What did she say, Rachel? We're burning daylight here."

"For starters, she told me a little bit about your family, and you'll never believe what I found out."

I snort. "That I'm poor? Big whoop."

"No, not that." She gives her hand a dismissive wave. "I found out you're the new palace gardener's daughter."

My blood runs cold. I'm not ashamed of it, but I *am* afraid of the repercussions if this gets out. I was expecting it to happen, but not this soon. *What will happen to Kaz? To my dad? Are they going to fire him? Will the queen deny Kaz the throne for doing something nice for us? Fuck.*

MADDIE

Another voice, an unfamiliar, slightly accented one, speaks up from behind me. "We also know that you've been spending time with the RP outside of your assigned events."

When the female moves to stand next to Rachel, I recognize her vaguely as the Omega from one of the Scandinavian countries. *Sweden, maybe?*

I haven't spent any time with her since she's always sitting with Rachel at meals, so I don't know her name, but she's clearly not happy with me. Her pretty features are arranged into a tight scowl. "It's not fair, you bottom-feeder. Are you so desperate that you've been spreading your legs to get them to keep you here?"

"Slut-shaming? That's what you're going for here?" I sigh, but I try to stand up again now that the Omega who was behind me is standing next to her friend.

I straighten and bend over to brush the grass off my bare skin. *Big mistake*.

This time, both of them lunge at me, catching me off-guard and off-balance as they grab my arms and yank me forward. The ground rises up at my face fast and I yelp, but thankfully, I've learned how to handle this kind of situation, too.

I don't try to stop my fall, simply tucking in my knees and rolling into it. The impact isn't so bad. *I probably only have a few scrapes and bruises.*

"What the fuck is the meaning of this?" Kaz's voice booms suddenly, his tone crisp and furious.

"Prince Kaspian," Rachel squeaks. "It's not what you—"

"Actually, I don't care," Kaz barks, his tone so rough and dangerous it makes goosebumps rise on my arms. I try to keep my face hidden, the embarrassment on it no doubt turning it ugly tomato red. I clench my fists, carving half-

CHAPTER TWENTY-SEVEN

moons into my palms, praying for this to be over quickly so I can run back to my room and be alone.

"But, Kaspian," the other Omega attempts.

"It's His Royal Highness to you," he spits. "You're not fit to be here. Neither of you. You should be fucking ashamed of yourselves. Pack your bags and get off our grounds before I have you escorted out."

I freeze. *What? He can't dismiss them just like that, can he?*

There's protocol and procedure. And surely, he has to check with the queen.

"Your Highness," Rachel says imploringly, clearly trying to turn on the charm as a fake giggle escapes her. "It's not what you think. We were just having a little chat and then Maddie fell over. You know how she is. Always so clumsy."

She gives me a light kick with the toe of her shoe, speaking again through clenched teeth. "Isn't that right, Maddison?"

"Get away from her."

The two Omegas fall back a few steps as Kaz's sure steps approach.

I look up to find him towering over me, his posture rigid and his glare positively glacial. "I am not in the business of repeating myself. Didn't I say you were dismissed? I have no qualms about having the guards escort you out the main gates. I hear the paparazzi have been stationed there around the clock since the Trials started. I'm sure they'd love to know the reason you've been unceremoniously turned out. I'd be happy to share that information with them."

I gape at him, shaking my head to show him this isn't necessary, but the other two Omegas' protests fall on deaf ears. As he raises an arm to signal the guards, they shut up

MADDIE

and stalk off, and Kaspian drops down to gingerly gather me into his arms.

When I realize what he intends on doing, I frown and wiggle to get out of his grasp. "What are you doing? I'm fine. I can walk."

"I'd rather not take any chances," he murmurs, dark eyes on mine as he picks me up and carries me toward the palace, cradling me against his chest until his scent is everywhere and I can't escape the things it's doing to me. "Where does it hurt, Maddie?"

"I said I'm fine." I sigh, but I loop my arms around his neck and rest my head against his chest anyway, wanting to soak him in for as long as I can. At least until the palace looms above and I know we can't stay like this anymore. "Someone could see us. Just put me down."

He ignores me completely, simply continuing to stride up the path that leads to their wing. I *am* fine, but if he insists on carrying me, I'll take my last opportunity to breathe in his scent.

As the smooth bourbon, musk, and caramel wash over me, my throat constricts, and I suddenly feel tears coming on. Since I don't want him to know, I simply bury my head in his chest and breathe through the pain.

Kaspian carries me to his chambers and, to my surprise, sets me down gently on his bed as he goes to fetch a first-aid kit. "How are you going to treat bruises with that?"

He shrugs. "There are some scrapes too that need cleaning."

I glance down at my knees, seeing the crisscrossing pattern of tiny cuts on the skin there along with bits of grass and dirt clinging to me, but it's nothing I can't brush off and be on my merry way.

CHAPTER TWENTY-SEVEN

He sets to inspecting every cut, every nick. "I should have gotten rid of that bitch as soon as you told me what she was. This is my fault, Maddie. I'm so sorry."

"I'm fine, really. I'm always getting injured, especially around you guys. This is nothing to worry about."

My attempt at a joke falls flat. Kaz doesn't laugh. Doesn't even smile. He kneels in front of me and opens his kit, extracting a piece of gauze and some wound cleanser. Without saying a word, he wets the gauze before gently lifting my leg and dabbing my knees.

I suck in an involuntary breath as the burn of the cleanser sears into me. His eyes snap to mine. "Sorry," he whispers, wiping more gently.

I hold his dark gaze for a moment, seeing the concern etched into his regal features. "About the other day—"

"Yeah, I'm sorry about that," he says, cutting me off with a certain weariness in his tone I'm not sure I've heard from him before. "You caught me at a bad time. I shouldn't have said those things to you."

"I'm sorry, too. I didn't have any right to come at you that way. I just—I wanted to be honest, you know? I had a *seize the moment* thought stuck in my head, but it wasn't fair of me. You've been honest with me right from the start. I shouldn't have...well, anyway, I'm sorry."

He blows out a long breath, raking a hand through his rich black hair before he returns his attention to my knee and his face scrunches up in concentration. "I'll try to do this as fast as I can, yeah? Just hold still."

As he says it, he brings the gauze back to my skin and quickly swipes away the dirt before cleaning the scrapes. It's not so bad, but he acts like he's performing brain surgery, his attention squarely focused on my injuries, his movements swift and sure.

When he's done, he surprises me again by pressing a soft kiss to each knee before he looks up at me. "All patched up."

His gaze darkens. "Why would they do this? And so close to the end of the competition."

"Jealousy," I say immediately. "And they're just mean. They knew I've been spending time with you guys outside of our dates and they also found out that my father is a gardener here now. Honestly, I'm not surprised."

He pushes to his feet, and the mattress dips as he sits down beside me, his expression gentle as he looks deep into my eyes. "There is no shame in being the gardener's daughter. It's honest work, which is more than I can say about either of their parents."

"Isn't Rachel's dad a politician?"

He dips his chin in a nod. "Sure, but not one of the honest ones. He's power hungry, and he's not above breaking some rules to get what he wants. It seems the apple doesn't fall very far from the tree."

"What about the other girl?" I ask. "You dismissed her too, even if she was probably only doing Rachel's bidding."

"I doubt it," he says. "Besides, it doesn't matter. If she's that easily manipulated, she would've posed a danger to the pack if we bonded with her. Either way, anyone who treats another Omega that way isn't someone I want in our lives."

"Antonio isn't like that."

Even as I say it, I realize though he isn't mean, there is something he's hiding from them. Something big enough to mean that he will not be the one Kaz ultimately selects.

CHAPTER TWENTY-SEVEN

A soft smile tugs at the corners of his lips. "I know. Neither is Casey Sinclair."

My heart breaks into little pieces once again when I see the fondness on his features as he speaks about them. He's right about Casey, the Canadian Omega who's never mocked me about my mishaps in the dining hall or looked down at me even though she must've heard by now that I'm not exactly in the same social circles as the rest of them.

Since Antonio is in love with someone else, Casey is probably the best choice for the RP, but as much as I like her, it still hurts that it can't be me. Kaz sighs, and his expression changes as he keeps looking at me.

"There's just one problem with both of them," he says quietly. "They aren't you."

My throat closes up, and I blink back the sting of tears.

He sighs again, shutting his eyes before bringing his hands to my face and then opening them again.

His voice is watery when he speaks again and the sound of it cracks something open deep in my core. "No one will ever be you."

My hands move up to cover his on my cheeks. The moment between us stretches to eternity before finally, slowly, he leans forward and presses his lips to mine. The kiss is soft and sweet at first, but as my hands travel into his hair and his slide to the nape of my neck and the small of my back, it grows deeper. Harder.

Kaz's lips are just as soft and firm as I remember, his scent more caramel than bourbon and musk now. Without conscious thought, I pull him closer, scooting up until I'm pressed to him as I devour his mouth like he's already mine.

When an accidental whine slides out of me, he stiffens and abruptly breaks the kiss, his eyes blazing with determination as he gets up. "*Wait,*" he breathes, something churning behind his shifting eyes. He looks back at me for a moment, lips swollen and chest heaving. "Just...wait here. There's something I have to do. I'll be right back."

Our eyes remain locked for another beat, then he spins and strides out of his chambers like he's on a mission, leaving me alone in his bedroom, confused, turned-on, and wondering what the hell he's up to now.

TWENTY-EIGHT

—

KAZ

I STORM into my mother's office, not bothering to knock and not stopping until I'm right across the desk from her. She looks up, seemingly unsurprised by my intrusion. "Kaspian."

"I dismissed two of the Omegas. California and Sweden are gone."

She blinks, sitting up straighter before leaning back in her chair and giving me a disapproving look. "Rachel and Elsa both come from powerful families. They have good connections. You shouldn't have done that."

"They may have good connections, but they're not good people. They're nothing more than your average, garden-variety, mean-girl bullies." I seethe quietly. "But you knew that already, didn't you?"

Clearly hurt as my words hit home, she flinches, but before she can say anything in her defense, I hold up a hand because I'm not done yet. "Who we choose should be *our* decision, and if you want to run to the press about it, then do it. I can't stop you, but know you'll be doing yourself as much harm as you'll be doing to us. We're choosing Maddison Darling, Mother."

Since I'm not inclined to listen to the arguments she'll inevitably have, I spin on my heels and storm right back out again.

She's been pulling the strings for far too long and seeing Maddie hurt right in front of me made me realize the Trials have been a farce from the moment we laid eyes on her.

We've known all along that she's meant to be ours and that she belongs with us. Our choice was made as far back as the Scenting Ceremony, and I've been a fool to deny it. I'll regret it until the day I die that it took her getting hurt for me to pull my head out of my ass, but not even *I* have the power to turn back time.

At least I came to my senses before we did something we couldn't come back from. And I know she wasn't injured badly, but as soon as I realized what was going on, I saw red. Stuff I didn't know I had in me rose up and those fucking Omegas are lucky I didn't do worse than dismiss them. The way I was feeling at that moment, I'd have dragged them both to the guillotine personally by their goddamn hair.

Okay, so we don't have working guillotines anymore, but still.

As I slam her office door behind me, I smack into something solid.

"Kaz?" My dad's voice filters to my ears. When I blink out of my thoughts, I find him frowning at me, his hands on my shoulders to steady me.

For once, his eyes are clear, and I don't smell any alcohol on him. "Are you all right, Son?"

"Do you care?" I snarl, backing away from him and fully

CHAPTER TWENTY-EIGHT

intending on heading back to our quarters to find Maddie instead of wasting time talking to him.

"Of course, I care." The raw pain in his voice stops me. Turning to face him again, I'm taken aback by the depths of the hurt in his eyes. "You left the door open before."

I frown, my pulse pounding hard in my ears as I stare him down. "So what? I don't care if you heard, and I don't care if anyone else did either. Now, if you'll—"

"I never wanted any of this," he says suddenly, his face falling as he waves his hands around in the air. "The rules. The spotlight. *The royal life.*"

His shoulders slump as he shakes his head, and he jerks a thumb at the office I just emerged from. "I love her. I always have, but I wanted her without all of the pomp and pageantry that came along with her."

"You knew exactly who she was," I hiss. "If you didn't want her life, you shouldn't have burdened her with your poor decision-making for the rest of hers."

"I sacrificed my happiness for her. To live her life," he argues gently. "You're right. I did know who she was when I chose her, but I don't want you to make the same mistakes I did, Kaz. Don't sacrifice your own happiness for a life that wouldn't do the same for you. Fight back. Take it from me, you'll never be able to live with yourself if you don't at least try."

"Perhaps that's true, but I wouldn't go looking for solace at the bottom of a bottle or in another female's cunt."

His eyes flash with bright shock, but he doesn't deny it. Just because I've never spoken to him this way doesn't mean I'm wrong, and he knows it. "Kaspian, I—"

"Nothing you can say will negate what you've done," I

say, stepping forward to get in his face. "If you were so unhappy with the royal life, you could've severed your bond with her years ago. Don't pretend that you didn't have a choice."

"I might have choices and I've made a lot of wrong decisions, but neither of us really want to sever our bond. We do love each other, even if you don't believe it."

"If you love her, how do you not know how much you're hurting her? Why don't you care? She doesn't send you on all these overseas trips for nothing. She sends you away because having you here is too painful for her."

"You think I don't know that?" he asks mildly, blinking rapidly in surprise. "Of course, I know all that, Kaz. I feel every single little thing through our bond. Like right now, I feel her disappointment and I know she feels mine in return."

"You should be talking to her about all this, then," I respond coolly, finally breaking eye contact with him and getting back on track with my original plan to go back to my chambers.

My parents' relationship has been broken since I can remember and neither of them seem to care enough to fix it. I never knew my father felt the way he said he does, that he never wanted this life or the rules that come with it, but that's no excuse.

I may not agree with the way he's handled it, but he's right about one thing: I'll never be able to live with myself if I sacrifice my own happiness along with that of my pack. How this will play out, I don't know. It's probably not going to be pretty and I've no doubt that my mother will try to put a stop to us bonding with her, but with Tai, Wolf, and

CHAPTER TWENTY-EIGHT

Maddie in my corner, I'm certain we'll endure whatever she sends our way.

Shit, we'll do more than just endure it. Together, we're going to thrive. It's simply a matter of getting to that point.

And Tai's right. There are still so many things I can do without Mother's endorsement. Things I can do with my boots on the ground and my own influence. They may not move mountains or change laws, but they could still make a difference.

Before any of that, I have to let her know what I've done. My pack will know already or, at the very least, they'll suspect it. With what they're sure to be feeling from me through our bond, the confrontational determination and the intense relief, I'm sure they'll put two and two together.

As I walk back into my chambers, my heart nearly stops when I don't see Maddie. Her scent is still strong, but she's not—

"Kaz?" She steps out from around a bookshelf, smiling cautiously as she pads toward me on bare feet. "Are you okay? Where did you go?"

"I'm more than okay." I grab her hands and tug her into me, one arm banding in a steel-like vise around her waist while the other snakes up so I can capture her beautiful face in my palm. "I choose you, Maddie. I wish I could say it's going to be smooth sailing from here, but that's not fucking likely. I think I've just brought a storm down on us unlike any we've ever weathered, but I still choose you. If you'll have me, that is. If you'll have *us*, regardless of what we might face because of it."

A wealth of emotion passes behind those stunning green eyes. There's shock, surprise, disbelief, and finally, the same intense relief I've been feeling as she winds her arms around my neck and pulls my head down to whisper against my lips. "I'll always choose you, Kaspian Eaton. All of you. It doesn't matter what's coming our way. We'll face it together, and we *will* win."

"That's my Omega," I murmur before my mouth crashes down on hers, and I kiss her like the ship is going down. Which it very well might be.

The decision I just made might've altered the course of my future and all of theirs along with it. There's no way of telling until we know, but for now, I won't let worry hold me back. I finally have my Omega in my arms, in my bedroom, and I have a lot of lost time to make up for.

Picking her up, I carry her to my bed and lay her down before climbing up after her, grabbing the hem of her dress in my fists as I do. Our lips part for the fabric to pass between us after she helpfully raises her torso to let me get it off her. Once it's free, I toss it away.

My mouth finds hers again as soon as the dress is gone. Her kisses are hot and hungry, her lips so soft, and her taste so sweet that a growl tears out of me. My cock swells against my fly, and she moans when I grind into her, her hands immediately pushing between us to undo my slacks.

As soon as she's got the button undone, her fingers fumble on my zipper. I roll us over, reaching between us to shove the zipper down and pushing my pants and underwear off in one go. Lifting my shoulders as far as I can without dislodging her from my lap, I pull my shirt off over my head and look up at her, seeing her for the first time in just a bra and panties.

Beige, washed-out cotton has never looked so good. Soon, I'm going to deck her out in all the finest lingerie money can buy, but my packmates and I will need several

CHAPTER TWENTY-EIGHT

uninterrupted weeks with her before that can happen. Groaning as I notice the flushed skin of her chest and her nipples straining against the fabric, I run my hand up the smooth skin of her back, my fingertips brushing along every nub of her spine until I reach the metal clasp of her bra.

Deftly unhooking it, I pull it off while her hooded gaze remains on mine, her eyes dark with desire and the scent of her arousal so intense now that it's driving me mad. "Kaz," she breathes before she tucks her hair behind her ears and lowers herself down on me as I lie back. "Are you sure about this?"

"I've never been as certain about anything in my life," I reply soothingly, the need to assure her and eradicate that uncertainty in her eyes rising like a beast from deep within me. "You're ours, Maddie. You always have been. It's just taken me some time to come to terms with it."

"And you're mine." She runs her fingertips along my jaw before bringing her mouth back to mine and kissing me like she's making me a promise.

I take her nipples between my fingers and squeeze until she's squirming on top of me, her breathing ragged as slick leaks through the fabric of her panties and brands my length with the only scent I ever want on it. Growling into her mouth, I bunch the waistband of those bothersome panties between my fingers, tightening my grip until I feel the material starting to give.

"Kaz," she squeaks, clearly surprised, but then the flimsy elastic snaps and I pull it free, never more relieved that a garment has been worn so many times that it didn't take much doing to tear it off. "I didn't know that could happen in real life."

"Anything can happen if you want it bad enough." I run

my hand down to her ass, teasing the puckered hole before reaching past it and coating my fingers in her slick. "One day, we'll take that, too."

She breathes out, smiling against my lips as she nods. "I'm looking forward to it."

As she presses down in an attempt to slide my fingers into her, her folds are so warm around my shaft that I can't hold back. I don't want to. My knot is already swelling, and I want her to have it.

With my hands flexing on her hips, I lift her up and position her on top of me, groaning at the searing hot, drenched feel of her against my broad tip. She braces herself on my forearms, her fingers squeezing as her breathing falters when she lowers herself down.

Her lids shutter, her cheeks a gorgeous rosy pink as she moans when I thrust up into her, unable to wait any longer. I hold her hips, helping her stay above the rapidly swelling knot as she fucks herself on my cock until my arms shake with the need to knot her.

"I want your knot," she says, her breath hitching. "Please, Kaz, I need it."

Pain crosses her eyes, and I clench my jaw, nodding. "Take it, Maddie. It's yours."

She shudders, bearing down on me until my knot begins to push into her. She moans, a knot forming between her brows as she works to take it into her but struggles to get it past the tight circle of her entrance.

I grip her hips and her lips part in surprise and desire as I pull her down, thrusting up with my hips at the same time until my knot slips past her slippery folds and locks inside.

The air in my lungs leaving in a rush as I feel her constrict around me, her scent so potent in the air that I

CHAPTER TWENTY-EIGHT

could drown in it. Maddie's eyes shoot wide open as she gasps. "Kaz..."

"I know," I groan as I look into her eyes, my hips struggling to keep still as I give her time to adjust. "Fuck, I've never felt anything so—"

"Perfect," she finishes for me in a breathy groan.

My heart races as my balls tighten, and the urge to let go overwhelms me. Maddie whimpers, rolling her hips and moaning as her clit brushes across my pelvis. "That's it," I whisper, my grip on her hips tightening, helping to move her as she grinds against my pelvis, her core flexing and tightening against my cock and my knot as she rolls her hips.

Her movements become stuttered as she reaches her climax and it's the look in her eyes that gets me the second before she comes. I explode into her, shouting a curse as she calls my name, her fingernails digging into my chest through my shirt. Her channel constricts around me like an angry boa as I pour myself into her, my knot pulsing with aftershocks so strong they make my entire body come alive with pleasure.

She collapses down on my chest in the aftermath, her heart pounding as she peppers my throat with soft, loving kisses. "You knotted me."

She says it so incredulously that I almost laugh, but I hear in her voice what she's not saying. What she means.

You chose me.

"Yes." My heart is pounding just as hard as hers as my hand travels into her hair. I stroke the soft strands, kissing her temple while I wait for my breathing to return to normal.

Reality will come for us soon, but this moment means

everything to me, and I intend on making it last for as long as I possibly can before I'll have the fight of my life on my hands.

Because it *will* be a fight. A fight for our happiness. Our joy. Our future.

But it's one I won't give up on. Now that I have Maddie in my arms, I'm never letting her go again. No matter what, I've chosen her. My pack has chosen her. She is our Omega, and I'll spend the rest of my life making that clear to anyone who would dare challenge it. It's what I owe my packmates.

It's what I owe her.

It's what I owe myself.

TWENTY-NINE

—

MADDIE

ALTHOUGH THE RP have made it quite clear to me that I'm going to win this thing after all, the Trials have to continue. We need to go through the motions, even if it kills me to be separated from them for a minute at this point.

"Down to the final three," Mary clucks as she fits me for my outfit for the ball. "I'm so proud of you, Maddie."

Beside me in the parlor where the fittings are taking place, Antonio's chest puffs out as he tests the boundaries of his shirt. "I think this one is a bit small, but it won't matter. No one is going to be looking at me anyhow. Not with you two in attendance."

He glances at me in the mirror in front of us, winks, and then turns his attention to Casey. "I'm glad you're here with us. The others were vile, weren't they? Let's hope you caught the attention of a wonderful pack during this process."

My elbow shoots out and connects with his ribs. A whoosh of air comes out of him, but he smirks and shakes

MADDIE

his head as he brings his eyes back to mine. "What? I'm just saying."

Casey smiles kindly. "You look wonderful, Maddison. I love the emerald green, it really suits you."

"Thank you. Turquoise is definitely your color." I haven't spent much time with her, but she doesn't seem surprised or offended by Antonio's statement. She doesn't argue with it, either.

She nods at us and then climbs off the small dais she was on, waving at her lady-in-waiting to step back. "I think this fits beautifully. I'll see you two at the ball."

"See you there," Antonio says happily, turning to me as soon as she's out of earshot with her lady-in-waiting in tow.

Mary and Antonio's lady-in-waiting exchange a glance before they rise, excusing themselves to give us some privacy. Every member of the staff I've met here has been exceptionally good at sensing when people want to talk alone, and they bow out so discreetly that I'm a bit jealous of how gracefully and effortlessly they move.

Not a clumsy bone in any of them, I swear.

Meanwhile, Antonio is obviously more used to having such instinctive servants around him and he doesn't skip a beat once they're gone. "Why did you elbow me? You already know who they're choosing and so does everyone else."

Since I promised my Alphas I wouldn't confirm anything to anyone, I only smile instead of giving him the information he's fishing for. He sighs, but then he winks at me. "It's okay, Maddie. I'm perfectly happy with it. I'm bringing my own Alpha back to Barcelona, remember? Everything is working out as it should."

CHAPTER TWENTY-NINE

I nod, but I can't help the nerves bubbling deep down inside me. The RP has made their choice, but it's not official yet. *What's that saying? Oh! It's not over until the fat lady sings.*

In this case, the fat lady is a queen and although she's not fat and she certainly won't be singing, I wouldn't put it past her to make her opinion known some other way. The ball is the final test before an Omega is chosen, and there's time yet for her to make a move.

"What do you think will happen at the ball?" Antonio asks reflectively. "Do you think it's going to be much like the Scenting Ceremony? Us getting all dolled up only to be in the room for a couple of minutes? I hope not. This suit is snazzy."

I laugh, looking him over in his *snazzy* tuxedo before I shrug. "I don't know, but I doubt it. There are so few of us now, and it's a ball as opposed to a Scenting. We're being presented as the final three. Surely, we'll be in the room for longer than it took them to sniff us."

He chuckles. "Fair enough. I'm only there to cheer you on, anyway, so I guess it doesn't matter if they dismiss me a few minutes after we arrive. As long as I get to keep the tux, I'm happy. Francis is going to have a hard time keeping his hands off me in this."

"I'm sure he is." I giggle, but then the door opens again and a decidedly nervous-looking Mary comes rushing back in.

Her pretty features are knitted together, and she's fidgeting with her hands as she looks at me with something stricken in her gaze. My pulse skyrockets, but it gets even worse when she tells me what she came in to say. "The queen has requested an immediate audience with you,

MADDIE

Maddie. We better get you changed and fast. She doesn't like to be kept waiting."

Confusion races through me, making my very blood feel heavy in its wake, but I nod. Antonio leaves to let me change by myself, but before he goes, he sends me a thumbs-up and mouths, "Good luck."

I'm too nervous to do anything but give him another smile, and then Mary helps me out of the dress. For once, the older woman doesn't say anything, but she definitely seems worried. There's a haste to her movements that isn't usually there and although she manages just fine, her fingers aren't as sure and swift as she undoes the delicate buttons running along my spine.

She eyes the jeans-and-sweater ensemble I was wearing before the fitting, then she sighs almost mournfully as she shakes her head. "I wish we had time to rustle up something more appropriate, but the clock is ticking. If you're late, it won't matter what you're wearing."

I nod woodenly as I change into my clothes when she hands them over, then I follow her at a clipped pace to a wing of the palace I've never been in before. I can tell when we're in the queen's territory as soon as we enter what is mostly her domain.

The air itself seems thick with tension here, the servants stone-faced and the guards standing stock still. Everyone who's moving does so fast, racing by us without taking a second look at Mary or the Omega she's escorting.

"Remember to curtsy when Stuart opens the door. Address her as Your Majesty. Do not argue. Do not shrug. Don't even breathe too loud." Mary rushes through the instructions in a quiet, urgent tone. "Gosh, I wish I had time to prepare you for this. Just...don't go with your natural

CHAPTER TWENTY-NINE

instincts. Regardless of what she says, you nod and agree. With anything. And you curtsy again before you leave."

My brows sweep up, but I nod. I can't make any promises, but I understand what she's saying. When we arrive outside an ornately carved door with two guards stationed outside, my palms are sweaty and my skin feels strangely itchy, but I do what Mary said when the door swings open after one of the guards gives it a firm, short knock.

"Enter," a male voice says.

I'm met with a stocky man I haven't seen before, but this must be the Stuart Mary mentioned. I nod at him, curtsying like I was told to as soon as I clear the door. The thing is, I have no idea how to curtsy properly, so I simply bend my knees and position my feet like I've seen ballerinas do on TV.

The queen herself is sitting behind her desk, one eyebrow arching slightly as if she disapproves of my lame attempt at a curtsy, but she doesn't come right out and say it. Instead, she cuts a look at her secretary. "Leave us."

The man scurries out after giving her a quick bow, and my heart is in my throat once he's closed the door behind him. Queen Catherine the Sixth is every bit as intimidating in person as I thought she might be. Tall and statuesque with features as sharp and regal as her son's, she rises elegantly and purses her lips at me.

"Maddison Darling," she says, her tone crisp and her gaze assessing as she looks me up and down. "Sit. We have much to discuss."

We do? Since I was told not to question her, I move to the chair she inclines her head toward. Once I've managed to perch my ass at the edge of it without falling over or missing the chair in its entirety, she sits down herself and slowly looks me over again.

"How is your father enjoying his employment with the palace?"

I swallow past the dry patches in my throat and force a tight smile. "He loves it so far. Thank you, Your Majesty."

She regards me like she might an enemy she doesn't quite know what to make of just yet. "Your mother has Cervus."

My heart flips and my stomach knots. "Yes, Your Majesty."

Lowering her chin, she slides open a drawer and extracts some sheets of paper from it that she sets down on her desk and pushes across to me. "Those are airplane tickets to America for yourself and your family, as well as confirmation from the Woods clinic that she'll gain immediate access to their foremost clinic for the Cervus program there. She'll start receiving the treatment as soon as she arrives, and we've arranged inpatient care for her at the clinic. Yourself, your father, and your brother will stay in a rental we've secured on your behalf nearby. I'm sure you know how valuable this offer is."

My entire body goes ice cold as my heart and mind start racing. Her offer is more than just valuable, it's a lifeline unlike any other. My mother is already receiving the treatment, but at one of their clinics as an inpatient, they may even be able to get even better results. It's possible they could even send her Cervus into a permanent remission.

Technically, there is no *cure* for the disease itself, but the treatment has been so effective in some that it has stopped the progression of the disease completely as well as reversed a lot of the damage it's already caused.

CHAPTER TWENTY-NINE

What she's offering is a second chance for my mother, and I'd be a fool to refuse it. As I open my mouth to say yes, however, I hear her voice in my head, making me promise not to sacrifice my happiness for them.

I'm concerned about what you've given in return.

"If I accept your offer, what do you want from me?" I ask quietly, my voice barely above a whisper. "It doesn't come without strings attached, I imagine."

She nods curtly, lifting her fingertips off the papers I haven't taken and folding her hands gracefully on her desk.

"I know you've entered into something of a relationship with my son and his pack. All I ask is that you end things with them and go to America with your family. I'm sure you'd like to be with your mother when she receives this new drug they're using in the program. It's said to be more effective and more powerful than the treatments out-patients are receiving. We have also been able to arrange for your scholarship to be transferable. You can choose which Academy in the States you'd like to attend, and we'll see to it that you're enrolled. Finally, there will also be suitable employment waiting for your father near the clinic."

"You want me to quit the Trials and move to America to stay there with my family?"

"The plane leaves tonight." She glances at the papers. "Those tickets are for first-class travel and your mother could be admitted to the clinic as soon as tomorrow morning. It's up to you, Ms. Darling, but I trust you'll choose wisely."

I stare back at her, almost unable to believe she'd do all this for my family. Entry into a Woods clinic as an inpatient. Accommodation. First-class airfare...

She must really be desperate.

MADDIE

But so am I, and she's called my bluff. *As Tai would say...*

There's nothing I want more in the world than for my mother to be pain-free. For her to have the chance to see Kevin grow up. For her to be there to meet her eventual grandchildren.

The thought of leaving the Royal Pack behind is so painful that I have to hold back a scream when agony rips my soul apart, but my mother would be receiving the very best care out there if we go. We'd have a home. School. Work.

It's everything I ever would've been able to dream of, but... "I'm sorry, Your Majesty. Your offer is so incredibly generous, but I'm afraid I can't accept it."

My mother would never forgive me for turning down a chance at love. She'd rather die than feel responsible for me being torn away from my soulmates, and I know the guilt itself may well kill her before the disease ever could. Besides, I have to believe that if the queen could arrange this for my mother, then maybe my pack could, too, *without* her help.

The queen blinks in surprise, but then she shrugs it off, swipes the papers off her desk, and drops them in the trash. "Very well, Ms. Darling. I'll see you at the ball, then."

The words sound a little ominous, but it doesn't matter how she feels. The Alphas have made it clear to me where they stand, and nothing and no one can take that away from us. I push to my feet, dropping into another clumsy curtsy before I turn to leave, but as I do, she speaks again, halting me in my tracks.

"Kaspian, Wolfgang, and William may have feelings for you, Ms. Darling, but make no mistake that they've been

CHAPTER TWENTY-NINE

raised for a life of duty. They will not shirk it indefinitely. This is a phase, nothing more."

I glance at her over my shoulder. "His name is Taiyo, not William."

Her eyes flash with fury, and I realize this is probably the final nail in my coffin, but what is done is done. She was way out of line summoning me like this, and the fact she did means her attempts to sway the Royal Pack have failed.

This was her hail Mary, and it was unsuccessful. *Let her be angry. I'm pissed off too.*

I know she's the queen, and that frightens me because I realize she has more power in her little finger than I'll ever have, but screw her. It's not like I'm a terrorist who has threatened her reign. I'm also not an anti-monarchist who will stop at nothing to bring down her family.

I'm just an Omega who doesn't have any connections to bring to the table, but what I do have is more love for her son and his pack than anyone else will ever be able to offer them. It may not seem like much to her, but it is what it is, and what it is, is enough for them. And right now, that's all that matters—whether she likes it or not.

THIRTY

—

MADDIE

OUTSIDE IN THE HALL, Antonio, Casey, and I are waiting to be announced. The sounds of music and chatter drift to us from the ballroom. While it's so like that first night in many ways, it's also so different.

As I stare at myself in the same mirror as I did when my name was called for the Scenting, I'm not wobbling on my heels and my freckles are out in full force. Mary and I reached a compromise on my shoes, and while they're not the pumps I liked, they're also not skyscrapers.

They're modest kitten heels, broad and low enough to allow me not to feel like I'm teetering and high enough to make my ass look good—according to Antonio, anyway. He grins as he comes up behind me, putting his hands on my hips and resting his head on my shoulder.

"You're beautiful, Maddison," he says happily before he frowns. "Very flushed, but beautiful. Are you still experiencing those heat symptoms?"

I sigh, nodding at him in our reflections before he turns me abruptly to face him, his expression serious and more than a little scared. "Haven't you been taking my suppressants?"

"I have, but only half a tablet of yours a day and one and a half of mine."

"Why?" he asks urgently. "Yours clearly aren't working and—"

"And I didn't want to burn through your stash at the same rate that I've burned through mine," I say stubbornly. "I'm okay, I promise. I took a whole one of yours this morning just in case. Gotta give it time to kick in."

"Are you in any pain?"

I shrug, but he doesn't miss the wince that follows. My lower stomach has been aching since I woke up the morning after Kaz knotted me. There's a tightness there that doesn't seem to want to ease no matter how many warm peppermint teas I drink or how many cold showers I take. And the slick. Don't get me started on the slick. I've borrowed a few panty liners from Mary, who's promised to keep the request hushed until I can get my heat dialed back and under proper control.

"A little," I admit. "But I brought another one of your suppressants with me."

I pat my chest, where I've tucked the little pill into the boning of my emerald dress.

"Maybe you should take it," he suggests. "But what you really need is to go to a doctor, Maddie. Now. This isn't right. If the dates on your suppressants were good, then this should never have happened."

His gaze sweeps across my face and his nostrils flare as he breathes in deeply. "Every Alpha here will know if you're going into heat." He swallows, eyeing me up and down. "And I suspect you are."

CHAPTER THIRTY

"I'm not," I protest, playfully shoving him away and taking a step back to use the delicate fan Mary gave me as an accessory to cool myself down. "I'll be fine for the next couple of hours. I can't not attend the final event. Besides, I already scrubbed myself to death with scent blocker in the shower. Look, I'll even take the extra pill."

Before he can protest, I pull the little tablet out from where I've hidden it and swallow it dry, showing him my tongue afterward to prove I've done it. "There. I should be right as rain within the hour."

"So that's *three* suppressants today?" he asks, looking completely unimpressed as he shakes his head. "Maddie," he murmurs more gently, but then our names are called and I shove my discomfort aside as we line up behind Casey to make our entrance.

The truth is that my stomach hurts and my head aches dully. My heart rate has been out of control all day, but I took one of Antonio's suppressants just a few hours ago. So if the problem was mine I should be fine by now.

Unless it's too late, my mind whispers, but I shove the intrusive thought away.

It's not possible. It's got to be something else, and at this point, I'm quite sure it's stress. After my conversation with the queen, I haven't had the opportunity to see my Alphas yet, and I'm terrified they've changed their minds.

I asked Mary about them. She looked at me funny but then told me they're preparing for the ball and to welcome their Omega to their quarters afterward. There have also been a lot of preparations to be made for the days after they announce who they've chosen—there will be an actual fucking parade through the city streets, a charity concert, a day of volunteering together, and a whole host of other public appearances. In addition to all that, they've apparently been inundated by requests for interviews with the media.

None of which has done a thing to ease the anxiety swimming around deep within me. I'm quite sure that's all it is when a tremor passes through me as the doors open and we make our way into the ballroom.

"Maddison Darling." My name is announced as I enter behind Casey with Antonio bringing up the rear.

Thankfully, everything goes smoothly this time as I make my way to the Royal Pack, who are gathered on the same dais as before. I don't trip, don't stumble, and I keep smiling all the way through.

Tai embraces me first, his arms warm and loving as he pulls me into him. "Maddie, you're breathtaking."

Some of the knots of tension in my stomach dissolve when I hear the sharp breath he takes as he holds me. Clearly, nothing has changed. He's just as in love with me and my scent as he was before.

He passes me off to Wolf next, and those blue eyes are soft on mine as he takes my hand and makes me do a little twirl before spinning me right into his chest. "Damn, Maddie. Green's your color."

My heart skips at his words, but after he brushes a light kiss to my cheek, he puts my hand firmly in Kaz's. The prince stares at me like he's never seen me before, a gentle smile on his lips as those dark eyes rise at the corners.

"It's almost over," he promises.

He lets go of me after that, sending me to join Casey beside the dais as they greet Antonio. I can't help but notice that they're friendly with him, but not overly warm. It was the same with Casey. They were kind to her, but

CHAPTER THIRTY

none of them look at her or Antonio the way they do at me.

Casey smiles when she sees me staring at them and I think she knows it, too, and I don't think she's upset about it, either. I'm grateful. The last thing I want to do is fill my heart at the expense of breaking another.

Once Antonio has descended from the dais, the music starts back up again. With the formalities done, the ball is underway. We were told earlier that we're supposed to mingle and prove that we can hold our own among some of the most influential people in the country, but Wolf catches my wrist before I can think about who to approach first.

He smiles as he spins me into him again and leads me out to the dance floor, those blues alive with laughter and joy as he circles his arms around my waist. "Where have you been, love? It feels like it's been forever."

"A day or two at most," I tease. "I've been here, though. The real question is where have you been?"

He lets out a dramatic sigh. "Stuck in meetings, studios, and interviews, I'm afraid. There are only so many exclusives to be given without giving too much away, but Lord knows, the vultures sure tried."

"Tired of all the attention already? I know you don't love the spotlight, but I'd have thought you enjoyed being so in demand."

His head dips back as he laughs, pearly whites on display before he drops his chin to look at me again. "I've always liked being in demand, but these days, I suppose I'm pickier about who I'd like to have making the demands. Here's a secret for you, it's not the press."

"It's not?" I joke, feigning surprise. "Who would you have preferred to be spending time with, then?"

MADDIE

He waggles his eyebrows at me. "Oh, you know. My pack. My parents. Some friends. Perhaps the Omega we've chosen."

"Perhaps?"

He laughs, bringing his head closer to mine, his lips moving against my temple as he responds. "No, not perhaps. I'd definitely have preferred to spend the time with you. Unfortunately, these interviews have been set up months before the Trials even started. As much as we've hated being kept so busy, we had to fulfill our responsibilities to the media and the palace. We'll need as many people as we can get on our side soon."

"Fair enough," I agree, thinking back to my argument with Kaz. We might've put it behind us, but that doesn't invalidate the points he made that night and before, nor does it mean we're not facing those storms he mentioned. "How did it go, then? Did you get them on our side?"

He shrugs. "Hopefully."

When his gaze catches on something behind me, his chest expands on a big breath and he pulls me even closer, his voice low against my ear. "I need to go, but I'll see you soon, okay?"

"Okay." After pressing a brief, light kiss to my cheek, he releases me and strides off toward an imposing man who's speaking to the king consort.

I'm only alone for a few seconds when another hand closes around mine. As soon as I take my next breath, the scent of bergamot and nettles settles over me and I smile. "Taiyo," I murmur while he's still turning me to face him. "I heard you guys have been knee-deep in interviews."

He blows out a frustrated breath, those warm brown eyes flickering with annoyance until it melts away when his gaze meets mine. "The press has been a bother, but it's all part of it. Besides, it'll be over soon and then we can go back to only making appearances in the news or on silly talk shows on occasion."

"Have you spoken to Kaz?"

This brings a warm smile to his face. "We have. He's torn up, but he seems certain in his choice. I still can't really believe it."

I smile sadly.

He slides a finger under my chin and smiles when I lift my eyes back to his. "That doesn't mean it won't work out. There's nothing to worry about, okay?"

"So you keep saying," I murmur, holding him tight and playing with the long hair on top of his head as we sway together, using the opportunity more as an excuse to hold each other than actually dancing. "I'm just paranoid, I'm sure."

He tightens his grip on me. "It's natural to be scared, Maddison, but you need to trust us."

"I do trust you." I close my eyes, breathing in his comforting, warm scent as I gently drag my nails along his scalp. "It's just not nice being separated for so long, is all. It hurts."

Physically hurts, but I don't say that. They're doing their best, and it's not going to do anyone any favors if they know I feel this strange, painful discomfort when we're apart. Okay, so I've been feeling it anyway, but it's better when I'm with them. Being held by them. I've been trying to find comfort in their scents when we're apart, but as much as I've made a *not-nest* with the items I've *borrowed* from them, it's not the same when they're not with me.

I don't care what anyone says. The shrine I've built to

them in my chambers is *not* a nest. I'm *not* going into heat. I've been taking my suppressants religiously and although they're definitely not working like they should be, this is just stress. Uncertainty.

It's simply a matter of being in love for the first time under such very unusual, very stressful circumstances. *That's my story and I'm sticking to it.*

"We're not enjoying the separation either," Tai murmurs before he sighs. "Soon, though, we won't ever have to endure it again. For now, however, I need to go have a quick chat with my mother. She keeps trying to grab my attention. See you soon?"

"Very soon," I say hopefully, and then I watch as the crowd swallows him as he walks away from me.

Yua smiles when she sees me looking at them, but there's something tense about the set of her jaw and shoulders. As soon as he reaches her, she bends her head to his and starts talking, leading him away until I can't see them anymore.

Kaz is dancing with Casey, but when he sees me standing in the middle of the dance floor by myself, he releases her immediately and strides over to me, wordlessly offering me his hand. I take it, drinking in those glittering black eyes as he keeps his gaze on mine while we dance.

He doesn't say anything at first, but somehow, his silence speaks volumes as he guides me across the floor with sure, commanding movements that make me feel more graceful than I ever have before. Eventually, he wraps a tender arm around my waist and cradles me against him. "Are you all right, Maddison? You're somehow flushed and pale at the same time."

CHAPTER THIRTY

"I'm just nervous," I admit quietly. "I haven't seen much of you for the last couple days."

"It was unavoidable," he says, but there's an undercurrent of something disconcerting in his voice. "I can't be seen dancing with you any longer than I have with Antonio and Casey. We need to keep up appearances until the final announcement is made."

"Of course," I murmur, but his words stir up the uncertainty that's been swirling in my belly all along. "You haven't changed your mind, have you?"

"No, Maddie. I haven't, but it's more complicated than you think," he says as he spins me out and then dips into a bow. "This is where I leave you for now, love. Try to have some fun tonight and don't worry about leaving a shoe behind when the clock strikes twelve. We'll find you later anyway."

He winks quickly, and then he's gone, but Antonio saves me from once again standing all alone in the center of the dance floor. "You look like you could use a drink, girlfriend. Let's go to the bar. I could sure do with another glass of that fancy wine before it's all over."

Forcing down the fear that's threatening to choke me, I smile and take his arm. "Yeah, so could I. It's been a hell of a night, hasn't it?"

"I'd imagine it has been for you. A romantic moment with every member of the RP in front of all these cameras must be rather intimidating. We'd better get you an extra big glass of wine."

I blink, noticing all the cameras for the first time as I look around. I'm not sure how I missed them before, but I've been so focused on my Alphas—and on not making a fool of myself—since I walked in here that I really haven't been paying much attention.

"It has been a bit of a whirlwind," I agree. "To be fair, it wasn't so much a romantic moment with each of them as it was a minute to catch up."

"It looked romantic to me," he says, smirking before his face suddenly drops and his eyes go wide just as we reach the bar. "Don't look now, but the queen and the king consort are coming our way."

My eyes go round, but when I peer over my shoulder, I realize he's right. They're not only coming our way, they're walking directly to us.

When they stop only a few feet away, the king smiles kindly but the queen's lips purse again as she looks me over. I think it must be her default when she sees me, the disapproving, royal lip-purse. "Maddison," she says coldly. "It's incredible how a well-designed dress can make a pauper look like a princess, isn't it?"

I blink, my retort dying on my lips when I remember how many cameras are in this ballroom right now. Any kind of exchange with her will almost certainly draw the attention of at least one cameraman. Although I'm sure someone has already caught this on film, I absolutely cannot risk a confrontation.

The king, however, rolls his eyes and pats her hand almost patronizingly. "Knock it off, Catherine. The Omega hasn't done anything wrong."

With that, he inclines his head at me, smiles again, and then drags his stunned wife away while I'm so shocked, I can't move for a moment. Antonio, on the other hand, does a gleeful little dance as he squeals softly once they're gone. "That was epic. I can't believe I just heard the king tell the

CHAPTER THIRTY

queen to *knock it off*. You've really not kept a low profile at all, have you?"

"Unfortunately not," I say, my voice breathy as shock reverberates through me. "I'm not sure *epic* is quite the word I'd use to describe that, though."

Whether he meant to or not, I'm pretty sure the king just signed my death warrant. Or at the very least, the death warrant of my hopes of a relationship with the RP. I need to talk to them. They need to know about this. Something isn't right. I didn't like the way she was looking at me.

Like she already won.

Urgency simmers in my gut as I look around, but I don't see them anywhere. None of them are where they were before. The king clearly isn't talking to the man he was speaking to anymore, and Wolf was with them last I saw.

Yua has appeared back where she was before she led Tai away, but he's nowhere to be found. As for Kaz? Well, he's vanished into thin air as well.

"Excuse me," I mutter to Antonio as I take off to find them. I don't know how I know, but I need to find them right away.

I really needed that drink to cool off, but to hell with it. This is more important. It's so important that it makes my stomach hurt even worse than before when I imagine what the queen might do if she gets to them before I do. If she makes some kind of announcement of her own or does something else designed to keep us apart.

I don't know if they know what she offered me before, but I have a feeling that woman knows how to put a spin on every conversation. After her husband chastised her in the presence of two Omegas, I have no doubt she'll want to take vengeance on me.

MADDIE

As I rush out of the ballroom, it feels like a small gremlin with a pickaxe has taken up residence in my brain and is slowly chipping away at my scalp. Strangely, my muscles are aching, but that might be because I'm so tense, and I'm suddenly incredibly cold.

It must be the shock. It has to be shock. Or fear. It's not fever. It's not allowed to be fever.

Regardless, I hurry down the hall toward the pack quarters. I don't know if they're there, but their scents are strong in the air as I make my way down the corridor leading to their place. When the faint sound of Kaz's voice reaches my ears, relief sweeps through me until I process the words he's saying.

"She's nothing. A worthless, poor Omega with no power and no connections that we'll tire of eventually, but by then, the mistake will have been made and we'll have bonded with her."

For a moment, my lungs seize. I feel like I'm about to faint. My head swims and I blink, but I'm still swaying on my feet and I can't quite think.

Get away from here, Maddison. Get out. Right now.

I have no idea what changed his mind, but it seems like my paranoia was for good reason. I knew all along that this was too good to be true, and I was right.

Spinning around, I run as fast as my feet can carry me, needing to get outside. Get some air. Get to my parents. Just...something.

But as I reach the corridor leading back to the ballroom, the queen steps out. Though she seems surprised to see me, she smiles as her gaze rakes over whatever expression is on my face. "I tried to warn you, Omega."

"I'm leaving," I choke out, fighting back tears as I back

CHAPTER THIRTY

away from her like a cornered animal. "You won't see me again."

"Farewell, Maddison Darling," is the final thing I hear as I take off down yet another corridor and find myself near the Omega wing, but maybe that's a good thing. Maybe it's fate.

At least I'll be able to gather my meager possessions before I go. They might not be much, but they're mine, and apparently, they're also the only things that ever really will be.

THIRTY-ONE

KAZ

AS I LOOK at my packmates, my jaw is clenched so tight that my teeth may just crack. "Okay, so we're all still on the same page, right?"

"Yes," Wolf says without hesitation, his voice low as his eyes dart from side to side to make sure we're still alone. "We'll choose Maddie at the Final Ceremony, but I think you were right about what you said before."

"Which part?" Tai asks quietly, also looking around. We're all on high alert for this impromptu meeting, even if talking about this outside of our quarters is risky, I needed to check with them before I did what I'm going to do when we go back into the ballroom and we don't have time to go all the way back to our chambers right now.

Wolf gives me a knowing look. "You were going to do it anyway, weren't you?"

Tai sighs. "Oh, that. I've been thinking about it too, and I agree. Whispering in a few ears may not be the worst idea."

"That's exactly what I was going to say," Wolf says. "I

know I wasn't a fan of the idea of leaking it before, but something is making Maddie uneasy. I wasn't the only one who felt it earlier. We can't make it official before it becomes official, but it might be nice if she wakes up tomorrow morning to the news that the whole world is talking about a rumor that we've chosen her."

I nod. "That's why I pulled you out of there. I was planning on going back in there and giving a couple of journalists a few strong hints, but I wanted to talk to you first to make sure you're still good with us choosing her. Push is coming to shove, gentlemen. If anyone has any doubts whatsoever, now is the time to speak up."

Tai scoffs. "I haven't had any doubt for weeks now. Hell, Wolf and I were going to break our bond and leave for her if you hadn't come around."

Pain ripples through me again at the reminder of what I might have lost if I hadn't decided to follow my instincts when I did. After I knotted Maddie that day and she left, I went to find Wolf and Tai. They were waiting for me in the rec room to ask what was going on. After I told them I had chosen her, they were even *more* relieved than I thought they would be.

A whiskey or two later they revealed their plan to me. I was so shocked that I'd have toppled right over if someone had so much as brought a feather anywhere near me. Frankly, I still am, but it also only served to reaffirm my belief that she *is* the one for us.

I know they wouldn't have made a plan like that lightly, and honestly, I'm glad I saw reason before they had to follow through. Nothing would've been worth anything without them and Maddie by my side—not even the goddamn throne.

CHAPTER THIRTY-ONE

"Okay," I say as determination surges through me. "We need to be careful who we choose to drop these hints to, though. My mother will try to stop us from officially choosing her, and I wouldn't be surprised if she's already whispered a few things in a few ears herself."

"What is her *problem*?" Tai asks, beyond frustrated as his eyes narrow and his spine goes ramrod straight. "This is our choice and it always has been. Why can't she just fucking let us make it?"

"Because according to her, she's nothing. A worthless, poor Omega with no power and no connections that we'll tire of eventually, but by then, the mistake will have been made and we'll have bonded with her."

A soft noise from around the corner makes us all stiffen and we exchange a horrified look. If the wrong person has overheard this conversation, we may need a new plan—and if that wrong person was Stuart, then we may need to go back into that ballroom and make the announcement right now.

At first, none of us move, all of us tense, and I don't think any of us are breathing, but then Wolf recovers. He gives me a look to warn me to stay put, then he goes to investigate, but he's back a second later, shrugging as he jerks his head back.

"There's no one there," he says, but he seems uneasy himself all of a sudden. "Let's get back to the ball and check on her before we start spreading rumors."

As one, we nod and head back to the ballroom, but Maddie's not there. Panic rises within me the longer we look without finding any trace of her. When I finally catch a glimpse of the back of Antonio's head, relief surges through me until I realize she's not with him.

She was with him before, though. I saw him approach her as I went to round up my packmates. *Fuck. Something's wrong here.*

Antonio's eyes widen when he sees me making a beeline for him, but then he steps around the Alpha servant he was looking mighty comfortable with and the guy takes off. "Kaz? What's wrong?"

"Where's Maddie?" I ask urgently. "Where did she go?"

"I, uh, I don't know," he says, but then he shifts on his feet and his gaze hits the ground. *He's lying. Motherfucker.*

"What is it, Antonio? Now, please. I don't have time to drag it out of you."

He looks up again, and he seems uncertain, but then he sighs and shrugs. "Well, you know how she's been showing symptoms of heat?"

"Of course."

"Well, I, uh, I told her earlier that she needs to see a doctor, but she said she was fine and that it was the stress. After that conversation with your parents though, she might've decided to go see the doc after all. She wasn't looking so good, you know?"

"What conversation with my parents?" I hiss as my eyes narrow. "And why didn't you tell us sooner if you suspected she needed medical attention?"

My voice is hostile now and I'm beyond controlling it. I know this isn't on Antonio. That's what makes it so much worse. It's on us. On *me*. I did notice that she seemed to be in some discomfort. I did notice the perfume of her scent getting stronger. I did notice how flushed she was. How warm.

I should've gotten her medical attention at the first sign

CHAPTER THIRTY-ONE

of an oncoming heat despite her religious use of suppressants. Damnit. What if she's sick. What if it's...

But I can't think it.

Antonio blanches. "I don't know much more than you, all right? I just know that her suppressants haven't been working since she got here. I offered her some of mine, but she didn't take me up on it immediately and then she told me earlier she's only been taking half a tablet of mine a day. She was already super stressed about everything, and then after you guys left, your parents came up to us. Your mother said something snippy about Maddie's dress turning a pauper into a princess, and then she ran off. You should've seen her face, though, mate. Her stress levels were high before that conversation, but after...it looked like her heart was about to give out."

"Where did she go?"

"I don't know," he says honestly. "I swear. I thought she was going to find you guys."

"Fuck," I mutter, but since I believe him, I spin around and march away to confront my parents. My Alpha instincts are in high gear now that my suspicions about her heat have been confirmed.

Tai, Wolf, and I have been speculating about it, but we knew she was taking her suppressants so we thought we were being ultra-protective and extra sensitive about something that might've been as simple as nerves. It comes as absolutely no surprise to me that it's been heat symptoms for real all along, though, but that only makes me more desperate to find her.

Wolf appears at my side again first, his expression aghast as he blinks at me. "Did I hear what I think I just heard?"

"Yep," I say, furiously looking around for my parents. "Maddie might be going into heat. We need to find the king and queen. Apparently, they had a confrontation with her that might have sent her spiraling."

Tai is there not a moment later, his eyes bouncing from mine to Wolf's. "Do you smell that? It's like Maddie's all around us but we can't find her."

"Yep," Wolf says worriedly. "She might be going into heat, mate."

Tai doesn't look surprised, instead his brows lower and something fierce and protective crosses his features. I can't say I don't feel the same.

"We need to find Kaz's folks. Have you seen them?"

"We need to find Maddie," Tai argues.

"They might be the ones responsible for her disappearance," I press.

He nods. "Right. Okay. I just passed them on their way out."

"What?" I ask, but I'm already moving. "Where were they going?"

"No idea. I just saw your mother whisper something in your father's ear, and then they left together."

"Fuck."

"Double fuck," Wolf echoes after me. "Should we split up?"

"No," I say immediately. "We need to track them down and find out what they said to her, and then we need to find Maddie. If she's going into heat..."

Tai sucks in a sharp breath, his voice pained when he says, "She can't be alone in the palace or outside it. Too many Alphas. It isn't safe."

Thankfully, the crowd parts for us like we're a hot knife

CHAPTER THIRTY-ONE

and they're butter as we rush back out of the ballroom. No one knows for sure what's going on, but I'm certain it's very clear something is going on with us.

Thankfully, no one stops us to ask, just giving us strange looks as we rush by, but right now, I don't care. We'll do damage control later. Once we've found her. When we know she's okay.

My mother and father are never on the greatest of terms, so for her to have gone to seek him out, something big must've happened. And whenever something big happens, she celebrates on their private balcony with a glass of her special brandy.

As we burst into their quarters, the greatest relief sweeps through me when I realize this time is no exception. She and my father *are* on their balcony, but she's holding the decanter, about to pour the brandy when she straightens.

"What are you doing here?" she snaps at me. "Your father and I would like some privacy. Now."

"What did you do to Maddie?" I ask, not stopping until I'm standing in the open doors leading from their sitting room to the expansive balcony. "She's gone, Mother. Until I know where and why, we're not leaving."

Mum gives me a cold smile, but she bats her lashes innocently. "I haven't done anything to her, Kaspian. I'll admit that I made her an offer, but the stupid girl turned me down. She left of her own accord. She's gone, and I wish her all the best of luck."

Horror zaps through me and my jaw unhinges as my father rears away from her. "How could you be so cruel, Catherine? It's no fucking wonder William left you as well. What did you say to the Omega to scare her off? What offer have you made that sent her packing in the belief that she'll never be good enough?"

When she doesn't respond, my father shakes his head. He picks up his empty glass and hurls it against their wall. It shatters in a spray, but before the pieces have started hitting the ground, he storms out, and for once, I understand why.

My mother seems both triumphant and upset, but her face crumbles when first Tai, then Wolf, and then I leave her alone, all of us turning our backs on a queen we're no longer loyal to. Once again, I'm uncertain about what this means for our future, but I can't think about that right now.

Besides, it doesn't matter to me at the moment. She could banish us all on the spot for all I care. Maybe there's a property on the market close to Yua's. We could all move to France, and at this point, if there's a guest room, I may even offer it to my father until he's back on his feet.

Before any of that, we need to find Maddie. My instincts are screaming at me, roaring that she's in trouble. We need to get to her before it's too late. I have no idea where she might've gone, but she can't be too far away just yet.

At least, I pray she isn't. If something happens to her, I'll never forgive myself and Wolf and Tai won't either. We should've fucking bonded with her already. And I know why they haven't. What I don't know is why it's taken me this long to realize I should've gotten out of all of our ways and let our nature take its course.

THIRTY-TWO

WOLF

FURY UNLIKE ANYTHING I've ever felt rips through me, coursing hot and heavy through our bond from the others as well. As we race out of the queen's quarters, none of us say a word. We don't have to.

We just run.

As fast as we can.

Find her. Find her. Find her.

The mantra echoes through my mind with every smack of my feet against the tiled corridor. When we reach the end of the hall, Tai goes left and Kaz goes right, so I keep going straight. Splitting up might not be the best idea, but it needs to be done.

Find her. Find her. Find her.

Our Omega is gone, and she's probably going into heat. I'm not sure if she's been through an unsuppressed heat since she first presented, but probably not.

Fuck.

When Tai, Kaz, and I went through our first rut together, I'm pretty sure I'd have died if they hadn't been there to help me through it. Hell, even with them there, I felt like I was dying at times. *Good God, it was* not *the most fun I've had with my clothes off, I'll say that much.*

Not only is it not fun, however, it's downright dangerous. If we don't find her...

Fuck that. We're going to find her.

My feet keep smacking against the tiles until I skid to a stop in front of her room, but her door is open and she's not in there. The problem? Neither is any of her stuff. Her closets look like they've been ransacked, hangers strewn around on the floor and the doors hanging open.

Curiously, I do spot some of our stuff on the chaise lounge in the corner. I recognize Tai's jacket immediately. My tie. Kaz's embroidered handkerchief. Some other odds and ends like the towel I gave her to dry off at the dowager cottage and an open package of Tai's favorite tea. Kaz's...*first-aid kit?*

For a moment, I just stop and stare. I mean... *What the fuck?*

But then, slowly, my eyes widen and my mouth turns into the Sahara. She built herself a little nest. *And we didn't know.*

We're fucking idiots, is what we are. We should've seen this coming long before we actually did. None of us were surprised to learn about her heat symptoms, but this was happening right under our noses and we didn't do shit about it.

We—*I*—should've gotten her to a doctor as soon as I realized her scent was getting stronger and stronger. Instead, I told myself she was on suppressants and left it at that.

Frankly, I don't know how this is possible. It shouldn't

be, and yet here we are. None of this matters right now, though.

The only thing that matters is finding her. Satisfied that she's not in her chambers, I turn and run back out into the hall, looking up and down, but there's still no sight of her.

Huffing out a breath, I rack my brain for where she might've gone. The next obvious answer aside from her chambers is her parents' cottage, but an Omega going into heat wouldn't run to her folks. She'd go... *Where, Wolf? Think!*

I meet back up with the others outside of the palace, but judging by Tai's clenched-fist pacing and Kaz's muscles being wound so tight that he's practically vibrating, they haven't found her either. "She's not inside?"

"Nope," Kaz bites out. "Mary hasn't seen her either."

"Her stuff is gone," I tell them dejectedly, wondering if maybe, we really are too late.

Tai stops pacing at my words and spins toward me. "Gone?"

I nod. "Cleared out. Where to next?"

"The stables," Kaz says decisively. "It's closer than the clearing and the archery field, though we'll check those if she's not at the stables."

As one, we take off running again, flat-out sprinting as we head toward the horses. Kaz is right. We haven't officially bonded with her or anything, but she is ours. It makes sense she might've gone someplace that reminds her of us and the stables are closest to the palace.

I beat the others there, my feet surer on the path than theirs as I round the corner and slam to a halt. Because there, on the ground in front of Sergeant Pepper's stall, is my Omega. Her knees are drawn up to her chest and she's moaning softly, her hair damp with sweat as she hugs her legs.

"Maddie," I murmur, kicking into gear again until I'm collapsing on my knees beside her. "Maddie? Are you okay?"

She moans again, but then slowly lifts her head to frown at me. "Wolf?"

Her scent hits me like a goddamned freight train, the spicy sweet scent magnified times a thousand. My cock jumps to attention and my immediate instinct is to rip every shred of her clothes off and fuck her right here in the hay. Knot her. Bond her. Claim her as mine forever.

I struggle to touch her gently, to keep myself under control, holding my breath and only allow small sips of air as I run my hands up and down her arms.

"I'm here, Mads. I'm here." I reach up to cup her face, startled by how blazing fucking hot her skin is against my palm. Her eyes are glazed over, too, and she's shivering like a leaf as she leans into my touch, whimpering as she presses her legs together.

Fuck. We are too late.

I don't know if she's in full-blown heat or if she's still on the verge, but we won't be able to get her symptoms under control now. With a wealth of medical knowledge behind me—or none, really—I already know it's progressed too far. She's going to have to ride it out.

She's clearly in pain, cramping, if the way she's hunched over, moaning whenever she shifts to ease the discomfort, is anything to go by. She's definitely got a raging fever, and when she sways as she tries to lean into me, I know she's dizzy, too.

Take her, my inner animal roars, and I grit my teeth against the intrusive thought, my groin aching as my erec-

CHAPTER THIRTY-TWO

tion grows and my knot swells. Precum dampens the front of my pants and I am dying to get out of this suffocating suit.

"Wolf?" she says my name again softly as she reaches for my face like she's trying to make sure I'm real. "I'm scared, Wolf."

"I know, Mads," I wrap my arms around her just as Tai crashes to his knees on her other side. Kaz stands behind him, chest heaving as he regards the scene and then nods, his eyes wide and wild as he shoves his hands into his hair, nostrils flaring.

"The dowager cottage," he says immediately. "Lady White was saddled for that display before the ball, right? Let's fucking hope she still is."

He takes off at a run toward the paddock where the grooms tend to the horses after they've been ridden, and he comes back a moment later leading my favorite mare by her halter. She's not saddled anymore, evidently, but I can ride her bareback and use only her mane to guide her if I have to.

At this point, the leather straps around her face with the rope clipped to them is a luxury. Kaz hands her over before crouching down to slide an arm around Maddie's waist.

"You're going to be okay," he murmurs soothingly. "We're going to get you through this, okay?"

Her eyes narrow when she manages to focus on his face. "You!"

"Yes, me." He frowns, brushing a lock of damp hair off her forehead and tucking it gently behind her ear. "Maddie, what is it?"

She raises a shaky hand to his chest and pokes him, feisty despite her pain. "I. Am. Not. Worthless." Each word is punctuated by another poke. "I. Am. Not. Nothing. I don't need your help."

Kaz jerks like she slapped him, his features contorting with pain as he realizes the same thing I do. *She overheard us, but she doesn't know he was quoting his mother. Fuck.*

Another cramp passes through her and she collapses against him before she realizes what she's doing and tries to push away, but she sways again, looking like she's about to faint until Tai moves in behind her.

"I've got you, Maddie," he says softly into her ear, and he leads her to where I've mounted Lady White. "I can explain, I promise, but not here and not now."

She groans and finally drops her chin in a curt nod.

Tai lifts her up effortlessly by her thighs and she mewls. He and I both wince at the sound, but we'll get there. I'm already hard as hell and ready as I've ever been, tempted to give her some relief on the way to the cottage. While I'll probably be able to stay on Lady White while I do, I'm not sure the same can be said for her.

Instead, I simply help her get settled, wrap my arm tight around her waist, and then dig my heels into the horse's flank. She responds immediately, breaking into a canter before we've even cleared the stable yard.

Maddie gasps, but I'm not sure if it's fright or because she can feel how hard I am for her. Maybe a little bit of both.

"Hang on. We'll be there in no time, okay."

Behind us, I'm sure Tai and Kaz are running again, but we'll beat them by a few minutes at least. Possibly enough time to clear up what she thinks she heard—or to get her off. *Choices, choices.*

My head starts to swim, though, so I might not make

CHAPTER THIRTY-TWO

this particular choice with my brain. Her scent is fucking strong, and I'm fast losing my bearings. Thankfully, Lady White breaks through the trees at the dowager cottage as I consider pulling her up short and taking Maddie right there on the forest floor.

Right. The cottage. That's where we were going. Fucking focus, Wolf. A soft snarl sounds, and it takes me a second to realize it came from me.

"Are you okay?" Maddie asks as I draw the mare to a halt and slide off before helping her do the same.

As our eyes meet, hers are still hazy. Her cheeks are more flushed now than before and her breathing comes faster the longer she looks at me. "No, I'm not. Neither are you. Let's get you inside."

"Wolf, I need—"

"I know, Mads. But there's one thing we need to get real clear first."

She frowns before she blinks hard and yanks her hand out of mine. "Oh. Right. How worthless I am and how you're all going to get bored of me in no time."

"That's not true," I say as I shove the door open and lead her directly to the fireplace in front of which I knotted her the last time we were here. The memory makes my cock swell even further and I groan.

Even though she's not holding my hand anymore, she trails after me and sits down heavily on the thick rug as she watches me pack the timber for the fire. A few seconds later, the first flames are flickering, and I drop to my ass to sit in front of her.

"First things first," I say, reaching for her hands and squeezing them. "You misunderstood what you heard. That's not what we think of you, Maddison. Kaz was quoting his mother. If you'd started eavesdropping a second earlier or stayed a second longer, you'd have known that."

She narrows her eyes at me. "So, this is my fault?"

"No, that's not what I'm saying." I drag in a deep breath, cursing when it fills my very soul with her scent. What was I saying?

"You don't think I'm worthless?"

I shake my head, remembering. "You're everything to us, Mads. *Everything*."

"Wolf and Tai were going to break our pack bonds for you," Kaz says as they enter the room, faces red and chests rising and falling fast, but they're here. They made it at a run. A full sprint, I'm sure.

A fact for which I plan on taking credit in every one of our workout sessions from now on. Let them fucking complain that I'm pushing them too hard again...

I've known the prince half my life and I've never seen him in as much agony as I see reflected in his eyes when he says those words out loud. I felt it through our bond before, when we first told him the plan, but I see it now, amplified by everything else that's going on as he falls to his knees beside her.

"As soon as I allowed myself to admit the truth, I was willing to abdicate for you," he says quietly. "I still might have to, depending on how it all plays out, but the point is that Wolf isn't lying when he says you're everything to us."

"You have to believe us," Tai implores her as he sits down behind her and pulls her into his lap. "Please believe us."

She moans and burrows into him, her ass pressing into his crotch as her lids flutter closed. His desire shoots like an

CHAPTER THIRTY-TWO

explosion through the bond, so strong that Kaz lets out a quiet *oof*. Don't get me wrong, the desire's been there all along, but it was simmering on the backburner while we did what we had to do.

It's not on the backburner anymore, though.

"I believe you," she whimpers, her eyes closed as she rests her head back against his shoulder. "I still have the card. I believe you."

The card? I don't know what she's talking about, but I don't care. I'll buy her a hundred cards if it means she really does believe us. And apparently, it does, because she reaches for Tai's hand and moves it to the waistband of her pants.

It dawns on me then that she changed out of the dress before she left the palace. And it saddens me that she left even that behind. The dress. Her little nest. She really was planning on going. On leaving. For good.

Thank fuck we found her before she did.

Tai's fingers disappear into her worn yoga pants, and her lips part as she breathes out a sigh of relief when his hand moves under the fabric. His eyes are closed now too, his breathing choppy as his gorgeous face scrunches in concentration.

Maddie mewls and whines, the sounds hitching with broken breath as Tai fucks her with his fingers until she screams her release as we all watch, and then I'm on my feet and shucking my clothes. We need to get this show on the road before I lose it without even being touched. I feel the same feral desire coming from Kaz as he hastily unbuttons his shirt, his mouth slightly open as he watches Tai lay Maddie down.

Alphas, start your engines. Shit is about to get very real in here, and although I hate knowing she's in pain, I can't say I mind that the four of us are going to be holed up in here together for however long it takes to get her through this.

I look at each of my packmates in turn and I can see the same feeling reflected in their eyes. It doesn't matter what's going on outside these four walls. None of us will leave her until she's through this.

THIRTY-THREE

—

MADDIE

I WENT to say goodbye to the horse. I don't know why. One minute, I was tossing all my stuff into my bags and running out of that godforsaken hellhole of a palace and the next, I was rushing into the stables, a hazy memory of my first encounter with Wolf there replaying in my mind as my body rebelled against itself.

My heartbeat stutters and I choke out a breath.

The stables.

No...the cottage.

What's happening?

As Tai's loving brown eyes meet mine when he rises up above me, I remember where I am. It's like I'm stuck in a weird fever dream, but as long as he's here, I don't want to wake up.

A moment of clarity brings the rest back and I gasp, remembering.

They *do* want me. Even Kaz.

Am I really at the dowager cottage with my Alphas?

MADDIE

I groan, confusion clouding my thoughts as I try to recall what I was thinking about before.

Tai's cool palm touches my cheek and concern clashes with the raw need blazing out at me from between his miraculously long eyelashes. "Maddie?"

"Yes?" I blink, reaching up to caress the edges of his amber eyes, but the movement is sloppy and my arms are heavy and I almost poke his eye.

The dull ache between my legs grows sharper again as Tai smiles but blinks so I can feel those soft lashes brushing my fingers. "I'm really here," he says and I realize I muttered my thought out loud. "You're not dreaming. Or hallucinating."

"Okay, but are you sure?" I murmur, spreading my legs and realizing there are no constraints around them.

Frowning, I glance down to see my pants have been removed. Relief slams into me, but it's slightly worrying that I don't remember who did it or when. As I'm looking down, however, I realize I'm not the only one who's suddenly pantsless.

Tai is naked too, his hard cock glistening with precum at the top as he hovers above me. Intense need crashes into me, and I moan, winding my arms around his neck as I pull him to me. No words are spoken between us as he kisses me feverishly, deep and hard while his cock presses at my entrance. Then he thrusts in, and I cry out, already halfway to heaven as soon as he starts moving, spreading me open and filling me up again and again and again, easing the ache deep in my core.

Something broad at the root of him brushing against my entrance makes me blink my eyes open to stare into his as a feral need takes me and I arch into him. "Your knot, Tai. I need it. I need it so bad."

He looks at me for another beat, then he drops his head in a nod before burying his face in the crook of my neck as he bears down into me, stretching my entrance, filling me with his knot.

My core spasms around him and I arch up, gripping him tight to me, clawing at the tattoos on his back as an orgasm is wrung out of my core and I muffle my scream into his collar.

With him no longer filling my field of vision, I suddenly catch a glimpse of what's going on behind him. The sight of it alone rolls one orgasm into two and Tai groans as my core flexes around him again, drawing him to his own release.

Wolf is naked, miles of golden skin on display and his blond hair shining in the orange glow of the fire behind him. Seeing those muscles rippling as he moves his hips, his head thrown back in pleasure, his eyes screwed shut, and his mouth slightly agape would've done it for me in and of itself. *But wait, there's more.*

The Crown fucking Prince of the Kingdom is on his knees in front of his packmate, sucking his cock like it's an ice lolly on a hot day, his own dick in his hand and his fist flying up and down his long length. The second orgasm barrels into me and Tai groans before he rocks against me, stretching out the orgasm as he spills his seed into me.

I scream my release into the relative darkness of the room, my toes curling as my back arches and white-hot bliss flows freely through my veins.

Tai lifts his head, looking right into my eyes and flashing me the most beautiful, most confident smile I've seen from him. "Better now?"

MADDIE

I do a quick mental check, and I'm about to nod until Wolf groans, his hand in a fist around Kaz's black hair as his hips jerk. I tighten around Tai's knot, and he sucks in a breath. Then he chuckles and rests his forehead against mine, making me feel so loved and protected that I relax instantly, purring against him.

My thoughts are scattering, my brain apparently on the fritz until Tai brings me back from the edge by running his nose along the length of mine. "Just breathe, Maddie. You're going to be okay. We're going to get you through this."

"Where are my bags?" I ask as suddenly it occurs to me that I didn't have them on the horse with Wolf.

Tai grins. "Kaz and I found them in the stables. They're by the door. Don't worry. Like I said, we've got you, Maddie."

Wolf lets out a strained cry as he comes into Kaz's mouth and Kaz drinks him down. I watch with rapturous hunger, that ache in my core already starting up again even with Tai still locked inside me, slowly deflating.

I wince and Tai begins to purr. The strong vibrations soaking into me like warm water. Like salve on a wound. It's the most beautiful sound I've ever heard.

He brushes his fingers through my hair, soothing me with hushed sounds until the tremoring stops and the ache subsides a little.

I wake to the feel of his knot slipping out of me and let out a sound I'm not proud of. Something halfway between a whine and a fearful cry.

He offers me a hand as I blink myself back awake, "Let me help you up?"

I shake my head, squeezing my eyes shut as another

CHAPTER THIRTY-THREE

wave of cramps takes me, almost stealing all the air from my lungs.

I don't remember it being like this. I've only been through one unsuppressed heat, and it was when I first presented. They say that's the worst one, but they're liars. This one definitely takes the cake and technically, this should be at least partially suppressed from all the damned suppressants I've been taking. But it doesn't feel like it. It feels like this heat is trying to tear me apart from the inside.

Doctor. I will definitely see a doctor if—no, *when*—I get through this.

When *we* get through this.

My gaze locks on Kaz. He's by the fire now, running his fist over his thick shaft, but he's slowed his movements. Unlike me, Tai, and Wolf, it seems my prince hasn't found his release yet.

Guilt twists in my stomach for ever believing he would've said those cruel things about me, especially after he stood up to the queen to have me.

Sitting up, I clench my teeth against the aching and crawl to him on all fours, my clit already aching again as slick coats the inside of my thighs.

Half-hoping that this is, in fact, a fever dream and I'm not really presenting myself to an Alpha who will rule the country one day, I look at him over my shoulder and stick my bum up a little higher in the air. "Please, Kaz?"

His jaw is tight, and he frowns as he moves in behind me, standing up on his knees as he guides his cock to my entrance. It's so hard that his veins are bulging along the shiny, perfectly straight length of him.

"You never have to beg me, Maddie." His hand drops to the small of my back, hot and firm as he pushes into me, burying himself all the way to the swollen start of his knot with one single, powerful thrust.

Wolf gets down on the ground with me, then he winks before he slides in underneath me, his head where Kaz and I are joined and his growing cock right in front of my face. It takes some doing, but I manage to take him into my mouth just as I feel his on my clit.

Logically, I know he's probably propped up on his elbows, but it still blows my mind that he's going down on me while his friend is thrusting into me and I'm going down on him all at the same time. On instinct, my eyes open and even though pleasure is already sparking through me, I have to find the last piece of our puzzle.

Tai. Where is he?

When I don't see him immediately, I panic, frantically looking around until I find him sitting beside us on his knees. Like Wolf, he's recovered fast, my heat seemingly having reduced their refractory period to basically nothing.

Talk about zero to a hundred in sixty seconds or less. I'm impressed, I won't lie, but with Kaz's cock hitting all the right places inside me and Wolf's hot tongue on my clit, I can't hang on to the thought for long enough to tell them. *Later. I'll tell them later.*

I moan around Wolf's length, pleasure and relief lighting me up from the inside out, but I still don't feel complete. My weight is resting on my elbows and it may be slightly precarious, but I can't leave him out of this.

As I reach for Tai's cock, though, someone else's hand is already on it. I don't know whose it is, but I don't care. Since his are braced behind him, his head tossed back as he thrusts into the fist around him, I know it's not his own hand and the thought of us all giving each other pleasure at once does me in.

I fucking love that my Alphas love each other so much. I swear, it's going to be the end of me one day. *Death by orgasm's not a bad way to go, though.*

As I constrict around Kaz's shaft and moan around Wolf's, the Alpha behind me loses it, filling me with his knot.

I scream around Wolf's cock and the evidence of my pleasure sends him over his edge. Wolf finds his release in my mouth, and I swallow every drop of it as I shudder through the most intense orgasm I've ever had with Kaz still locked inside, his fingers digging deep into my hips.

A wave of intense dizziness takes me and my arms give out.

"Whoa," I hear wolf's voice echo as if underwater and then, Kaz: "Get her some water. Hurry."

When the blackness at the edges of my vision subsides I notice the beautiful pulse of warmth in my core, a replacement for the pain, and I smile to myself as Kaz wraps his arms around me from behind and I'm enveloped in his scent.

I'm not sure how long it's been when Wolf presses a kiss to my forehead and I come back to the moment to watch him stroke his fingers through the prince's hair.

"You should try to get some sleep," Tai murmurs as he crawls up on my other side and rests his head on my shoulder. "Or would you like to take a shower first?"

I shake my head. I probably *should* shower, but I don't want to wash their scents off me. Not yet. Besides, I don't think my legs could hold me up right now. My knees are numb and my thighs are still quaking. The ache is a dull

MADDIE

thing in my core. Sated enough to allow a few hours rest. Or at least, I'm praying for that.

"Okay," Wolf agrees softly. "Can anyone reach a blanket?"

Kaz chuckles, but then he sits up before pushing to his feet. "I'll get it."

Wolf laughs and waggles his brows at his royal packmate.

The prince arches a dark brow at him as he walks backward out of the room.

It's nice to see them this way. Playful. Happy. And completely naked.

With that, he winks and spins around, but he's not gone long before he's back with a massive, plush blanket that he carefully settles over us all before he lies back down and burrows into Wolf's side, reaching for me to rest a hand on my hip. My lids are heavy, and I don't try to fight it when they slide shut.

I must fall asleep, because the next thing I know, I'm waking up to them whispering to each other. "...with all three of us repeatedly knotting her, it could potentially subdue her heat faster, but my best bet is still at least two days."

I open my eyes to find Wolf already smiling at me. "How are you feeling, Mads?"

Shifting and pressing my legs together to ease the growing discomfort there, I shake my head. "Not great. Need you."

He nods and glances at Kaz. "Personally, I hope it's more than two days." He flashes me a goofy grin before he settles between my legs. "Unless it's really bad. Don't like seeing my girl in pain."

CHAPTER THIRTY-THREE

Sweat breaks out on my brow and slides down my neck as an ache spears through me, and I nod. "It's bad," I grind out. "Wolf..."

"Got you," he says immediately, already hard as he presses my dripping pussy with a loud roar. Without breaking the pace he instantly sets, he winks at Kaz. "I guess it's a good thing we're not in the palace for this, huh? We're pretty loud, guys. Not gonna lie."

Kaz rolls his eyes, but then he beckons Tai to him and wraps his hand around the nape of his neck, pulling him in for a deep kiss that fills the air with wet, passionate noises as the two Alphas surge together. Wolf's mouth descends on me then, and I lose myself in his taste and the firm feel of his lips against mine.

I hook my ankles together behind his firm ass, kissing him back with everything I've got as I get the distinct sense of being warmed by sunlight. It wasn't like this before when he made love to me, but they've chosen me now, and no one is holding back anymore.

Wolf has reminded me of sunshine since almost the first time I met him, and it's like he's letting me bask in him now. I pull him closer, and I don't have to ask for his knot before he gives it to me, his teeth scraping against my throat, but he's careful not to mark me. And I can't say I'm not a little disappointed. I want him to. Badly.

I want to wear their marks for the entire world to see.

I tremble underneath him as relief races through me again. As I catch my breath in the aftermath, I look over just in time to see Tai's head drop back, his hips jerking as he thrusts into Kaz one last time. My prince goes over the edge with his packmate, his cock swelling in Tai's hand as he comes all over the expensive fur rug we're on.

MADDIE

Locked together with Wolf, I return my gaze to him, and he smiles before he presses his lips to my forehead. "It'll be dawn soon. No one should be able to find us here, but we should probably close the drapes and make sure all the doors are bolted."

"On it," Tai says lazily, stretching his arms into the air as he yawns. "Just give me a minute."

Wolf cuddles me as we wait for his knot to go down. Eventually, he helps me to my feet and leads me back to the massive shower we were in the last time we were here. He climbs in with me, lathering his hands with soap before he washes me carefully, cleansing every inch of my skin.

Kaz and Tai join us when they're done ensuring our privacy, and Kaz's long fingers slide into my hair as he washes it for me. *God, it feels so good to have them taking care of me like this.*

And for the next couple of days, they don't stop. They tend to my every need, reading me so well toward the end that I don't have to say anything before they're there, making sure I'm looked after between brief bouts of snacking on the jars of peaches and pickles left in the canning shed, napping, and a lot of laughter.

The rug in front of the fireplace remains littered with our clothes that we took off that first night and haven't bothered putting back on again. There are also all the blankets we've used and the towels, and as I snuggle into Tai, it occurs to me that this is the best nest ever.

The thought brings a smile to my face as I drift off to sleep, wondering if somehow, I can convince them to stay here with me forever.

THIRTY-FOUR

—

TAI

LATE AFTERNOON light warms the lounge as Maddie and I lie together in our nest, panting and beyond sated. For now.

Wolf's back slams into the rug beside me as he collapses after taking Kaz hard and fast, and Kaz groans as he rolls over to press himself to my other side. We're all quiet for a while, but Maddie breaks the silence as she suddenly sits straight up.

"I still don't know how this happened," she says, frowning before she rests her face in her hands and sighs. "Why did I go into heat? I've been taking one and a half doses of my suppressants since the first week of the Trials, and I doubled it this last week or so. It doesn't make any sense."

I reach up to rub her back, but we've all been wondering the same thing. Since the intensity of her heat seems to be subsiding, we may actually be able to get to the bottom of it now. "Can I see your pills?"

She nods. "Sure, but why?"

I shrug. "It's just a hunch, but I've been thinking about this a lot and I suspect that whatever you've been taking hasn't been suppressants."

"But how?" She frowns again as she rises and heads over to her bags. She rummages through her purse and comes back with the package, handing it over as she shakes her head. "That's not possible. If they weren't suppressants, wouldn't I have gone into heat, like, a week into this thing?"

"Not necessarily," I muse as I inspect the little plastic container she gave me. "You've been drinking a lot of my tea, right?"

"Yeah, so?"

"Well, the herbs in the tea act as a naturally occurring suppressant. It's one of the reasons why all the Omegas' chambers were stocked with it as well. It's not strong enough to keep you from going into heat at all, obviously, but it would've been enough to stave it off. It was an added safety measure."

"Plus, Antonio mentioned he gave you some of his suppressants," Kaz says thoughtfully. "That would've helped as well. What's the verdict?"

He glances at me as I break open one of the tablets and then bring it to my lips. Tasting it with the tip of my tongue, I roll it around my mouth before I sigh. "This is sugar, Mads. There's absolutely nothing else in there. Like, I don't even get a hit of anything bitter or even vaguely chemical."

Her jaw drops open. "How? I got them from the same store I've been getting my suppressants from for years. If they got a dud batch, why wouldn't they have contacted me?"

"I don't think it's a dud batch." I grimace as I look back up at her. "The legal liability alone would've been staggering if they'd knowingly let a bunch of Omegas walk around with suppressants that are nothing more than placebos. The regulation of this stuff is also serious business. It's unlikely the problem lies with the batch. Has anyone ever had unfettered access to your things?"

"No." She starts shaking her head but suddenly stops, her eyes going round as she nods instead. "Clara."

Kaz's jaw grinds. "The Omega from Cambridge Academy, that Clara?"

Maddie's brow furrows as she glances at him. "Yes, but how do you know her?"

"I don't, but I've heard of her." He brings those dark eyes to mine and then to Wolf's. "She's the Omega my mother mentioned, the one who was supposed to have been chosen."

"She was supposed to have been chosen?" Maddie asks, but then she shrugs after thinking it over. "That makes perfect sense, actually. We all thought it would be her. Were you ever going to tell me about it, though?"

He shrugs. "Perhaps eventually. If she's responsible for this, I'm assuming you two aren't friends. How did she gain access to your bags?"

"We're definitely not friends. It was hate at first sight, if I'm being honest. She thinks scholarship students like me sully the name of the institution and I think she's a pompous, entitled brat who lets her privilege hang out much too often."

"Your bags, Maddie?" I prompt as anger sparks in her eyes while she talks about this...Clara. "How could she have managed to swap out your pills?"

"I knew there was a reason she agreed to watch my stuff so easily," Maddie mutters darkly. "Before I came here, I was called into the headmistress's office. She wanted a word, and they asked Clara to guard my bags while I was lectured about not embarrassing the school. I wouldn't be surprised if the old witch was in it with her. She certainly didn't seem to expect me to make it this far."

"I'll be paying them both a visit as soon as this is over," Kaz says with malice glittering in those eyes. "What Clara attempted to do is unacceptable. You could have been hurt if you'd gone into heat without us around to help you through it. She'll answer for this, I promise you."

I sigh. "Before we start planning our revenge, perhaps we should talk about the Final Ceremony?" I suggest, but Maddie's still looking at Kaz.

"Wait, if she was supposed to have been selected, then how am I here?"

"Fate intervened and saved us from eternal disappointment and unhappiness," he replies without skipping a beat. "In other words, there was a mix-up within the selection committee. Apparently, they were meant to review one of Clara's essays in her nomination package but somehow ended up with your essay instead."

Maddie looks like she might know something about how that happened but says nothing, smirking quietly to herself.

"What do we need to talk about for the Ceremony?"

He turns back to me, and I hold his gaze, hoping this won't lead to another argument between the two of us. "Are we going to do it, or are we just going to say to hell with it all?"

A knock interrupts us. We all stiffen until a voice calls out from the other side. "It's Antonio. I know you're in there. Is it over yet?"

CHAPTER THIRTY-FOUR

"Get dressed," I tell the others as I grab the nearest pair of trousers and pull them on. They're not mine. I think they're Kaz's, but they'll do for now. "Give us a minute!"

Laughter rings out from the other side of the door. "I'm assuming it's not over yet, then."

"No, it's basically over," Maddie responds as she jumps a little to get into her jeans faster, then shoves a sweater over her head. "Are you alone?"

He pauses for a beat, the laughter long gone. "No, Francis is with me."

I frown. "Who's Francis?"

"A palace guard," she says quietly. "One you're about to lose once the Trials are over, I'm afraid."

Wolf snaps his fingers. "Oh, that Francis. That's too bad. I like him. Why are we losing him?"

"You're about to see for yourself." She falls into step behind me as I head to the door, then she smiles and peeks out from behind my back to give her friend a wave once I've opened it. "Come to make your confession, have you?"

He arches a brow at her. "Says the Omega who's just ridden out a heat she wasn't supposed to have had with the royal pack who's supposed to be sequestered in their quarters, trying to decide between myself and Casey."

"Is that where they think we are?" Kaz asks as he motions for them to come in. "Please excuse the state of the place, but we weren't expecting company, obviously. I wouldn't have invited you in at all were it not for the fact that you may be seen if you stay out there."

Antonio waves him off as if he's an old friend. "No problem. We get it, and yes. That's where they think you are. Rumor has it Maddie was dismissed the night of the ball, and after you got rid of her, you locked yourselves in to make your final decision."

"So the queen has no idea where we are?" Maddie asks, incredulous.

Kaz scoffs. "I have no doubt she knows exactly where we are."

Honestly, I'm surprised we haven't been dragged out of here by our ears, but I have a feeling the queen likes it this way. Being able to influence the narrative while we've been 'busy.'

"That actually works out pretty well for us," Wolf says, grinning as he darts a glance between the two of them. "What's this, then?"

Francis shifts on his feet, but then he raises his chin and looks our packmate right in his eyes, which I doubt he's ever done before. "Antonio and I have chosen one another. If you'll accept my resignation, I'd like to leave with him once the Trials are over."

"Of course, mate," Kaz says, reaching out to shake the other Alpha's hand.

He seems taken aback, but he shakes with Kaz and steps back as he looks us over. We're all shirtless—except for Maddie, and Francis sighs as he shakes his head. "Things are heating up out there. I realize you've been tending to your Omega, but you ought to consider returning to the palace as soon as possible. Antonio and I have been doing what we can to fan the rumors of you being holed up in your quarters, but media speculation is becoming rife that you're in a deadlock or something."

"Clearly, we're not," Wolf says, still grinning. "We made our decision ages ago. As far as we're concerned, the only decision still to be made is whether we're going to attend

CHAPTER THIRTY-FOUR

the Final Ceremony or disappear into the sunset with our Omega."

"We're attending the Ceremony," Kaz decides out loud as a smirk tugs at the corners of his lips. "I have a plan." He turns to the other two. "How did you find us here? Did you check to make sure you weren't followed?"

"Maddie mentioned Wolf bringing her here last week," Antonio says. "After you ran out of the ballroom like your asses were on fire, and I discovered she was gone, it wasn't so much of a leap that you'd have come here. It's the closest, most private place I could think of."

"We weren't followed," Francis adds as he bows his head at us. "As far as anyone else knows, Antonio is freaking out about how long it's taking you to choose him, and I took him for a walk to calm his nerves. We, uh, we took the scenic route."

"With that, he means we walked around randomly for ninety minutes before eventually doubling back around the edge of the forest and following the perimeter fence here. No one would have followed us around for that long, and we kept looking over our shoulders. You're good."

"The perimeter fence?" I ask as my heart stutters in my chest. "You do realize there are cameras out there, right?"

"They've been hiding in the bushes?" Antonio frowns. "That's just weird. Hardly anyone ever comes back this far, so I doubt they'd be on that side of the grounds, but we also didn't see or hear anything out there."

Relief swirls through me, but at the same time, just because they didn't see the cameramen doesn't mean they weren't there. *One thing at a time, though.*

Besides, if they did get pictures of them, it would only have been a photograph of an Omega and a servant walking

373

around the grounds. Nothing too scandalous or harmful to anyone—unless they were caught holding hands or something. In which case, I suppose the whole world will know soon that we haven't chosen Antonio and he hasn't chosen us.

Francis starts backing out when Maddie suddenly folds her arms over her stomach and her shoulders hunch. "We'll leave you now, but come back to the palace soon."

"We'll see you tomorrow for the Final Ceremony," I assure him as I walk them out, locking the door behind them as Kaz peels Maddie's sweater off and Wolf drops to his knees before her.

"Need a little more, Mads?" he teases as he rolls her jeans off and glances at Kaz. "As soon as we're done here, you're laying out your plan for us."

He nods. "We're all in this together. If you don't like it, we'll revisit riding off into the sunset and becoming beach bums, okay?"

"I was looking forward to that," Wolf murmurs before he leans forward to breathe Maddie in. "I'm looking forward to this too, though. "Someone get my pants. This really could be the last time for this heat, and my knot wants to pass Go."

I groan but lean over to help him out. Even as I'm doing it though, trepidation runs through me about what's in store for us tomorrow.

Right here, right now, we're safe and happy in our nest. We're all on the same page. It feels like we've made it through the worst, but the real world is waiting for us out there and none of us have an idea how bad it's going to get once we rejoin it.

THIRTY-FIVE

—

MADDIE

OUTSIDE IN THE hall once again, music filters out from the ballroom. A ripple of anxiety runs through me as I look at myself in what I'm coming to think of as *my* mirror. I'm not wearing much makeup today, only a smudge of eyeliner and a coat of mascara.

I look more like myself than I have for any of the events we've been waiting for out here before. Mary even let me wear pumps this time. *No heel at all!*

Antonio and Casey aren't dressed up either. We're supposed to be, but after we brought Casey into the loop and laid out Kaz's plan for her and Antonio, the other Omegas and I decided together that we wanted to look like ourselves today. This is who we are, and the Final Ceremony is being broadcast live.

It's our last chance—or theirs, rather—to present themselves to the world. If all goes according to plan, I'll have a whole life's worth of chances in the limelight, but it seemed important to us all to be exactly who we are for the world to see.

MADDIE

For a month now, we've been their primary entertainment. We've followed everyone else's rules, and we've done it with a smile on our faces. Today, we're making a stand.

The Royal Pack and I are making a more dramatic one, but Casey and Antonio wanted to be part of it in their own way. Antonio plans on asking Francis to bond with him formally once my Alphas and I have made our spectacle, and it turns out that sweet Casey has a pack back home in Ontario she wants to belong to.

As soon as I started explaining my relationship with the RP to her, she burst into tears. At first, I thought she was hurt. She wasn't. It was relief. When her sobs eventually subsided, she broke down and told me she never wanted to be selected and that she's been terrified of being chosen.

I can't quite believe how perfectly this has all worked out, with all three of us getting the happy endings we were after all along. I smile at the thought, and Antonio comes up behind me just like he did the night of the ball, resting his chin on my shoulder as he holds me tight.

"You're beautiful," he says again, returning my smile in the mirror. "Positively glowing. Although, if I'd spent the past few days being repeatedly knotted by three gorgeous Alphas, I suppose I would've been glowing too."

"Stop it." I blush, reaching behind me to swat his side. "We're going to be called in at any moment, and I'm not going on live TV with a face as red as a firetruck."

Casey giggles at our sides, shaking her head as she glances between us. "I wish I'd have gotten to know you two sooner. I thought keeping to myself was for the best, but you guys aren't so bad."

Antonio sticks his tongue out at her. "*Not so bad?* We're

CHAPTER THIRTY-FIVE

magnificent. Marvelous. Darling and her pack are going to come visit me in Barcelona when Francis and I have our ceremony. You should come. Bring your pack, too. It'll be fun. We could catch up and say mean things about all the Omegas who made you feel like you had to keep to yourself."

"I'd like that," she says softly just as the announcer cries out from inside.

"For the last time during these Mating Trials, please help me welcome Antonio Ramirez!"

Casey pulls back her shoulders and takes his hand when he offers it to her. "We're really doing this, huh?"

"We are," he says confidently, taking my hand too before tucking mine around one elbow and Casey's around the other. "Let's do this. I have a Bonding Ceremony of my own to plan, and I don't want to wait any longer than I've already had to."

"It's been a month," I say as we walk together toward the doors. "It's not that long."

"So says you," he says, sassy as ever even as the doors open and we walk in together despite the fact that he should be making his entrance alone. "You have a whole palace to help you plan your Bonding Ceremony. I don't have the same manpower. So chop-chop."

The crowd murmurs as we pass between them, heads bending together as they speculate about what's going on. Queen Catherine is on her throne again, and she's clearly struggling to keep her expression neutral. More so when her gaze meets mine and her eyes narrow.

I'm not supposed to be here anymore. Rumors of my departure have been greatly exaggerated.

MADDIE

I won't even begin to deny the satisfied little thrill that runs through me as she tries to mask her surprise. King Edward seems much more pleased to see me, releasing the queen's hand and settling back on his throne with a small smile on his face, like he knows what's about to happen and can't wait for the show.

The Royal Pack are up on the dais as always, looking smug, proud, and loving—and really freaking hot in their tailored black suits. Kaspian is flanked by Tai on his left and Wolf on his right, and I know it was planned this way so that Wolf would be standing next to the announcer.

He's thrown off as well, but he improvises, grinning as he hastens to introduce the two of us also. "Joining Mr. Ramirez, of course, is Ms. Maddison Darling and Ms. Casey Sinclair."

As they watch us move toward the dais, Wolf turns to the announcer and takes the mic from him before he can say anything else. Lord Wolfgang Von Damme charms the gathered crowd and all those watching from home with a dazzling smile before he brings the mic to his lips.

"Maddison Darling, could you come up here, please?" he says, his blue eyes sparkling as they lock on mine and he beckons me to them.

Antonio releases my arm, he and Casey staying at the bottom of the staircase, taking the proverbial front-row seats for what's about to happen. I ascend the stairs carefully, more comfortable in my pumps than even the kitten heels, but still supremely aware that I've fallen over while barefoot before.

A lack of heels does not, in my case, guarantee a graceful, incident-free ascent. From the corner of my eye, I see the queen starting to rise but Wolf must see it too, because

CHAPTER THIRTY-FIVE

he doesn't wait for me to make it all the way to them before he makes the announcement.

"Kaspian, Taiyo, and I are proud to officially introduce you to our chosen Omega, the Cinderella of this story and the Darling of our hearts, put your hands together for Maddie!"

There's a moment of brief, stunned silence, but then to my surprise, a roaring cheer breaks out from the crowd as Wolf takes my hand and raises it into the air like I'm a fighter who's won the world's greatest match. In a way, I suppose that's exactly what I am, so I tighten my grip on his fingers and smile wider than ever before, allowing my relief and my love for them to break free.

Eat your heart out, Clara! Bet you're not going to pull my scholarship now, are you, Hartigan?

As much as I'm gleeful about having defied the odds, though, it's not a patch on how it feels to be publicly claimed by my Alphas. When Wolf lowers our joined hands but keeps speaking into the microphone, I frown, giving him a questioning look.

I thought we were leaving after he made the announcement?

He grins as he shakes his head at me. "You know, before the Trials started, I didn't think much about the tradition we had to take part in."

Gasps ring out across the room—and the world, no doubt—but Wolf simply rolls his eyes good-naturedly before he turns back to me. "What? Everybody knows it's true. We were skeptics, you were a skeptic. Everybody was a skeptic, and why not? It's an ancient rite of passage forced upon every third generation to prevent the likelihood of inbreeding among the Royals by bringing in fresh blood."

If I had a sip of anything in my mouth, I'd have spewed

MADDIE

it all over him right about now, but Wolf isn't known for keeping his mouth shut. Between the three, he's the straight-talker. Kaspian is the diplomat, and Tai is more famous for shutting up—which I intend to work on.

"However," Wolf continues as he wraps an arm around my waist and draws me closer. "I must admit that the twist of fate that brought Maddie here instead of somebody else has turned me into a believer. I love you, Mads, and I can't wait to spend the rest of my life with you."

Before I know what's happening, he seals his mouth over mine and kisses me hard, even dipping me back until my hair is likely brushing the ground before he finally lets me go. *The entire world just saw that. Holy shit.*

I'm still trying to wrap my head around the magnitude of it all when Wolf surprises me again by handing the mic over to Tai. The earl takes it easily, obviously having known it was coming—unlike some of us—and steps forward to take my hand out of Wolf's.

"Maddison Darling, you are a force to be reckoned with," he begins, his voice soft but sure as those warm brown eyes catch on mine. "No words have yet been invented that are adequate for me to describe how much I love you, but I do. I've been waiting for you since long before I knew you existed for real, and I can't believe we've finally found you. In front of our families and a few billion of our closest friends, I choose you, Maddie. Now and forever."

Tears prick at the backs of my eyes, but Tai kisses my lids gently, his lips lingering on my skin before he pulls away and hands the microphone over to Kaz. The prince's long fingers close around it and he brings it to his lips, but

CHAPTER THIRTY-FIVE

unlike the other two, he doesn't take my hand or step closer.

"Wolfgang might not have believed in the Trials," he starts easily, speaking more casually than he usually does in public. "I wish I could say I didn't agree with him before, but I did."

A ripple of surprise passes through the crowd and Kaz smirks. "Yes, I know. No one expected me to admit that, but I'm all about being true to myself these days. Traditions are meant to evolve over time, and this one didn't. That bothered me. Until now, that is."

He looks at the crowd and then straight into the closest camera. "See, in the past, the Omegas who were selected came from powerful, influential families who were seen as having something to offer to the crown. That will not be the case going forward. I've come to understand the importance of traditions such as this, but the monarchy will no longer stagnate. We will evolve, transform, and hopefully soon, my pack and I will give you lots of little royals to fawn over."

Way to break the tension with a joke, but jeez. If that's not an *up yours, you're not in control anymore* to his mother, then I don't know what is.

Finally, Kaz turns to me. "Thank you for putting up with me, Maddie. I wish I could say I'll be less stubborn from now on, but that's probably not true. Just remember that while I'm being stubborn, I'm also loving you."

He holds out his hand to me and I take it. When he tugs me into him, I catch another glimpse of the queen. Her lips are pursed so tight, they might permanently fuse together. *Although, that may not be a bad thing.*

Since we're on live TV, though, she has to accept the

choice they made. She can't have a tantrum about it—especially not after what Kaz just said. He hands the microphone back to the stunned announcer, who recovers as Kaz claims my mouth with his own for all the world to see.

"Well, there you have it, everybody. Your chosen Omega, Maddison Darling!"

EPILOGUE

MADDIE

"THIS HAS BEEN A CRAZY MONTH, HUH?" Antonio says from the chair beside mine. The makeup artist gives him a warning look, but he shrugs as he smirks at her. "What? I won't make her talk or cry. It was a rhetorical question. I'll catch up with her without her having to speak to me at all."

The hair stylist behind me gives him a sharp look in turn. "She can't nod or shake her head either, so you're on your own, I'm afraid."

"Yay." He lifts his hands and shakes them around a little. "Can you believe it's been a month since the Final Ceremony and I'm still getting requests to be interviewed about what happened behind the scenes?"

He sniffs. "I haven't told them anything about the queen having her knickers in a knot about you, though. The money they've offered me hasn't been enough to betray you."

The makeup artist pulls her sponge away from my face,

and I take the opportunity to arch an eyebrow at him. "Are you saying that you'll tell the truth if they offer you more?"

Humor sparkles in his dark eyes as he lifts one shoulder and slowly drops it again. "I don't know. Francis and I still have our own Bonding Ceremony coming up and *someone* has to pay for it. Not all of us have the Royals footing the bill for our I-do's."

"Oh, please. Your parents can afford it," Casey interjects from his other side, and I raise my fist to bump hers. I don't say what I'm really thinking. That most Omegas don't even get an official bonding ceremony with all the pomp and finery. Most are just happy to bond into a pack who love them. I know that if it weren't a royal requirement to go through with the traditional ceremony, I'd rather do this just the four of us.

"Can you imagine the reactions when the two of us walk out as your entourage? The press are going to cream themselves over this."

"I know," Antonio croons. "I can't wait. I knew keeping in touch was a good idea. Aren't you glad I made us that group chat?"

"You mean the one where you keep sending us selfies of you and your lover on the beach while Maddie has been working on softening up the queen and I've been just plain working?"

He laughs. "That's the one, but Maddie hasn't been working on softening up the queen. It's already done. You know I heard things have been going better with her and the king as well?"

"It's true," I murmur without moving my lips as the makeup artist smears a natural pink shade of lipstick on them. "She's even on neutral terms with Yua now, and with me. Things are still shaky, but I think she's finally starting to come around."

"Blot." The makeup artist hands over a Kleenex and I take it, carefully pressing it to my lips before dropping it in the bin beside me.

"She must really be giving some thought to everything they said at the Ceremony, huh?" Casey smiles gently. "Speaking of, how's your mother? She introduced herself to me while you lot went off to wow the world with the strength of your love."

"Oh, I met her too," Antonio squeals. "She's amazing. Nobody cared about my declaration after the ruckus you caused, but she did. You were giving interviews, and I was giving her details about."

I jerk my head toward him, but the hair stylist jerks it right back. "What details?"

"Nothing much," he says mischievously. "Just that you spent the entire Trials sneaking off with the Royal Pack, so we all knew you were destined for each other."

I roll my eyes at him. "It wasn't that bad."

Casey groans. "It totally was. How is your Mum, by the way? She mentioned Kaspian had gotten her on a new medication that was working well for her?"

"It's working *so* well."

It's now become public knowledge that my mother has Cervus, and while neither of the artists show so much as a modicum of surprise over the revelation, they also don't stop me from gushing or looking at my friends this time. Both of them pause for a moment to let me speak instead. "She's improving daily, but Kaz got her into the Woods Cervus Clinic in the States. She's starting treatment there as an inpatient the day after tomorrow. They're only sticking around for the Ceremony, and as soon as it's over, they're leaving."

My heart twists at the thought that I won't be going with them, but my Alphas and I are taking off after our Ceremony ourselves. We're in desperate need of some real time alone after the media feeding frenzy we've been caught in the center of since the Trials ended.

After we get back from a few weeks of travel, we'll be heading over to America to visit them. "My brother is super excited. It's the cutest thing. He keeps talking about all the sights he wants to see, but he doesn't realize how far apart they are. It'll be the first time any of us has ever been on a plane."

Casey chuckles. "It's hard being that small. How are your parents feeling about the treatment program?"

"They're excited. Optimistic. They haven't wanted to talk about it too much, though. I think they've been afraid of detracting from today if they go on and on about it, and they keep ignoring me when I tell them not to worry about it."

"Your mother's little girl found love," Antonio croons. "Of course, your Bonding Ceremony is the only thing she can talk about. She's only been dreaming about this day since you were born."

"Is your father going to escort you to do the traditional handoff?" Casey asks.

I nod. "The queen about had a meltdown about one of her gardeners playing such an important role in the RP's ceremony, but they insisted."

"No surprise there," he says, then he suddenly squints at my makeup artist. "It may be a bit late, but you did sign an NDA, correct?"

She sets down the light mist she just sprayed me with and then smiles. "We did, but we wouldn't say anything anyway. I was Team Maddie all the way."

"Same here," my hair stylist says, and my heart warms even if it is still really weird to hear people I've never met talking about rooting for me.

"Thank you," I say softly. "Am I done?"

They both nod as Mary walks into my chambers with my dress in its protective covering. Tears well in her eyes when she sees me. "Gorgeous, honey. Simply gorgeous. Great job on letting the freckles show, Mara. His Royal Highness demanded it."

She winks before she shoos everyone out so I can get dressed. Casey and Antonio head back to their own chambers to do the same. Before I know it, the time has come. Today is the day I bond with the royal pack.

Part of me still can't believe it, but the massive crowd of people waiting in the gardens proves it's real. The Ceremony has been set up in the Rose Garden where Kaz and I first opened up to each other—and where he told me I could never win. *Oh, how far we've come.*

There's a beautiful gazebo where all three of my Alphas are waiting. Nerves and excitement simmer in my gut as I walk toward my dad. He's waiting just around the corner, and as my dress swishes around my ankles, my red sequined pumps peeking out from underneath the hem with every step I take, I drag in a deep breath.

Somewhere, faint music is playing and I hold on to the sound of it, trying to drown out all my warring thoughts. Don't think about the cameras. Don't worry about tripping. Just walk.

This is it. The moment I never thought would happen.

The moment all of this has been building up to, but I don't even get to savor it before my dad grabs my arm and blinks at me. "I've never seen so many cameras."

Smiling as I lean in, I brush a soft kiss to his cheek. "Yes, there are, but we'll be all right, Dad. One foot in front of the other."

He nods, the music starts playing, and then he practically runs me down the aisle to my three Alphas. I barely have time to wave at Ms. Frampton in the second row before he hands me over to them, placing my hand atop their joined fingers.

Everything and everyone else disappears as I look at each of them in turn, the lord, the earl, and the prince who are about to become mine. A pair of black eyes meet mine, then brown, then blue, but what they've all got in common today is the slight shimmer that tells me they are fighting tears as we join together.

The king stands behind the podium, and he stretches his arms out to his sides to let everyone know they can be seated before he begins. He's stone-cold sober, and looking really happy as he welcomes our guests.

"I've been asked to keep this short and sweet," he says before rolling his eyes at us. "When we become parents, we're told that we're going to learn a lot from our children, but I don't think anyone really believes it until it happens to them. I myself have learned a lot from these four young people standing before you today."

"I've learned that life is what we make of it, regardless of the cards we've been dealt and that the most important thing any of us can do is to listen to our hearts."

He glances at the queen. "I've learned that sometimes, we need to be kind to ourselves and to those around us, and we need to trust each other even when times are tough and it's almost impossible to believe things will work out the way they should. Mostly, I've been reminded that love conquers all. It doesn't care about status or station, and it has the power to heal wounds even if they've been festering longer than they should. What you're looking at when you see this pack is the future, and I, for one, am excited to see what it holds for our family and for the kingdom as a whole."

Applause breaks out, and then he gets to the nitty-gritty. Our hands are bound together with a swatch of delicate white lace, and after that, we repeat our intention to bond with each other. When it's done, Wolf sticks our joined hands in the air again, and then he's kissing me hard.

I smile against his lips. "Love you."

"And I, you," he murmurs before releasing me.

Kaz takes my hand and brings it to his mouth, those dark eyes locked on mine as a slight smile curves on his lips. "I didn't think we'd ever get here, but you have a way of weaving your magic on us all, it seems."

I wink at him. "No magic. It's called fighting for what you want."

"Yes, and I'm afraid there will be a lot more fighting for that in our future," he says before his chest rises on a deep breath. "Thankfully, I'm certain you can handle it."

Tai slides his arms around me from behind, and although I can't see his face, I'm pretty sure he just rolled his eyes at Kaz. "Nah, the hardest part of the fight is over now. Think your mother is ready to retire yet?"

Kaz chuckles. "Let's hope not. We have a month in Thailand to look forward to. Perhaps after that."

A dreamy smile spreads on my lips. A whole month in

Thailand, alone at the beach with my Alphas. I can't freaking wait.

No responsibilities, no reporters, and no overbearing royalty. It will be amazing.

First, however, we have a reception to get through. Tai places my hand in the crook of his arm and leads me to the massive tent that has been set up in the garden for it, and my breath catches in my lungs. "Wow. This is beautiful."

Thousands of fairy lights have been strung across the ceiling and around the pillars. There are mountains of greenery so it looks like we're in an enchanted forest rather than a tent, but the table decorations are simple and elegant.

"The queen approved this?" I ask.

Kaz smirks. "A lot of it was her idea. You might not think you've weaved any magic around here, but I beg to differ. The proof is in the pudding, or the reception, in this case."

My jaw slackens. I honestly can't believe she'd have done this for us. For me. It's truly beautiful, and so romantic and perfect that he's right. Maybe the proof really is in the reception that the queen has finally accepted me.

Wolf comes up on his other side. "This is romantic and all, but how about we sneak away to the dowager cottage instead? We can always come back later."

My heart starts racing. The dowager cottage is important to us, and it's where we've agreed they're going to give me their marks. I thought it would only happen much later, but it seems Wolf isn't the only one who's eager.

Tai's grip on me tightens and even Kaz nods. "We've got some time. Let's go."

Sneaking away with all the cameras around proves a

chore but since we've been guaranteed privacy in the opulent tent to complete the bonds, it's not impossible to slip out the back undetected.

By the time we reach the cottage, I'm laughing and flushed with exhilaration. "Do you think they know we're gone?"

Wolf snorts. "Probably, but it doesn't matter. We're here now and no one but Antonio will know where to look for us."

The door opens, and Kaz wraps his fingers around my wrist, tugging me into the entrance hall and straight into his chest. His mouth descends on mine in a kiss that's as powerful as he is. With his arms around me, he walks us back to our nest, but before he lays us down, Tai starts unbuttoning all the satin-covered buttons running down my spine.

While he's busy with those, Kaz keeps kissing me. I feel Wolf crawl in under my dress and grin against the skin of my thigh as he pulls my panties down. "Have fun waiting, gentlemen. I have no intention of doing the same."

Then his hot, wet mouth is on me, and I shudder, my fingers flexing on Kaz's biceps as I moan. He holds me closer, silently letting me know he'll catch me if I fall. When the dress finally comes loose, Tai pushes it down until Wolf's head stops it from falling all the way to the floor. He pulls away from me to let the material slide down, then he stays on his knees as he holds out his hand to help me step out of it.

Since I wasn't wearing a bra and he's already taken care of my panties, I'm standing naked in the center of the loose circle they've ended up in. Three sets of eyes devour me, their gazes a perfect mix of heat, love, and adoration.

Slowly, Kaz undresses himself, his eyes never leaving mine. My mouth waters for him, but Wolf makes me laugh regardless. Somehow, he always does.

Instead of making a show of getting naked, he practically rips his shirt off—I've no doubt he would've ripped it for real if we didn't need to get back—then kicks his shoes away and shoves his pants and underwear off before throwing his arms out to his side and giving me a little bow.

"That's how it's done, mate," he says to Kaz before he steals me away from him, sealing his mouth over mine until I'm breathless and needy.

Tai's scent pervades my senses when he joins us, now naked as well as he presses up against my back. Finally, they kneel and bring me down with them. Then Kaz is there too, and it occurs to me that dreams I never even considered dreaming are coming true right now.

I'm about to have a pack, and as I receive each of their bites and feel the bond sparking to life inside me, I feel more whole than I ever have before. These are my Alphas. My pack, and I'm ready to explore our future together. Regardless of what it might hold.

CAPTIVATE: ALSO BY E. J. LAWSON

Available Now

I don't need a pack. I'm doing just fine on my own.

Until one tiny mistake has me perfuming enough to draw every enforcement officer in a ten block radius.

I know what awaits me if I go into custody as an unclaimed Omega, so when a *blazing* hot and surprisingly kind Alpha throws me a life raft, I grab hold with both hands.

Only problem? He didn't exactly clear his claim on me with his pack. They don't want an Omega. Especially Thane, who seems to be calling the shots.

At least they're letting me stay until they find another pack to take me. I should be grateful, but being trapped in a mansion with four unbonded Alphas that smell like heaven is pure torture.

Fox, Miles, Levi, and Thane are everything an Omega could ever want, but there's a reason I was in hiding.

I have to remember… I'm Knot Their Omega.

CAPTIVATE *is a standalone Omegaverse romance told in multiple points of view. It includes MM and MMFMM and a happily ever after is guaranteed.*

Available Now

HYPNOTIZE: ALSO BY E. J. LAWSON

Available Now

Available Now